The Hellcat

In which Lieutenant Al Wheeler is expected to

♦ solve the mystery of the decapitated head

♦ investigate the Sumner family without ruffling any entitled feathers

♦ keep the two mob killers from wiping out the Sumners

The Lady is Transparent

In which Lieutenant Al Wheeler is sent out on a stormy night to an old dark house

♦ where a ghost has just murdered someone behind a locked door

♦ where the whole family believes in a century-old curse

♦ where a tape machine holds the only evidence of death by avenging spirit

The Dumdum Murder

In which Lieutenant Al Wheeler responds to a call about a bloody murder

♦ in a house of old Vaudevillians and entertainers

♦ involving the shooting death of a former associate of an ex-bootlegger

♦ that sends him into the arms of an intimidating Amazon

The Hellcat

The Lady is Transparent

The Dumdum Murder

Three Novels by
Carter Brown

INTRODUCTION BY
JAMES REASONER

Stark House Press • Eureka California

THE HELLCAT / THE LADY IS TRANSPARENT /
THE DUMDUM MURDER

Published by Stark House Press
1315 H Street
Eureka, CA 95501, USA
griffinskye3@sbcglobal.net
www.starkhousepress.com

THE HELLCAT
Originally published and copyright © 1962 by Horwitz Publications,
Sydney, Australia. Reprinted in the U.S. by Signet Books, New York, 1962.

THE LADY IS TRANSPARENT
Originally published and copyright © 1962 by Horwitz Publications,
Sydney, Australia. Reprinted in the U.S. by Signet Books, New York, 1962.

THE DUMDUM MURDER
Originally published and copyright © 1962 by Horwitz Publications,
Sydney, Australia. Reprinted in the U.S. by Signet Books, New York, 1962.

Reprinted by permission of the Estate of Alan G. Yates, and licensed via
The Carter Brown Foundation Pty Ltd, Australia. All rights reserved
under International and Pan-American Copyright Conventions.

"Carter Brown and Me" copyright © 2025 by James Reasoner.

ISBN: 979-8-88601-130-2

Text design by Mark Shepard, shepgraphics.com
Cover design by Jeff Vorzimmer, ¡caliente!design, Austin, Texas
Cover art by Stanley Borack
Proofreading by Bill Kelly

PUBLISHER'S NOTE

First Stark House Press Edition: March 2025

Contents

7

Carter Brown and Me
By James Reasoner

11

The Hellcat
by Carter Brown

89

The Lady is Transparent
by Carter Brown

171

The Dumdum Murder
by Carter Brown

249

Carter Brown
Bibliography

Carter Brown and Me

James Reasoner

I blame it all on Robert McGinnis, Ron Lesser, and Barye Phillips.

I mean, there I was in the early Sixties, the stereotypical red-blooded American boy with an avid interest in both mystery fiction and the opposite sex, and the paperback spinner racks of the day were just full of books depicting beautiful, long-legged young women in skimpy outfits or various stages of undress, most of them with sultry expressions on their faces that promised delights the likes of which I could only dream of. Those covers were painted by the men I mentioned above, although their names meant nothing to me at the time.

And the titles that went along with the covers! *The Wanton, The Blonde, The Desired, The Stripper, Lament for a Lousy Lover, The Passionate*, and so many others. As I stared at them, it was like the books reached out, grabbed me by the shoulders, gave me a good shaking, and shouted in my face, *"BUY ME!"*

Did it matter that I'd never heard of the author, some guy named Carter Brown? No, of course not. The cover art, the titles, the sales copy on front and back breathlessly promoting hardboiled crime action and sexy hijinks, all formed a perfect synthesis crafted to make me (and millions of other potential readers in the drugstores, grocery stores, and bus stations of America) want to read them.

There was only one problem.

My mother hated sexy paperback covers.

I was a kid, remember, not quite a teenager, but I'd been reading adult mysteries ever since I'd discovered them on the bookmobile that came out to our little town in the country from the public library in the county seat. I'd been devouring novels featuring Mike Shayne, Perry Mason, Cool and Lam, James Bond, and other series of the day. As far as subject matter goes, the Carter Brown books didn't appear to be much racier than the stuff I was already reading. (I should note that the paperback editions of many of those books also featured sexy covers by McGinnis, Lesser, and Phillips, but I checked out the hardbacks from the bookmobile, and as long as a book didn't have a scantily attired dame on the cover, my mother didn't know or care what I read.)

Eventually, I found a Carter Brown book that probably had the least sexy cover of any in the series: the Signet edition of THE UNORTHODOX CORPSE from 1961. I think the cover art on this one is by Barye Phillips, but I'm not sure about that. It depicts five young, reasonably shapely women with their backs to the reader as they stand over what appears to be a man's corpse. The cover copy tells us that they're students at an all-girls school. Obviously, a murder has taken place there, and a police lieutenant has been assigned to investigate the case. His name?

Al Wheeler.

I don't remember any details of the plot, but I do remember sitting on the front porch of my parents' house, where I did most of my reading, one afternoon when I got home from school and opening this paperback. I remember laughing out loud at the breezy, first-person narration as Al Wheeler insults and banters with everybody he meets, including several beautiful young women. I remember him driving to the scene of the crime in an Austin-Healy sports car. (Man, how cool was that!) I remember whipping through that book and being incredibly entertained.

I knew right then and there that I had to read more of those Carter Brown books.

Over the next few years, I became quite skilled at book cover espionage, sneaking paperbacks with questionable covers in and out of the house in binders, stacks of textbooks, lunch boxes, any way I could. Not just Carter Brown books, of course. By then I was also reading the paperback editions of Mike Shayne, Shell Scott, Nick Carter, and a bunch more. In a way, those books *were* my textbooks, so it was appropriate that I smuggled them in school notebooks. I'm all for education, but honestly, I learned just as much to prepare myself for a career of writing genre fiction from all the books I read as I did from any of my classes.

As I read the Carter Brown books, I figured out they were published originally in Australia before Signet brought them out in the United States. They were copyrighted by a company called Horwitz Publications, a name I would recognize immediately a few years later when Bantam began publishing the Larry and Streak books and the Nevada Jim books by Marshall McCoy, which were also published originally by Horwitz. (Those books are a story in themselves, for another time and place.) The fact that the Carter Browns, evidently, were not written by an American explained the occasional, very occasional, word or phrase that just didn't quite ring true. But whoever wrote the books got it right nearly all the time, as far as I was concerned.

Al Wheeler was the protagonist of that first book I read, and he was always my favorite of the Carter Brown characters, although over the years I read plenty of Brown's books featuring other protagonists. I really liked the novels starring Hollywood troubleshooter and private eye Rick Holman. Brown wrote about another private detective named Danny Boyd who operated mostly in New York, and those books were very enjoyable as well. The books were all fast-paced, funny, and well-plotted, no matter who the protagonist was.

Speaking of well-plotted, some of the books are really complex and so well put together that they're prime examples of the mystery writing craft. Any time I read a Carter Brown book, I was surprised at just how much plot he could cram into a single short novel. I don't think any of them ran more than 40,000 words, which is just about the perfect length for most fiction, if you ask me.

So I loved the books, especially the Al Wheeler novels, and I continued to read them off and on throughout the six decades since I discovered them. Today, from time to time I still read one of the old Signet editions I missed somehow along the way, and I'm really enjoying reading, or in some cases rereading, the Wheeler series in order as reprinted by Stark House, including the books never published in the United States until now. This is an effort for which I'm profoundly grateful.

But I haven't talked about who Carter Brown really was, have I? Well, if you're reading this, you probably know just as well as I do that the name was a pseudonym for an Englishman named Alan G. Yates who moved to Australia after World War II. I think it was my friend Stephen Mertz, a mystery writer himself and a big fan of the Carter Brown books, who told me about that. Steve even loaned me some of the original Australian editions he'd gotten hold of somehow. If you've read the excellent introductions to the previous volumes in this series, and I assume you have, you've learned a great deal about Alan G. Yates and his career. It's a fascinating story, and if you're a Carter Brown fan and haven't read Yates's autobiography *Ready When You Are, C.B.,* I give it a high recommendation.

Instead of all that, I've chosen to write about my personal relationship with Carter Brown and Al Wheeler and what an integral part of my reading life those books were in my early years and on through today. I think it's fair to say that I love this series. There's really nothing else quite like it. I love a writer who has a distinctive voice, and that's Alan G. Yates, for sure. No other books sound like a Carter Brown—and damned few these days are as entertaining. The three novels in this volume, *The Hellcat, The Lady is Transparent, and The Dumdum Murder,* were written in the early Sixties when Yates was at the top of his game, and they're all just as much fun to read today as they were all those years ago.

I started out by saying that I blame Robert McGinnis, Ron Lesser, and Barye Phillips, who painted the covers on those Signet editions and created an instant, unshakable desire in me to read the books.

What I should have said was a big thank you to those guys for opening the door to countless hours of entertainment over the past six decades. Now you get to go follow Al Wheeler around for a while as he romances beautiful babes and catches some cunning killers. It's a damned fine way to pass the time.

—November 2024

....

A lifelong Texan, Reasoner has been a professional writer for more than thirty years. In that time, he has authored several hundred novels and short stories in numerous genres. Best known for his Westerns, historical novels, and war novels, he is also the author of two mystery novels that have achieved cult classic status, *Texas Wind* and *Dust Devils*. He lives in a small town in Texas with his wife, award-winning fellow author Livia J. Washburn.

The Hellcat

Carter Brown

Chapter One

It was a handsome head, young, masculine, and virile. The thick, coarse black hair was combed straight back from the forehead in neat waves; the full lips were set in a smug, slightly contemptuous smile. I wondered what the guy had to grin about—had been grinning about these last five years.

"A nice-looking boy," Sheriff Lavers said in a gruff voice. "Don't you think so, Wheeler?"

"I don't much care for his look of complete detachment myself, Sheriff," I said politely. "But I guess it's all a matter of taste."

"The Lieutenant doesn't approve, Charlie," Lavers grunted sourly. "So I guess you'd better put it back on the shelf now."

Charlie Katz, the mortician, grunted with relief as he pushed the heavy, outsize glass jar back on the shelf. Inside the jar the head, severed cleanly at the neck, bobbed up and down gently as the formaldehyde swirled. From the depths of boyhood memory, a sudden clear mental image of my Aunt Clemmie emerged. She had been a whiz at preservatives—I wondered idly what she would have thought of this one.

"Five years already he's been with me," Charlie Katz said in a slightly wistful voice. "I've kind of gotten used to him. It wouldn't seem the same not having him around anymore."

"You got a name for him, Charlie?" I asked, against my better judgment.

"John—what else?" he said with a sly grin on his face. "Get it, Lieutenant?"

"A morgue is no place to get cute, Charlie," the Sheriff snorted. He looked at me blankly. "So John. So what?"

I sighed deeply. "The Baptist, I suppose. Charlie keeps his feet on the ground in here by studying the Bible, Sheriff. Salome and stuff. Didn't you know?"

Katz looked chagrined. "You got all the answers, Lieutenant! You're so smart, why don't you find the rest of him, to match up with the head, huh?"

I shuddered. "After five years?"

"Let's get out of here, Wheeler," Lavers said abruptly. "If I stay around here and talk with Charlie for too long I start confusing the morgue with a nut-house!"

Katz giggled suddenly. "Is that real kind, Sheriff? I do a good job here and you know it."

"Sure," Lavers growled as he headed toward the door. "It's just that if it comes to a choice between you and one of the stiffs for company, I'll take a stiff anytime."

Charlie looked at me with patient inquiry after the Sheriff had disappeared outside. "You know something, Lieutenant?" he said plaintively. "There are times when I figure he just don't like me!"

"He thinks you're a very lovable guy, really," I said, in a consoling voice. "It's just that the Sheriff's a guy who hates to show any emotion."

I went out through the same door Lavers had used, into the bright clean day that bathed the walls of the morgue in brilliant sunshine. He was already sitting in the back of his official car, waiting for me with obvious impatience. By the time I got in beside him, the car was already rolling.

"What do you think of it, Wheeler?" he asked a couple of minutes later.

"The head?"

"What else?"

"Well," I said, "it was real nice of you to take me out sightseeing, Sheriff, and don't think I'm looking a gift head in the mouth—but what the hell has that been doing in the morgue the last five years?"

"It's been filed there under the heading of unsolved crime," he said tersely. "Now, after five years, we've got our first lead."

"Like a signed confession?" I said, without real hope.

"Right," Lavers said. "But not the kind you mean."

I sighed loudly, making it as rude and insubordinate as I could manage. "Do me a favor, Sheriff, and start talking in plain English, like words of one syllable that even a dumb lieutenant can understand?"

"I guess it had better wait until we get back to the office," he growled. "It's a long story."

He didn't seem to be in any big rush to start the long story after we'd gotten back to the office and he was comfortably established in back of his big desk with an enormous cigar stuck firmly in his face. I sat and watched patiently while he made a big production out of lighting the cigar, waited until he reappeared out from behind a mushroom cloud of evil-smelling, dense black smoke, and he still didn't say anything.

"Maybe it's a state secret?" I asked finally. "You want to get a clearance on me from the FBI first?"

"I was just wondering where to start," he said vaguely.

"Let's start with the head," I suggested. "How come I've never seen it before?"

"It happened before your time with my office," he said. "I guess everybody likes to forget their mistakes. We never even got to first base on this one—never got identification of the head. So after a while, like I said at the morgue, it was filed under unsolved crimes and Charlie had the head in a glass jar all to himself."

"Where did it come from? Out of somebody's nightmare?"

"You know Sunrise Valley?"

"I've heard of it," I said. "Someplace about twenty or thirty miles out of town, isn't it?"

"Right on the edge of county territory," he said sadly. "Another couple of miles and that head would have been someone else's problem."

"I wouldn't want to hurry you, Sheriff," I said, real polite, "but you mind if I send out for some coffee and sandwiches? At the rate you're telling this story we'll be here next week."

His face crimsoned. "It's important you get the background right, Wheeler," he snapped. "We're involved in a delicate situation here. As you saw, the head was very neatly decapitated. The body was never found. Some kids playing in scrubland at the far end of the Valley found the head tied in a sack. We combed the area for miles around over the next couple of weeks but never found the body—or anything else, for that matter."

"And you never got identification?"

"No." Lavers shook his head mournfully. "We circulated photographs of that head to every law enforcement agency in the whole damned country—and came up with a big fat zero. Nobody in the Valley had ever seen him. For a while there, I was convinced he never did have a body—it was just a head that a couple of Martians had dropped out of a flying saucer one night for the hell of it!"

"So it's been an unsolved crime for five years," I said, trying to get him back on the ground again. "Now you've got a lead, something about a signed confession, you said?"

"The Sumner family live in the Valley and own most all of it, I guess," he said sourly. "Their cook, a woman named Emily Carlew who'd been with them twenty-five years, died in the county hospital last night. She made her confession to her priest, and he persuaded her to make a signed statement."

The Sheriff's face disappeared behind another dense cloud of smoke for a few seconds. "Five years ago when the police showed her a photograph of the head she told them she'd never seen the man before, but it wasn't true. Lying to the police had frightened her but the thought of breaking her oath of silence given two days before to Eli Sumner had frightened her even more.

"The head belonged to a man who had been a house guest of the Sumners for five days. He'd arrived late one night and the first thing she knew of it was when Eli told her the following morning that they had a guest who was sick and confined to his room. She was to prepare his meals on a separate tray and Eli himself would take them up to the room. On the night of the fourth day Eli hadn't appeared when the tray was ready, so Emily Carlew decided she'd save herself the trouble of finding him and take it up herself.

"She knocked on the door, opened it, and walked into the room. The man lay in the bed with Charity Sumner bending over him, talking in an animated voice. She called him 'Tino' and seemed to be pleading with him about something, then flew into a violent rage when she saw the cook inside the room and pushed her outside. Later, Eli Sumner came into the kitchen and made Emily Carlew swear a solemn oath on the Bible she would never tell another living soul that she had seen the man inside the house. If she did, Eli told her, it would bring shame and ruin not only on his own family, but on all the other families who lived in the Valley."

Lavers shrugged his massive shoulders gently. "Emily Carlew was born and bred in Sunrise Valley and all her life she'd recognized one simple fact—the whole community existed only by the grace of the Sumner family. It made good sense to her, if anything destroyed the Sumners, it automatically destroyed the Valley along with them. So she swore her solemn oath on the Bible and kept it—until last night."

I stared at the Sheriff blankly for a few seconds. "You don't mind if I go look outside at the automobiles for a little while, Sheriff, just to make sure we're still in the twentieth century? Or maybe that Lavers jazz is just a pseudonym—you're one of the Brontë sisters in disguise?"

"It's an isolated community," he growled. "Orange groves are their only reason for existence, and the trees are nearly always planted on land owned by the Sumners. The nearest highway is ten miles away; the valley itself leads nowhere, just ends with a sheer wall of rock that goes straight up for three thousand feet. If you ever went further than the nearest bar on your vacations, Wheeler, you'd know there are many small communities like that scattered through the whole country!"

"Yes, sir," I said dutifully. "So last night Emily Carlew signed this statement before she died, and now the head has a name and a place where it rested before somebody severed it from its body. What else?"

He rubbed the back of his hand briskly across his jowls for a few seconds. "Like I said, it's a very delicate situation. The whole Sunrise Valley community will feel exactly the same way about the Sumner family as Emily Carlew did. They'll band together in a solid wall of silence and hostility toward us for opening up something that they'll feel was better left buried and forgotten. We'll have to handle the Sumner family with kid gloves."

"Why?" I asked mildly.

"What have we got? A signed statement from a woman who's now dead—who could have been rambling in delirium!" Lavers snorted violently. "Would you like to take that into court against the kind of lawyers the Sumners can buy?"

"I guess not," I agreed.

"Five years is such a hell of a long time," he said, feelingly. "Eli Sumner's been dead the last two years, and that doesn't help, either."

"How about Charity Sumner?—whoever she is."

"The daughter," he grunted. "She's still living there. Her elder brother, Crispin, inherited the bulk of the estate—but she has plenty of income in her own right. I guess she'd be about twenty-three or so now."

"You want me to go talk with her?" I asked.

"Do you read the morning papers?" he asked cryptically.

"Not lately," I told him. "I have enough problems in the mornings already."

"It made a front-page story," Lavers said coldly. "Fresh evidence from dying woman gives new hope of solving five-year-old bizarre murder, and all that crap. It hit all the wire services and they're running the photo again with a caption, 'Tino?' We just might get a break and have somebody recognize him."

"Did you mention the Sumners in the interview?" I queried.

"No—but I mentioned Emily Carlew by name. If there's any truth in her story, that girl Charity Sumner must be biting her fingernails by now!"

"You want me to go find out?"

The Sheriff sighed deeply. "It's against my better judgment, but I don't see what the hell else I can do. But don't forget, Wheeler, you handle her like she was made of spun glass!"

"I handle all my women that way, Sheriff," I said coldly. "Otherwise they bruise."

Chapter Two

Sunrise Valley in the afternoon was like hell in the off-season. The breeze off the ocean had sailed across the mountains, leaving the valley shrouded in stifling stillness. By the time I reached Main Street, I'd seen enough orange groves to last me the rest of my life. And Main Street wasn't that much either. If you weren't concentrating you could drive right through it and never know what you'd missed.

There was a post office, half a dozen stores, and two bars. An ancient pickup and two sedans, circa 1935, were parked out front of one of the bars. A panting mongrel stretched out on the sidewalk opened one bleary eye at the staccato sound of my Austin Healey's exhaust. I figured there would be one great comfort about living in Sunrise Valley anyway—when the end of the world came, you wouldn't notice it.

The Sumner house was further into the valley, about a mile past the town. It stood on top of a lightly timbered knoll so it dominated the whole valley, and from a distance it looked like a bad imitation of *Wuthering Heights*. The two white-barred gates that flanked the driveway were invitingly open, so I drove straight through. After a quarter of a mile, the driveway ended in a wide semicircular sweep in front of the house. I parked the Healey beside a dusty late-model Continental and walked toward the six wide steps that led onto the front porch.

A massive front door that looked like it was built to withstand an Indian siege had a tiny doorbell button concealed in its center, like a blush-white navel. It seemed almost indecent to jab it with my index finger, and the resultant peel of muted chimes sounded like the nervous giggle of a debutante who's realized for the first time that tickling has a sexual basis.

It took a long thirty seconds before anyone opened the front door, but the wait was worthwhile. A statuesque brunette studied me for a long moment with impersonal gray eyes. She wore a mandarin-type dress, made from a rich, shimmering brocade, with a high collar. It emphasized her regal tallness and flattered the slender curves of her body. All in all, she looked like something out of the society pages of a fashion magazine and I guessed maybe she was.

"Miss Sumner?" I asked politely.

"Mrs. Sumner," she corrected me in a pleasant, low-pitched voice. "I am Mrs. Crispin Sumner."

"I'm Lieutenant Wheeler, from the county sheriff's office," I told her. "Is Miss Charity Sumner home?"

Her eyes were still impersonal. "I think so. Won't you come in, Lieutenant?"

Inside, the house was even more depressing than from the outside. Apart from the wide circular staircase that led up to the top floor, there was a labyrinth of long narrow halls which would have confused a homing pigeon. Mrs. Crispin Sumner led the way with all the confidence of an Indian scout, and after four or five right-angled turns we wound up in a huge living room, with the whole valley neatly laid out like a patchwork quilt beyond the wide bay windows.

"Please sit down, Lieutenant," she said, "and I'll see if I can find Charity for you."

"Thanks," I told her and sat cautiously on the straight-backed couch which was uncomfortable enough to be a genuine Sheraton sofa.

Mrs. Sumner went out of the room, closing the door behind her, so I was shut in with the austere furnishings and dignified silence. I lit a cigarette, got up from the couch that felt like it was upholstered with iron filings, then walked across to the huge open fireplace. Above the mantel was a large portrait in oils, mounted in a hideous gilt frame. A head and shoulders study of a patriarch with a thatch of straight white hair that emphasized the pallor of his face and intensified the piercing quality of the cold blue eyes. The ruthless, predatory look of his hooked nose was underscored by the tight-lipped mouth.

"That was my father, Lieutenant," a masculine voice said suddenly from someplace in back of me. "Eli Sumner. He looks like a man who knew his own mind, doesn't he?—and I can assure you he most certainly did!"

I hadn't heard the door open but it must have, unless he'd simply materialized in the center of the room. For a moment before I turned around to look at him, I wondered why a man needed to catfoot his way around his own house.

"My wife told me you were in here, Lieutenant," he went on in a casual voice. "I am Crispin Sumner." By then I was turned around facing him. He made no move to offer his hand. "I understand you want to see my sister Charity?"

He was tall and lean, dressed like the country squire with an elegant cravat tucked into the open neck of his silk shirt and whipcord gabardine pants tucked into highly polished riding boots. Somewhere around thirty-five, I guessed, with a thatch of straight black hair and a slightly hooked nose. But there the resemblance to his father ended abruptly. Crispin's eyes were a composite of aquamarine and mud, and they kept on moving the whole time like they were scared of being caught out. His lips were full, and the lower lip had a slightly petulant pout which gave his mouth a soft, almost feminine look.

"That's right, Mr. Sumner," I said finally. "I wanted to see your sister."

"Jessica—my wife—made an unfortunate mistake," he said, smiling vaguely. "She didn't know Charity had already left, maybe an hour ago, for Los Angeles. She's going to spend a couple of days with friends in Bel Air."

"That's too bad—for me," I said, and smiled vaguely back at him. "Maybe you can give me their name and address?"

He laughed shortly. "I can't. I know it sounds stupid but Charity is all grown up now—runs her own life. She doesn't bother to tell us any of the details when she takes off. I'll certainly have her call you when she gets back, Lieutenant. Or maybe I can help you?"

"Maybe you can," I said. "You read the morning papers?"

"About poor old Emily's dramatic statement?" He shook his head ruefully. "She was a dear sweet woman—did you know she'd been with the family for twenty-five years?—but at the end there, I'm afraid she built herself a fantasy. The dear old girl always did love a touch of the dramatic, you know?"

"Dramatic enough to make her lie in a deathbed confession to her priest?"

He shrugged irritably. "Maybe it was just the ramblings of a dying woman in delirium. Anyway, I can assure you the whole thing was pure nonsense!"

"You were here at the time of the murder, Mr. Sumner?"

"Murder?" His voice sharpened. "I was here when the head was found, if that's what you mean, Lieutenant."

About then I realized he'd already rubbed my veneer of politeness almost raw. "If you want to think he committed suicide by decapitation and afterwards his headless body walked away because it couldn't stand the sight of blood, that's your privilege," I snarled. "For me, it was murder."

Crispin's face reddened slightly. "I was here in this house at the presumed time of the—murder—Lieutenant. So was poor old Emily Carlew—she hardly ever left the place after her mother had died a year before. I don't know the details of the rambling nonsense she told, but you can take my word for it, she never saw that man in her whole life. Whatever craziness she babbled on her deathbed came strictly out of her own imagination."

"So you didn't have a house guest at that time?"

"House guest?" His mouth dropped open for a moment as he stared at me. "Of course not. There was only the family here, and the servants, of course. My father, myself, my brother and sister. Did Emily actually imply that man was staying—" He laughed incredulously. "Well, I have to hand it to the poor old girl—she certainly had a colossal imagination."

"You wife wasn't here then?"

"No, we've only been married for three years," he said shortly. "As I have already told you, there was only the family here in the house at the time—my father, brother, sister, and myself. I trust I make myself absolutely clear this time, Lieutenant?"

It would be about the usual luck of the Wheelers, I figured silently, to find myself drowning with Crispin Sumner the only guy in sight on the beach. From the way he'd been such a big help up until now, I guessed I'd be lucky to get even a farewell wave of the hand from him as I went down for the third time.

"Is your brother still living in the house?" I asked.

"Barnaby?" His eyes sneered at the thought. "Good God, no!"

"Well, thanks for your time, Mr. Sumner," I grated, "and you'll have Miss Sumner call me when she gets back from Bel Air?"

He frowned. "If it's absolutely necessary, Lieutenant. But I've already told you that story of poor Emily's was nothing but delirium, you remember?"

"I remember very well what you told me, Mr. Sumner," I said in a pleasant voice, "and it's still absolutely necessary for Miss Sumner to call me as soon as she gets back from Bel Air."

"I don't care for your insolence, Lieutenant!" he said sharply.

"Nobody does, mostly," I said sympathetically.

"I'm not without influence in Pine City," he said stiffly, "both with the county and City Hall. You'd do well to remember that, Lieutenant."

"I left my notebook in the car," I told him, "but I'll write it down first thing when I get back to it."

His face flushed angrily again. "I'll take good care to see you do remember it, Lieutenant, without the use of your notebook!"

"Good day, Mr. Sumner," I told him.

"Good day, Lieutenant. I'm sure you can find your own way out?"

"If I don't, I'll make soft, birdlike cries for help," I said, and headed toward the door.

It wasn't that damned easy, either, to find my way back through the maze of angled, narrow halls to the front door. But I finally made it, and found Mrs. Crispin Sumner waiting there for me.

"I'm sorry about that stupid mistake of mine, Lieutenant," she said, smiling easily. "I expect my husband told you?"

"That his sister had left already?" I nodded. "He told me."

"She lives her own life—"

"—and doesn't bother to tell you any of the details when she takes off," I finished for her. "Your husband told me that, too."

"Oh?" Her smile wavered a little. "You don't seem in the best of tempers, Lieutenant. I do hope Crispin wasn't difficult?"

"More like impossible," I said truthfully. "But I guess there's no fun in being a feudal baron if you can't be feudal some of the time."

"I don't think I understand," she said dubiously.

"He owns the Valley, doesn't he?" I explained. "And his father owned it before him. I guess your husband just isn't used to people who talk back, Mrs. Sumner."

"Oh, I see what you mean!" Her smile was confident again. "I think maybe you're right, but please don't quote me."

"Are the rest of the family the same?" I asked.

Her gray eyes were suddenly bleak. "Charity was a misnamed child if ever there was one," she said softly. "She's a hellcat, Lieutenant. Compared to her Crispin is a paragon of all the virtues. Again, please don't quote me."

"My lips are stamped with the county seal," I assured her. "How about Barnaby?"

"I wouldn't know about Barnaby. I've never met him," she said simply.

"You've been married three years and never even got to meet your brother-in-law?"

"He had left the house before I ever saw it." She nearly giggled. "We don't talk about Barnaby in the Valley, Lieutenant. He's the black sheep of the family."

"What did he do? Ruin all the orange groves by drinking grapefruit in the mornings?"

This time she did giggle. "I'm sure I don't know what it was, but it must have been something dreadful. I do know his father disinherited him, cut him off without the proverbial penny."

The faint sound of measured footsteps approaching through the labyrinth of halls made her stiffen, then she swung open the front door in a quick movement.

"I think this is your cue to disappear, Lieutenant," she said in a soft voice. "It was nice talking with you. Maybe we could talk again sometime soon?" She sounded almost wistful.

"That would be nice," I said politely. "Goodbye, Mrs. Sumner."

The door closed in back of me almost before I was outside the house. I walked back toward the Healey, wondering if Jessica Sumner was really scared of her husband or just playing the conventional bit women sometimes like to play about their lords and masters. And why that final wistful gambit about talking with me again soon? There was a variety of possible answers, and I decided regretfully that Wheeler's magnetic personality was the least possible one. Maybe she was just lonely for some conversation—or it just could be she had some interesting information. Either way, I realized with a nasty jolt, I was beginning to sound like the cliff hanger of a morning television soap opera, even to myself.

I drove the mile back into the town and parked outside the first bar. The view hadn't changed any, except the mongrel had rolled over onto his back and was fast asleep. If anything, the stifling blanket of heat had gotten worse. A cigarette tasted like charcoal-broiled hay, but it gave me something to do while I waited.

Maybe thirty deep-fried minutes later, a dusty late-model Continental went past me at a fast clip. I got a momentary blurred glimpse of a determined-looking face surmounted by copper-colored hair in back of the wheel—then she was gone. I wheeled the Healey out from the curb and drove fast enough to keep the tag end of her car in sight without gaining on it. If she really was going to Bel Air I had a hell of a drive in front of me.

Chapter Three

Some thirty miles and twenty-five minutes later, I felt a lot happier when she turned off the highway, heading toward Pine City itself. The traffic thickened and I cut down the distance between us to three cars; after all the trouble I'd taken I would have hated to lose her at a stop light. Now, she wasn't in any hurry at all. She meandered aimlessly through the downtown streets with no apparent purpose, then finally, just when I figured she'd gotten wise to the fact she was being tailed, stopped outside a hotel on a side street well off the main drag. I drove on past, made a left at the next cross street, and parked halfway down the block. When I came around the corner, the Continental was empty and a bellhop carrying a couple of bags was just disappearing inside the hotel.

I lit a cigarette and spent five minutes window-shopping in front of a salon that devoted itself exclusively to the sale of girdles, specializing in the long-legged variety that make a girl inviolate from waist to knee. I wondered idly just how much training a girl needs before she can wrestle one of those things on and off by herself. It's getting so the free-wheeling bachelor will have to carry a can opener along with the bottle opener on his key ring.

The desk was clear when I walked into the hotel lobby and the clerk looked lonely all by himself, busy cleaning his glasses like they'd suddenly gotten steamed over or something. I walked across and leaned my elbows on the desk like I was a stockholder and watched him interestedly.

"Yes, sir?" he said in a dreamy voice, after he'd gotten his glasses back onto his nose. "Can I help you?"

"The girl who checked in five minutes back," I said. "The redhead?"

He considered deeply for a moment, then shook his head firmly. "I wouldn't say redhead, exactly. More like a tomato-blonde?"

"Copper-colored, maybe?" I suggested helpfully.

"That comes close," he admitted, "but it's still not the exact—"

We both considered deeply in respectful silence for a few seconds.

"Like a certain kind of Persian cat almost," the clerk said suddenly. "How would you describe that color?"

"It's a good question," I told him. "Let's not louse it up trying to get an answer."

"What a dame!" His voice was still tinged with awe. "I bet she'd purr the way my Persian did, if you stroked her back the right way. I never saw such a *feminine* dame in my whole life before."

"What name did she sign in the book?"

"Huh?" The nostalgic gleam slowly faded from his eyes. "Who wants to know?" he asked coldly. I showed him my badge and he smiled nervously. "Well, of course, that's different, Lieutenant!"

He checked his card index with a spurious air of efficiency, like he was worth two IBM machines all by himself.

"It shouldn't be too hard to find," I pointed out. "It's the last card in the index, right?"

His eyes closed for a moment while he muttered some silent incantation under his breath. "You're right, Lieutenant!" He flipped the card onto the desk in front of me like he'd just extracted it from a magician's top hat. *Celia Shoemaker* was written in a bold, outsize handwriting, with a San Francisco address.

"What room number?" I asked.

"It's on the card." The clerk gave me a triumphant smirk. "I gave her the penthouse suite, Lieutenant. She wanted nothing but the best—and for my money, she's entitled!"

"I don't think you have enough money, friend," I said honestly. "I'll go see her. You wouldn't do anything stupid like calling her to say I'm on my way up, would you?"

"No, sir!" The apple in his throat jumped convulsively. "If you don't mind me asking, Lieutenant—is it like real trouble? A nice-looking, classy dame like her, and all?"

"No trouble," I told him. "Just a couple of questions. I don't want her to have any time to think up the answers, that's all."

"You can trust me, Lieutenant."

"I don't have too much choice," I said bleakly.

The elevator took me up to the penthouse suite, which was only twenty floors above the desk clerk's head, whereas—I philosophized all to myself—the girl inside was a million light-years way over his head. I knocked sharply on the door and a muffled voice from inside asked who the hell I was.

"Assistant manager, Miss Shoemaker," I said loudly. "Sorry to disturb you but there's a slight formality you overlooked when you registered at the desk."

"Can't it wait?" Her voice was still crackling when it came through to my side of the door panel.

"I'm afraid the manager is very strict about correct registrations," I yelled apologetically. "He always checks them himself before he quits for the day and he's about due to quit any minute now. He's got some bug about people using false names and all. I know it's ridiculous but it would save a whole lot of trouble if you would—"

"All right!" The door opened six inches and a bare, bronzed arm flapped wildly a few inches from my nose. "Give it to me and tell me what the hell I did wrong—or didn't do right—or whatever!"

"Well, for a start," I said in a normal voice, "how come you managed to change your name so quick in the short ride over from Sunrise Valley to Pine City, Miss Sumner?"

Her arm stopped flapping suddenly, and hung motionless for a second. I put the flat of my hands against the door quickly and gave a sharp push. There was a startled yelp from inside, followed by a slight thump; then the door swung open wide and I stepped into the suite.

Charity Sumner glared up at me with hot, malignant hatred flooding from her eyes. She was sitting awkwardly on the carpet with her legs sprawled all ways, which accounted for the slight thump I'd heard—and how was I to know she was all set to take a shower? Her ripe, naked body was perfection in a light bronze color that covered her from head to foot, with no telltale white streaks to mar the smooth patina. For sure, that desk clerk had known what he was talking about—she was the most *feminine* dame I'd ever seen in my whole life.

A grunt of choked fury came from deep in her throat as she scrambled furiously onto her feet; the violent movement started her high, pointed breasts swinging with a breathtaking freedom that paralyzed my vocal cords faster than curare, even.

Considering the circumstances, I figured she could do about anything, from making like that old classic "September Morn" to bursting into hysterical tears. Then a split second later, she did the very last thing I could have expected. She came straight at me, her face set in a savage snarl, her long, ivory-tinted nails raking toward my face.

"You!" she hissed. "You—I'll kill you!"

I made a frantic grab with both hands and caught hold of her wrists, pushing them down, then out from her sides. There was a solid thud as the momentum of her charge brought her body into sharp collision with mine. Suddenly it was like a lovers' meeting—I could feel the firm weight of her breasts pressing against my chest, the yielding roundness of her hips locked to mine, the smooth flat thighs pressed hard, as if in sensual abandon, against my thighs.

For a while she writhed impotently, struggling to free her wrists, then she suddenly gave up so that her whole body relaxed in a catlike limpness. Her face was only inches away from mine, and there was almost a physical impact from the naked violence that shone in the tawny-colored eyes.

"All right," she whispered savagely. "Let me go!"

"Why the hurry?" I said. "I'm just beginning to like it."

Green flecks danced in her eyes as if something inside had suddenly exploded. The full lips curled back from sharp white teeth in a snarl of fury that was purely feline, as her whole body flexed with a sudden muscular tension. "You dirty son of a bitch!" she said in a slow, husky whisper that accented each word with an immense deliberation. Then her knee slammed brutally into my groin, and nauseating pain rose like a cloud in my insides. I let go of her wrists and was dimly aware that she moved away from me; but by that time she was an out-of-focus blur in a world full of blurred objects—only the pain was real.

I moved slowly like an old man, doubled up, hugging myself with both arms, and by the time eternity had run out I reached the nearest chair and slumped into it. For a long time it didn't get any better at all. Then, out of the fog that pressed tight against my eyeballs, a voice said, "Here! You'd better have this." A lighted cigarette was pushed firmly between my lips and I drew on it gratefully.

Gradually the pain faded, and the white fog in front of my eyes went along with it. I managed to straighten up a little, and a small hope crept into my mind that maybe I wasn't about to die after all—I was just maimed for life.

"You'll get over it!" the husky voice rasped.

Like someone had adjusted the tuning, my eyes suddenly came into sharp focus again. Charity Sumner was standing a few feet away from the chair, watching me with a sharp, attentive look, her arms folded under her breasts. "Now—get out!" she snapped. "Before I call the desk and tell them to send up a couple of cops."

"That's very funny," I croaked, and fumbled for my badge with my free hand.

Her eyes widened in horrified disbelief when she saw It. "You—a police lieutenant?" She gurgled with helpless laughter. "And I had you figured as some kind of sex maniac!"

"You took care of that possibility real good," I growled.

She stopped laughing as she watched me wipe my saturated face with a pocket handkerchief. "I'm sorry, Lieutenant, I really am." Her husky voice sounded almost contrite. "But you have to admit you asked for it, busting in here the way you did."

"If you're real sorry, you could get me a drink instead of just standing there," I said bitterly. "Not that I normally wouldn't admire the view, but right now my need for alcohol is infinitely greater."

She glanced down casually at the magnificence of her own nakedness, then shrugged elegantly. "I guess I should go put some clothes on. I was just out of the shower when you arrived. What do you want to drink?"

"Scotch on the rocks, a little soda," I told her. "A bucket of Scotch and a bottle of soda would be about the right proportion."

The view of those taut, undulating bronzed buttocks as she turned and walked toward the phone was strictly medicinal. I was feeling a hell of a lot better already, I realized in sudden surprise.

"This is Miss Shoemaker in the penthouse suite," she told room service. "I want a bottle of Chivas Regal, soda, ice—and two brandy Alexanders right away." Her voice had that unconscious, inbred arrogance that could only come from a long line of ancestral feudal barons. "If it's not here within five minutes, I shall call the manager." She hung up before room service could argue. "I'll go put those clothes on now," she told me and disappeared into the bedroom.

It didn't seem any time at all before there was a knock on the door and room service appeared with a tray full of liquor. There was a haggard look on room service's face, like he'd just run up twenty flights of stairs, carrying the tray. He dumped it onto the coffee table, then straightened up with an audible sigh of relief.

"Miss Shoemaker?" he asked in an uncertain voice as he looked at me nervously.

"I shouldn't be surprised," I told him.

"Four minutes, thirty-five seconds," Charity Sumner announced as she appeared from the bedroom. "That's not bad. You just remember it's the kind of service I want always, while I'm staying in this fleabag!"

"Yes, ma'am," room service croaked.

I figured Charity's idea of putting some clothes on was strictly a minimal approach. She wore a pair of mules on her feet, made from a rich brown velvet and decorated with what looked like genuine platinum bows; the rest of her outfit was simple, consisting of a white satin bra and matching briefs. Room service's face was a study in scarlet as she took the pencil and tab from his limp hand and scrawled her signature across it. He still just stood after she had thrust them back into his hand.

A faint frown of irritation showed on her face as she looked at him. "I added twenty per cent," she said tartly. "What else do you want—the key to the city?"

"Yes, ma'am," room service stammered. "I mean—no, ma'am, that is—"

"If you never saw a girl before, you should start getting some practice," she said coldly. "I'd say you don't have too much time left."

"No ma'am." With a glazed look in his eyes, he backed straight into an armchair, ricocheted off at a tangent so he slammed painfully into the wall, then blindly felt his way along it until he reached the door. After a lot of fumbling he found the doorknob and backed out of the suite, his gaze still riveted on Charity Sumner.

"You striptease for all the help?" I asked her, after the door had finally and reluctantly shut on room service.

"It never worries me one way or the other," she said in an unconcerned voice. "The concept that a girl should go into a dead faint if a man happens to see her adjusting her garters is a little old-hat, don't you think?" She lifted the nearest Alexander off the tray and sipped it appreciatively. "You can make your own drinks, Lieutenant."

I got onto my feet very carefully and walked across to the coffee table even more carefully. It wasn't too bad—another couple of years and I figured I wouldn't even notice the pain. I made myself an emperor-sized drink and took it back to the armchair. Charity sat facing me and crossed her legs and right then I knew those golden thighs would haunt my waking dreams for the rest of my life. I lowered the level in my glass by a couple of inches in one long swallow and felt the mellowed warmth of fine Scotch spreading joy along my alimentary canal.

"Feeling better now, Lieutenant?" Charity asked. "What comes after 'Lieutenant,' anyway?"

"Wheeler," I told her. "Al Wheeler."

Her lower lip pouted. "You're the one who was at the house!"

"Right," I said. "I guess it was brother Crispin's idea you shouldn't talk to me, huh?"

"Sure it was," she said, nodding. "That screaming headline this morning made him so nervous he just didn't think it was a good idea for me and the law to get together. For some screwball reason, he thinks I'd have made a bad impression or something."

"I can understand how he feels," I said. "Was Tino sick, he had to stay in bed all the time?"

Her face was carefully blank. "Who's Tino?"

"The house guest who got himself decapitated," I grated. "The one Emily Carlew saw in the bedroom—the one you were talking to—the one you called Tino."

"Poor old Emily!" She shook her head slowly. "Her imagination must have been doing cartwheels there, at the end."

"You don't imagine deathbed confessions to a priest," I snarled. "You don't imagine signed statements either."

Charity yawned deliberately. "Well, if you won't believe me, Al, I guess you'll just have to talk to our lawyers."

I lit a cigarette, resisting the temptation to start a fire under Charity Sumner at the same time. Handle it with kid gloves, Lavers had told me, and for the second time, with the second Sumner, I couldn't handle it at all. Their lawyers would laugh that statement out of court, and the Sumners knew it.

She watched my face with a mocking gleam in her eyes. "I can give you the name and phone number of the lawyers, if you want, Al." she suggested innocently.

"Never mind," I snapped. "How long do you figure on staying here under a false name?"

"Now you've found me already there isn't any logic in staying at all." She looked at me thoughtfully. "But now I'm here I just might stay for a few days. You met my brother, of course?"

"I met him," I agreed.

"Then you know what kind of garbage he is, already," she said casually. "That wife of his isn't much of an improvement, either. She had to marry him for the money—he didn't have anything else—and I wouldn't mind that so much if she'd only mind her own goddamned business. Through some psychotic reasoning of her own, she's decided I'm her responsibility—she has to save me from myself. I keep on telling her it's only psychosomatic, and if she slept with the butler a couple of times it would probably make her a different woman. But she won't take my advice—or I haven't been able to catch her at it yet, anyway."

"I thought she was a very nice person, what I saw of her this afternoon," I said.

"That was a little naïve of you, Al," she said coolly. "Of course Jessica is the sly one, all right. But maybe you have to live in the same house with her to find out."

"Seen anything of Barnaby lately?"

"Not since I was sweet eighteen and Pappy booted him out of the house," she said lightly. "There are times when I miss good old Barnaby—life might have been unpleasant sometimes when he was around, but at least it was never dull."

"Why unpleasant?" I queried.

"Barney was the impetuous type." She grinned. "Had his own idea of fun, like the time he set up a midnight date with one of the more amorous maids in the back of the family vault, then stripped her naked and locked her inside the vault until morning. He figured that was a riot—and the maid didn't lose her mind the way they'd thought she would for the first couple of weeks after it happened."

"The family vault?"

"Didn't you see it?" She looked mildly surprised. "In back of the house about a hundred feet. Grandfather Sumner built it because he was damned if he was going to be dragged through the valley in a hearse after he was dead, and make a public spectacle of his mortal remains. Grandmother's in there too, of course, and Mother and Father—but he built it real big so there's still plenty more room inside."

"What else did Barnaby do?"

"It would take a couple of weeks—if I could remember! I do remember the time he brought home a Chinese cook off a ship in San Francisco. Barney had him dressed in the most beautiful robes you ever saw, and introduced him to the family as the deposed emperor of the Chinese Provinces—His Imperial Majesty, Sun Yat-sen. The Sumners never were too hot on either politics or geography, and the old boy looked real impressive in his robes. Barney explained that the Emperor had to observe the customs of his former imperial court and the whole family would have to observe them along with him, or else he'd be mortally offended."

Charity gurgled with laughter. "For two weeks we ate specially imported shark's fin soup and salted almonds for breakfast. We always had to back out of the room because you couldn't turn your back on an emperor, Barney explained. Father and Crispin had to plan fan-tan with the Emperor every night—the Chinese were great gamblers, Barney told them—and the cook cleaned up a small fortune. Whenever they caught him blatantly cheating, Barney would tell them it was an emperor's privilege.

"He might have stayed forever, only he got violently drunk one night and burst into Father's bedroom around four in the morning, brandishing a carving knife and calling Father 'Captain.' While poor old Pappy sat rigid with a knife at his throat, the Emperor told him his fortune back through ten generations, then wound up asking him what he wanted cooked for breakfast."

"If your old man didn't throw him out of the house after that, it must have been something real wild Barnaby did to get booted finally, and disinherited at the same time?"

Her face blanked out again. "I guess it must have been," she said tonelessly. "Only it's so long ago now that it happened, I just don't remember."

The Scotch had done me a whole lot of good. I stood up almost briskly while Charity watched me curiously.

"I won't say it was wonderful," I said, wincing only slightly. "But the Scotch was good, and your body beautiful."

"You're going already, Al?" Her heavy eyebrows puckered into a frown. "What for? The night hasn't even started yet."

I checked my watch. "It's a little after seven—and I've aged about twenty years since I first got here, remember? I plan to go home to my apartment, have a nice hot bath, and go to bed!"

She came smoothly onto her feet. "I'm sorry you have to go, but I understand, Al." When we got to the door she put her hands on my shoulders so I turned toward her.

Her body pressed hard against mine for a few seconds, her hips moving gently with a ruthless intimacy. "I'm sorry you have to go," she repeated softly, her voice suddenly a lot huskier. "We could have had a lot of fun, baby. Maybe I would have danced my special dance for you, even!"

She looked up into my face through half-closed lids. "I took lessons in San Francisco one time from a genuine Egyptian belly dancer. Only this isn't the kind of dance they'll allow in this country—not even in the real tough joints."

"You make me breathless, just listening to you talk, Charity baby," I said drily.

The rhythmic movement of her hips hard against mine increased in tempo. "You come back another time, baby," she whispered, "and I guarantee a lot more than just breathless." She bit into my lower lip casually for a moment, like it was an olive in a martini, then moved away from me. "Don't let on to old sourpuss Crispin you found me already," she said evenly. "Or he'll come charging into town and drag me back to the ole plantation, and I ain't a-ready to go yet!"

"I wouldn't give him the time of day if he was wired to a time bomb," I said sincerely, fingering my already swelling lower lip. "They should have christened you Mayhem, not Charity!"

Chapter Four

The long hot bath, the long night's sleep—both did wonders for the Wheeler frame, so long unused to kindly treatment. I woke up feeling alert and healthy—to my horror, at six the next morning. I ate breakfast for the first time I could remember, and got so bored sitting around reading the morning paper the second time through, that I arrived at the office at five after nine.

Annabelle Jackson, the Sheriff's secretary, gaped at me in open-mouthed concern as I came into the office.

"Al Wheeler! You-all is sick!" In moments of stress, her Southern accent thickened to the consistency of molasses and made me wonder if it was the McCoy after all. "Or maybe you-all is walking in your sleep, honey chile?"

"Garbage!" I said briskly. "I'm just feeling healthy, that's all."

"Healthy—you?" She shook her head sorrowfully. "Now I know what it is—you've flipped."

"I am merely brimming over with vitality and lusting for life," I said warmly, and to prove my point, gave her an appreciative slap where her skirt was tightest.

She backed hastily around her desk, watching me closely with a kind of haunted look in her eyes. "If you're like this at nine in the morning," she moaned softly, "I sure don't aim to be here around five this afternoon!"

"You don't need to be scared," I told her with a reassuring, friendly smile. "It's just that I appreciate girls who are blonde, beautiful, and sexy!"

She made a sudden lunge across the desk and grabbed a heavy steel rule. "You just twitch in my direction, Al Wheeler," she panted, "and I'll let you have it right between the eyes!"

"Okay." I shrugged helplessly. "If I'm going to be misunderstood all the time around here, I'll go talk to the Sheriff, see?"

"You can't," she said regretfully. "He just called. He won't be in until after eleven—he has to go talk with some of the City Hall brass."

"So I'll go sit in his office and make like I'm a county sheriff and read the file on the case of the missing body," I told her.

"The file's right there on his desk," she said, still poised for aggressive action if I even leered at her. "And don't you dare try sneaking back out here while I'm not looking, Al Wheeler, or I'll beat your head down into your chest!"

"All this from one appreciative slap?" I muttered as I headed toward the Sheriff's office. "What would a playful tweak, just a little on the sneaky side, have gotten me, I wonder?"

"Instant burial!" Annabelle shouted, as I closed the door.

The file was on Lavers' desk like she had told me. I lit a cigarette and started to read. It was a thick file—Lavers had done a hell of a good organizational job throughout the whole Valley trying to find the rest of the body and anyone who could identify the head. The list of names of the people questioned ran into fifteen closely typed pages. Only one set of names meant anything to me, and they all ended in Sumner. They were bunched together toward the bottom of page ten: Eli Sumner, Crispin Sumner, Charity Sumner. Then the servants, starting with Emily Carlew. No mention of Barnaby Sumner—maybe it was a typographical error. I was about to check if Annabelle had another copy in the file, when I heard a lot of noise and movement outside, and then the sound of voices. I figured Annabelle would be busy handling whatever it was, and I'd wait until she was free again.

A couple of minutes later Annabelle came into the office, and carefully closed the door behind her. "There are some people outside," she told me in a piercing whisper as she came up close to the desk.

"You're kidding?" I looked at her in surprise. "I figured they must be Martians."

"Please, Al!" There was almost a pleading look on her face. "There's three of them—two men and a girl—but one of the men does all the talking. He—frightens me. I never saw a man before who looked evil!"

"What does evil look like?" I asked seriously.

"He's tall and very dark—swarthy complexion—and he's got a

horizontal scar right across his forehead."

It rang a bell vaguely in back of my mind, but all I got from the memory banks was a busy signal. "What does he want?" I asked her.

"To see the Sheriff." Annabelle twisted her fingers together nervously. "I told him Sheriff Lavers wouldn't be in until eleven or after, but he said I was a liar. He could see your shadow in here and I can't convince him you aren't the Sheriff. If the Sheriff doesn't see him inside two minutes, he said, he'll break the door down!"

"What's so urgent he can't wait three minutes?"

"I don't know." Annabelle shrugged helplessly. "He won't tell me. All he said was, 'You tell that fat Hicksville bum in there that Gabriele Martinelli's here to see him!' What will I do, Al?"

"Gabriele Martinelli?" I stared at her blankly for a moment as the memory banks opened up like sluice gates. "What the hell would Gabriele Martinelli be doing in Pine City?"

"You know him?" she asked hopefully.

"Every law enforcement agency from here to Alaska does," I grunted. "He was a protégé of Lucky Luciano. He's beaten every rap in the last twenty years from grand larceny to murder—you name it, he's committed it."

"Then what will I do?" Annabelle was close to tears.

"Send him in, honey," I told her. "And if I don't come out of here in ten minutes, maybe you'd better call a cop."

"Where's the nearest—oh, you!" She managed a facial twitch that bore no resemblance to a smile, then opened the door again. "Would you come in, please, Mr. Martinelli?" Her voice shook slightly.

"You're damned right I'll come in!" a harsh voice snarled. "Your boss cut it real fine—another ten seconds and that door would have been across his desk!"

The three of them came into the office, two men and a girl, and once they were inside, Annabelle slipped out, closing the door behind her. The tall, painfully thin man with the hatchet-face and the horizontal white scar across his forehead stepped up to the desk. "You're the county sheriff—or whatever fancy name you give yourself—the law around here, anyway?"

"I'm Lieutenant Wheeler, attached to the county sheriff's office from city homicide," I told him. "Like the girl told you outside, the Sheriff won't be in until later."

He slammed a copy of yesterday morning's newspaper, from Detroit, onto the desk in front of me. The familiar picture of the unidentified head seemed to leap up at me from the page.

"You got anything to do with this case?" Martinelli snarled.

"Sure," I said. "I'm handling the investigation."

"Yeah? Great!" His voice was thick with sneering contempt. "You hear that, Georgie? This is the genius been handling the case for five whole years, and he ain't got to first base yet!"

"I hear you, Gabe," the girl said in a tight voice. "And I think it's dreadful—absolutely dreadful!"

"You hear that, cop?" Martinelli said savagely. "Georgie thinks it's real dreadful. How about you, Ed, what do you think?"

"I think it's appalling inefficiency, Gabe," the other guy said in a quiet, cultured voice. "I think there's probably a case for an indictment on the grounds of criminal inefficiency. There should be a state investigation."

"You hear that, too, cop?" Martinelli grated. "Ed figures you're so goddamn lousy at your job, they should put you in the pen for ninety-nine years. What have you got to say to that, huh?"

"Some advice, Gabriele," I snarled. "Get the hell out of here before I book the three of you for breaking the peace."

For a moment his eyes widened with disbelief, then his face darkened with an erupting fury. "Listen!" he nearly choked. "You ever talk to me like that again, and I'll take you apart and toss the pieces out the window!" He leaned forward across the desk, his hands lunging for my throat. "You know who I am?"

With the desk as a cover, it had been no trick to ease the thirty-eight out of the belt holster. I lifted my right hand above the desk and pointed the gun at his chest. His hands suddenly stopped moving and hovered uncertainly in mid-air while his eyes widened again. The click as I eased off the safety sounded very loud in the sudden stillness of the room.

"I know who you are, Gabriele," I said softly. "With the kind of backing I'd get from the girl outside when she told her story to a court, about the most I could get for killing you would be a medal. So don't push it, huh? I'm almost tempted enough already."

He dropped his hands to his sides and pushed himself away from the desk, a fixed grin on his face. The black eyes glittered as they studied my face intently for a moment, long enough for a mental picture to register and be filed away for future reference.

"Take it easy, Lieutenant," he said, almost pleasantly. "So I got a little excited. Is that a Federal offense?"

"With good reason, Gabe," the other guy's cultured voice said earnestly. "With good reason! I think you should tell the Lieutenant."

"Yeah, Gabe," the girl said with an oddly triumphant sound to her voice. "You tell him."

Martinelli looked almost completely relaxed now. I put the gun down onto the desktop, and took a good look at the other two for the first time. The girl was a brunette and very young, twenty at most I figured, with a face that was real pretty without looking over-bright. Her pleasantly plump curves were accentuated by a skintight black satin sheath which, along with the string of plump pearls around her neck, looked out of place at around nine-thirty in the morning. Maybe she was still having a very late night, I figured, or she'd gotten ready real early for a heavy date this coming night. I didn't care much either way—in a setup with a guy like Martinelli, she made obvious, if not very interesting, sense.

The guy called Ed—the one with the cultured voice—didn't seem to make any sense at all. A short fat man, with graying tufts of hair stuck at random all over his shiny skull, wearing an immaculate Brooks Brothers suit along with a matching expression of complete serenity on his face. But there was something wrong about him— something that disturbed me because it didn't jibe. I looked at him again, at each separate feature of his face, and then it hit me. It was the eyes that were off key, the pupils were completely covered with a film of opaque whiteness. With a sudden sense of shock, I realized Ed was blind.

"So, I'll tell you, Lieutenant," Martinelli said, dropping his voice to a whisper. His fist smashed down onto the newspaper photograph with sudden violence. "That picture—that face—it belongs to my kid brother, Tino Martinelli!"

"You hear that?" the girl asked in a shrill voice. "Tino!"

"His kid brother," the blind man said in a sepulchral whisper. "Five years dead, and only now can Gabriele mourn his loss."

"It ain't right," the girl shrilled. "There should be a law!"

"We're working on it," I told her, through gritted teeth. "And there's a city ordinance here that makes it legal to muzzle young girls who run off at the mouth all the time."

Her eyes widened and she clamped a hand over her mouth in nervous uncertainty. I looked into Martinelli's dark eyes and they could have been dead a hell of a lot longer than his kid brother.

"If I asked are you sure," I said slowly, "I guess that would be a stupid question, huh?"

"You think I don't know my own kid brother?" he asked passionately. "In all these five years, not a word! I spent a fortune trying to pick up a lead on him—all over the whole country, I tried! But always I kept on hoping he'd show up one day—and it was just a lousy, stinking pipe dream. All that time he was dead."

"There's one way to make sure," I told him. "We can take a ride down to the morgue."

"So why don't we do that?" he asked tonelessly.

I put the gun back into the belt holster and stood up. "We can pick up a car and driver here," I told him as I walked toward the door. "You can leave the girl with Miss Jackson outside. She'll take good care of her while we're gone."

"I ain't staying here," the girl said nervously. "Where Gabe goes, I go—that's the way it's gotta be, right, Gabe?"

"So put on your hat," he said irritably, "and stop making a big production out of it!"

I stopped and stared at him for a moment. "Are you out of your mind? You know what you're taking her to see?"

"You still have the head, Lieutenant?" the blind man asked in a gentle voice. "After all this long, long time?"

"Pickled in formaldehyde," I said, and the girl cried out suddenly on a thin note of terror.

"It won't worry Ed, anyway," Martinelli said easily. "This is one time a blind man's got the laugh on the rest—right, Ed?"

"There are many times, Gabe," the blind man corrected him softly. "This is just one more of them."

I opened the door and Martinelli walked through into the outer office with Ed following him closely, his head cocked to one side.

"Gabe!" Georgie came out in a rush and clutched hold of Martinelli's arm. "I don't care about what it's like. All I got to remember is he's your brother and how could anybody so close to you ever scare me, huh, Gabe?"

"You please yourself, Georgie," he said absently. "I got a lot of other things on my mind right now."

I asked Annabelle to get us a car and driver out front right away and she dutifully lifted the phone. We stood in silence for a couple of minutes while we waited, then I saw the car stop at the curb outside.

"So let's go, huh?" Martinelli said impatiently and strode out of the office with Georgie, still clinging desperately to his arm, half-running to keep up with him. Ed picked up a white stick from the chair where he must have parked it on his way in, and tapped steadily toward the door. I caught up with him in a couple of strides and took his arm.

"Thank you, Lieutenant." His voice was a melodious benediction. "I could manage alone, but as time seems to be the essence with Gabriele at this moment, I appreciate your help."

"Has it been very long?" I asked him, in spite of myself.

"I have been blind for fifteen years now," he said placidly. "One accepts it, Lieutenant, even if one never grows used to it."

We reached the car, where Gabriele was already sitting in the back seat with Georgie wedged in real close beside him. I helped Ed into the car beside them, then walked around and sat beside the driver. Nobody said anything on the way to the morgue.

Charlie Katz blinked in surprise when we walked into the sparse whitewashed office. "Hey, Lieutenant," he said in his reed-like voice. "You're getting to be a regular visitor. Maybe I should fix you up with some permanent accommodation, huh?" He laughed heartily at the joke that was invented the same day they built the world's first morgue.

"Charlie," I said in a pleasant voice while I bared my teeth at him in a warning snarl, "this is Mr. Martinelli. He thinks he can identify the head."

"John? My John?" A look of sudden alarm showed on Katz's face.

"What the hell's he muttering about?" Gabriele snapped.

"Don't worry about Charlie," I said in what I hoped was a reassuring whisper. "You work in a morgue as long as he has and you get to talking to yourself a whole lot—at least," I added with fervent hope, "I hope that's who he's talking to!"

The mortician blinked rapidly at me again and shook his head firmly. "There must be a mistake, Lieutenant." His voice quavered a little. "There's got to be a mistake—who'd want John after all these years?"

"Well now, Charlie," I said in a too-loud voice, "let's get on with it, shall we?"

I grabbed his elbow savagely and propelled him toward the freezer-room, walking fast so we left the others behind for a few seconds.

"Keep a clamp on that big mouth of yours, Charlie," I said in a murderous voice. "This Martinelli is convinced that head belonged to his kid brother, so watch it!"

"That's crazy!" he said, his voice loud with scorn. "John belongs to me and no one else!"

"You say that name again," I hissed in his ear, "and I'll have you fired before noon!"

"You wouldn't do that, Lieutenant?" The apple jumped violently in his scrawny throat.

"You open your big mouth once more and that's just what I will do," I grated. "Now, go get that jar so Martinelli can take a look."

Katz scuttled away like a frightened rabbit and I could have felt sorry for him, only I had enough troubles of my own right then. The other three caught up with me and came to a halt. Georgie was trembling violently, her face more pale than a mountain mist.

"So where is it?" Martinelli asked abruptly.

"He's gone to get it," I told him. "It won't take long."

"It's so cold in here!" Georgie's teeth chattered uncontrollably. "Why can't they warm it up a little?"

"Because it'd unfreeze the stiffs," Gabriele told her casually. "This is the one place you got to really keep 'em on ice all the time! Right, Ed?"

"Right," the blind man said and sighed gently. "This is where the loneliest of them all lie frozen in their neat, hygienic cabinets—the unclaimed!"

"Ed!" Georgie whimpered. "Don't!"

Charlie Katz came hobbling back toward us, carrying the large jar awkwardly in front of him, bent over it with both arms wrapped around it so it was almost hidden from sight. By the time he reached us, he was panting for breath.

"You okay, Mr. Martinelli?" I asked.

"Sure," he growled. "Show it to me!"

"Lift it up to the light, Charlie," I said, "so Mr. Martinelli can take a good look."

The morgue attendant gave a deep grunt, then hoisted the jar up until it was on a level with his face. The handsome head bobbed up and down gently, while the full lips gave us that same smug, slightly contemptuous grin. Georgie moaned softly, then slid into an ungainly heap on the cold cement floor. I guessed Martinelli wasn't even aware she'd passed out; all his concentration was wrapped up in a fixed stare riveted on the contents of the glass jar. Ed stood beside him unmoving, a look of polite boredom on his face.

I watched Gabriele's face closely for any reaction and didn't see any. Time stopped, as if not to disturb the grotesque tableau unnecessarily, until I finally broke the silence.

"You recognize him, Mr. Martinelli?"

His head snapped forward in a tight nod. "Yeah," he exhaled deeply. "That's Tino, all right. I knew it from the first time I saw that picture in the paper!"

"You're wrong!" Charlie Katz said shrilly. "You've made a mistake. How can my friend John be your brother?"

Gabriele looked at him blankly for a moment, then turned his head toward me inquiringly. "What is this creep?" he asked thickly, "Some kind of a nut, or something?"

"Shut up, Charlie!" I said softly to the attendant. "You remember what I said about noontime?"

Katz swallowed convulsively, then jerked his head up and down.

Martinelli wiped the back of his hand across his mouth. "It's not right," he said, his voice thickening even more. "It's not decent, seeing him like this. If that's all that's left of my brother, Lieutenant, I want to claim him and see he gets proper burial."

"Sure," I said gently. "There's a couple of technical formalities but we'll get you through those real quick and—"

"No!" I gaped at the sudden ferocity of Charlie Katz's face. "You can't do it!" he said wildly. "John, he's my friend—nobody takes him away from me, nobody!" He lowered the jar to the level of his stomach and wrapped himself around it again. "You won't ever take him away from me, you hear!" he yelled hysterically, then turned away, heading toward the far end of the refrigerated room in a crazy, wobbling run.

"He's a nut!" Gabriele said dully. "I told you he was a nut, didn't I? What do we do now?"

"You'd better get the girl outside," I told him. "Take Ed with you, and I'll see if I can soothe Charlie down a little. I guess a guy can work too long at this kind of job."

Martinelli grabbed Georgie under the arms, hoisted her onto her feet, then tossed her over his shoulder, where she hung limply, looking like something headed for the nearest garbage truck.

"Okay, Ed?" he said to the blind man. "You want to hang onto me until we get outside?"

"Thank you." Ed reached out and found his arm. "So it was poor little Tino? I weep for you, my good friend. Inside of me I weep for your sorrow and—"

"You can cut out that kind of crap!" Gabriele snarled savagely at him. "I'm not interested in crying over Tino—I did that yesterday when I saw his face looking out at me from the front page! Somebody killed him, Ed, right? That's what interests me right now—and they're still walking around five years after, like it never happened!"

I went after Charlie Katz, who'd vanished in the dim recesses at the far end of the refrigerated room. It took around five minutes before I finally located him. He was sitting on top of the refrigerating plant, his face turning blue with cold and his whole body shuddering in violent spasms. The jar rested on his knees, his arms still protectively encircling it.

"You won't get it, Lieutenant!" he shrilled as he saw me coming toward him. "You get any closer and I'll smash it, you hear? I'd rather do that than have that lying bastard bury poor little John under the ground."

"Take it easy, Charlie," I told him, and stopped right where I was.

"You keep away from me, Lieutenant," he repeated dully. "Ain't nobody going to take John away from me—I'm his friend."

"Charlie," I said reasonably, "you can't sit up there forever, you'll freeze to death."

"You come anywheres near me, I'll smash the jar," he said, with a kind of gloomy satisfaction. "And that ain't all—poor old John, he ain't going to last long—not after five years in his bottle and then the air hits him."

Charlie had flipped his lid okay, I thought sourly, and what the hell I could do about it, I didn't know. For maybe half a minute I stood there trying to come up with a flash of inspiration. Then I thought the hell with it—I'll call the Sheriff and let him worry. As I walked away, I could hear Charlie gently crooning to his buddy in the jar, and it raised the short hairs at the nape of my neck.

When I got back to the others, I saw that Georgie had recovered and was sitting in the car, staring numbly ahead of her at nothing special. "Well?" Martinelli ejaculated as soon as he saw me. I explained the situation wearily, and how the only thing I could do was call the Sheriff's office and get a bunch of men down to the morgue to take care of the situation.

"If he does anything to Tino, I'll—" The veins stood out from his forehead while he minutely detailed the obscenities he'd wreak on the morgue attendant.

Ed just stood there listening sympathetically until he'd finally finished. Then he cleared his throat gently. "Lieutenant, I think I could help."

"That's fine, Ed," I told him, "but how?"

"The lights—there's a master switch outside the building?"

"I guess so," I said blankly. "With the meter that's on the outside wall."

"Then if you'll describe the far end of the room where the crazy man's sitting, we don't have any problems."

"I guess I'm dumb, but I don't get it!" I said.

"Another of the strengths of the blind man," he said with a beatific smile on his face. "Total darkness is where I live, Lieutenant, it's my world."

"Hey, that's right!" Gabriele said excitedly. "That's a great idea, Ed. Lieutenant, you tell him where the refrigeration plant's situated and I'll go find that switch!"

Five minutes later, Ed disappeared into the blacked-out morgue like a wraith. I lit a cigarette and looked uneasily at Gabriele Martinelli. "I don't like it," I told him. "Katz is clean out of his mind—there's no telling what he could do—and we're standing around here while a blind man's gone in there after him."

Gabriele shook his head confidently. "You got nothing to worry about, so relax! For Ed, this is nothing—easy—like falling off a log! Why, I can remember the time when he—" He stopped abruptly.

"When he what?" I prompted.

"Forget it!" he muttered irritably. "But don't worry about Ed—I'm telling you."

Another five minutes dragged by, and then the door opened slowly. I watched tensely for a moment, then relaxed as I saw Ed step out into the bright sunshine, his face wrinkling a little in the sudden warmth.

The fingers of his right hand were hooked into Charlie's collar, and he dragged the limp body of the morgue attendant along behind him.

"That's great work, Ed!" Gabriele slapped the blind man's shoulder delightedly. "How about—"

"Everything's fine, Gabe," Ed smiled happily. "I put the jar back on a shelf. I figured that was the safest place for it—right, Lieutenant?"

"Right," I told him. "How about Charlie?"

"He's okay," he said in a disinterested voice. "Be out of it in a few minutes. Just a little pressure on the carotid artery—I was very gentle."

"How did you manage to get the jar away from him and apply that pressure at the same time?" I wondered aloud.

"I didn't," he said and chuckled softly. "Just a little applied psychology, Lieutenant. Even when I was standing right next to him, the morgue attendant had no idea I was even inside the building, you understand? So when the voice whispered, 'Put me down, my good friend, I'm tired of being up here'—who else could be talking to him but his good friend John? So he obeyed without question, and put the jar carefully on the floor."

He held his hands out in front of him, and for the first time I noticed the thick, sinewy fingers that hinted at a frightening and brutal strength when used as a weapon.

"Then," the blind man continued in a dreamy voice, "as he straightened up again, my hands were waiting for him." His fingers flexed with a sudden exultation. "I felt the touch of his shoulder, and while he was still opening his mouth to scream, I had already found his neck, and the artery. It was much easier than catching a rabbit!"

"You did a wonderful job, Ed," I told him sincerely. "So thanks again."

"Anytime you feel like some violent exercise, Lieutenant," he said good-humoredly, "we could play tag in the dark."

There was a sudden coldness in the pit of my stomach as I thought about that for a moment.

Chapter Five

I left the driver behind to take care of Charlie until another car arrived, and drove the other three back into town. Gabriele asked if I'd drop them at the hotel where they were staying and I said that would be fine. Ten minutes later I parked outside the hotel where a certain Miss Celia Shoemaker was occupying the penthouse suite.

"You plan on being in town long?" I asked casually.

"Long enough to take care of Tino," Gabriele said. "Get everything tidied up. How about you, Lieutenant? The law's had all of five years to do something about it already."

"I think we're moving in the right direction," I said vaguely. "There's something that bothers me. That picture of your brother was published in about every newspaper in the country right after it happened five years back. How come you never saw it then?"

"I was in Europe—in Italy—for six months," Gabriele said bitterly. "None of my pals back here even knew I had a kid brother. I figured on keeping him out of the rackets—make a college bum out of him, even. So there was nobody to recognize him as Gabe Martinelli's kid brother and let me know."

"It makes sense," I said. "It was a bad break for you, Gabe."

"Gabriele from you I don't mind," he said coldly. "But only my friends get to call me Gabe—and I don't ever make a friend out of a cop yet!"

"Sure," I said, "it makes me feel real proud of all us cops, Gabriele."

"That old dame that shot her mouth off before she croaked," he said icily. "What was her name? Emily Carload?"

"Carlew."

"Yeah. I guess that statement of hers didn't help much—right? A smart lawyer could laugh it off like it came from a nut, or something? But now I've identified the 'Tino' she mentioned as my kid brother, that'll make her statement stand up, or start to, anyway—right?"

"Right," I grunted.

"I got a couple of connections in this town," he went on. "The old dame worked for the bunch that about own the whole damned valley where they found my brother—" his voice dropped suddenly"—my brother's head, I mean. Sumner is the name—and the old lady saw Tino inside that house just before he was rubbed out, and she heard somebody use his name."

"You're trying to say something to me, Gabriele," I suggested brightly.

"It's got to be somebody that lives in the house that killed him," he said tautly. "That figures it's got to be somebody called Sumner. So how many of them are there, Lieutenant?"

"Sixty-five at the last count," I snarled. "You stay out of this, Gabriele—or else you might finish up staying in Pine City forever."

"Gabe!" Georgie's voice was a tremulous whine. "I need a drink like I never needed one before."

"Shut up," he said absently. "Are you threatening me, cop?"

"I never threaten anybody, Gabriele," I told him softly. "It's more like a gypsy's warning. Your brother was murdered in Pine City County and that made it the Sheriff's business—and he made it my business. Stick your nose into it and I'll chop it off for you."

"You get the guy who done it, cop," he said savagely, "and you get him quick. Or maybe there'll be a whole bunch of noses chopped off around here—including yours, even!"

"C'mon, Gabe!" Georgie tugged at the sleeve of his coat. "If I don't get a drink I'll go crazy, just sitting here with nothing to do!"

There was a sharp, explosive sound as the back of its hand slapped across her mouth. She just sat there with a glazed look in her eyes, not making a sound while a trickle of blood ran slowly down her chin.

"Now you got something to do," he said viciously. "You got to keep on remembering to keep your at mouth shut when I'm busy—because that's what happens when you don't."

"Get out of the car, Gabriele," I said harshly. "Just having you this close to me makes me want to puke."

"You talk a real tough fight, cop," he sneered. "Maybe we'll get to find out how you shape up when all the talking is finished."

He opened the car door and got out onto the sidewalk, then leaned back in, grabbed himself a handful of black satin neckline, and yanked Georgie out of the car like extracting a cork out of a bottle.

The blind man edged himself along the seat until his probing white stick located the open door and the curb outside.

"It's been a most interesting morning, Lieutenant, most interesting." The soft, cultured tones soothed my eardrums like a soporific. "I hope we meet again, I find you an intriguing personality."

"Thanks, Ed," I said politely.

He was almost out of the car when he obviously remembered something important. The shining dome of a head, with its weird tufts of graying hair that sprouted like cactus all over it, was thrust inside the car again. Then he lifted his head and those unseeing eyes were much too close for comfort.

"You must forgive me, Lieutenant," he said with a serene smile. "In all the excitement I never did get around to introducing myself properly—I am Edward Duprez."

"Well, thanks for your help this morning, Mr. Duprez, with the morgue attendant," I said, still keeping it very polite, wondering vaguely why he should make a big deal out of a formal introduction. A guy traveling around with Gabriele Martinelli, and he wants to be like real polite and friendly with a cop yet.

His head disappeared out of the car again, and a moment later the door slammed shut. I heard his stick tapping rhythmically across the sidewalk toward the hotel entrance the moment before I pulled out from the curb. And it was five whole minutes after that before the dam burst again inside my head, and all the memory banks flooded out for the second time that day. Sheriff Lavers, I thought wonderingly, is going to be real wild about this.

I stopped off for a drink and a steak sandwich before I went back to the office because, like Georgie, I felt a great need. My luck was better than hers—I didn't get a slap across the mouth for an appetizer.

Annabelle Jackson gave me a wide-eyed, breathless look as I walked in. "Are you all right, Al?" she asked in a muffled voice.

"Sure." I blinked at her. "Why shouldn't I be?"

"Those horrible men," she said incoherently, "and that morgue attendant running amuck." A sudden deep breath billowed out her white blouse like the proud canvas of a sailing ship—and now I knew why ships are always presumed to be feminine: they, like Annabelle, have wonderful jutting curves.

"I listened outside the door when you were inside the Sheriff's office with them," she went on in a scrambled torrent of words. "You were wonderful, Al! Simply wonderful!"

"I was?" I said cautiously.

"The way you handled that dreadful, evil man, Martinelli." She sighed deeply, and it was like her blouse had suddenly picked up a trade wind. "I honestly thought you were going to shoot him right there and then, and I was all set to cheer!"

I squinted at her suspiciously, then leaned across the desk toward her and sniffed deeply. If she was fried, it must have been vodka because I couldn't smell any liquor at all. So there was only one way to find out if this was the greatest rib of Annabelle's career, or if it was for real. I had to apply the acid test.

"Annabelle, honey," I said gently. "Stand up, huh?"

"Sure." She stood up and gazed at me with a look in her eyes like melting ice cream.

"Turn around," I told her, and she turned around obediently.

"You dropped an eraser on the floor," I said, reprovingly.

She bent down to pick up the nonexistent eraser and I gave her a playful tweak, just a little on the sneaky side, then held my breath.

She straightened up slowly, then gave an explosive giggle as she turned back toward me. A faint blush stained her delicate cheeks and she batted her eyelashes at me modestly. "Oh, Al!" She giggled again. "You are a naughty man!"

"Is that all you've got to say?" I asked cautiously.

"Well—" she looked down at her feet demurely "—you don't expect a well-bred Southern girl to say she liked it, do you, honey?"

"You don't have any urge to pick up a steel rule and beat my brains out with it—nothing like that?" I gurgled.

"Girls like l'il ole me are made to 'preciate great big heroes like you, honey chile," she murmured.

"You doing anything tomorrow night, Annabelle?" I asked with elaborate unconcern.

"Not a thing!" she said eagerly. "Not one cotton-pickin' thing."

"So we got a date?"

"We sure do have a date!"

"I was thinking we could have dinner someplace, then go back to my apartment," I said carefully. "I could put some records on the hi-fi machine and we could sit on the couch and—uh—listen to them." I grinned evilly. "How about that?"

"Al Wheeler," she said, with an almost worshipping note in her voice, "I do declare you have the most divine ideas of any man I've ever known!"

"I'll pick you up around eight," I said hoarsely and tottered into the Sheriff's office, not sure if I'd suddenly discovered the Lover's Stone—which is the alternative to the Philosopher's Stone if you don't care much for heavy metals—or if I was simply losing my mind and had daydreamed the whole bit.

The look that Sheriff Lavers gave me as I sat down facing him said eloquently that, compared with me, Benedict Arnold was a man of honor, integrity, and wore his loyalty like a badge of shining faith. He lit a cigar, the look of brooding hatred on his face momentarily transferred to the match, then exhaled heavily, enveloping me in an impenetrable cloud of black smog. I couldn't see him for a while, but the sound of his voice would have sawed through reinforced concrete walls.

"Yesterday morning," he said, making it sound like he was giving a Presidential address, "I gave you an assignment—a delicate assignment—I stressed that fact many times. To be handled with kid gloves, I said, you treat the Sumners like they were made out of spun glass. Stupidly, I imagined that a lieutenant who had been so carefully briefed would return to this office at some stage to make his report. On that naïve premise, I waited here until eight last night."

He took a deep breath and a look of terrible concentration knotted his forehead for a moment before he exhaled. I decided he'd been practicing for the last hour before I got into the office, and he figured the sound he made was the gentle sigh of a kindly executive, treacherously betrayed. The way it came out, it sounded more like the full-blooded roar of a young bull the first time they turn a cow loose in his pen.

"This morning," he continued, "I was put on the D.A.'s carpet and stayed there for a couple of hours. There had been a savage complaint from a certain Mr. Sumner concerning a certain lieutenant working out of my office. Just to be sure I appreciated who Mr. Sumner was, the D.A. insisted I read through all the lists of contributors to campaign funds during the last four elections. That took me seventy-three minutes, and I skipped a page here and there when the D.A. wasn't looking. Need I tell you, Lieutenant, who was the biggest single contributor during each one of those political campaigns?"

"Why, Sheriff," I said admiringly, "I didn't realize you bought that chair with your own money?"

"*Shut up!*" he bellowed at the top of his lungs, and all of Southern California took it for another earth tremor, for sure. With a conscious effort he dropped his voice down to its previous level and launched into an informal discussion of the state of the sheriff's office.

"While I was being bruised and battered in City Hall this morning," he said bitterly, "you take it into your thick head to be on time—a splendid 'first' by the way, Wheeler—I think it's commendable, considering you've only been with this office for three and a half years!

"When I arrived at eleven-thirty, I was greeted by a wild-eyed, psychotic female who was a highly competent secretary when she left the office last night. She gave me a frenzied, incoherent, and maniacal story about the man who was evil—you could tell by just looking—the sleazy girl who needed to diet, and the blind man who was growing asparagus on top of his head."

The look on his face was too awful to contemplate, so I looked out the window instead. But I'd goofed, coming in without earplugs.

"This trio—who must have been spawned out of her fertile imagination—proceeded to threaten you with incredible violence. But because you're a natural hero, you soon put a stop to it by aiming a gun at the evil man's head and promising to blow his brains out all over my newly polished desk! Then you rushed them off in a car to the morgue. Presumably to save the meat wagon a trip?"

He buried his head in his hands and groaned with a despairingly hollow sound. "The best is still to come! While I'm still trying to calm the girl down—at least enough so they can slip her into a straitjacket—I get an urgent call from a prowl car. Acting on Lieutenant Wheeler's instructions, they've picked up the morgue attendant—who's flipped his wig, to use their own words—and what do they do with him now? Then, as I'm trying to think up an answer to that, the hysterical female remembers an item of vital importance—the evil man's name is Gabriele Martinelli."

He smiled wanly. "You remember Martinelli, of course? I can just see a hood with his rating in the syndicate coming into Pine City!"

"Your press release paid off, Sheriff," I said politely. "Gabriele had a good reason for coming—he identified that head this morning as his brother, Tino Martinelli."

Lavers' cigar dropped out of his open mouth and started to burn a neat round hole in his leather desk pad. He didn't even notice it—I guess his cigars smelled about the same as burning leather, at that.

"It's true?" he croaked, with a stricken look on his face. "I am not surrounded by a bunch of hysterical screwballs who should all be out at the loony bin, tied down in warm baths?"

"It's all true," I agreed. Then it was my turn to take a deep breath and give him a run-down on what had happened since I'd left the office the previous morning. I gave him most all of it, censoring the detail of my meeting with Charity Sumner in the hotel penthouse— mainly because if I told him about her savage and successful attack on my person, it would be like giving him a Christmas present in July. When I'd finished, there was the same happy, carefree look on his face that Chicken Little had the day the sky fell in.

"Maybe World War III will start this afternoon?" he said hopefully. "*Zwammm!* No more worries for anybody!" He smashed the palm of his hand down onto the desk pad for emphasis, then gave a yell when it landed smack on the burning cigar.

"There's one more little item, Sheriff," I said, giving him the kind of cheerful smile that was first copyrighted by the Marquis de Sade. "The blind man called Ed? When I dropped them at the hotel around an hour back, he was the last one out of the car. Then he suddenly insisted on ducking his head back in and introducing himself formally."

"That's a fascinating story, Wheeler!" Lavers said savagely. "Now, about the—"

"I hadn't finished," I said icily. "His full name is Edward Duprez and it didn't mean a thing to me until maybe five minutes afterwards."

"Duprez?" Lavers frowned in concentration for a few seconds, then shook his head. "It doesn't mean anything to me."

"You remember when they busted Murder Incorporated, it didn't upset the syndicate too much," I said. "It hadn't been a real efficient organization, and if it had, it could have gotten too powerful for their own comfort. So the professional gun came into his own to fill the gap. If a hood could build himself a reputation with a number of nice, clean rubouts, he could make himself a six-figure income just for killing half a dozen people."

"I'd love to mull over FBI case histories with you, Wheeler," Lavers said feverishly. "Maybe some other time when we're not quite so busy?"

"It's relevant," I snarled. "Gabriele Martinelli was one of Luciano's protégés and when Murder Inc. went out of business, he saw an opportunity to branch out on his own. But in his own little way he was unique. Every profession spawns the man with the new idea—and Gabriele was the guy in the murder-for-money business who came up with a new idea. 'You pay all this dough just for a killing,' he told the bosses. 'Mostly you rub a guy who's been double-crossing you as a warning to the rest of them to stay in line. But apart from the one guy who's a corpse already, who's scared? The rest of them figure he was just unlucky, that's all.'"

"Wheeler?" the Sheriff pressed the palms of his hands tight against his forehead. "I'll listen—but, please! You don't have to act out the dialogue. Just tell it, please?"

I was disappointed—I'd thought I was making quite an impact with the dialogue, the hatchet-faced sneer, and all.

"All right," I said bleakly. "Gabriele said why didn't they plan on doing the next few jobs in a different way?—make it so nasty that the chiselers who hadn't been found out yet would quit out of sheer terror. So they finally made him a deal—he could do it on his own time, in his own way, and no payment. If it worked out, they'd make him their official executioner on a permanent percentage basis.

"Gabriele had an ace in the hole—a man with a college degree from one of the top eastern universities; a man who had been a crusading lawyer and had gotten lye thrown at his eyes for his trouble, which had blinded him. After that he'd turned into a psychotic with a homicidal streak. He started to educate himself to blindness with all the eagerness he'd once applied at law school. At the same time he worked at strengthening his hands and his fingers, the way a professional fighter will work out every day in a gym. There are a lot of different stories— some say it was a couple of years before he was ready, others say it only took a few months. Either way, by the time he got together with Gabriele, he could move around a room quieter than a cat. They say that for a bet he'd have you sit in a darkened room with a flashlight you could only flick on or off, and if you caught him in the beam you won. But if his hand reached out and touched your neck first—he'd won.

"So the two of them went into the terror business. Always the same technique—pull the fuses from the outside and then the blind man would slip into the house or the apartment, and stalk his prey in the dark world of his own choosing, where he was king. After the first three killings they called him the 'Creeping Terror.' One of his victims died of fright when he felt a brush of fingers against his throat."

"And this is Edward Duprez?" Lavers said bleakly.

"He hasn't lost any of his old techniques, either," I said comfortingly. "This morning he went into the morgue after Charlie Katz and that jar with Tino Martinelli's head in it, and he got the jar away from Charlie and brought Charlie out unconscious."

"We'll have to call Homicide in on this," the Sheriff said suddenly. "We don't have enough men to adequately guard the Sumners twenty-four hours around the clock against a team like Martinelli and Duprez."

"Are you out of your mind, Sheriff?" I yelped. "Here we got a good chance of solving a five-year-old murder and you want to ball up the whole deal!"

His first reaction was to blast me out the window; the second was a sudden nasty feeling I could be right; and the third and final reaction was the hell with it, anyway. If things got real tough he could always take over Charlie Katz's old job.

"Gabriele identifies the head as belonging to his kid brother Tino," I said carefully. "That gives a hell of a lot of backing to Emily Carlew's statement. So, just before he was murdered, Tino was inside the house, apparently sick and confined to one room. Eli Sumner knew he was there, and so, obviously, did Charity. She was talking to him inside the room, and called him Tino—according to the Carlew woman's statement, she heard Charity say it as she came into the room. Charity was only about eighteen at the time, so if she knew about Tino, it's impossible to believe the oldest son, Crispin, didn't."

"So the Sumners are lying—have been all along," the Sheriff said, nodding. "That newspaper story reviving the whole thing again must have scared them pretty badly yesterday morning. Crispin did his damnedest to whip Charity into hiding so you couldn't question her— then used his influence in City Hall to try and deter any active investigation from this office."

"Sure," I nodded. "Now we've got a lever to make them talk—fear. The 'Creeping Death' all over again—Martinelli out to avenge his kid brother's murder, helped by Duprez. You surround the Sumners with cops and give them a nice, safe feeling, they'll never talk in a million years!"

"I see your point," he grunted. "The theory's just fine, but what if it doesn't work out in practice—and one of the Sumners is murdered?"

"I don't think it will happen," I said with more confidence than I felt. "As soon as we're through here, I figure on driving out to the Valley again and injecting a little healthy terror into my old friend Crispin. Then I'll see Charity tonight and do the same thing."

"I wonder?" Lavers sniffed derisively.

"The original file on the case," I suddenly remembered. "The one right there on your desk—I read it through this morning. It doesn't mention Barnaby Sumner being questioned at all."

"Barnaby Sumner?" The Sheriff stared at me blankly.

"The second son who was kicked out and disinherited by Eli," I said impatiently. "According to what Crispin said yesterday morning, Barnaby was there at the time of the investigation."

"He's mistaken—or lying," Lavers said with sure conviction. "I never heard of any Barnaby Sumner before. But if he'd been in the house at the time, I would have known it."

"Maybe he got his old man's boot a few days before the head was found, and he'd already left the Valley," I said. "I'd like somebody to run a check over all the available records, even if it only proves he did really exist and nothing else."

"I'll get somebody onto it right away," the Sheriff said briskly. "Anything else?"

"Not that I can think of, right now," I told him. "I'll get started out to the Valley."

"You know, Wheeler," Lavers said slowly, "there's something been bothering me for, a long time now—maybe you can help?"

"If it's Mrs. Lavers, sir," I said cautiously, "I never think an outsider should come between a man and his—"

"Stop babbling damned nonsense!" he roared at me, his face a dangerous purple color. "This is the problem. Why are all our homicides such screwball cases? Is it because they just happen that way?—or because this is the only way you can handle an investigation?"

"I wouldn't know, sir," I said politely. "Although if you check back through the records of this office, you will find a number of bizarre—or screwball if you prefer?—cases that happened before my time. There was a real dilly about five years back. A bunch of kids fooling around in a valley came up with a neatly decapitated head, tied neatly in a sack, and—"

"*Out!*" Lavers screamed.

Chapter Six

The same stifling heat lay over the Valley like a shroud as I drove through Main Street. There had been one startling change since the previous day. The mongrel had moved right across to the opposite side of the street. He lay in a supine position with his head buried between his paws, like he just couldn't stand the sight of the Valley anymore. This was only my second visit, but I could understand how he felt.

I parked the Healey out front of the Sumner baronial home about five minutes later, then went up the six steps to the front porch. Maybe it was strictly my imagination, but I could have sworn the blushing bell button centered in the door winked at me the moment before it was rudely violated by my index finger. This time the door opened a hell of a lot quicker than it had the time before, and it was again the statuesque brunette who stood there, smiling pleasantly at me.

"How nice to see you again so soon, Lieutenant," she said in that pleasant, low-pitched voice. Her gray eyes searched my face in a candid appraisal. "We still haven't had any word from Charity, I'm afraid."

"That's okay, Mrs. Sumner," I told her. "It was your husband I came out to see."

"Oh, dear!" She smiled ruefully. "This isn't one of your good days, Lieutenant! He's out, right now, at one of the groves on the other side of the Valley. But I don't think he'll be that long, if you'd care to wait?"

"Thanks," I said. "I'll wait outside, if you don't mind? A walk around out here for a while might do me some good."

"Of course." She hesitated for a moment. "Lieutenant—would you think me very presumptuous if I asked if I might join you?"

"I'd like that," I said sincerely.

We walked around the side of the massive, rambling house until we finally came onto the wide lawn at the back. Right where Charity said it was stood the squat, ugly mausoleum, about a hundred feet back from the house.

"The family vault, Lieutenant," Jessica Sumner said lightly. "I think it's dreadful, so close to the house, but it's family tradition—and that's something inviolate with the Sumners!"

"It sure is big enough," I murmured.

"Grandfather Sumner looked after the next three of four generations to come after him—and that's also in the family tradition." She pulled a wry face. "You've no idea how it cheers me up on a wet morning to look out at the family vault and think that one day I'm going to join the rest of them who are there already!"

"Just how many would that be?" I asked casually.

"Four, exactly," she said. "Crispin's parents and Sumner grandparents."

"You ever take a look inside?"

She shuddered faintly. "No, thank you! Time enough for that when I don't have any choice. It would be impossible anyway, even if I did want to take a look."

"How's that?"

"Another family tradition—what else?" She sighed. "The Sumners are simply loaded with traditions. There's a massive bronze door to the vault—honestly it's absurd!—like something out of Fort Knox. Tradition decrees that the door only be opened when one of the family is ready to take up permanent residence inside."

"It would make things a little hard if somebody lost the key?" I grinned faintly at her.

"Oh, it's much more complicated than that!" She grinned back. "You're not giving the Sumners enough credit, Lieutenant. It has a combination, like a safe!" She started walking again. "I think we've had enough of that mausoleum for now. Let's go around the other side of the house, shall we? That's where the view of the whole Valley is, right at your feet. I never grow tired of looking at it."

A couple of minutes later we stood and admired the view. She was right, it was a magnificent view—but I hadn't come to look at it, and neither had she, I figured.

"When I left the house yesterday, Mrs. Sumner," I said easily. "I got the impression you wanted to talk to me about something—or maybe I was wrong?"

She smoothed the front of her immaculate silk blouse gently with the palm of her right hand and frowned at the magnificent view.

"You're right, I did, Lieutenant," she said steadily. "But it's hard to know where to begin—and harder still to try and make any sense out of it."

"So don't try," I told her. "Say what's on your mind."

"All right." She turned her head toward me quickly, her troubled gray eyes searching my face again.

"What's it all about, Lieutenant? I don't understand any of it. Why was Crispin so angry because you came out to the house yesterday? He's been completely impossible these last two days. Why?"

"You must have read about it in the papers, Mrs. Sumner?" I suggested. "How we just got a new lead on an unsolved murder five years old?"

She closed her eyes tight for a moment. "That disgusting picture of a man's head that had been completely severed from his body—and he's *smiling!*"

"What opened up the case was a deathbed statement from a woman named Emily Carlew—but you'd know about that, too?"

"I know," she said. "Poor Emily was a wonderful cook."

"If her story is true, then just before his death the murdered man was staying in this house as a house guest who was apparently sick. But that was categorically denied by your husband, his father, and his sister, at the time. Your husband still denies it—we're not sure he's telling the truth. That's what it's all about, in answer to your question, Mrs. Sumner."

She bit down hard on her lower lip for a long moment. "I don't know what to think, Lieutenant. I love my husband, but I don't always understand him. And ever since the first day we came back to this house after our honeymoon, I've been aware of the constant friction between the two of them—Charity and Crispin, I mean."

"Friction?" I queried the word.

"That's a polite word for it!" she said despairingly. "Hate is the right one. They hate each other in a way I wouldn't have believed possible for two human beings to hate each other—let alone brother and sister. At first, I thought it would blow over—that everyone finally gets over a temper. But if anything, over the last three years it's gotten even worse. It's as if they want to destroy each other." A baffled look showed on her face. "But there's something even more than that—just between the two of them. Nobody else can share it, or even be allowed to understand whatever it is."

She turned her face away suddenly as her voice broke. "I've pleaded with him more times than I care to remember, to take me into his confidence so I could try and help—but every time he'd just turn away and say he didn't know what I was talking about. Once, I even swallowed my pride enough to ask Charity what was it that kept them at each other's throats the whole time. I was even stupid enough to suggest I might be able to help! Charity suggested in her own charming, inimitable manner that the best way I could help would be by leaving Crispin for good, so she wouldn't have to stand the sight of my miserable face around the house anymore. Or, failing that, I might form an illicit attachment with one of the servants and invite her along as a spectator—she thought she might find it sufficiently diverting to distract her from needling Crispin!"

"Do you think Charity is really as tough inside as she likes to make out?" I asked her.

"Indeed I do!" she said feelingly. "Tougher, even! I don't know whatever happened to make her the way she is, but there have been many times when I've seriously wondered if she's human!"

She looked back over her shoulder toward the house and suddenly the polite mask of the gracious lady of the manor house was clamped back tight onto her face.

"Oh, here's Crispin now, Lieutenant." Her voice was determinedly bright. "You wait here for him, he's on his way across already."

She walked toward him with an eager stride, like he was just home from the wars after a four years' absence. So who can ever figure out what makes a woman? I watched her greet him with apparent enthusiasm, talk animatedly for a little while, then walk on toward the house. I lit a cigarette while I waited for Crispin Sumner to join me.

He was still the country squire and, except for a different shirt and cravat, dressed in the same clothes he'd worn the previous day. The petulance of his pouting lower lip looked even more pronounced. His muddy eyes glared at me for a moment, then slid away at an oblique tangent for a momentary look at the view, then focused back onto my face again.

"You're getting to be an intolerable nuisance, Lieutenant!" he said acidly. "I thought I'd taken care of that with a couple of phone calls last night. Now I see I'll have to take more drastic action."

"If you have the time," I said.

"What?" It startled him badly, and his eyes jumped around like they were trying to see all ways at one time. "What the hell do you mean by that?"

"You may be dead before you have the chance," I said mildly.

His face reddened. "Are you threatening me, Wheeler?"

"Don't be a damned idiot when there's no reason you should be!" I snapped. "Of course I'm not threatening you. I'm warning you, your life can be in danger at any moment from now on."

A facial muscle in his cheek twitched slightly, then he laughed raucously. "This must be your own crude idea of a bad joke!"

"If you'd just shut up and listen to me for five minutes," I snarled, "it might save your life."

He stopped laughing as abruptly as he'd started, and then I told him about the head being identified as Tino Martinelli, the brother of Gabriele Martinelli. I gave him a very detailed run-down on just exactly who Gabriele was and what kind of business he was in. After that I gave him an equally detailed run-down on Gabriele's partner, Edward Duprez.

For a long time after I'd finished, he didn't say anything at all. He just stood there, staring out across the Valley, his teeth nibbling reflectively at his lower lip.

"You're trying to tell me, Lieutenant," he said finally, "that because these two men—known gangsters and killers!—choose to believe the ravings of a dying woman, they are prepared to kill me?"

"You—or your sister—or maybe both of you," I agreed easily. "You've got just one chance to be safe, Sumner, and that's by telling us the truth."

"I've told you the truth"—he almost spat the words it me. "And if you'd like a little more of the same truth, I think you're a near maniac masquerading as a law enforcement officer! I don't believe for a moment there's a word of truth in that fantastic story about those two men— an official executioner for a crime syndicate with a blind man as a partner who's known as the 'Creeping Terror'? And, of course, they both share a blonde mistress! What's her name—Goldilocks?"

"You can check with the Sheriff," I told him. "Both men are staying at the Pines Hotel. You could call the desk clerk. Ask him if Mr. Martinelli is a tall, painfully thin man with a hatchet face? Ask him if Mr. Duprez is the same one you're thinking of—a short fat gentleman with a beautiful voice, who is unfortunately blind?"

"I'm too old for childish games of fantasy!" he said in a contemptuous voice.

"Again, I have to tell you the Sheriff's office doesn't have the men to give you the kind of protection you need against an expert combination like Gabriele and Duprez," I said, trying to make my voice sound both official and somber at the same time.

"Give me protection?" he sneered. "I've got all the protection I could ever need, and more, right here." He pointed down at the Valley. "All that owes its very existence to the Sumners. An oaf like you, Wheeler, might find it hard to understand, but the people in this valley respect and admire the Sumners on the hill! If I thought it necessary I could have fifty men with rifles and shotguns up here within a half hour! Don't talk to me about your protection because I don't need it—I have my own!"

And that did it up real good, I thought, because he was obviously telling the truth.

"Okay," I said in a resigned voice. "Have it your way, Sumner. There's something else before I go."

"Make it brief," he snapped. "My patience is wearing thin."

"At the time the decapitated head was found, five years back, you said the only people in the house at the time, other than servants, were your father, brother, sister, and yourself?"

"I said it twice yesterday to you," he said coldly. "How many more times do I have to say it?"

"I checked the official records, the complete lists of all the people questioned in the Valley. Eli, Crispin, and Charity Sumner in this house—but no mention of Barnaby Sumner at all."

"Maybe your records are wrong?"

"No," I said firmly. "They're right."

He shrugged stiffly. "Then I must be wrong. I must have confused the time exactly when Barnaby was thrown out by my father—I don't think you can blame me for that, Lieutenant. Five years is a hell of a long time to remember back to exact days and dates."

"Sure," I said evenly. "You've never seen your brother from that day to this?"

"Never!" he said curtly.

"Not even a postcard?"

"I don't find this a very amusing topic of conversation, Lieutenant," he said in a bleak voice.

"You just don't have any idea what he did after he left? Where he went after he quit the Valley?"

"I don't know how many ways there are to say 'No!' exactly, Lieutenant," he grated. "But we must have used up about all of them by now."

"I guess so," I said. "Thanks for your time, Mr. Sumner—and don't forget to make those calls and check on Martinelli and Duprez!"

"May I go now?" he snarled.

"Good day, Mr. Sumner," I told him, and looked out at the magnificent view again. "Please don't bother showing me to the entrance to your valley—I'll drive my own way out."

Chapter Seven

The same desk clerk was on duty at the Pines Hotel, and his glasses fogged slightly in recognition as I came up to the desk.

"Good evening, Lieutenant. Miss Shoemaker is in her suite."

"Thanks," I said. "How about Mr. Martinelli? Is he in his?"

"Martinelli?" He frowned at me worriedly. "We seem to have more guests who interest the police at this moment than we normally get in a whole year!"

"It probably has to do with the color schemes," I said idly. "Done any redecorating lately?"

His eyes widened in sudden admiration. "By George! You're right, Lieutenant! Just two weeks back we finished redecorating all the suites on the top three floors."

"You did?" I said, real surprised.

"And where is Miss Shoemaker?" he asked triumphantly. "In the Penthouse suite! Mr. Martinelli—suite 1901 on the floor below!"

"Thanks," I told him.

He shook his head admiringly. "I guess crime detection's gotten to be a pretty scientific business these days, Lieutenant. I bet they have to be real smart operators to put anything over on you!"

"You're damned right they have to be!" I agreed. "By the way—I don't suppose I could interest you in some Golden Gate Bridge stock? It's an absolute steal!"

His glasses fogged over completely that time, so I traded the front desk for an elevator and got off at the nineteenth floor. Martinelli opened the door of his suite and didn't look overjoyed to see me. "What the hell do you want?" he rasped.

"To talk to you, Gabriele," I said patiently. "What else?"

"We're about ready to have a night out on the town!"

"So you give me the first ten minutes?" I pushed my way past him gently, into the suite.

"Honey lamb!" A shrill voice called from inside the bedroom. "You figure I should wear the pearls again, or maybe the emeralds go better with this dress? I'll come show you what I mean—you wait right there, cuddle-pie!"

Five seconds later Georgie bounced gaily into the room, the string of pearls in one hand and the emeralds in the other. Georgie was built along generous lines so when she came to a stop, most of her just kept right on bouncing. She was obviously still dressing and so far she'd only reached the bra and panties stage—both of matching black satin with a heavy motif of pink satin rosebuds running riot. The overall effect reminded me of the chocolate box cover that put me off eating chocolates for the rest of my life.

She suddenly realized she had company and dissolved into a bouncy giggle. "Oh! 'Scuse me!" Then she bounced right back into the bedroom again.

"Dames!" Martinelli said in a morose voice. "She drives me halfway out of my mind! She keeps on talking all the time and she talks like a jerk!"

"I see she's still got all her teeth," I observed. "That's real good after that backhander you gave her this morning."

"One of these days I'll take a chair and break it over her stupid head if she don't stop talking all the time! And that reminds me—you had about five of those ten minutes already, cop!"

"I don't like making deals with punk hoodlums," I told him, "but in your case I'll make an exception. I don't call you 'Gabe,' and you stop calling me 'cop'—okay?"

He shrugged irritably. "You come all the way up here just to say that?"

"No," I snarled. "I wanted to ask you about Tino."

"More?" He rubbed his face energetically with the palms of his hands. "So what do you want to know?"

"What was he doing in Southern California to get himself killed here?"

"If I knew that, you figure I'd still be sitting around in a one-horse town like this?" He jerked his head up and glared at me malignantly. "You done anything about those Sumners yet?"

"We're working on it," I said patiently. "It all takes a little time, Gabriele."

"Just so it don't take too much time," he grated. "All I want to see is whoever it was knocked off Tino gets his. If you don't do it—then I do!"

"There are times when you fascinate me, Gabriele," I told him truthfully. "You keep on saying things like that right out loud in front of me. Suppose, for a moment, that you went out to the Valley tonight and killed Sumner. How would you hope to get away with it? What kind of an alibi would you have?"

"Alibi?" he sneered. "You want an alibi anytime, Lieutenant, you come to me. For one grand, I can lift the phone and by tomorrow morning early there'll be forty guys ready to swear you spent the last week with them in Detroit! There's another thing—hold it!"

He walked quickly to the bedroom door and yelled violently, "I don't aim to stand around here the rest of the goddamned night! You got another five minutes, then we go, you hear? If you don't got any clothes on by then, you go just the same, you hear?"

"I'll be ready, Gabe—honest!" Georgie's voice quavered nervously.

He came back to where I was standing in the center of the room.

"Maybe I should get smart and rip all her clothes off before I take her down to the lobby," he muttered. "I might be able to get a good price from a jerk town like this—they'd be stupid enough to figure Georgie's got some real class or something!"

"White-slave all you want, Gabriele—it's inside the city limits and doesn't interest me," I said wearily. "You must know something about Tino. He was your kid brother, right?"

"Yeah," he said softly. "That's right."

His lifeless black eyes bored into my skull for a long moment. "Listen"—his voice was still soft, almost velvety in its tone—"you did me one small favor by getting us out to that morgue real quick this morning. You also pulled a gun on me, and I don't go for that from anybody. But here it don't matter so much—like I said, it's a jerkwater town and you're a jerkwater cop. I don't got nothing to tell you about Tino. What's there to know? He's been dead five years already!"

"All right, Gabriele," I said. "If you don't want to talk with me, maybe Ed does. Where do I find him?"

"Right next door, to your left," he said. "I'm getting real tired of this dump I just decided, Lieutenant—so you got twenty-four hours to fix things up real neat. If you haven't got those Sumners by then, I'll have them inside the next twelve hours. You got that?"

I shook my head admiringly. "You're one of a kind, Gabriele, and you worry me. Sometimes I get to thinking you mean what you say."

"Me and Ed," he said reflectively, "we been around a long time now. With us a rub's gotten to be a matter of professional pride. We got to make sure it's done right, even if it's only a free sample. So if it works out we have to take care of the Sumners and do the job ourselves—do yourself a favor and stay out of our way, will you, Lieutenant? Or you'll be dead."

"You know something, Gabriele?" I said softly. "I think you're nothing but a big bag of wind. You're living on your past glories. The both of you should have a theme song, 'When you and I was young, Eddie.' How about that?"

"You want to get me mad, you got to do better than that," he said calmly. "A whole lot better, Lieutenant."

"I figure I can take you anytime I want," I said. "Then and there—

here and now, even—you want to try and prove me wrong?"

"So you can pin a minor rap on me and keep me out of circulation for a couple of weeks?" He grinned slowly. "I told you before, Lieutenant, I been around a long time."

"I guess you have at that, Gabriele," I said sadly. "Have a wild time tonight. Get good and fried and fall under a truck maybe?"

"The same to you, pal," he said. "And you still got twenty-four hours!"

I went back out into the corridor and knocked on the next door along to my left. "Come in," a musical voice said. "The door isn't locked." So I did as the man said and stepped into total darkness.

"The light switch is to your left," Duprez said. After an awkward, fumbling moment, my fingers found the switch and the room was flooded with soft light. He was sitting placidly in an armchair in the center of the room, his hands folded neatly in his lap.

"Good evening, Mr. Duprez," I said politely.

"Lieutenant Wheeler. How nice of you to call on me!" He smiled vaguely. "Please sit down."

"About five minutes after I left you this morning, I remembered exactly who Edward Duprez was—and is, I guess," I told him.

"I'm flattered," he said easily. "Have you seen Gabe this evening?"

"I just left him. He's about to go out on the town for the night. Georgie can't make up her mind between the emeralds or the pearls."

"Always he gets the same type of girl." Duprez shook his head wonderingly. "Wouldn't you think that once, in twenty-five years, he might find something a little different? But not Gabe—they're always blonde and plump and brainless, and most of the time they just sit around and whine. Sometimes I wonder if Gabe just hates himself. What did you want to see me about, Lieutenant?"

"Tino Martinelli," I said. "Gabriele won't talk about his kid brother at all. I figure it's kind of important. The only thing I ever heard from him was that he wanted to make Tino a college bum, yet."

"He would have gotten old trying," Duprez said contemptuously. "I can tell you about Tino Martinelli—he was a bum. Worse, he was a punk. A penny-ante hood with no more real guts than a rabbit. He ran out on Gabe just before we went to Europe that time. You know why? Because Gabe was working hard, trying to train the kid, groom him for the big time—and it scared little Tino half to death! He was meant to be a grifter and that's all. Gabe could have sweated over him for a million years and it wouldn't have made that much difference!" He snapped his fingers sharply. "For me, I'm glad the kid is dead. A life like his was pure waste anyway. But I don't say this to Gabe because he's the best friend I ever had in my whole life, you understand?"

"I understand," I said. "You have any ideas what Tino would have been doing in Southern California to get himself murdered?"

He shrugged his shoulders eloquently. "Who knows? When people will murder for pennies, maybe whatever Tino was doing wasn't that bad. One thing is for sure, Lieutenant. Whatever he was doing would be both piddling and dishonest!"

"Thanks, Ed," I told him. "Gabriele is getting impatient. He just gave me twenty-four hours to take care of the Sumners, or he says the both of you will do it by yourselves."

Duprez leaned his head back against the chair and smiled. "Then it sounds to me as if you have twenty-four hours, Lieutenant," he said softly.

"I don't dig you guys," I said wonderingly. "You go around announcing a forthcoming murder like it was a wedding or something. You make it so damned hard for anyone to take it seriously, and least of all a cop."

"I thought you didn't like that word, Lieutenant?"

"Cop? It's fine by me when I use it," I said. "And that doesn't answer any of my questions at all."

"You're right," he said, "it doesn't."

I lit a cigarette, remembering how Ed had performed at the morgue that morning. Remembering that the semiofficial tally of murders done by the "Creeping Terror" over an eight-year period was somewhere around twenty-seven, and to my knowledge Duprez had never even been arrested.

"What is your problem that twenty-four hours is not enough time to resolve it in, Lieutenant?" he asked suddenly.

"On a case that's been cold for five years? Are you kidding? Just to find a motive, let alone concrete evidence, is a tall order. And even when they showed that picture of Tino's head five years back to just about everyone who lived in Sunrise Valley, not one of them had ever seen him before."

"Maybe he'd only just arrived, and was murdered the same night?"

"Not if Emily Carlew's dying statement is true—he'd been a house guest of the Sumners for five or six days before. And that's another thing that worries me. What the hell would they have in common with a grifter, a punk like Tino Martinelli, that they should want him as a guest in their house, with the old man running up and down with food trays to keep him happy?"

"It's a very good question, Lieutenant," he said comfortably. "Maybe you can begin to appreciate that our more direct method can have certain advantages?"

"The book credits the 'Creeping Terror' with twenty-seven corpses, Ed," I told him. "Would you say that's accurate?"

"Very probably—we never bothered to keep count."

"Did it ever bother you, Ed? I mean—killing a man?"

"Of course not." His fingers flexed unconsciously. "I've always quite enjoyed it, in fact. It is an experience not realized by many men. The ultimate experience, I would call it. The supreme act in life, where for a few moments a man can be as a god, willing life or death. I thought about writing a book on the subject once, but there were certain formidable complications, such as how a court might regard it." He chuckled comfortably. "Would you like a drink, Lieutenant?"

"No, thanks," I told him. "I have to be going in a couple of minutes."

There was something about Edward Duprez that fascinated me in spite of myself. Gabriele Martinelli I could understand up to a point, but the blind man was different, horribly different.

"Have you ever been scared yourself, Ed?" I asked him.

His hands lifted from his knees and the fingertips made a delicate exploration of his face, pressing lightly against the sightless eyeballs.

"Only the one time—when they aimed the lye at me," he said softly. "Before you go, Lieutenant, I would like to ask you a few questions also."

"Sure," I said.

"You have told the Sumners about Gabe and myself, naturally. To try and panic them into thinking of the police as a preferable alternative?"

"That's right."

"Did they take you seriously?"

"Not Crispin Sumner, anyway," I growled. "He figures if he should really need protection he can get fifty men up from the Valley, all armed with shotguns and rifles, within a half hour."

"I'm sure he can," Ed said nodding, "but he won't."

"How can you be sure?"

"Because he would look so stupid if we never came—if just nothing happened," he said complacently. "All men would much prefer to risk their lives than risk being made to look a fool, Lieutenant."

"I guess that's true," I said. "Thanks for information on Tino. Good night, Mr. Duprez."

"Good night, Lieutenant. Oh, wait! There is just one other thing before you go. Did Gabe tell you to stay out of our way if we have to take action ourselves?"

"He told me," I said flatly.

"But you won't?"

"Not if I can help it."

He sighed gently. "I think that's a pity. You have the makings of a conversationalist, Lieutenant—however! Please switch off the lights on your way out."

Chapter Eight

I knocked on the penthouse suite door and while I waited, I thought about life's little coincidences which are a great thing to think about while you're waiting. Like right at that moment, for example, on the nineteenth floor of the hotel, a blind man sat in total darkness, planning how he and his partner were going to murder two people. While on the floor above him, the girl who was one of the intended victims was— doing what? I hammered harder on the door a second time.

Just as I was getting real nervous, Charity's voice called out to know who was there. The door opened a couple of seconds after I'd told her and I stepped into the suite.

"Well!" Charity looked at me with an almost pleased expression on her face, and it was definitely encouraging. "You must be all recovered and everything, Al, baby?"

"Like resilient," I said, with my fingers crossed.

"I guess you'd better go make yourself a drink," she said. "I've got a quartet of Alexanders to keep me company already."

She wore an orange silk scarf loosely knotted across her breasts, and a pair of long bikini pants that started at her ankles and finished abruptly at her hips. Charity watched me watching her with appreciative interest. "What's the matter?" she asked finally. "You never saw a navel before, baby?"

"Not in bronze," I said honestly. "I think it's kind of cute."

By the time I'd made myself a drink, she was draped all over the couch, her drink balanced precariously on her bare midriff.

"So what's new in the outside world today, Lieutenant?" she asked idly.

"That five-year-old head being identified positively as Tino Martinelli by his brother, Gabriele," I said casually.

The glass went flying as she sat bolt upright and stared at me fixedly. "What?"

I repeated what I'd already said.

She lay back onto the couch again and stared at the ceiling for a few seconds. "I've heard that name Gabriele Martinelli before someplace," she said slowly. "Who is he?"

"A highly successful businessman. As far as I know, he's still the official executioner for the syndicate," I said. "Works in partnership with a blind man called Edward Duprez, who specializes in killing people in total darkness."

"Get me another Alexander," she said in a small voice, her gaze still riveted on the ceiling.

I brought her a fresh drink across to the couch and looked inquiringly. "Where will I put it?" I asked finally. "And from where I'm standing, I can see nothing but rude answers to the question."

Charity swung her legs off the couch and sat up, then took the glass out of my hand and sipped the contents slowly.

"So what else is new?" she asked finally.

"I went out to your old ancestral mansion again this afternoon," I told her. "Had a long chat with your brother's wife—like intimate."

"That bitch," she said without any particular inflection in her voice. "All about the evil influence of the hellcat on her married life, I bet! Meaning me, of course."

"She worries what is this big, brooding thing between you and your brother, you have to try and destroy each other the whole time," I said lightly.

"Jessica's one of those natural born do-gooders who get real desperate when their do-gooding doesn't work out," she said reflectively. "I think I'm better adjusted than she is—I'm a bitch and know it—so is she but she won't admit it even to herself. I often wonder why my dear brother ever married her in the first place." She shook her head, "No, I don't," she corrected the statement quickly, "but he had no need to marry her for that. I'll bet she was available to any guy who said just being with her improved his mind!"

"I wouldn't say Crispin is about the ultimate in marriage for a woman either," I suggested. "If I was married to him, I'd slap him across the mouth first thing every morning in the devout hope that after ten years of it, he might have learned a little humility."

Charity gurgled with laughter. "I'd love to see that! Only if you preferred Crispin to me so much you'd marry him even, it would kind of spoil our relationship, wouldn't it?"

"I didn't know we had a relationship—beyond the maiming stage?" I snarled.

She shrugged bare, beautiful, and bronzed shoulders. "You have to give it time, baby, like another fifteen minutes!"

"After I talked with Jessica this afternoon, I talked to your brother," I said.

"That must have been jazzy!" She wrinkled her nose disdainfully. "You still trying hard to prove Tino slept there, the way old Emily claimed?"

"I'm still trying to prove it because I'm a cop and have to do it the hard way," I said. "Gabriele and Duprez aren't trying to prove it because they're convinced it's true already."

"Why?"

"Don't ask me—and maybe you'd better not ask them either. I had an ultimatum from Gabriele about thirty minutes back. If I don't take care of the Sumners in the next twenty-four hours, then they will."

"How does he define that plural?" Her voice had a brittle edge to it.

"The Sumners who were living in the house at the time Tino was murdered," I said, "Eli's dead—that leaves you and Crispin, honey."

Her tawny eyes watched me intently over the rim of her glass. "You wouldn't kid about something like this, Al, baby?"

"Not with Martinelli and Duprez living one floor below this, I wouldn't," I told her.

Under the bronze tan, her face was white. "Do they know who I am?" she whispered.

"Not to my knowledge," I said truthfully. "It's what's known as a complicated situation, right?"

"Maybe this Martinelli is just talking a good murder?" She didn't sound as if she'd even convinced herself.

"I'd like to think that, but not with his background," I said. "He's a pro—a top pro—and Duprez you could call an artist, even."

Charity shuddered: "In the dark! Stalking people like they were animals. It's *horrible!*"

"Duprez says it's the ultimate experience in living. A few seconds of ecstasy when a man can be a god—grant the gift of life, or take it away."

"He sounds like he's crazy!"

"I'm sure he is," I agreed. "Only you'd have a hell of a job proving it."

Charity got up from the couch in a sudden, restless movement and got herself a fresh drink—that last one had gone pretty damn fast.

"I tried to tell your brother he had a choice of the law or the professional assassins, but I don't think he believed me," I said evenly.

"And I've got the same choice—is that what you're saying?"

"Sure."

"They're crazy!" she said vehemently. "Out of their minds! And so are you, Al Wheeler! Nuts!" She swung around and hurled the full glass at an inoffensive painting on the far wall, and a moment later there was a loud explosive noise as the glass fragmented into a shower of milky pieces. "You heard what I said!" Charity stormed at me. "You're crazy, too! Why won't you believe me when I say I'm telling you the truth! There never was any Tino Martinelli or anybody else staying in the house?"

"Because an old woman who knows she's dying has much less reason to lie than you have," I told her." But if you want to stick with your story, that's fine by me. I'll just keep right on sitting here. But Duprez won't, of course. He'll have the lights out and be moving around."

Her head shook slightly as she scowled at me. "You sadistic bastard, Al Wheeler! I think you're enjoying it!"

She picked up the last remaining Alexander and I got ready to duck. But she sipped it instead of throwing it, so I relaxed a little.

"Why don't we talk about something else?" I suggested brightly. "Let's talk about Barnaby, for a change?"

"What about Barnaby?" she asked moodily.

"What was his last and greatest practical joke that got him thrown out of the house and disinherited at the same time? I'm fascinated to hear it, honest!"

"It wasn't funny," she said in a tight voice, "it wasn't funny at all!"

"Barney suddenly lost his sense of humor?"

She stared down at her glass for a few seconds before she answered. "One of the farmers in the Valley went for a vacation to Long Beach and brought back a wife with him," she said slowly, a perceptible reluctance in her voice. "He was in his early fifties and she was a twenty-year-old waitress out of a drugstore. For the first year or so, I guess everything was okay, then she started to look around—and like all the females in the Valley when they feel the same way, she looked toward the hill."

Charity shrugged helplessly. "I saw her a few times—she wasn't anything very much. She was cheap and tawdry—she was also pretty in a tinsely kind of way—and she was available. I guess it took Barney about five minutes to find her. He had a homing instinct like a pigeon for that kind of female!

"It wouldn't have meant anything—it wasn't the first time Barney had sneaked into a Valley bed when the husband was safely a long way from the house—only this time he got caught. One afternoon the farmer got home a couple of hours earlier than expected and found Barney in his bed with his wife. So he took him outside and beat the hell out of Barney in a fair and square, stand-up fight.

"I guess that was what really hurt so bad—the whole Valley heard about it and it was the stock joke for weeks. There was Barney, an athletic twenty-five-year-old, having the tar knocked out of him by a man twice his age. So Barney got an obsession about it—he had to get even, somehow. Some real cute practical joke, he figured, that would make the farmer look an absolute fool—that was the perfect answer."

She walked back to the couch and sat down again, staring at the carpet for a few seconds. "The wife was still friendly. The farmer had taken off his belt and beaten the hell out of her, too, after he was finished with Barney, so she was eager to help. It was the craziest thing. Barney rigged a booby trap—something he'd read about natives using in Africa to catch game. You bend a sapling almost to a right angle, or even further, I don't remember. Then you lash it down, conceal a net on the ground, and you have some kind of trigger mechanism that's automatically released when your victim steps on it. The sapling whips back into the air, and if everything's gone right, your victim's dangling helplessly in a net maybe thirty feet off the ground.

"Anyway, Barney spent weeks practicing until he figured he'd got it down to perfection. Then he got the whole thing ready. The farmer's wife, according to plan, made lousy excuses for having to leave the farm that afternoon, making sure she aroused her husband's suspicions, and he followed her. When he caught up with them, they were making violent, play-acting love on the grass and he blew his stack and charged straight into the booby trap."

"And it worked?" I queried.

"Everything worked just fine," she said bitterly, "except for one minor detail. Knowing he'd have to compensate for the weight of the farmer inside the net, Barney had picked a real strong sapling for the job. What he hadn't realized was, just how strong. When it whipped back to its normal upright position, the momentum and the farmer's weight were just too much—and something had to give. It was the rope holding the net to the tree, so the farmer was hurled some fifty, sixty feet into the air, and then fell straight down again. He landed fiat on his back across the limb of a tree; it broke his spine and left him permanently paralyzed from the waist down.

"Father threw Barney out of the house the same night, and cut him out of his will the next day. He settled something like a hundred thousand dollars in an outright payment to the farmer, but I guess he'd much rather have had the use of his legs back. About three months later the wife was killed in an auto accident. She was driving back alone from a Pine City dance hall and ran straight into an oncoming truck. She was loaded, of course."

"Well, thanks for telling me," I said. "You never heard from Barney after that—not even a single word?"

"Nothing," she said flatly.

"Were you very close to each other?"

"Not really." She shrugged. "Closer than either of us were to Crispin— but then he was born in a stuffed shirt!"

Charity got up again and walked quickly across to the phone. "I'll go crazy just sitting around here rehashing deaths and disasters," she said tautly as she picked up the phone. "Let's liven it up a little, Al Wheeler. Anybody would think you came to gossip with a girl instead of seduce her!" She glared at the phone, then spoke into it. "No, not you! I was talking to my uncle—the cross-eyed one that spits when he talks. This is Miss—yes, that's right. Send me up—yes, that's right, only make it six this time." She hung up and grinned at me. "Treat me right and I might dance for you yet, before the night's out, baby!"

"I hate an orgy to be interrupted by the hired help, don't you?" I said confidentially. "Why don't we wait until he's been and gone, then we can roll Aunt Jessica out from under the bed and drop her out the window? I always say there's nothing like a good laugh to get an orgy started, don't you?"

"Indubitably!" she said, with the zing back in her voice. "Later on, we could play a little prank on dear Uncle Crispin, maybe? Something like—let me see now—oh, we could stuff his stuffed shirt down his throat and while he's choking to death we could soak him in gasoline and set fire to him. How about that?"

"Sounds like fun," I agreed. "Save on electricity, too!"

A knock on the door heralded the arrival of room service, who deposited his tray on the nearest table, then departed.

"Now we can relax," Charity said enthusiastically. "A couple of games for the kiddies first would be an excellent idea, don't you think, Uncle Al?"

"Wonderful!" I beamed at her. "Do you have any suggestions, Aunt Charity? —and not that, they're too young!"

"Bullfights!" she said triumphantly. "You're the bull and I'm the matador."

She undid the knot in the silk scarf across her bosom and casually removed it. "Now, remember! This is my cape." She waved the scarf a couple of times. "And you have to keep on concentrating on the cape the whole time!"

"Honey," I said weakly. "Are you kidding?"

"I hope so." She looked down complacently at the high, swelling curves of her breasts. "Or else I'm going to have to start exercising first thing in the morning!"

We horsed around and drank some more, like a couple of kids left alone in a house for the first time. Maybe an hour later, Charity held up her hand for silence, with a solemn expression on her face.

"I think," she said in a dramatic whisper, "the time has come!"

"That's a phrase fraught with fascinating alternatives!" I said enthusiastically. "Let's work our way through them, one at a time?"

"For me to dance!" She winked carefully. "I told you—this was taught me by a genuine Egyptian belly dancer from the Bronx, and is practically guaranteed to be obscene!"

She turned her back on me suddenly. "Unzip me!" I pulled down the zip at the back of her bikini pants and she wriggled out of them like a setting-up exercise for a professional contortionist. Then she looked reflectively at the white silk briefs and shook her head. "They'll have to go. We need lots of space!"

She raised her arms over her head in an arch and tensed her body. "Watch!" she commanded breathlessly and then became an immovable, rigid statue for the next three minutes.

"I love it!" I told her when she took time out for a drink. "What is it?"

"It's a belly dance, you peasant!" she said coldly. "I'll do it yet."

Back went her arms over her head, and immediately her body became a rigid statue again. It sure was no belly dance, unless I'd been misled by the Egyptologists. Maybe ten minutes later when I was busy making myself a drink at the opposite side of the room, she squealed ecstatically.

"Al! I did it!"

"What?" I stared at her blankly.

"The dance, you moron! It moved! It really moved!"

"It did?" I shook my head a couple of times and made another try at it. "What did?"

"My navel!" she said in a breathless voice. "I know it moved—I felt it—maybe a whole quarter-inch even!"

"And that's the end of the dance?"

"What did you expect? —the Russian ballet for an encore?"

Her tawny eyes had a warm, fiery glow as she looked at me steadily for a few moments. Then she turned away and walked toward the bedroom. She stopped for a moment when she reached the door and looked at me over her shoulder. "You want to see the greatest show on earth?" she asked casually.

"Sure," I said, nodding vehemently. "I wouldn't miss it for the world."

"Well!" She flounced her hips in a wildly exaggerated gesture. "You won't see it standing out there in the living room, that's for sure!"

"Is this the main attraction of the evening?" I asked anxiously.

"For you, baby"—her voice floated back to me from the open doorway of the bedroom—"it's the one and only!"

Chapter Nine

The Sheriff and I were having a quiet little chat in his smoke-filled room. He must have stopped puffing for thirty seconds because I suddenly could see him peering at me as the clouds thinned. His look was one of obvious distaste and he only barely managed to suppress a shudder.

"I know it's early for you, Wheeler, and ten-thirty is about the crack of dawn in your life but do you have to look like that?"

"Like what?" I mumbled.

"Like something that's been thrown away when its owner can't find any further possible use for it!" he snapped.

I shuddered. "How did you know?"

"What?"

"Nothing, sir," I said quickly. "It's just that the wonderful healthy, life-giving rays of sunshine streaming in through your window are steadily blinding me!"

"Well, look the other way!" he snorted.

I pulled a pack of cigarettes out of my pocket, looked at them dubiously, then had the sudden reassuring thought that how could anything make me feel any worse than I already did? So I lit one with great confidence, and felt the first puff of smoke flinch as it entered my mouth.

"For Heaven's sake, Wheeler, can't you even assume a look of intelligence?" Lavers growled. "Anything but that submoronic, open-mouthed, vacant stare!"

"I could do my belly dance, if you want?" I mumbled at him.

"What?" he roared like a rogue elephant full of native spears.

I frantically covered both ears with my hands. The Sheriff talked to me for quite a while—I could tell that by the way his mouth kept moving all the time. When he finally took time out to light a cigar, I cautiously removed my hands from my ears.

"I think I finally got the answer to the whole problem last night," the Sheriff said tersely. "I couldn't sleep so I was just lying there, counting votes, and the whole thing came to me in a flash!"

"You dropped your cigar again?" I offered helpfully.

"It's pretty tricky," he said confidentially. "But I'm sure that's what they've done."

"Who?"

"The authorities," he said vaguely. "But they just haven't told us yet. Maybe we'll get an official announcement any day now."

"About what?"

"The new zoning, of course," he said impatiently. "That's what came to me in a flash."

"A new zone?"

"They've declared the whole of Pine City, including all the county territory, as one big sanitarium." He smiled at me benevolently. "That's why we're getting such crazy cases lately. It makes sense, doesn't it? It's a perfect explanation why I'm out of my mind right now—and you're out of your mind, too."

"You wouldn't like me to open the window a little further, Sheriff?" I asked doubtfully.

"No!" he thundered. "I'd like you to pay some attention to this investigation you're supposed to be handling! If you can listen to me talk gobbledigook, you can damned well listen to me talk official business!"

"Yes, sir," I said humbly.

He immediately lapsed into a morose silence and just sat there, scowling at me across his desk. After a couple of minutes of it, I started to feel restless.

"I told you the story of the practical joke that got Barnaby Sumner thrown out of his father's house and disinherited from the will?" I asked nervously.

"You did," he said grimly. "But what Barnaby Sumner has got to do with the murder of Tino Martinelli, I'll never know!"

"I'm sure he has somehow," I said confidently. "Crispin Sumner told me Barnaby was definitely in the house at the time of Tino's death. Then, when I told him the official records said he definitely wasn't there at the time, he mumbled something about being confused because it was such a long time back."

"So he could have been!" Lavers growled.

"In something a little over five years since Barnaby was kicked out by his father, nobody's heard a word from him," I said. "The obvious theory is he left the Valley and kept on going—the hell with the whole bunch of them he'd left behind. But I think the alternative theory's just as interesting—that he never left the Valley at all."

"He grew a long white beard and bought a farm?" Lavers sneered.

"More likely he was buried on one," I grunted.

"We've had one unsolved murder for five years already!" he grated. "Now you're trying to find us another one!"

"I've got a hunch if we could find out what happened to Barney Sumner, we'd know what happened to Tino Martinelli," I persisted.

"Never mind that now," he snapped. "I'm a damned sight more worried about Gabriele Martinelli's threat. Why don't we simply grab the both of them and toss them into jail for a few days?"

"Because we won't be able to keep them there. They won't be in the cell, even, before their lawyers arrive," I said. "And there has to be more to it—the threat, I mean. It's a calculated move on their part. A team like Martinelli and Duprez don't play anything off the cuff, Sheriff. Maybe this is an elaborate bum steer—a cover for their real plans?"

"I talked with Captain Parker at Headquarters," Lavers said, almost defiantly. "Both of them are being tailed night and day, so if they even point in the direction of the Valley, we'll know of it."

"I don't have too much confidence about that, either," I said. "They'll let the tall sit right behind them as long as it suits them and if it doesn't, they'll lose him in less than two minutes."

"The way you talk about these two cheap murdering hoodlums,

anyone would think you admired them, Wheeler!" Lavers said in a coldly disapproving voice.

"I don't admire them for what they are or what they do, Sheriff," I said, with equal coldness. "Only for their professional competence. I'd hate to underrate them in any way at all—they're the biggest challenge we've had yet!"

"Challenge?" He gaped at me for a moment. "What are you talking about?"

"I'd like to see us in a position to offer them our hospitality for an extended period into the future—something like twenty to thirty years."

"It would have to be something very big to bring that kind of sentence!"

"Like attempted homicide?" I suggested cheerfully.

"Are you out of your mind again?" He closed his eyes tight and shook his head slowly. "You mean you want to encourage them into an attempted homicide, Wheeler? What if they're successful?"

"You have a point there," I admitted grudgingly. "Anyway, it was only a thought, Sheriff."

"Then destroy it!"

"Duprez says Tino Martinelli was nothing but a bum, a small-time grifter," I said conversationally.

"The hell with what Duprez says," Lavers said angrily. "You want to make him an honorary sheriff or something?"

"It's important," I said acidly. "Gabriele won't talk about him, so Duprez is the only person we know who can tell us something about the executioner's kid brother."

"So now we've established Tino was a bum and a grifter—thank you, Lieutenant Wheeler!"

"As always," I said, bouncing the syllables like ice cubes at him, "I hadn't finished! Duprez also said that whatever Tino was doing in Southern California would be piddling and dishonest."

"So?"

"So did anything piddling and dishonest happen in the Valley in the few weeks before the decapitated head was found? That's another thing, Sheriff—whatever happened to the rest of the body?"

"How the hell would I know!" he yelped.

"Is that your answer to both questions?" I asked coolly.

"Yes! And I told you right in the beginning that the body had never turned up!" He slammed his elbows onto the desk and buried his head in his hands. "Wheeler, do whatever you want—organize a murder contest for your two new friends, if you want. Anything—but just get the hell out of here!"

"Yes, sir," I said politely. "I'm not the type to stay where I'm not wanted."

"Then how come you've been hanging around this office for three years already?" he asked happily.

I went out of his office without answering, because I guessed it was about his turn for the punch line and I couldn't think up one to top it, anyway. The filing cabinets were the first most obvious place to look, so that was where I started.

Maybe a couple of minutes later, I felt a burning sensation right between my shoulder blades which grew steadily worse. I turned around and was nearly knocked off my feet by the blast of fever-pitch adoration that gleamed in Annabelle Jackson's eyes.

"Hi, Al," she said dreamily in a voice that was full of tinkling southern belles. "I just can't wait for eight o'clock tonight to come around!"

"Why, what's happening?" I said absently, then remembered just in time. "Me, neither!" I added hastily. "Do we have anybody working in here who lives in the Valley?"

"Oh, sure," she said sweetly. "Valleys, mountains, suburbs—they come from all over."

"I'm glad to hear it." I just managed to keep the snarl out of my voice. "I mean Sunrise Valley in particular."

"You want me to check the l'il ole files for you, honey chile?"

"Thanks," I said tersely. "And while you're at it, you could file the magnolia and harvest moon until tonight, honey. This looks like it could be my busy day."

"Fine," she said briskly.

There were two uniformed men who lived in the Valley. I checked and found one was off duty and the other out on patrol—the one off duty looked like the best bet, I figured, and crossed my fingers he hadn't gone fishing for the day already.

An hour later I was back in the steam heat of the Valley, and praying for rain like I'd never prayed for rain before. A shimmering curtain of heat haze danced along the road in front of me and any moment I expected the whole surroundings to explode in one single sheet of flame.

Joe Daly was the man I wanted, and he was home all right—sitting comfortably in the shade of his veranda, wearing a pair of indescribable shorts and a pipe. He lumbered onto his feet as I came onto the veranda, a look of blank surprise on his face.

"Lieutenant Wheeler—what are you doing out here?"

I told him I was looking for help, gave him a capsuled run-down on why, and then the vital question—Did he remember any crime at all, however small, in the Valley in those few weeks before the discovery of the decapitated head?

He puffed his pipe solidly through thirty agonizing seconds of silence, then shook his head slowly.

"Not that I recall, Lieutenant—you checked the files, of course?"

"Miss Jackson checked them for me—that's why I'm confident they were checked."

He grinned sympathetically. "I know what you mean, Lieutenant. So it's no good, huh?"

"Looks like it," I said. "It was only a hunch and it could have fitted in real well—but it doesn't."

"I was just thinking," he said blandly. "The Valley's a pretty tight community, like most isolated ones are. They can be a little funny in their ways, too."

"You mean they don't trust strangers anyway, and most times they'd rather look after their own affairs instead of calling in an outside authority?" I grinned at him. "They don't like calling for a cop when they can sort it out real well by themselves?"

"Sure," he said nodding. "Hank Williams would be your man—runs the general store on Main Street. Why don't you drive down there, Lieutenant, and talk with him? I'll call him as soon as you leave and let him know you're coming."

"I'd appreciate it very much," I told him. "Thanks again."

Fifteen minutes later I walked into the general store, where it was ten degrees cooler, and had no trouble finding Hank Williams at all— he was the only other person in the store.

"Joe Daly said you'd be dropping in, Lieutenant," he said as we shook hands. "Told me what you're looking for." He hesitated a second too long before he shook his head. "I'm sorry, but I can't help you. Nothing happened around that time, not that I remember, anyway."

"Thanks, Mr. Williams," I said, "and I think you're lying."

His face darkened a little. "You can think what you like, Lieutenant!" he snapped.

"I think you're lying for a good reason—or what looks like a good reason to you," I said. "This is desperately important to me. It can be the missing link in the proof that maybe two men were murdered in the Valley, not one. My guess is the second body has never been found because it was so damned skillfully hidden in the first place. You can help find out—and catch a murderer, too. It's up to you."

His hesitation was a lot longer this time. "It's kind of hard to explain, Lieutenant," he said uncomfortably. "It's other people. Their privacy's involved—even more than that. I don't know that I've got the right."

"I'll give you any kind of personal guarantee you—or the people involved—want," I said. "Even if they broke the law themselves, I don't give a damn. The information is all I'm interested in."

"If I could persuade one of them to talk with you, Lieutenant, would you give your word not to mention anything they didn't want mentioned?"

"Sure," I said. "A blank check!"

He scratched his head and grinned at me. "There's a bar right next door. Why don't you wait in there, Lieutenant? This won't be easy, and I got a nasty feeling it's going to take some time."

It took just over an hour. I was sitting in a booth wondering if I should have another beer or switch to Scotch when somebody stopped beside the table. A tall, powerfully built guy with a face that looked like it had been punched out of concrete. "You Wheeler?" he grunted.

"That's right," I told him.

He sat down opposite me with slow, deliberate movements, his openly hostile eyes studying my face with minute care, without being either embarrassed or hurried.

"You having a drink, Mr.—?" I asked him, when the checkup on my face was finished.

"No," he said abruptly, "and we'll keep names out of this. I didn't want any part of it—still don't. I wouldn't be here now if Hank Williams hadn't told me why you're sticking your nose into what don't concern you. Hank figures you can be trusted." His voice dropped a fraction. "I hope he's right, mister, for your sake!"

"He's right," I said briefly.

"Yeah." He wiped the back of his hand slowly across his mouth. "You know something? It is hot in here. Maybe I'll change my mind and have a beer."

I got two fresh beers and carried them back to the booth. He drank deeply, then stared at me again for a long half-minute.

"It was like this," he said with a sudden abruptness. "A week, maybe eight days before they found that chopped head, I took my wife to visit with some friends about three miles further up the Valley from where we are. We left after dinner, around eight. Our two girls were left in the house. The eldest was sixteen then, and the other a couple of years younger. Nobody even thought about leaving their kids alone in the Valley then—the biggest crime we'd ever had was when some kids stole somebody's pickup and drove it a couple of miles away."

His eyes clouded slightly. "Oh—yeah, there was some money in the house—around three hundred dollars. The buyer had paid me too late that afternoon to get it into the bank. When we got to the friends', the wife found out she'd left a birthday present at home and she got kind of upset about it. We had a couple of drinks and I could see she wouldn't enjoy the party unless she could hand that present over to where it belonged. So I said I'd go back and pick it up.

"I was driving my pickup, and I had a double-barreled shotgun in it—we'd been after some birds a few days before without any luck."

He took a sudden deep breath. "I parked and was halfway up to the front door when I heard the youngest crying inside the house. But I'd never heard her cry like that in her whole life before—like she was ashamed."

His eyes were glacier-like in their coolness as he stared at something a foot above my head. "Then I knew there was something wrong—badly wrong. I grabbed the shotgun and a handful of shells, loaded it, and came in through the front door just as they were leaving out the back. The girls' clothing was torn and scattered everywhere across the floor. I found both girls in our bedroom, tied down side by side on our bed. Whatever you can imagine, mister, it was worse.

"I didn't stop to untie them then because I knew I was too late to save them any hurt—it had all been done while I was sitting having a drink three miles further up the Valley. But I figured if I moved real fast I'd stand a good chance of catching up with them. I knew every inch of the country for miles around and I didn't think, whoever they were, that they'd come from the Valley.

"I used to hunt a lot—I don't anymore. So I could move pretty fast without making much noise. It didn't take any time at all to catch up with them. I could hear them talking—and *laughing*. I wanted to kill them so bad it nearly choked me—I couldn't wait maybe another ten seconds to take it quietly.

"So I came running at them like a crazy man, and that gave them a chance. What I wanted was to give them one barrel each, closeup, in the belly, then I was going to leave them out there. But I never got the chance." His voice was still tinged with faint regret. "They were a lot younger than me and they could run faster, so I had to stop and see what the gun would do for me. I got one of them in the leg and he veered away from his pal, screaming his head off."

He drained his glass and wiped the back of his hand across his forehead again. "Sure is hot in here. Anyway, the other one lost his nerve and came to a dead stop with his hands in the air. He kept on yelling out, 'Don't shoot! Don't shoot!' So I told him to turn around and walk back toward me. When he was maybe six feet away I gave him the other barrel. I meant for it to hit his belly, but I guess I was shaking a little and it went a little high—in his chest, mostly. He hit the dirt and didn't move any. The other one had disappeared by then, of course. So I turned around and went home."

"Did you recognize either of them?"

"The one I hit in the leg—it was his head they found about eight days later."

"How about the other one?"

"He looked kind of familiar but I figured I'd killed him and it didn't matter too much then who he was!"

"I can see your point," I told him.

"Nobody in the Valley ever got treated by the doctor for gunshot wounds in the next few weeks," he said. "I know, because I checked with the doctor."

He leaned forward across the table, bringing his face closer to mine. "Up until this morning, mister, only six people ever knew that story. Me, my wife, the two girls, the doctor—and Hank Williams. That's why when Hank said he trusted you, I had to go along with it."

"You know what I am?" I asked him.

"Sure—a police lieutenant," he said steadily. "What difference?"

"You took a hell of a chance," I said softly. "I appreciate it—that fills in nicely the missing pieces of my own problem."

"Okay," he said. "So I'll be moving along—got some things to do."

"Sure," I said. "How are your girls, these days?"

"Just fine," he said bleakly. "The oldest is married already and the other one's still at school, but she figures she's going steady."

"That's nice," I said soberly.

"We like it—the wife and me, we just keep things going exactly the way they are." He got up from the booth. "I guess I won't be seeing you again," he said slowly. "Will I?"

"Maybe you'll see me again sometime," I said. "But I won't see you. I've got such a lousy memory for faces that yours is blurred already."

"That's what I figured." His voice was a little more friendly, but not too much. "You should get yourself a pair of glasses, mister."

Then he was gone.

Chapter Ten

It was around three-thirty in the afternoon when I got back into the city. I parked close to the Pines Hotel and just sat in the Healey for a while, thinking over what I was going to do. I thought about it long enough to make up my mind it was worthwhile, but not long enough to change my mind again. The one thing I couldn't afford right then was to get nervous in my thinking, or in no time at all I'd be sitting right alongside Charlie Katz, cutting out paper dolls all called John the Baptist.

I didn't bother to check with the desk but took the elevator straight up to the nineteenth floor. If they'd jumped the deadline, that was too bad and I could go someplace quiet and cut my throat. After I'd knocked three times real loud on the door of 1901, it finally opened and a bleary-eyed Georgie blinked at me.

"Is Gabriele inside?" I asked her.

"Yeah!" She yawned loudly and I could almost hear her nylon pajama top squeal in terror. "But he's sleeping," she said. "We had a kinda late night and didn't get back until morning."

"I'll be in with Ed," I said. "Now, you wake Gabe up. Tell him I said it's real important and for him to come into Ed's suite. You got that?"

"Oh, sure!" She ran her fingers through her tousled hair. "Gee! I bet I look just awful!"

"You look real great," I said, lying in my teeth. "A real doll, Georgie. If Gabriele wasn't in there already, I'd say the hell with it and jump in beside you right now!"

She giggled delightedly. "I'll tell Gabe what you said!"

"Hey, you wouldn't squeal on a guy just because he's crazy for the classiest dame in town, would you?" I said, wondering where I'd dredged that line of dialogue from—one of those late, late shows on television, I guessed, when they show all those movies that were made around the time Wallace Beery was playing juvenile leads.

"All right," she said coyly, with one hand tactfully tucking a hairpin out of sight around the back of her head. "For you, lover-boy, I'll keep quiet!"

"Thanks, Georgie," I said, gritting my teeth. "Now don't forget—you got to get Gabriele out of bed right away."

"Sure," she said confidently. "I'll get him in there in no time at all. Who will I tell him said to wake him up?"

"Me," I said blankly.

"Oh, yeah!" she giggled shrilly. "Aren't I the stupid one!" She blew me a liquor-loaded kiss all to myself, but I got lucky and dodged it as she closed the door.

I had my hand raised ready to knock on Duprez's door, when the other one popped open again and Georgie's head shot out frantically, a relieved smile showing up on her face when she saw I'd only moved along about six feet. "Hey, lover!" She winked, and it was a mistake because the mascara started to run all ways.

"Yeah?" I said cautiously.

"What's your name?"

I closed my eyes so she wouldn't see the bloody murder in them, then told her.

"Oh, yeah!" The smile slowly faded from her face and was replaced by outraged indignation. "Hey! You're that cop—and you making all them cracks about jumping in with me!"

"Wouldn't you jump into bed with a cop?" I asked curiously.

"Not," she said distantly, "on my own time!" The door closing wiped her out of my sight.

At the first knock, Duprez's voice said, "Come." So I opened the door and stepped into his suite. He was sitting in the same chair he'd been in the night before.

"Lieutenant Wheeler," he said, smiling. "An official visit?"

"How did you know it was me?" I asked him.

"I've heard your footsteps often enough now to pick up their individual characteristics," he said. "Sit down, if you're staying long enough, Lieutenant."

"Georgie is getting Gabriele up and in here as fast as she can," I told him. "I wanted to talk to both of you together. It's important."

"I think we'd better allow fifteen minutes," he said with a chuckle. "Gabe is a passionate riser."

Maybe it wasn't any more than a quarter-hour before Gabriele came into the room, but it seemed a hell of a lot longer. He didn't look exactly full of the joys of living, either.

"What the hell's so important you got to get me out of bed in the middle of the night?" he snarled at me balefully.

"I want to make a deal," I said.

For a brief moment, surprise showed in his eyes. Then he shrugged and lit a cigarette. "What kind of deal?"

"I can tie the rap onto the Sumners all right—where it belongs," I said. "But I got to go a couple of places first where I can't go legally right now. That's why I want your help."

"So what's in it for us?" Gabriele said, shrugging.

"Tino's body," I said, and he stiffened. "The satisfaction of seeing the Sumners on their way to the gas chamber. No strain."

Duprez turned his head toward me for a moment. "You have to go a couple of places—illegally—first? Where and what are these places, Lieutenant?"

"The Sumner house out in the Valley—and the family vault in back of it."

"That's where the rest of Tino's body is?" Gabriele asked quickly.

"I think so—I'm almost certain," I said. "It would take me a week to get the official authority and that would tip off Crispin Sumner. We can't afford that."

"There is only he and his wife at the house right now," Duprez said easily. "The girl—Charity—hasn't been there for days now. I think Gabe would like to be sure she would also be there?"

"Yeah," Gabriele said slowly. "I'd want her along, too."

"I'll bring her with me," I agreed.

"If you say so, I would like to be a gentleman and take your word on the subject," Gabriele said very politely. "But if she's not there?"

"The deal's off," I said casually. "No girl—so you had a ride out into the Valley. Maybe you can take care of one-half of the job you've got in mind—it's up to you."

"I think that sounds reasonable, Gabe," Duprez said. "When?"

"Tonight!" I said sharply. "I figure Crispin Sumner is getting nervous already. I don't want to give him a chance to get into that vault before us."

"We are being tailed, night and day," Duprez said.

"Sheriff's idea," I said briefly. "I'll get that lifted right now."

The hotel switchboard put me through on the direct line into Captain Parker's office. His voice was cool when he learned who it was. The Captain prefers the more orthodox kind of cop who'll listen respectfully when the Captain shoots off his mouth, and that happens most of the time. I told him I was calling for the Sheriff, and we wanted the tail lifted on Martinelli and Duprez right away, until the next morning at least. I made a nice polite vote of thanks to the Captain on behalf of the Sheriff, and he was almost purring when I hung up.

"Good," Gabriele said. "This family vault—you've seen it?"

"It has a heavy bronze door that works on a combination, and Crispin has the combination, of course." I gave Gabriele a particularly blank look. "I don't imagine you'd have any trouble persuading him to open the vault for us?"

"It will be no trouble," he said.

"How do we get into the house without raising his suspicions?" Duprez asked, practically. "A quick phone call and that would be the end."

"The sister—Charity," I told him. "I'm figuring on her for sure, even if you aren't convinced. I'll have her call him and say she's coming home. She has a big car, there'll be plenty of room for the three of us to stay out of sight while she drives in."

"Will she do it?" Gabriele said. "When she sees me and Ed she'll start getting real worried!"

"I think it'll be okay. She trusts me," I said modestly.

"Maybe the Lieutenant is wasted where he is, huh, Ed?" Gabriele said, grinning. "So what else is there?"

"You drive out to the Valley yourselves and park on the main drag anyplace," I said. "We have to see you—the place isn't big enough to lose anybody. We'll stop and pick you up at, say, nine?"

"That will do fine," Gabriele nodded. "I can get a little more sleep right now!"

"How many other officers will there be, besides yourself, Lieutenant?" Duprez asked.

"Just me," I said. "I like the official glory all to myself."

"I appreciate your feelings." He chuckled. "So now, we are organized—

there is nothing else?"

"Not that I know of," I told him.

"Just one little thing, Lieutenant," Gabriele said curiously. "I had it figured we would have to rub them out and you'd try and buck us. For a jerkwater-town cop, you got quite a lot going for you. So what made you change your mind?"

"The combination," I said easily. "It cuts down the odds a long way too far. I'd take a chance on a playoff against either of you on your own—but together?" I shook my head slowly.

Gabriele bellowed with laughter. "You know something, Ed? This boy could go a long way—if he was in an honest business!"

It was after six when I walked into Police Headquarters, but the guy I had to see was a kind of genius-nut in his own right, and he thought clocks were only designed to break up the monotony of walls. He was hunched over a microscope when I walked into his lab and I almost had to yell in his ear before he lifted his head.

"Hey, Al!" He grinned widely. "That Sheriff finally flip his lid and send you home?"

"Not yet, Mac," I told him. "But tune in tomorrow, it could happen. I want a favor—two favors—and I want them both fast and unofficial."

"Like what?"

"Gimmicks," I said. I want a dummy pen that will squirt water."

"That you got."

"Fine—this may be a little tougher. I want a magnetized thirty-eight, Mac, that will clamp on the underside of a dashboard—loaded, of course."

"None of that's any problem," he said, smiling bleakly. "Except you don't want to sign for the gun?"

"No," I said meekly.

"You must have your reasons, I guess." He shrugged. "So I'll sign for it and just hope nobody reads the signature and wonders what the hell I want to take a gun home nights for."

"Mac, you're a very sweet guy and can you get them for me right away because I'm running out of time and I have to use your phone to tell the Sheriff I'm following a hot lead down in the Valley?"

"Al Wheeler," he said bitterly, "you should have been a con-artist!"

Chapter Eleven

I looked sideways at Charity's profile, which was worth the look in its own right, but also to see how she was making out.

"I think I must be crazy," she said in a bleak voice. "The way I let you talk me into this! Calling up my stuffed shirt of a brother, like I'm the prodigal daughter on my way home. Hiding you and these two other men we're picking up in the Valley so you can all get into the house! All this I'm doing for you on the strength of a couple of orgies!"

I checked my watch and saw it was a little after seven-thirty.

"Pull off the road up ahead, we got plenty of time, baby," I told her. "Let's talk a little more?"

"That's about the most original approach I've ever heard for pulling off a deserted road!"

The Continental whispered sedately onto the grass shoulder and Charity cut the motor.

"Okay." Her fingers still gripped the wheel tensely. "I'm listening."

"I know most of the story now, baby," I told her, "and I can guess the rest. When brother Barney was thrown out of the house by your father, he ran into Tino Martinelli someplace, sometime—it's not important. What is important is that they teamed up together, and one night they came back into the Valley."

Charity closed her eyes tightly. "Do I have to go through this again?"

"You haven't been free of it in five years," I reminded her gently. "One more time might make all the difference."

"All right," she said in a low voice.

"They went into a house and—well, let's skip that—but the father came back as they were leaving, and he caught up with them finally and let off both barrels of his shotgun. Tino got hit in the leg, but Barney got the full blast from one barrel straight into his chest. So they were stranded in the Valley, both hurt, Barney certainly incapable of traveling any distance at all, knowing that if the police caught them they were through. So they took the only possible chance they had— Barney went back to plead with his father for sanctuary. Eli Sumner gave it to his son, and to his son's friend.

"Tino appeared safely as a sick guest confined to his bed, but Barney would have been recognized instantly by the servants, so he had to be hidden away?"

"The cellar," Charity said tonelessly. "Overnight I developed a craze for developing my own films, so the cellar door had to be locked and the key kept by me in case anyone ruined my films by letting light in at the wrong moment."

"You imagined the police were hunting through the whole district for the wanted men, so you didn't dare call a doctor for Barney, right?"

"It was dreadful!" she whispered. "Father managed to get enough drugs to keep him out of pain most of the time, but we all knew he was dying. One night Father decided he would call a doctor and Tino nearly went berserk."

"And after Barney was dead, his body was put in the family vault," I went on. "And Tino got well again."

"He was busy planning the rest of his life—as a member of the Sumner family," she said bitterly. "Expose me and I'll expose your dead son unlawfully buried out in the backyard, was the theme, if not the words. From gratitude to blackmail in one easy step!"

She turned her head away from me toward the window on her side of the car. "Father and Crispin hated him, not only for what he was but for the magnitude of the threat he constituted against the Sumner family. I was just eighteen then, and because they hated him, I made myself like him, and after a while I thought I was in love with him. He fascinated me—his crude good looks, the way his complete lack of moral values seemed to get him anything he wanted." She laughed mirthlessly. "I guess I was the right age for it, too!"

"What made it all blow sky-high?" I asked her.

"Me," she whispered. "Father had gone to San Francisco for a couple of weeks to visit some friends. All the servants were given a week's vacation except Emily, the cook, who'd go home after dinner every night. On the second night, Tino came into my room and got into bed with me. I was panic stricken at first—about being caught, I mean—but he said who else was there to worry about and laughed when I mentioned Crispin. I gained confidence from his attitude and soon we were talking in our normal voices and laughing out loud.

"Then Crispin came charging in to rescue his virginal sister and found she was enjoying herself. Tino was openly contemptuous of Crispin and delighted in mocking him. He said Crispin had better get used to the idea, because that was going to be the permanent arrangement in the future. Tino was grinning the whole time he watched Crispin writhe. He couldn't resist the chance to push him as far as he'd go—so he said Crispin should remember that when he married and brought his bride back home, Tino, as his new brother, would expect equal marital rights. At that time, Crispin was seriously considering asking Jessica to marry him on the understanding of a long engagement. And it was the sudden vision of a future of unending horror while Tino grew more arrogant and contemptuous every day that pushed Crispin over the edge."

Charity began to weep softly. "He hardly seemed to have left the room before he was back with that axe in his hand! Oh, God! I saw him standing there, his eyes gleaming like a maniac's, and then he swung the axe and I saw Tino's head roll!" She sobbed uncontrollably for some time, while I tried to comfort her and got no place at all. Then gradually she calmed down again, and lit a cigarette.

"I fainted then," she said in a tight voice. "When I woke up I was in Father's room with the door locked from the outside. Crispin must have carried me in there. About nine in the morning he came into the room, still with that crazy look in his eyes, and said we alone shared the secret of how he'd saved the family from evil—then he rambled on and on.

"During the night he'd done an incredible amount of work. All my bed clothes had been burned. He'd scrubbed the floor clean of bloodstains. There wasn't a trace of anything to prove that Tino had ever existed. In the afternoon, Crispin told me he'd walked a long way through the scrub to get rid of something, then must have had a blackout, because when he came to his senses it was after dawn and he was miles away from the last place he remembered. I didn't worry about what it was he'd walked so far to get rid of, until I saw Tino's head looking up at me from the paper!"

"Did he ever tell you what he did with Tino's body?"

"I never asked him."

"In the vault for sure—otherwise it would have turned up. He really flipped that night, didn't he?—not to put the head in the vault too?" The picture of her brother plunging through the underbrush on his crazy errand with a sackful of human head wasn't pretty. "What did your father say when he found Tino was gone after he got back?" I asked her.

"Nothing," she said. "I don't think he wanted to know. He was frightened about what he might hear of his own children. After Barnaby died, I guess Father lost the will to live."

I checked my watch again and saw we still had plenty of time.

"Why don't we pull off the road further down and have some coffee— a drink?" I suggested.

"No, thanks, Al!" She shuddered at the thought. "I look like the wrath of God!"

"It's confession time all over, baby," I told her. "Listen hard, and start figuring chances!"

I told her how I'd made the deal with Gabriele and Duprez—they were the two men we were to pick up in the Valley. How she had been made part of the deal, and how she was, as she already knew, the decoy to get us into the house without raising an alarm.

Charity was staring at me wide-eyed with horror by the time I had finished. "Now let's figure the percentages," I told her. "No chances in a million for Crispin—if Gabriele doesn't get him, the law will. Jessica's got to lose a husband anyway, and other than that, I don't think there's much risk for her. Gabriele wants you dead because you're one of the two surviving Sumners who were in the house when his kid brother was killed.

"I want you alive and I desperately need you as the decoy or the whole thing's a bust. I also want to frame Gabriele and Duprez with enough of a rap to put them away for a long time.

"You got a choice, baby. You can let me out any place you like and drive straight back to Pine City, or you can play decoy down in the Valley."

"I—I don't know, Al."

"You take the risk with me," I said soberly, "and I can lift the burden of guilt from your magnificent bronze shoulders."

"Don't kid around, Al!" she pleaded.

"I know you had nothing to do with Tino's death. Technically you were an accessory after the fact—but that's crazy, when you consider the minimal amount of free choice you had. You have to face up to something right now. Crispin will be either dead or insane before the night's out, and that leaves you—with a police lieutenant looking over your shoulder to see everything works out fine. If you're still alive, that is."

"Al, baby!" she said, and laughed hysterically. "You kook! How could any girl refuse a cast-iron guarantee like that!"

"That's great!" I said enthusiastically. "Just don't forget—when Gabriele and Duprez get into the car in the Valley, you don't know who they are. You're just vaguely assuming they're friends of mine."

"I won't forget," she said, shivering slightly.

I prodded around under the dash until I'd found enough metal for the magnetized gun to grip onto firmly. All the rest of the way through the Valley until we reached Main Street, I devoted the time exclusively to gun instruction for Charity's benefit, getting her to say out loud at least fifty times, "The safety catch is off!" I figured it would be ironical if she grabbed the gun in an effort to save me and blew my brains out in the attempt.

It went like clockwork, like there had been a general staff planning the operation for months. Gabriele and Duprez got into the back seat of the car when we stopped on Main Street. The three of us sat on the floor from the time the car was in sight of the house until the time Charity parked beside the front steps. Jessica and Crispin came out to greet her, and found themselves being shepherded back into the house by Gabriele's gun. Inside five minutes, we were a tight, if not exactly cozy, group in the living room.

"It was the planning and the coordination that made it simple," Gabriele said happily. "You did a nice job, Lieutenant. Now you got some idea how Ed and me figure out the precise moves in a job before we ever make a move."

"Lieutenant?" Jessica Sumner asked in a completely bewildered voice. "What on earth is happening here? Has everybody gone mad? Aren't you supposed to be in charge? I don't understand what—"

"Why don't we leave Mrs. Sumner locked in one of the other rooms?" I said to Gabriele.

"Sure. I'll take care of it," he said tonelessly.

Jessica was led away still firmly protesting that either this must be some kind of practical joke or else there must have been a hideous mistake. Then Gabriele came back a couple of minutes later and grinned at me.

"I put her into the bathroom. I figure what more could she want? There's a view from the window, even!"

Crispin cleared his throat gently. "Lieutenant! Up until now I assumed you were in charge here—as did my wife! And if you are, I demand to know who are these other two men that forced their way into my house at the point of a gun and—"

"Let me introduce them, Mr. Sumner," I said politely. "This gentleman is Gabriele Martinelli, the elder brother of Tino Martinelli, deceased; and the gentleman over there is Mr. Edward Duprez, popularly known as the 'Creeping Terror.'"

The blood drained from his face and he shrank back into his chair, his body trembling uncontrollably.

"We want to see inside that vault," Gabriele said coldly. "You have the combination?"

"Yes, yes!" Crispin nodded vigorously. "I'll come and open it right now for you."

"Gabe," Duprez said gently, "I'd like to stretch my legs a little. Why don't we all go out to the vault?"

"Fine by me," Gabe said easily.

As we walked through to the back of the house and then out onto the lawn, Charity managed to get close to me for a moment.

"What do I do if we get separated?" she whispered frantically.

"Run like hell for that gun under the dash if you're left alone with Gabriele," I told her, and there was no time for any more.

The moment we reached the vault, Crispin started work on the combination as if his life depended on how fast he could open it. Finally there was the last click and the last tumbler rolled. Crispin lifted his sweat-drenched face triumphantly, almost as if he expected applause. The massive bronze door opened smoothly without the slightest sound.

Cold steel nosed into the small of my back, while expert fingers lifted the thirty-eight from the belt holster.

"You're doing fine, Lieutenant," Gabe said generously. "No sudden nervous reactions that can only get you a slug in the back! Now, all you got to do is walk into the vault!"

"Gabriele!" I said tensely. "What the hell is this? We made a deal! You would—"

"Now we made a new deal, cop!" he chuckled. "A nice clean sweep all around—one dies, they all die. No witnesses, and since you had the tailing job removed for us, who's to say we ever left the hotel? Not Georgie, that's for sure!" The gun nudged harder against my spine. "So walk!"

I didn't have any choice and the entrance to that vault looked about as inviting as an open casket. Almost as soon as I'd gotten inside, Crispin was pushed in behind me. Then Duprez stepped through the open door and paused for a moment.

"No light switches on the inside? You're sure?" He smiled happily. "Close the door tight shut after me, Gabe, but don't go away—the air won't last that long! Give me five minutes exactly."

He moved two paces further into the vault and the bronze door closed tight. Crispin shrieked as the claustrophobic qualities of the absolute darkness twisted his already battered nerve ends. I heard Duprez's exultant chuckle from somewhere still close to the entrance. Then his voice sounded, surprisingly loud.

"Welcome to my kingdom, gentlemen! This is where the blind reign supreme and those who have sight are the scurrying rabbits doomed to extinction!"

"You must have been practicing that, Ed," I said evenly. "Nobody could dream that up on the spur of the moment!"

He didn't answer and I felt the first prickle of fear walk up and down my spine. There was a faint scuffling sound that only lasted two seconds at most, then silence again.

"One little rabbit taken care of, Lieutenant," Duprez's voice said, from somewhere much closer than before. "You have a few moments left. As you know, I like to savor the minute taste of infinite power. To rush is to lose a little of the ultimate pleasure!"

"Ed, baby," I said softly, "remember what I said when we made the deal?—the combination of the two of you would be too strong for me to take on alone, but I wouldn't mind my chances with each of you—one at a time?"

"You may talk for a little while more, Lieutenant," he said dreamily.

"If it amuses you."

"Why do you think I told both of you I had to get inside this vault, huh?" I laughed softly. "I knew you wouldn't be able to resist it, Ed, baby. Divide and conquer—you on the inside, and Gabe on the outside. Now do you start to get the picture?"

"You think you have a chance against me in the absolute dark?" he said confidently. "You'll never know what happened until it's already over, Lieutenant!"

"Don't forget I set this up, Ed," I said reprovingly. "I offered the deal—made sure we'd get inside the vault—so I wouldn't stop there, would I?"

"Just what are you talking about now?" he snarled.

I slid the gismo pen Mac had given me from my inside coat pocket and unscrewed the top gently. "One of those trick pens, Ed, baby," I said slowly. "You press a button and it squirts a stream of water straight into somebody's face!"

"Are you out of your mind?" His voice sounded genuinely amazed. "How do you think that will save you?"

"You press a button and it squirts a stream of water into somebody's face," I repeated. "That is, if you've got it filled with water. I haven't. Guess what my pen's loaded with, Ed, baby—special for you!"

He didn't answer and my spine twitched apprehensively at the silence. "It's lye, baby," I said softly. "Lye!" I sank down onto my knees soundlessly the moment I finished speaking, and a split second later, there was a faint, brushing sound, like a small bird flying over my head. I flung my arms out sideways, and my left arm bounced off his leg. But as I came up into a standing position, I felt the brutal strength of his fingers closing around my throat. I aimed the pen wildly in the direction I hoped he'd be, and pressed the knob.

The steel fingers fell away from my throat and he screamed horribly and repeatedly until my fumbling hands grabbed hold of his shoulders and half-walked, half-ran him toward the bronze door that was slowly opening at the far end of the vault. I kind of hunched down in back of Duprez as we came up to the entrance itself, praying that he'd get any of Gabriele's slugs if Martinelli cut loose.

We ran maybe twenty feet outside the vault onto the lawn, and still nothing happened. I took my hands away from Duprez's shoulders and chopped the side of my hand down across his neck and he stopped screaming and crumpled to the ground. I spun around, frantically looking for Gabriele, when I heard a piercing feminine shriek which sounded vaguely like "Al!"

A couple of seconds later a bundle of bronzed curves hurtled into my arms. "Al, baby!" Charity yelled happily. "I thought you were dead!"

"Where's Gabriele?" I asked, the sudden panic returning fast.

"Over there." She pointed casually to what looked like a beanpole stretched out on the grass.

"What happened?"

"When there were only the two of us left outside the vault and he pointed that horrible gun at me, I was about to die!" she said fervently. "But then—you know what he did?" Her voice rose on a strident note of indignation. "He tucked the gun away and tried to make a pass at me!"

"So then what happened?" I growled.

"I clobbered him," she said calmly. "What girl wouldn't?"

Duprez started to moan and twitch, so I walked over to him and knelt down beside him. "Ed," I said in a very calm voice, "it wasn't lye. It was water, you understand? It was all in your mind. Not lye—only water! When you felt it hit your face you remembered the time before when it was real. You didn't wait to find out if it burned your flesh or not."

He felt around for my arms as he sat up, and I helped him up onto his feet. He hung onto my arm for a few seconds until he had his balance.

"It wasn't lye?" he whispered.

"Only water," I repeated firmly.

"Only water!" He started to laugh and couldn't stop. There was nothing we could do about it except watch helplessly until the hysterical guffaws died away to occasional gurgles.

"What was so funny, Ed?" I asked.

"I was just thinking of the syndicate, when they read about it." He gurgled for another ten seconds: "The 'Creeping Terror'—vanquished by a water gun!"

I walked into the office real early the next morning, around five after nine, feeling almost good enough to stay awake for the rest of the day. Martinelli and Duprez were already safely in the county clink. It was like Happy New Year in the Sumners' family vault—out with the old, in with the new—now that what was left of Tino had been removed from his stone casket and Crispin was about to move in, keeping it all in the family. Another cheering thought was Charity—she was a promise of the near future. She was going to take Jessica Sumner away someplace for a month but then she'd be back, but definitely back. Meantime, Wheeler was a bachelor of free-wheeling destiny ready to tilt at—

Right in front of me was the delicious, delightful Annabelle Jackson bent almost double as she picked up her eraser from the floor. I figured you could almost call it a sign—a good omen. How could I ignore it?

I gave Annabelle a playful tweak—well, maybe a little on the sneaky side—and waited confidently. She straightened up in a rush and spun around in a continuous circular motion, grabbing the heavy steel rule on the way. A split second later the rule slammed across the side of my head with brutal force that sent me staggering halfway across the office.

"Al Wheeler!" Annabelle said in a fierce snarl. "Don't you ever dare do that again!"

"But I'm a hero!" I protested feebly.

"Not to me!" She advanced steadily, waving the rule above her head in a murderous arc.

"I thought you worshipped heroes!" I yelped, still backing off fast.

"I lost that feeling in a real hurry from eight o'clock on last night!" she hissed. "We had a date, remember?"

My back hit a solid wall and I was trapped. "But that's why I couldn't make it last night," I said frantically. "I was too busy being a hero!"

"Well!" she said breathlessly. "This will teach you never to be a hero on my time again!"

THE END

The Lady is Transparent

Carter Brown

She rose her head from her down-soft pillow,
And snowy were her milk-white breasts,
Saying: "Who's there, who's there at my bedroom window,
Disturbing me from my long night's rest?"

—Verse from "The Lover's Ghost," on old English folk song

Chapter One

The sudden crack of thunder right outside the window made the brunette with the intriguing silver streak scream suddenly, as her whole body quivered in a delectable combination of full, rounded curves and frothing black lace.

"I hate storms!" she whimpered nervously.

"I love them," I said. "An hour back, as I remember, you were sitting on my couch like a quick-frozen ice cube, making polite conversation. Then the storm hit—"

"And look at me now!" She sighed deeply. "One thing's for sure, Al Wheeler, I'm a lot sadder—if no wiser—girl."

"Jackie, honey!" I said in a shocked tone. "You mean the mutual experience we just had is something you won't cherish as a favorite memory in your old age?"

"I never knew a guy to move so fast in my whole life before," she said sourly. "Before I'd gotten around to realizing this damned storm was the least of my problems, it was too late already."

"I figured we worked up a storm of our own that even Mother Nature couldn't touch," I told her in an aggrieved voice. "You mean, all the time you were worried about an itty-bit of thunder?"

"I guess I should never have taken off my shoes in the first place—it always undermines a girl's defenses," she reflected out loud. "Al, are you *sure* they attract lightning the way tall trees attract lightning?"

"You know what you use to keep your shoes neat, honey?" I said. "They call them shoe *trees*, don't they?"

The phone rang with sudden shrill brutality, and Jackie screamed as she reacted so violently that the top half of her body jumped clean out of the frothy black lace. I backed off toward the phone and finally lifted it, reluctant to be distracted from the magnificent pastoral scene of towering peaks and deep-shadowed valley in front of my eyes.

"Weather bureau," I said into the mouthpiece. "We forecast a fine clear night, and this storm is strictly in your imagination, lady."

"Wheeler?" The deep growl belonged to Sheriff Lavers, of course. Who else would call a guy around midnight?

"You mean the Wheeler who's a cop?" I asked cautiously. "I'm his brother—the one with the lisp like thith—thee?"

"Cut out the clowning!" he said irritably. "We've got a problem—a homicide. You'd better get out there right away!"

"Where?"

"Old Canyon Road. You take the right fork in back of Bald Mountain—

the house is about a half mile down on the right. You can't miss it, there isn't another place within a couple of miles."

"Okay," I said. "Who's dead?"

The County Sheriff paused a couple of seconds too long before he answered. "I'm not real sure," he said with the first hint of uncertainty in his voice. "But they seem pretty damn sure he's dead all right."

"They?" I queried.

"The rest of them inside the house," he explained obliquely. "They heard the scream, then a thud."

"They heard a scream—and then a thud?" I repeated in wonder. "Nobody took a look at him to make sure? Just to check whether he'd been murdered or maybe was suffering a bad case of heartburn?"

"They were too scared to look," the Sheriff said simply, "and anyway, the door is locked from the inside."

Jackie was busy covering her goose pimples and my pastoral scene was fading fast, so there was nothing to stop me giving him my full concentration. Or maybe one little thing—my brain was tottering on the brink already.

"They could break the door down, couldn't they?" I asked, without any real hope.

"I guess they could," he admitted in a strangled voice. "Only the ghost might still be there inside the room, do you see?"

"Sheriff," I said gently, "have you been at the applejack again?"

Maybe the noise in my ear would have had a familiar sound to the white hunter stalking a wounded rhino through the deep bush, but I'd never heard anything like it before.

"Don't start getting cute with me, Wheeler!" Lavers bellowed. "Maybe they are a bunch of nuts out there, but then again, they could have a genuine stiff on their hands. One thing I do know for sure, they aren't about to check on whatever it is inside that locked room, and that means you're elected."

"You sure you don't want to have the place exorcised first?" I asked desperately.

"I want a detailed report from you inside the next two hours, Lieutenant," he said coldly. "If you haven't called in by then, you'll be detached from my office and back with Captain Parker in Homicide before noon tomorrow!" It made a nasty crunching sound in my ear as he hung up on me.

There was a questioning look on Jackie's face as I walked back toward the couch. She had gotten all dressed again, except for her shoes, and now that the storm seemed to have quieted down a little outside, there was a calculating look beginning to show in her eyes. I had an instinctive feeling it would do me no good at all.

"Who was that?"

"The call of duty, Jackie, honey," I said sorrowfully. "The County Sheriff, no less. Either he's flipped his trolley, or we have us a brand-new homicide in the county. I have to go find out."

"And what do I do while you're away finding out?" she snapped. "Knit you some new shoe trees?"

"I was thinking maybe I could drop you home on the way?"

"Men!" She made it a dirty word. "Now it's all over, you just can't wait to get rid of me, can you?"

"That's not true." Well, it was only a half-truth, anyway. "You want to stay here until I get back, that's fine with me," I said in my real sincere voice. "Stay the night, if you want."

"No, thank you!" She made the usual feminine switch with the usual feminine lack of logic. "I wouldn't stay here another minute, not if you offered me Fort Knox along with breakfast!" She got up from the couch and padded toward the door in stockinged feet, carrying her shoes gingerly in her right hand. "Take me home right now, Al Wheeler, or I'll call a—" She shook her head wearily. "Oh, hell! I keep forgetting. Just take me home, huh?"

"Sure," I said, and caught up with her at the door. "When will I see you again, Jackie, honey?"

"How about the fall?" she said icily. "You'd fit real well then—along with everything else that's dying on its feet!"

The ride home was strictly short on conversation. I dropped Jackie outside her apartment building and the only farewell I got was a sharp scream of terror as the lightning flashed again just as she reached the entrance. A split second later she'd vanished inside the building, and the only remembrance left was the pair of shoes she'd dropped on the sidewalk outside the front door. With Duty calling like crazy, I figured it was no time for Wheeler to play Prince Charming, not with Cinderella about to beat me over the head with her broom if I showed up in her life again any time within the next six months.

By the time I reached Old Canyon Road, the storm was back in full strength. Thunder played an almost continuous rolling symphony and rain lashed down upon the landscape with a brutal indifference, making a mockery of the windshield wipers' futile efforts. Within a couple of minutes the canvas top of my Austin-Healey was leaking steadily, splashing big cold drops of water onto my neck in an unending stream.

A vivid flash of forked lightning showed momentarily the brooding silhouette of Bald Mountain, then the fork in the road came up ahead in the watery gleam of my headlights. I made a cautious right turn, drove slowly for another couple of minutes, and another lightning flash split the sky. It gave me a quick glimpse of the house maybe a hundred yards ahead—a solid mass, bone-white in the lightning, with a fantastic roof line that looked like it was all turrets and gables—the architecture by Disney, Hans Andersen, or Count Dracula himself. Then the landscape was blacked out again, and there was only me and the Healey pushing a small area of light ahead of us through the sheets of rain.

The driveway was neglected gravel the rain had churned into a couple of small river beds, flanked on either side by sodden overgrown bushes. I parked the car as close to the house as I could, then got out and ran across to the front porch. The whole house looked to be in complete darkness, and without the comforting sound of the Healey's motor, I started to wonder why the hell I ever became a cop when I could have gone on relief.

Another convenient flash lit up the porch for long enough for me to see the huge bell hanging at one side of the massive front door and the rope that hung from it. I gave it a couple of sharp tugs and it rang like the knell of doom above the muttering chorus of thunder.

Maybe ten seconds later I knew I was rapidly losing my mind. A small square of the front door, immediately level with my eyes, suddenly began to glow with a feeble yellowish light that steadily grew stronger. At the last moment before my mind plunged over the abyss, I realized there was a peephole cut in the door—a square of glass heavily guarded by a stout mesh of thin iron bars—and the light came from inside the house as someone approached the front door, carrying a lamp. A pair of ice-cold eyes peered implacably into mine for around five whole seconds, then I heard the sound of a heavy bolt being withdrawn, and the door swung inward slowly with a loud creak.

It looked like Dracula's daughter on her way back to the tomb, and I wasn't about to get in her way. A tall, regal-looking brunette, her thick dark hair hanging loosely down her back, stared at me with an aloof expression on her face. She wore some kind of a white robe that seemed to flow from her neck right down to her ankles, gathered at her waist by a thin chain of silver mesh.

"What do you want?" she asked in a deep resonant voice.

"I'm Lieutenant Wheeler," I croaked, "from the County Sheriff's office."

She moved her arm so the oil lamp she held in her right hand shone full on my face. "How do I know you're telling the truth?" she demanded imperiously.

"You figure anybody in his right mind would be out selling brushes on a night like this?" I snarled at her.

"On such a night one cannot be too careful," she snapped. "Have you any identification?"

I showed her my tin and she studied it carefully, like it was my credit rating. Finally she was satisfied and stepped back a pace.

"Please come in, Lieutenant—and please wipe your feet!"

Once I was inside, she closed the front door and bolted it again carefully. "There is evil outside the house as well as inside tonight," she said in a matter-of-fact voice. "The lightning hurls its balls of fire to the ground, and *they* travel with it."

I wasn't about to ask who *they* were, in case she told me. "Sure," I said vaguely, and cleared my throat. "Don't you have electricity out here?"

"It failed," she said, "sometime before he screamed."

"The guy in the locked room?"

"Henry Slocombe." She nodded gravely. "He's dead, of course. The poor fool thought he could pit his puny science against *them*."

"Oh?" I swallowed. "Well, how about I take a look?"

"Entirely at your own risk, Lieutenant," she said, with a bittersweet smile on her face. "Please follow me. Or do you wish to talk with the others first? They're all in the dining room at the moment."

"Let's check on Slocombe before I talk to anyone else," I said quickly, stiffing a dangerous impulse to ask her just how many legs apiece the *others* had.

She went ahead of me, gliding along in a flowing, unbroken movement down a wide hall, then up a winding staircase to the top floor of the house. By the time we finally stopped outside a door, I had lost all sense of time and direction. It was the familiar feeling of nightmare, when you know you have to get the hell out of wherever you are—but how?

The statuesque brunette held the lamp high and the yellow rays revealed a door that looked like it was made from solid oak around three inches thick. I rattled the knob a few times in a futile effort to open it, then gave up.

"It is locked from the inside, Lieutenant," she said placidly. "Henry Slocombe was a brave, as well as stupid, man."

"After you heard the scream, I guess nobody thought of putting a ladder up to the window and taking a look to see what had happened inside the room, exactly?" I suggested moodily.

"It would have been a pointless procedure," she said. "The window of this room has been boarded up ever since I can remember."

I eased the thirty-eight out of my belt holster, then looked at her questioningly. "You mind if I shoot in the lock?"

"Do whatever you consider necessary, Lieutenant," she said firmly. "Only—if you don't object—I would prefer not to wait here while you do it. It could still be there, inside the room, you see?"

"It?" I gurgled.

"The manifestation that killed Slocombe," she explained in the patient kind of voice people normally use with a backward child. "I think it must have been the Gray Lady, although it isn't impossible for Ashtoreth or Asmodeus, even, to appear on a night like this."

I plunged straight to the heart of the matter: "So who gets the lamp?" I asked coldly.

"I don't need it to find my way around this house in the dark," she said in a compassionate voice. "Please take it, Lieutenant."

Numbly I took the lamp from her outstretched hand, then watched her glide away. For a few seconds her white robe shimmered like a wraith, then was finally enveloped in the darkness.

I took a deep breath and fired two shots into the lock. The deafening noise hammered and rehammered my eardrums as I lifted one foot, then slammed it against the oak paneling. The door stuck for a moment, then swung inward with an ugly rasping sound.

Two reluctant steps brought me inside the room, with the short hairs at the nape of my neck bristling uneasily. The atmosphere was stuffy, the air foul with a heavy fetid smell, as if some unclean animal had made its lair inside the room. I held the lamp above my head with my left hand, the right still clutching the gun. The rays dimly lit the dark, mildew-stained walls. The boards nailed across the window were cracking and riddled with dry rot.

The furnishings were sparse—a high-posted bed with a drab cover thrown across it; a circular pedestal table and two carved-back chairs; the flowery pattern of the carpet had been worn almost threadbare. In startling contrast, an expensive-looking tape recorder stood on top of the table humming gently to itself, while an attaché case rested on one of the chairs. It was presumably their owner who lay face down on the carpet at the foot of the bed.

I put the lamp on the table beside the recorder—that damned humming was starting to get on my nerves—and switched off the machine before I knelt down beside the outstretched body on the floor, then rolled it gently over onto its back. The face was young—around twenty-five—and handsome in a dark aquiline fashion, the eyes wide open and staring with glazed horror.

The strong, fetid smell of the room stank in my nostrils as I stumbled hastily up onto my feet, fighting the wave of nausea that threatened to engulf me. Maybe thirty seconds later I had it under control, enough to take another look at the corpse at my feet. Henry Slocombe was dead all right—something had torn out his throat with the cruel efficiency of a mountain lion.

Chapter Two

At the bottom of the stairs, a shimmering white wraith waited for me patiently. When I got close the oil lamp showed up the highlights in her thick, glossy black hair and the untroubled look on her face, its skin smooth and white like alabaster.

"He's dead, isn't he?" she said softly.

"He's dead," I said.

"Was it—" she hesitated for a long moment "—his throat?"

"How did you know that?"

"Then it was the Gray Lady," she said, almost to herself. "Poor Henry! Poor Martha, too! I begged him not to be a fool, but he had all the arrogance of youth and the confidence that only ignorance can give." She shook her head slowly. "Now, of course, Lieutenant, you'll try to find a logical answer for his death?"

"That's what I'm paid for," I told her. "Who are you, for a start?"

"I am Justine Harvey," she said evenly. "This house belongs to my father, Ellis Harvey."

"Is he here now?"

"In the dining room."

"With the others?" I remembered out loud. "Who are the others?"

"My younger sister Martha, my Uncle Ben, and George Farrow," she answered promptly.

"And the man upstairs—he was Henry Slocombe?"

"That is correct, Lieutenant."

"A friend of the family?"

"He wanted to marry Martha," Justine Harvey said in an even voice. "Father didn't approve, that was why Henry was so determined to spend this night in the room alone. We warned him—begged him, even—not to do it, but nothing would make him change his mind."

The lights came on suddenly, and I blinked a couple of times—once, because my eyes were dazzled by the glare, and the second time because Justine was startlingly beautiful, far more so than I'd suspected under the feeble light of the oil lamp.

She smiled momentarily and took the lamp from me. "You won't need this anymore, Lieutenant." She blew it out, then stood holding the lamp in front of her like some kind of talisman while she waited for me to ask more questions.

"Maybe I'm out of my mind already," I said truthfully, "so I need help before there's no doubt left at all. If there's a beginning to this thing, tell me fast, please? Why was Slocombe determined to spend the night alone up in that room?"

"Because of the Gray Lady," she almost whispered. "She is our—family ghost—if you like. That was her room originally, and she put a curse on it—but it's a long story, Lieutenant. Do you want to talk with the others first?"

"No," I snarled. "They'll only give me some more of this 'Gray Lady' jazz you've been feeding me. I don't care how long a story it is—time is the one thing I've got plenty of right now."

She gestured toward a door halfway between the foot of the stairs and the entrance. "We could go in there and be a little more comfortable, Lieutenant."

"Fine," I told her. "You go right ahead. I'd better call the sheriff's office first. Where's the phone?"

"In the same room." The corners of her mouth quirked a little. "Would you prefer I wait outside while you make your call?"

"I don't have a thing to tell him you don't already know," I growled.

What the hell the Harvey family called this room, I wouldn't know. The furnishings were about as attractive as they had been in the room upstairs—only the carpet looked in better condition—and I figured the room would do just fine for a mortician's front parlor, with maybe a stuffed parrot perched on the mantel. Justine Harvey sat in one of the wing chairs, her hands folded in her lap while she waited patiently for me to use the phone.

I gave it to Lavers straight, strictly the facts, with no reference to things that went *EEEK!* in the night, because I figured we had enough problems already. He said he'd send the doctor and the meat wagon right out, and did I want him to borrow the crime lab boys from Parker. I said that was a fine idea and while he was about it, he could send out Sergeant Polnik, too. And furthermore, if he had any of that applejack left I could use maybe a couple of jugs. This time I hung up on him while he was still rumbling deep in his throat.

Sitting opposite the brunette in one of the wing chairs, I was suddenly aware that her white robe was made of very thin silk indeed, which tightly molded the rich curves of her deep breasts and the full rounded sweep of her thighs. I had figured her for some kind of a nut all through the weird bit with the oil lamp and all, but now I was almost uncomfortably aware of her as a beautiful and highly desirable woman. Maybe she sensed the change in attitude—there was a challenging look in her dark liquid eyes as she carefully watched my face.

"The story starts with my great-grandfather, Nigel Harvey," she said in that deep, resonant voice. "He was an English country gentleman with a son and daughter—Arthur and Delia. His wife had died giving birth to the girl. They lived on Nigel's estate, close to a small village in the west of England. On Delia's nineteenth birthday he told her he'd arranged a suitable marriage with the eldest son of a neighboring landowner.

"This didn't suit Delia at all—she was in the middle of a passionate affair with one of the gypsies camped on the other side of the village. They hadn't been exactly discreet, and already people in the village were talking. She pleaded and fought with her father, but Nigel was adamant. The banns were read and the ceremony arranged for the tenth of May."

"It brings a lump to my throat," I said tersely. "Can we skip the hearts-and-flowers routine and get down to cases?"

"I guess we can," Justine said easily. "Ten days before the wedding day, the prospective bridegroom was found dead in the woods close to Nigel's estate. His throat had been torn out by some savage beast. A woodcutter swore he saw a huge gray wolf loping through the trees shortly after it happened. One of the village maidens, up to no good in the woods with the blacksmith's son, swore she had seen Delia running back toward the house with wet bloodstains down the front of her dress. The stories swept through the village like a flood and the people turned nasty, accusing Delia of being a witch.

"Within weeks, Nigel Harvey discovered there was a plot among the villagers to kidnap Delia from the house and burn her as a witch. Meantime, none of them would work his land, his friends avoided him—he thought he would soon face ruin, both socially and financially. So he decided to get out while he could—take his children to some faraway place where his daughter would only be known by her rightful name, for the villagers were now whispering of her as the 'Gray Lady.'

"Delia didn't want to go. She pleaded with him that if he took her away from her gypsy lover, she would die within the year. It made no difference at all to her father. He sold up the estate and brought both his children to California. He built this house way out in the wilderness deliberately, shunning all contact with the outside world. From the first day they moved in, Delia went into a decline and kept to her room.

"She prophesied she would die on the anniversary of her prospective bridegroom's death, the thirtieth of April. On the morning of that day she made her father solemnly swear he would keep her room empty for all time. If anyone else ever slept in her room, she swore they would die before the year was out, on the anniversary night of her own death. She would return from beyond the grave to see her curse was carried out."

"It's a real wild story," I grunted. "Is that all there is to it?"

"Almost," Justine said. "Delia died that night and Great-grandfather buried her the next day at the foot of an oak tree on the grounds. He left her grave unmarked, locked her room, and it was left empty through his lifetime, through his son Arthur's lifetime, and through my father's time up until tonight."

"You really think the Gray Lady came back and tore out Slocombe's throat tonight?" I said disbelievingly.

"All the growth within twenty-five feet of the oak tree died of a mysterious blight within a month of Delia's burial," she said flatly. "The story always fascinated me, Lieutenant, from the time I first heard it as a little girl. I've done some research on the subject; the night of April thirtieth is Walpurgis Night—May Day eve—by ancient law one of the most important witches' sabbaths of the year."

"So what decided Henry Slocombe to spend the night in the room?" I grated.

"There is a portrait of Delia on the wall of my father's study," she said. "There's a remarkable resemblance to my younger sister Martha. It's worried my father for years." She saw the expression on my face and smiled. "This has a point, Lieutenant. George Farrow wants to marry Martha—and has Father's approval. George is rich, one of the landed gentry, you might say. Henry Slocombe also wanted to marry Martha—and he didn't have any money at all. But he was very handsome in a dark kind of way, almost like a gypsy, you might say."

I closed my eyes for a couple of seconds, but Justine Harvey was still there when I opened them again. "Are you saying there's a parallel situation between Martha and Delia?" I asked bitterly.

"That's how Father saw it," she said in a mild voice. "He thought the family curse had been revisited upon this generation, that's why he was so set against Martha marrying Henry, or even thinking of the idea. There was almost a fight about it two weeks back. Henry said the whole thing was a lot of damned superstitious nonsense and Father should be ashamed of himself. It got worse and worse, with the men shouting at each other and Martha having hysterics. Finally Henry said he would disprove it for once and all—he would sleep in Delia's room on Walpurgis Night."

"Your father agreed to that?"

"After a lot more argument," Justine said, nodding. "He didn't like the idea any more than I did, but both Henry and Martha were determined, so finally he gave in."

"What happened tonight—from the time Slocombe got to the house?"

"He arrived around seven-thirty," she said. "We had dinner about eight, then Henry went up to the room about an hour later. He took his tape recorder and attaché case with him, and locked himself in."

"Was he nervous, do you think?" I queried.

"No, more defiant, I would say." She thought about it for a little while. "He said nobody had better try any damn-fool tricks on him, because he had a loaded revolver in his attaché case and he'd use it if necessary."

"Was that all?"

"Oh, a lot of stuff about how he was going to tell the Gray Lady exactly where she got off, if she did actually materialize in the room. Sheer bravado, I thought at the time—the little boy whistling loudly in the dark, you know?"

"What happened after he'd locked himself inside the room?"

"Martha went to her own room. She was very upset, tearful. The men went downstairs and I went to my room and tried to read, but I had the horrible feeling all the time that I was just waiting for something inevitable to happen. Then, at midnight, I heard this horrible scream followed by a thud. I rushed out of my room and found Martha pounding on the door, screaming Henry's name over and over. While I was trying to calm her down, the men appeared. George Farrow helped me get Martha to her room, and we gave her a strong sedative. I stayed with her until she went to sleep, while George came back down here to call the police."

"When did the lights go out?"

"Right after the storm started, about ten, I think. It nearly always happens when we have an electrical storm. The power lines across the valley get hit by lightning."

"After Farrow called the sheriff's office—everyone just sat around and waited in the dining room?"

"I think so," Justine agreed. "All three of them were there when I came downstairs again, and we stayed in the dining room until you arrived."

"Do they think it was the Gray Lady who killed Slocombe, the same as you do?"

"I wouldn't know," she said coldly. Her eyes flashed for a moment. "Why don't you ask them, Lieutenant?"

"I guess it's an idea," I said without any wild enthusiasm.

The door swung open violently at the same moment I got onto my feet, and a girl stumbled into the room. She was younger than Justine, but the family likeness was unmistakable. Her hair was the same glossy black, but cut short so it neatly framed her elfin face. She was smaller, more delicately built than Justine, but the knee-length nightgown made of lavender nylon revealed, in proportion, the same voluptuous curves.

She grabbed the edge of the table with both hands for support, breathing heavily as she stared into Justine's surprised face.

"Martha, dear!" her elder sister said tenderly, "you shouldn't be out of bed—"

"He's dead!" Martha Harvey snarled in a low voice that was almost frightening in its naked ferocity. "You killed him—you filthy witch!"

Her eyes went blank as the heavy lids closed slowly over them, then her hands let go of the table and she swayed alarmingly to one side. I moved fast and caught her as she fell, holding her limp body awkwardly in my arms.

"Poor Martha!" Justine's voice was a lot sharper and a lot less tender when she spoke again. "I don't know how she woke up so soon from that sedative—if she was awake? She obviously didn't know what she was doing or saying!"

I lowered the girl into the nearest chair cautiously and stepped back. Her head slumped to one side and she was breathing heavily with her mouth wide open; the hem of her nightgown had ridden halfway up her thighs and she looked like the end product of a five-day orgy.

"Why don't you go into the dining room, Lieutenant?" Justine suggested firmly. "I'll take care of Martha here."

I listened to the stertorous breathing for a few seconds. "That must have been one hell of a sedative you gave her."

"We gave her a strong dose because there was nothing else we could do," Justine snapped. "She was hysterical, half out of her mind!"

"Saying all kinds of wild things," I said casually, "the way she was just now?"

"I really don't remember," she snapped. "Now, if you'll excuse me, Lieutenant, I have to see to my sister. I'm sure she'd be embarrassed if she knew a strange man had been leering at her while she was dressed in a flimsy nightgown!"

I got as far as the door, then looked back at her for a moment. "You know something, Justine?" I said, admiringly. "With your sharp nails showing, you get to be real cute."

"Get out of here," she said evenly, "you cheap son of a bitch."

Chapter Three

I leaned my shoulder against the doorpost and looked at the three men sitting close together at the far end of the big table. The brandy balloons in front of them looked as if they had just been refilled from the decanter in the center of the table. A faint haze of rich cigar smoke hovered in the air above their heads, giving the whole scene a comfortable atmosphere like the smoking room of a not too exclusive men's club.

"I'm Lieutenant Wheeler," I said formally, "from the sheriff's office."

A tall thin guy at the head of the table stood up slowly. He was getting close to sixty, I guessed, and life had rubbed off all the surplus fat so only the skin and bones were left. The opaque dark eyes looked startlingly large against the surrounding translucent white skin.

"I am Ellis Harvey, Lieutenant," he said in a thin, dried-up voice. "We heard you arrive, of course, and then the shots. We thought it best to wait here until you wanted us."

"Sure."

"You forced your way into Deli—the room?"

"I shot in the lock," I said.

"And the young man, Henry Slocombe, he was dead?"

"With his throat ripped out," I confirmed.

Beneath the loose fold of skin at his throat, the apple jumped convulsively. "I pleaded with him not to do it," Harvey said in a low voice. "But he was determined—and Martha was also determined. What could I do?"

"Nothing!" a gruff voice suddenly exploded beside him. "Not a damn thing, Ellis. Stop sniveling, will you? The young fool ran up against the Gray Lady and what we warned him would happen, happened! There's an end to it."

I transferred my attention to the owner of the voice. A man some ten years younger than Ellis Harvey, the same height, and around twice his weight. A massive guy with a voice to match. He sat easily to the right of Harvey, a cigar held negligently between the thumb and finger of his right hand, while his left gently agitated his glass so the brandy swirled inside. His thick, curly gray hair was close-cropped, and he wore a neat matching goatee beard. His complexion was ruddy, the sharp blue eyes almost submerged in thick creases of fat. For no good reason at all, I disliked him on sight.

"I'm Ellis' brother, Lieutenant, Ben Harvey," he snorted at me. "I suppose you're wondering what the hell I'm talking about?"

"No," I told him, and looked pointedly at the third man, facing Ben Harvey.

Right then he looked like the promising young executive in the accounting office caught with his hand in the cash register. An awkward-looking guy who had an air of being a lot younger than the firming lines on his face said he was—about thirty, I figured, give or take a year. What once had been a flaming thatch of red hair was receding fast back across his head, giving his forehead that elegant, egghead, high-domed look. But the rest of his face didn't match up at all; the watery blue eyes and the weak mouth, with the full lower lip slack, looked as if they were in mutual agreement that they should never have left Mother in the first place.

"I—I'm George Farrow, Lieutenant," he said nervously, speaking rapidly like he had a whole bunch of second words to unload. "I'm engaged to be married to Martha Harvey and—"

"I know," I snapped.

"Oh?" His mouth hung open in surprise.

I moved in from the doorway, pulled a chair out from the opposite end of the table, and sat down facing Ellis Harvey. The three of them watched me intently, as if I was a conjuror about to perform a new, unannounced trick—something I had up my sleeve, maybe.

"Justine told me what happened tonight," I said slowly. "Why Henry Slocombe was in that room."

"Then you know about the Gray Lady?" Ellis said eagerly.

"In detail," I said. "Slocombe arrived at the house around seven-thirty tonight, you all had dinner about eight. An hour later he went up to the room taking his attaché case and tape recorder with him. Is that correct?"

"Yes, I think so," Ellis said, nodding. "I think those times are right as I remember. Do you agree, Ben?"

"Yes." Ben let go of his brandy balloon long enough to stroke his goatee a couple of times with loving affection. "Slocombe went on with a lot of amateur dramatics about how he had a gun so nobody had better try and play any tricks on him and so on—but I expect Justine has told you that already, Lieutenant?"

"She mentioned it," I said briefly. "After Slocombe locked himself inside the room, Martha and Justine went to their own rooms, and you three came back downstairs, right?"

"That's right, Lieutenant!" George Farrow was obviously happy to find some accord between us. "We went into the living room and had a drink, then—well—we just sat for a while, listening."

"For how long?"

"I'm not sure exactly, Lieutenant." Farrow worried his fat lower lip with horsey teeth while he concentrated. "I guess—maybe an hour— until the lights went out."

"It was the storm, Lieutenant," Ellis interjected. "It always happens with an electric storm, the pow lines—"

"Justine told me already," I said wearily. "What then?"

"We've gotten used to it after long experience," Ellis explained. "The power failing, I mean. So whenever a storm is forecast I have oil lamps filled and put into every room of the house—"

"I lit the lamp in the living room, then came in here to do the same," Ben Harvey grunted comfortably. "Ellis is a shrewd feller—always keeps his best brandy in here so you only get one chance at it, and that's after dinner. I helped myself and thought I might as well stay in here—sitting in the other room together, we were only getting on each other's nerves the whole damned time."

"So that left you and Mr. Farrow in the living room?" I asked Ellis.

He shook his head mournfully. "No, Lieutenant. After Ben left us, I felt I couldn't stand the strain of just sitting there, waiting for something to happen, any longer. I had to do something, so I went to my study and read a book."

"What did you do?" I said to Farrow.

"I just sat in the living room," he said simply.

"You'd be good at that," I reflected out loud.

His face flushed brick red. "I—I resent your sarcasm, Lieutenant, it's completely uncalled for!"

"I'm sorry, Mr. Farrow," I told him politely. "I've had a bad night—I guess it hasn't been too good for any of us."

"Of course!" If he'd had a tail, right then he'd have wagged it at me. "You're quite right, Lieutenant, this has been a dreadful experience for all of us. I understand perfectly!"

"So when the scream came, the three of you were in separate rooms?" I went on doggedly. Maybe it was Farrow's influence.

They looked at each other slowly, then nodded in unison.

"About what time would that have been?" I prodded.

"A minute to twelve," Ellis answered promptly.

"How can you be so accurate?" I asked in a disbelieving voice.

"It has to do with the Gray Lady, you see, Lieutenant?" He swallowed hard. "Even though Walpurgis Night—the witches' sabbath—would normally last from sunset to cockcrow, Delia's curse was specific. Anyone who slept in her room would die on the anniversary of her death—and that would end at midnight. For the last quarter-hour before twelve, I just sat and looked at my watch. If nothing had happened to Slocombe before midnight, he would have been safe then, you see?"

He winced at the look on my face. "I know it's hard for you—an outsider to the family—to understand this, Lieutenant, but you have to appreciate that here you are dealing with the supernatural!"

Ben Harvey's whole body suddenly shook with rumbling laughter. "I feel sorry for him, Ellis," he chuckled. "All those years of hard factual training don't mean a damned thing now, do they, Lieutenant?"

"Right now they mean a hell of a lot to me," I said truthfully. "By the time I'm ready to believe that the ghost of a girl who's been dead for over a hundred years materialized in the form of a gray wolf and tore out Slocombe's throat, I'll be a hot candidate for the nearest loony bin!"

"There are some things you just have to accept, even if they are wildly remote from your own experience, Lieutenant," Ellis said soberly. "You have to accept them because they afford the only possible explanation."

"Meantime, I'll stay with the theory that somebody in this house murdered Slocombe," I told him. "Let's get back to the scream at one minute to midnight—when it happened, the three of you were alone in separate rooms, right?"

Again they looked at each other slowly, then nodded in unison.

"What did you do when you heard it?" I asked Farrow.

"I ran upstairs to the room," he said. "Martha was already there, screaming her head off and pounding on the door, while Justine was trying to comfort her. I helped Justine get her back to her own room, then found Ellis and Ben outside Slocombe's door when I came out again. We tried the doorknob, but it was locked, of course, and we had no chance of breaking it down—"

"Did you try?"

His face colored rapidly. "Well, no, we didn't—"

"George wanted to," Ben boomed sympathetically. "But no, Harvey wanted to get inside that room while there was a chance the Gray Lady was still present! I told George the best thing he could do was call the police and let them handle it."

I heard a faint swishing sound in back of me and turned my head to see Justine gliding toward me.

"I got poor Martha back to bed," she said evenly, "and she's sound asleep again now."

Farrow jumped to his feet eagerly and pulled out a chair for her. She sank into it gracefully, folding her hands in her lap, then looked at me expectantly.

"Are you making any progress, Lieutenant?"

"I'm not real sure," I said. "So far it looks like all of you had equal opportunity to kill Slocombe."

Ellis looked at me more in sorrow than in anger. "While he was behind a door made of solid oak and three inches thick, Lieutenant? A door locked from the inside?"

"I'll worry about that one when I come to it," I snarled. "After opportunity, comes motive. So who wanted Slocombe dead?—apart from Farrow?"

George's eyes popped like I'd pulled a lever inside his head. "Me?" he squeaked. "Why should I want Slocombe dead?"

"You both wanted to marry Martha, didn't you?" I growled at him. "With Slocombe dead, it doesn't exactly leave her much choice, right?"

"Don't let the Lieutenant upset you, George," Ben Harvey shouted at him. "The poor feller's only trying to do his duty the way he sees it."

"Nobody's got an answer to my question? Who else besides Farrow wanted Slocombe dead?" I repeated.

Ellis shook his head sadly. "None of us had any reason to wish the poor boy any harm, Lieutenant. The reverse, in fact. I admit I certainly preferred George as a suitor for Martha, but even more important was the inherent danger to Slocombe through the family curse. I tried—we all tried—countless times to warn him, but he was a pigheaded youth, I regret to say."

"Maybe they'll make that his epitaph," I said. "Have it inscribed on the headstone: 'Here lies the body of a pigheaded youth—who wouldn't believe in ghosts, forsooth!'"

"That's a bad joke, in poor taste, Lieutenant!" Ellis said stiffly.

Ben suddenly exploded into violent laughter again. "But damn funny, Ellis, you have to admit that!" He tugged his beard happily. "A cop with a sense of humor—I like that, Ellis."

I wondered wistfully for a moment whether, if I took out my gun and shot him clean through his goatee, Lavers would call it justifiable homicide.

"How long has that window been boarded up?" I snapped at Ellis.

"Since my grandfather's time," he said bleakly.

"Has the door always been kept locked since his time, too?"

"It has."

"How many keys are there to the door?"

"Only the one." He rubbed the palm of his bony hand the taut, translucent skin of his cheek in a sudden gesture of irritation. "All these questions are a ridiculous waste of time, Lieutenant! There is only the one key and it has been handed down from father to son since the time of my grandfather, Nigel Harvey. It has always been kept safely locked away, secure from curious children and cheap sensation-seekers! I took it from my desk tonight and gave it to Slocombe at the dinner table."

"I think the Lieutenant suspects we invented the family curse, and the Gray Lady, just to explain what happened tonight," Justine said in a slightly contemptuous voice. "I think you should show him Delia's portrait in your study, Father."

"That's ridiculous," George Farrow said hotly. "I've known all about it since almost the first time I met the family—and that must be more than three years back!"

Right on cue, the outside bell suddenly tolled loudly, rescuing me from an impossible situation. Farrow almost jumped out of his chair, his eyes popping again. Even Ben's goatee quivered interestedly.

"I'll answer the door," Justine said calmly and got to her feet.

"Don't bother," I told her. "That will be the doctor, and more police. I'll get it."

She sank back into her chair again. "What do you want us to do while you're gone, Lieutenant?"

"Wait right here." I smiled at her pleasantly. "You have my word that if we find a big gray wolf hiding under the bed, I'll call you!"

Her dark eyes blew up a sudden storm. "Peasant!" She almost spat the word at me.

"In this house I'm real glad to be one," I said cheerfully, "when you remember how the Harvey family once treated the landed gentry!"

Chapter Four

Doc Murphy scrambled onto his feet again, his saturnine face a couple of shades paler than usual.

"I've seen some bodies in my time—" he muttered.

"What do you think, Doc?" I asked him.

"Cause of death is painfully obvious," he grunted. "The weapon—don't ask me! Three or four butcher's hooks?" He sniffed audibly. "You smell something in here, Wheeler? Apart from your own decaying mind, I mean?"

I sniffed loudly, then thought about it for a few moments.

"I can tell that another case history for your files has been brought to a successful conclusion," I told him finally. "You reek of formaldehyde!"

"I'm serious," he snarled.

"Sure, I can smell it," I agreed. "It was a lot stronger when I first got in here, right after I shot in the lock. It was like a zoo at the end of a hot day."

"Animal?" Murphy said, wondering. "It's possible, but what kind of animal could get into an upstairs room and—"

"It would have to be something with a strong bite," I said distastefully. "Something like a wolf, maybe? A big dog, even?"

"It's more like his throat was ripped out, not bitten," Murphy said without a qualm. "It's not teeth you have to worry about, Wheeler, it's something with talons—or sharp claws."

"A mountain lion?" I croaked.

"Or, like you said, a wolf?" He shook his head suddenly, as if to clear it. "What the hell are we talking about?—wandering around the top floor of a house—a wolf?"

"You don't know the half of it," I said bitterly. "How about time of death?"

"Between three and four hours—" he checked his watch "—thirty minutes either way of midnight."

"You hit it right on the button," I admitted with reluctant respect. "He screamed—and the rest of the inside the house heard the thud as he fell—at precisely one minute of twelve."

"Science triumphs again!" he said smugly. "You should try a little science yourself sometime."

I ignored that. "There's something else you could do for me, Doc." I told him about Martha Harvey—how Justine had said she'd given her a sedative, then she's suddenly appeared downstairs and collapsed again.

"Sure, I'll take a look at her." Murphy brightened perceptibly. "Young and beautiful, wearing a nylon nightgown, you said?"

"You nasty-minded old satyr!" I said disgustedly. "Don't you ever think of anything else but young, beautiful girls with not enough clothes on?"

"Sure, I do," he answered happily. "Most of the time I think about young, beautiful girls with no clothes on at all."

"Justine—her older sister—is in the dining room," I told him. "She can tell you whatever it was she gave Martha—only I'd prefer you didn't take her word for it, Doc, and check for yourself."

"It would be a pleasure," he said promptly. "I'll send the boys up for the body, if you're all through with it."

"Do that," I agreed.

Ed Sanger, the senior of the two guys from the crime lab, came over to me and lit a cigarette.

"You got a real nasty one here, Lieutenant!"

"You're so right," I muttered.

"We got all the photos you'll need," he went on. "How about the other junk—the attaché case and the tape recorder?"

"Hey!" His partner joined us, holding up a door key between his thumb and index finger. "Look what I found."

"Where was it?" I asked him.

"Hidden under the bottom of the door. I pushed the door open a little further—and there it was on the carpet."

"If the door had been closed, how far away would the key have been from it?" I queried.

"A couple of feet, maybe a little less."

"It figures," I said. "When I shot in the lock, the key bounced out onto the carpet, but thanks, anyway."

"That's okay, Lieutenant." He looked a little disappointed as he drifted away.

"Wait a minute," Ed Sanger said slowly. "That would mean the door was locked from the inside?"

"Right."

He looked around toward the boards nailed across the window, then back at me. "And when you got in here, there was just the corpse?"

"Right!" I snarled.

"Oh, brother!" He whistled softly. "Have you got troubles, Lieutenant!"

"My troubles have got troubles, even," I said bleakly. "Sure you can have the attaché case and the recorder. Let me have them back right after you're through with them, huh?"

"Sure thing, Lieutenant."

He walked back to the table and I stood there watching him, and there was something in back of my mind, something bugging me that hadn't been there before I'd talked to Sanger.

"Polnik didn't come out with you?" I asked him.

"No, sir." He shook his head. "There was only the two of us and Doc Murphy, with the meat wagon following."

"That lousy sheriff never listened when I asked him to get Polnik out here," I said bitterly. "Now you see the lousy way a lieutenant gets treated when—" Then I remembered. "Hold it!" I told him.

He gave me a dubious look over his shoulder, then shrugged and put the tape recorder back on the table. I walked across to where he stood and stared down at the machine.

"Now I remember," I told him. "When I first got into this room that thing was switched on. The humming noise it made got on my nerves, so I switched it off. But the power failed here around ten in the evening. The recorder's battery-operated?"

"That's right," Sanger said.

"Then it's probably recorded every sound in that room since sometime before Slocombe died! My God, Ed! Let's play the tape back!"

But just then the two boys in white coats came into the room.

"Okay if we remove the stiff, Lieutenant?" one of them asked cheerfully.

"Sure, go ahead," I told him.

"This one's a real dilly, Joe!" Ed Sanger told him.

Joe looked like something that had been fashioned out of dried mud by a myopic witch doctor who suffered with an uncontrollable tremor in both hands. A superior sneer spread across his face, adding to the macabre landscape it presented.

"I've seen 'em all," he said loftily. "After fifteen years on this job, buddy boy, there just ain't any surprises left!"

He walked up real close to the body, then stared down at it intently. Ed and I watched interestedly while his face slowly turned a bright shade of green. The whites of his eyes showed as he looked at his partner. "Get that stretcher and sheet over here quick!" he said huskily. "Or this will be the first time I quit on a job halfway!"

Both of them worked fast, carefully keeping their eyes averted until there was only an anonymous white bundle resting on the stretcher.

They carried it out of the room at a fast trot and I wondered if they'd make the stairs.

"All they want is for that storm to start up again on their way back to town," Ed said gleefully, "and there'll be three slabs needed at the morgue!"

"What have you got against Joe?" I asked him. "He just looks like a normal, repulsive ghoul to me."

Sanger looked almost embarrassed for a moment. "Nothing, I guess, when it comes right down to it. Only sometimes, they can stay on that job too long, and I figure that's Joe's trouble. It's getting so he enjoys it." He cleared his throat irritably. "Why don't we just forget it, huh, Lieutenant?"

"Fine," I said. "Let's get with it on the tape recorder."

I lit a cigarette and watched while he rewound the tape and reran it at full speed. Nothing at all happened at first, then there was that weird babble indicating something recorded. Ed backed it up, fixed the speed properly, and pushed the button again.

"Here we go," he said.

For a few seconds there was only the hum of the machine, then a low-pitched voice spoke with startling clarity. An icy coldness fingered my spine as I remembered it was the voice of the man whose body I had seen carried out of the room only five minutes before.

"This is Henry Slocombe," the voice said. "I switched on the recorder some while back because the room suddenly got colder. Then nothing else happened and I figured it was my imagination, but I just checked on the thermometer, and there's been a drop of over ten degrees. But it feels a lot more than that—as if I'm freezing to death. My fingers are numb and I know I couldn't move out of this chair if I tried."

The tape ran silently for a long half-minute before he spoke again.

"It's gotten worse," he said huskily. "There's something in the room with me, I can feel it. The coldness was the beginning, but now there's fear as well. I feel half frozen to death, and at the same time the sweat is pouring down my forehead into my eyes. Somewhere—real close—just beyond the range of vision, is—"

Again the tape ran silently, and Ed Sanger stared me with raised eyebrows.

"*Oh, my God!*" Slocombe's sudden cry seemed to leap out of thin air.

Then a few seconds later another voice spoke, with delicate, crystal-like quality, almost liquid in its purity.

"Who dares to defy the wrath of the Gray Witch of this night of nights?" it asked coldly.

"Who are you?" Slocombe whispered. "Where did you come from?"

"I lie at the foot of the oak, where no flowers bloom," the liquid voice answered. "I fly with the wind and nestle at the foot of the mountain. I rot with the winding sheet and dance in the moonlight. I strike with the snake and hunt with the pack!"

"You're Delia Harvey's ghost?"

"If you like." Her voice was scornful. "What difference? I placed my curse on this room and it was respected for more than a century. Now you have defied me, and your retribution has come."

"Wait!" Slocombe's voice was frantic. "You've got to listen to me, Delia. You must understand why I did it!"

"The reasons are not important," she said coldly "It is done, and that is an end of it—for you."

"I love Martha Harvey!" he almost shouted. "Her father wants her to marry another man—a much richer man. Martha is Delia—you—all over again, he says, and it would invite disaster if she were to marry me."

"Martha is me all over again?" She sounded vaguely amused. "What drives her father to this profound conclusion?"

"He looks at your portrait on the wall and then he looks at his daughter," Slocombe said slowly, "and the face is the same. Her mother died giving birth to Martha, as your mother died giving birth to you. Your father wanted you to marry a man you didn't love, and take you away from the man you really loved. *Her* father is trying to do exactly the same. He is frightened for his daughter; frightened that her life will somehow parallel yours, and the Harvey family will produce another witch."

"This is why you defied my curse?" Her voice was cold again. "You risked death and worse, to tell this puking story of lovelorn youth?"

"Not only that!" he said urgently. "But to ask your help, Delia. Martha looks like you, sounds like you. Somehow, she must be a part of you! If you lift your curse, you'll give her the chance of happiness that was denied you. Don't you see that?"

There was a flutelike, trilling sound as she laughed gently. "You think one lifespan is important in the scheme of eternity?" she sneered at him. "That the spasm in time which is no more than a tear in the ocean is important to me—condemned to lie beneath the oak, wrapped in everlasting awareness?"

"I beg you, Delia," he said in a muffled voice, "grant this one small favor and receive the everlasting gratitude of Martha and myself!"

The machine hummed softly for what seemed a long time before she spoke again, and the change in her voice tightened my nerve-ends to a fine pitch. The crystal-clear liquid tones had vanished, replaced by a rasping, throaty whisper that vibrated with a cold, repellent hate.

"I grow tired of your whining pleas," she whispered. "The Gray Witch walks the night only in search of the prey that is rightfully hers." She cackled throatily. "Defy the foul fiend if you can, mortal! The worms await!"

The silence shrieked at us briefly, then came a hoarse scream of terror—absolute and complete—that was cut off abruptly in full cry. A moment later there was a loud thud; the machine hummed steadily on, and when the tape ran out, Ed flipped the switch.

He stared at me silently for a couple of seconds, then grinned shakily. "Did you hear what I heard?" he asked in a thick voice.

"Sure," I admitted, "and I'm not about to believe it, either."

"It was—was—" He gestured helplessly with his hands. "How the hell do you start fitting words to something like that?"

"It's a good question," I grunted, "and I'm almost sure that someplace there has to be a good answer. Right now I'm thinking of handing in my shield inside the next hour and taking up knitting wire backstops for tennis courts. There must be a good living in it. Think of all the people who play tennis, Ed."

"You're right, Lieutenant!" He nodded emphatically. "Anyone for tennis? I could use a game myself right now."

The door swung open suddenly and Doc Murphy marched briskly back into the room with Justine gliding along in back of him.

"The girl's all right, Wheeler," he said crisply. "I told—uh—Justine here, that she was a little heavy-handed with the sedative but there's no harm done. She'll sleep like a log until noon is about all."

"Thanks, Doc," I told him.

"You don't need me anymore?" he asked hopefully. "I'd like to get on home and pick up what's left of the night's sleep, which isn't too damned much already!"

"Sure, go ahead."

"I'll see you to the front door, Doctor," Justine said in a low, intimately pitched voice.

"You mind finding your own way, Doc?" I asked politely. "There's something I want Miss Harvey to hear."

"I mind," Murphy growled, "but what good will it do me?" He gave an exaggerated shrug of resignation, then walked quickly out of the room.

"Rewind the tape and play it back again, will you, Ed?" I asked Sanger.

"Sure thing, Lieutenant." He busied himself with the machine.

Justine folded her arms beneath her jutting bosom and looked at me frigidly. "Is this anything important, Lieutenant? It's almost morning already, and we've all been through a harrowing experience!"

"I meant to ask you before," I said, real interested. "You always wear that kind of wild outfit?—the long white robe, with a silver-mesh belt—

or is it for special occasions only?"

"If you kept me up here just to insult me, Lieutenant," she said tightly, "I'll—"

"I'm serious," I told her. "Is it some special kind of outfit?"

"It is," she snapped. "But you wouldn't understand, or you'll pretend not to understand, anyway!"

"Try me."

"The curse of the Gray Lady was very real to any member of the Harvey family, even before the dreadful thing that happened to Henry Slocombe tonight," she said slowly. "To be in the same house with someone who was openly defying the curse was dangerous for all of us. White is the color of purity, Lieutenant, and as such is a protection against witches. Spun silver is another more potent charm against evil." Her dark eyes burned as she glared at me.

"So now you know—and you can laugh your fool head off if you want!"

"I don't think it's funny at all," I said politely. "I'm glad you're well protected, because we just found a direct line to the Gray Lady, and I want you to listen in on it."

Her eyes widened and she opened her mouth to say something, then listened in stunned silence as Slocombe began to speak on the tape. I watched her closely the whole time the tape was running, and saw a variety of expressions cross her face, ranging from numb shock in the beginning, to stark horror at the end. By the time the tape finally ran out, she had her face buried in her hands.

"It was horrible—horrible!" she said in a muffled whisper.

"Did you recognize either of the voices?" I asked her.

"That was Henry Slocombe's voice, beyond any doubt," she said flatly.

"How about the other voice—Delia—from the foot of the oak tree?" I rasped.

She lifted her head slowly and looked at me for a little time without answering. "Father was right," she whispered "It must be some kind of reincarnation—they're exactly the same!"

"What are exactly the same?"

"Their voices!" What looked like genuine bewilderment showed in her eyes. "You could never tell them apart."

"You mean Delia's voice is identical to Martha's voice?" I asked the obvious question.

"Yes," she said, nodding. "It—frightens me, Lieutenant."

"There's an alternative explanation," I grated. "Real simple—it's just Martha's voice on that tape."

"Martha's voice?" She gaped at me for a moment. "But that would mean she would have had to be inside this room with Slocombe while the tape recorder was running." A sudden shiver rippled her silk robe as she realized the full implication. "It would mean that she killed him!"

"That's right," I said coldly. "There's a whole bunch of questions I want to ask Martha—right now."

"But you can't," Justine said quickly, "she's—"

"—sleeping." I scowled at her. "And she'll sleep like log until noon—I've got the doctor's word on it! Because her big sister thoughtfully hit her with an overdose of sedative right off the bat!"

"What do you mean by that?" she said angrily. "I did what I thought was best for Martha at the time. I couldn't know—"

I waved my hand impatiently in the air and she stopped talking suddenly. "Only one thing bothers me," I rasped at her. "Martha can't answer any questions for another six or seven hours, and I figure maybe that's very convenient for somebody. Trouble is, I can't make up my mind who. Martha?—or you?"

Her eyes shone ferociously as they put me to death seventy different painful and humiliating ways. Then she made an obvious effort and spoke in a quiet voice.

"May I go now, Lieutenant?"

"Why not?" I shrugged.

I made a mental bet with myself as she walked toward the door, and collected when she stopped in the doorway, looking back at me over her shoulder.

"I told you once before tonight, Lieutenant, that you were a son of a bitch," she said in a thoughtful voice. "I hadn't realized up until now that it's not true."

"Thank you," I said cautiously.

"The whole truth is, you're a *subtle* son of a bitch," she said, even more thoughtfully, "and that makes a lot of difference!"

She glided out into the corridor and I turned back to Sanger to see that his eyebrows were permanently glued to his hairline.

"One thing's for sure, Lieutenant," he said in an awed voice. "They'll never hog-tie you to a desk with a nice white card on it that says 'Lieutenant Wheeler—Public Relations'!"

"The way things are going right now, I'm seriously thinking about asking Delia to move over and make room at the foot of the old oak tree," I said gloomily. "Like the girl said to the sailor, enough is enough for one night! So why don't we get out of here, Ed?"

"You just said the magic word," Ed agreed promptly. "I'll have the recorder and the attaché case back at your office around twelve—okay?"

"Real dandy, friend," I assured him. "I don't figure on getting to the office myself until after lunch."

Ed snapped the lid shut on the tape recorder and hefted it off the table by the carrying handle. With his other hand he grabbed the attaché case and we went downstairs. In the front hall we picked up his sidekick and Ed pushed the heavy recorder at him. "Thing's heavy," he grunted, giving me a reproachful look.

"Hey," I said thoughtfully as I pushed open the front door. "There's something missing."

"Now he tells us!" Sanger groaned.

"The oil lamp," I said happily. "What did you do with it?"

"What oil lamp?"

"The one in the room, stupid!"

"I never saw it." He looked at the other guy for confirmation and got a vigorous agreement. "There wasn't any oil lamp in there, Lieutenant, leastways not when we arrived. Maybe it was there when you busted in the first time?"

"Now I come to think of it, there wasn't any oil lamp the room that time, either," I said slowly.

"Well"—Sanger's voice sounded strained—"it's been a rough night, Lieutenant, and you don't only need that good sleep, you deserve it!"

Outside, the rain had gone, taking the storm with it. The half-light of early dawn drenched the driveway in a fine-spun mist, lightly pierced by the first slanting rays of sunlight.

Sanger took a deep breath and stuck out his chest. "Great morning!" he said heartily. "Makes you feel glad to be alive!"

"Speak for yourself, friend," I told him, and crawled into the Austin-Healey, where the fresh, rosy dew had generously saturated the leather seat.

Chapter Five

I got into the Sheriff's office around two-thirty the next afternoon and his Southern blonde secretary, Annabelle Jackson—the girl who was always successful in keeping Wheeler the wrong side of the Mason-Dixon line—looked up from her desk with a wildly exaggerated expression of surprise on her pretty face.

"Well, hush my mouth!" she said, in a deliberate burlesque of her own soft accent. "I do declare, it's Lieutenant Wheeler come to visit with us poor working people, and all!"

"You're maligning a hard-working cop," I told her in a wounded voice. "Nights, you get to sleep—or you have free choice, anyway—while I have to stay awake all the time."

"That reminds me," she said sweetly. "I have a message for you, from—Jackie?"

"You do?" I said cautiously.

"She said to tell you she broke her ankle running across the lobby of her apartment building last night, and she's going to sue!"

"She's out of her mind," I said firmly. "It was the storm that did it. Poor kid, she's scared to death of them, that's why she ran like that."

"Oh?" Annabelle smiled blandly. "I thought you must have been chasing her at the time?"

"Even a lousy runner like me would have caught up with her if she had a broken ankle!" I snarled.

"I assumed you did," Annabelle told her typewriter, "and that's why she's about to sue."

"Annabelle Jackson," I said sorrowfully, "you have a nasty mind."

"I owe it all to you, Lieutenant," she said in a demure voice. "If we'd never met, I guess I'd still be that innocent, fresh little ole magnolia blossom I was when I first came from Virginia to California."

"Which year was that?" I said, scratching my head thoughtfully. "Was that before or after the war?" I walked quickly toward the sheriff's office before she had a chance to annihilate me. "Well, not the *Civil War*!" I protested reproachfully as the door closing behind me caught her flying notebook.

The tape recorder and attaché case sat on the desk top, and a pair of bloodshot eyes glared redly at me over the top of them.

"Good afternoon, Sheriff," I said in a pleasant voice. "How is every little thing with you?"

His jowls quivered violently, giving a grotesque impression of an overweight bloodhound—and come to think it, that's something you don't see very often.

"You were up most of the night," he said in a low voice. "You have to get some sleep—this, I understand."

"Thank you, sir," I said appreciatively.

"*Ten* hours?" he roared.

"I'm still growing," I said in a defensive reflex, "and what happened to Sergeant Polnik, anyway? Around two this morning, you were going to send him right out there."

"I did." He jammed a cigar into his face and brooded over the match for a while before he finally lit up. "He got to the house around twenty minutes after you'd left."

"What did he do? Walk?"

"He got lost," Lavers said in a restrained voice. "I guess it was mostly my fault—I told him to take the right fork on Old Canyon Road."

"That's the right way to the house," I said.

"But I should have remembered to tell him you have a choice at a fork in the road," he said heavily. "Naturally, Polnik decided the left fork was the right one, and he was halfway to Nevada before it occurred to him he wasn't getting anyplace and maybe he should ask directions."

"Where is he now? Still out at the Harveys'?"

Lavers shook his head. "I finally sent a uniformed man out there at noon—even Polnik has to sleep, but don't ask me the logic of it. That was why you wanted him out there, wasn't it, to keep an eye on things?"

"No," I said. "But I was going to ask him to wait to talk to Martha Harvey when she woke up, before anyone else had the chance. It doesn't matter now."

He glowered at me for a few seconds. "You'd make it a lot easier for everyone around here if you'd just tell somebody what you had in mind, occasionally!" he growled.

"That would be about the quickest way back to pounding a beat I could think of," I told him.

"There's an even quicker way!" He patted the tape recorder on the desk in front of him. "I've run that tape twice already, and I'm halfway out of my mind. So start making some sense out of it for me, Wheeler, or I'll do something worse than send you back to a beat. I'll—I'll—" A beatific smile spread slowly across his face. "I'll have you demoted to the lowest grade detective, then assigned to Sergeant Polnik as his junior partner, strictly under his personal supervision at all times!"

I had already launched into a run-down of what had happened to me out at the Harvey house overnight, even before he'd finished speaking. It was the first time I'd been face to face with a fate worse than death, and I didn't care for it one little bit. As I kept talking, Lavers' face got longer and longer, and the O-shape of his mouth got rounder and rounder. By the time I'd finally finished, he looked like something that just shouldn't have happened.

"Maybe they were a bunch of nuts out there, I told you last night on the phone," he muttered. "What made me use the word 'maybe,' I wonder? A man is murdered inside a locked room—a second story room with the window boarded up—and the doctor seriously suggests his throat was torn out by the claw of some giant animal? Then we got a tape recording of the victim talking to a ghost right up until the time he was murdered!"

He stared at me with a pleading expression on his face. "Please tell me, Lieutenant, and be honest about it! Is this whole thing just the product of my imagination?"

"I wish I could say it was, Sheriff," I said, "but where would that leave me?"

"Do you have any ideas at *all?*" he asked.

"About fifteen of them, all going different ways at the same time," I told him. "Did Ed Sanger come up with anything?"

Lavers shook his head morosely. "Not a thing. All the prints belong to Slocombe."

"What was in the attaché case?"

"A thermometer, a gun which belonged to Slocombe, and a pack of Kleenex," he said glumly.

"What was a ghostbreaker doing with a thermometer and a pack of Kleenex?" I wondered. "Ready to take the ghost's temperature and wipe its nose when it cried for mercy?"

"It was a *room* thermometer, you imbecile!" the Sheriff snapped—he has a great sense of humor. "Probably Slocombe had a cold and was one of those health nuts. Don't kid around with me, Wheeler, this one is a natural for the newspapers. They'll laugh themselves sick at the idea of us running around chasing ghosts!" He winced as he used the word. "What are you going to do now?"

"Get to know the people I met last night a little better," I suggested. "I figure they all had the opportunity to kill Slocombe, so now I have to dig around for some motives to go along with the opportunity."

"The classic textbook approach?" He looked at me with a gleam of suspicion in his eyes. "When *you* start talking this way, Wheeler, I start getting worried."

"George Farrow is the one with an obvious motive," I went on, "so maybe I should start with him."

"You know where to find him?" Lavers asked, much too casually.

"I guess I can find him in the phone book," I muttered.

He tossed a sheet of paper across his desk toward me. "That dumb sergeant, Polnik, made a list of all the people in the house, and their addresses, right after he got there." The Sheriff leered at me nastily. "You know what your trouble is, Wheeler?"

"Sure," I said quickly. "I'm a genius, and all us geniuses are a little absentminded."

As I walked back into the outer office, I saw Annabelle was standing beside her desk with her back toward me, her rounded hips gyrating in a mad frenzy.

"What's the matter, honey?" I asked sympathetically. "Girdle chafe?"

She spun around toward me, her face a bright pink. "You always sneak up on people like that?" she demanded in a furious voice. "How many more times do I have to tell you, I *don't* wear a girdle?"

"Then it was ants in your—well—everybody has their own troubles," I finished nervously.

"If you must know, I was practicing a new dance," she snapped. "My date tonight is an expert dancer, and a gentleman—which is a pleasant change from some people I could mention!"

I was fascinated. "Does the dance have a name yet?"

"It's called the Patagonian twist," she said brusquely.

"It reminds me of a drinking dance they used to do once," I told her.

"Drinking dance?"

"Same kind of a thing like a drinking song, only you dance it, not drink it," I explained. "It was called 'Bottoms up!' and it was a big hit with the cancan set, I remember."

"Al Wheeler!" She grabbed the heavy steel rule from her desk and advanced toward me menacingly. "Get out of here!"

"I'm on my way already," I assured her, and headed toward the door at a fast lope.

It was around four in the afternoon when I parked the Healey on the driveway of the Farrow house. All trace of the storm had long vanished, along with the witches, I guessed, and the sun shone fiercely from a cloudless blue sky. It was the kind of day that even the native Californians don't really believe in.

The Farrow estate—in contrast to the Harveys'—was kept in immaculate condition. Trim green lawns ran off in all directions, neatly dotted with carefully shaped flower beds where all the flowers grew strictly to attention. Thy house itself was a rambling structure, maybe fifty years old, but it gleamed from the obvious, and lavish, application of care and money.

Instead of a barred peephole, there was a generous panel of clear plate glass cut into the front door, and I figured the Farrows must be open-minded people. With one finger poised on the buzzer, I suddenly had a startling firsthand confirmation of the Farrows' freewheeling approach to life.

Through the plate-glass panel I saw a girl appear at the far end of the hallway, then slowly saunter toward the front door. Either she was just out of the bath or the house was hot—I didn't care much either way. It's not very often a lieutenant, strictly in the line of duty, gets to see a stark-naked redhead walking toward him, idly trailing a robe from one hand. Like an idiot, I forgot to remove my finger from the buzzer and the next moment it squawked loudly.

The redhead reacted like it was the Doomsday Bell, going about a foot straight up into the air, then wrapping the robe around her body at the speed of light. By the time her feet touched down again, she was demurely swaddled from neck to knee in a thick toweling robe. I wondered bitterly if the curse of the Harveys had transferred itself into the curse of the Wheelers.

Then the door opened suddenly and I got the full arctic blast of her frigid glance. "I hate snoopers!" she said passionately. "Dirty, furtive little men who peer in through windows and doors, with their hot piggy eyes feeding the rotting garbage inside their minds!"

"I am not little," I said coldly.

"Whatever you're selling, we don't want any," she continued at full blast. "You can get off this estate before I have you thrown off! If there's anything I despise it's a foul-minded little—"

"Shut up!" I snarled.

Her eyes widened incredulously. "You can't—"

"Sure, I can!" I grated. "You should remember what they say about people who live in houses with plate-glass panels cut into their front doors—they should wear clothes when they walk down the hallway. I only got the merest glimpse, anyway, nothing beyond a swift guess of 37-23-38."

"38-23-37," she said slowly.

"And I think that little mole—right where it is—is real cute," I added warmly.

The flame-colored hair that was piled into a cone on top of her head teetered alarmingly. "Who are you?" she asked in a breathless voice. "I just changed my mind—I could buy some of whatever it is."

"Lieutenant Wheeler—from the sheriff's office." I told her. "I wanted to talk to George Farrow, but somehow it doesn't seem important anymore."

"You—a police officer?" Her green eyes had a stunned look.

"It's not that wild a thought, is it?" I grunted.

"And I thought you were a peeper." She gurgled with laughter. "I guess I was half right, you're a legal-peeper!"

"And you are—?"

"Loraine Farrow—George's sister. He's much older than me, of course."

"And not built the same interesting way at all," I agreed.

"Why don't you come on in and have a drink?" she suggested. "Or don't you drink on duty, Lieutenant?"

"I find it always works out to be a pleasure," I said, then stepped inside the house.

Loraine Farrow led the way back down the hall, then down three steps into a pleasant room with a business-like bar at one end and a glass wall opening onto an outside patio. She established herself in back of the bar and looked at me inquiringly.

"Scotch on the rocks, a little soda, thanks," I told her.

She busied herself making the drinks while I lit a cigarette and studied the sharp, attractive planes of her face.

"George went out someplace maybe an hour back," she said, putting the glass in front of me. "I don't know when he'll be back. I guess he's probably gone over to the Harvey house again. Did you hear about the dreadful—" Her eyes took on that familiar saucerlike shape. "But, of course! You must be the lieutenant investigating the murder, the one George was telling me about at lunch!"

"That's me," I said, or something equally profound.

"But I'm thrilled!" She put two ice cubes into an old-fashioned glass, then casually filled it to the brim with 100 proof bourbon. "Tell me, Lieutenant, do you believe it was that old ghost that done it?"

"If it wasn't, then somebody's done a real good job of framing her," I said.

"Why don't we take our drinks outside?" she said. "I always say a sun-tanned alcoholic is so much more attractive, don't you think?"

She slid back a section of the glass wall and stepped out onto the patio with me tagging along in back of her. There were a couple of chaises, obviously out of the deluxe class, with deep foam rubber cushions that looked real bouncy and were covered with an elegant Hawaiian design. Loraine sank luxuriously into the nearest chair and the toweling robe fell apart across the tops of her thighs as she lifted her knees. I flopped on the other chair beside her and concentrated on the magnificent panoramic vista that stretched almost as far as her sun tan, I figured.

"I love talking about people," Loraine Farrow said happily, "and for about the first time in my life I've got a legitimate excuse because I'm talking to a real live police lieutenant—ecstasy!"

"The name is Al," I said. "I don't want to be distracted from my thigh-gazing by you calling me 'Lieutenant' all the time."

She looked down at her bare legs complacently. "On the edge of decency," she said. "All part of my deep-laid plot to keep you long enough to dish up all the dirt I know about the Harveys and, believe me, that's plenty!"

"Seduction and character assassination," I said encouragingly. "That's two hobbies you got, already?"

"Alcohol for a third." She tasted her bourbon and approved. "You've met my brother George already—I'm not like him at all!"

"I can see that," I assured her. "He doesn't use lipstick, for one thing."

"I often wonder who his father was," she said idly. "It all happened before my time, but I'm still curious. When I was sixteen I made up my mind I was going to ask my mother straight out on my twentieth birthday. Then she died before I was nineteen—along with *my* father."

"I'm sorry," I said politely.

"Don't be, they had a lot of fun," she said in a casual voice. "They were at a party when it happened, both fried as usual, and the host ran out of liquor. So Daddy volunteered to drive into town and bring back fresh supplies. Mummy went along with him, not because she figured he wanted the company, but because she'd get a drink a lot quicker that way. They were driving a convertible with the top down, and a couple of people saw them heading toward a bridge at around ninety, passing an open bottle back and forth between them. They went off the center of the bridge into the lake, and suddenly, I was an orphan. But they sure had fun!" She sighed deeply.

"There's just the two of you in the house, you and George?" I queried.

"Check!" She nodded. "We see as little of each other as we can, but even that's too much. George is a mean creep! I don't like a man who's mean-mean, rather than nasty-mean, do you?"

"I never thought about it too much," I admitted. "I guess you'll be happy when George marries Martha Harvey?"

"Marries all that lovely rich oil just waiting to be tapped under the Harveys' ground, you mean?" She gurgled with laughter. "He's not getting married, Al, he's making an investment!"

"Oil under the Harveys' ground?" I said eagerly.

She stretched out her arm and neatly dropped her empty glass onto my chest. "Go fill that up again with some more of that wonderful hundred proof, and I'll give you the inside story when you get back," she promised.

I did like I was told, handed her the fresh drink, then sank back onto my chair. The foam rubber definitely was *bouncy*, and the robe seemed to have crept up a further half-inch, exposing a thin white line above the length of sun-tanned thighs. And I was making conversation about oil deposits! How dedicated could I get? I wondered bleakly.

Loraine drank some of her bourbon, then spoke again. "The Harveys have owned that place for a long time, you know, Al. My theory is that once the house was built the decay set in, and the two Harvey girls are about the end product of four generations of steady decay. That's why Martha and George are just made for each other."

"How about the oil?"

"I was coming to it." She lowered the level in her glass a good inch. "Don't rush me! They've got a hundred acres of land over there, and from what George told me about the oil company's survey, it should average out a couple of gushers an acre!"

"That's nice for Ellis Harvey," I said.

"Wrong!" She gurgled softly. "He's an even bigger nut than his two daughters. Not interested, he told the oil people. He liked the land just the way it was. His grandfather was the first man to build beyond Bald Mountain, and his grandson wasn't about to destroy a hundred years' heritage for something trivial, like money. And that's how it stands, Al. Ellis just won't budge, but George is awful sure he'll change his mind once he gets a brand-new son-in-law."

"He can influence Ellis Harvey that much?"

"It's more complicated than that, legal-peeper," she said drowsily. "They all have a piece of the estate—the Harveys have always been great ones for providing against providence! Ellis has the lion's share, but both the girls and dear, fungoid Uncle Ben have a sizable piece also. George figures to shift the balance of power once he's got his hands on Martha's piece, I think." She giggled. "And I am talking about her real estate holdings!"

"I guess George isn't exactly broken up by what happened to Henry Slocombe, then?" I asked.

"Given half a chance, dear George will dance on his grave," Loraine said vehemently. "With Justine to keep him company."

"Why would she do that?"

"Hal Slocombe was her boyfriend before Martha lifted him from right under her elder sister's nose," she said. "Hal had quite a reputation with the girls around these parts—and a whole bunch of female scalps hanging from his belt." She drained her glass in one long gulp and tossed it onto my chest. "The service is lousy around here!"

Again I made the trip back to the bar and made her another drink. The edge of her robe was hovering around the point of no return when I sank back into my chair again.

"A very attractive guy, Hal Slocombe," she said in a reflective voice. "A lousy poet with no money, and a wonderful arrogance that made a girl feel grateful after he'd tumbled her in the hay and left her to walk home alone. He was one of the biggest bastards I ever met, but it's kind of lonesome now he won't be around anymore, all the same!"

"Does George believe in the Gray Lady bit, the family curse, and all?" I asked her.

"George believes in George," she said flatly. "All the rest is only incidental, Al-peeper. Please don't mention his name again—not while I'm drinking. It spoils the taste of good booze."

"What kind of a girl is Martha Harvey?"

The glass came away from her lips, reluctantly "Martha? She's a bitch," Loraine said in a matter-of-fact voice. "Justine is a witch, but Martha's maybe a couple of degrees worse. You know the kind, Al-peeper? The don't want a thing until you've got it—then they've got to have it or die trying to take it away from you!"

"Like she was happy with George until Justine acquired Henry Slocombe?"

"You're real sharp, Al-party-pooper, you're still on your first drink!" She said all in one breath. "And I guess it didn't matter too much to old Hal. He was looking for some nice comfortable place to settle down—a reasonably rich family with a reasonably bedworthy daughter who could pay the bills while he wrote his lousy verses. Justine or Martha, it wouldn't worry him which one he finally led up to the altar. Remembering how he was, he probably figured that once the marriage cooled off a little, it could be kind of fun to have an available older sister around the house."

"I wonder he lived to the ripe old age he did," I said.

"He was twenty-six!" she said sharply.

"That's what I mean," I agreed. "How about Uncle Ben? Got any dirt you can throw his way?" I saw her arm start to move, and I got to my feet. "I know," I said wearily, and lifted the empty glass out of her hand.

"Just one ice cube this time, Al-pourer," she called after me. "It loses its flavor with too much ice."

"Uncle Ben," she said a few moments later, with the full glass clasped firmly in both hands, "the creep who carries his own shrubbery around with him so he can crawl into it and vanish if the going gets rough! Good old Uncle Ben—the explorer back from foreign parts. He's an explorer, all right. I found that out the first time they sat me next to him at dinner!"

"An explorer—for real?"

"Well, he she was a travelin' man for about fifteen years, anyway," she said with a shrug. "I can remember when we were kids, Martha had the best stamp collection for miles—all donated by Uncle Ben writing from various foreign parts. He had a wife who died of something revolting in Madagascar—so he said. My guess is they had nothing for dinner one night so he ate her. After that he came home and settled in the bosom of his brother's family—and that's where he's been the last couple of years. From the way he looked the last time he saw me wearing a swimsuit, I figure bosoms are getting to be a real big thing in his life!"

Her voice had been steadily getting thicker all the time, I realized, and her face had a flushed, drowsy look. I swung my feet onto the ground and heaved myself out of the chair reluctantly.

"I should be getting along. It's been real nice, Loraine. A new experience, like getting a capsuled education in stuff you never even knew existed before. See you again soon, I hope?"

She made an effort and lifted her head, her eyes working hard to bring my face into focus. "What's your hurry, Al-piker?" Her eyebrows knit together in a worried frown. "You getting bored or something?"

"I enjoyed every minute of it, Loraine," I told her. "It's the clarion call of duty, and all that jazz."

"Don't go now," she said petulantly. "Leave me all alone with nothing to do, 's no good!" She shook her head too vigorously, and good bourbon spilled from her glass onto her bare thighs. "Sit down again, Al-poker-face, and have another drink, huh?"

"I'm sorry, honey," I said gently, "I really have to go."

Her lips puckered like those of a small child. "I think you're lousy!" she said in a tearful voice. "We could have a lot of fun if you stayed a while longer." A calculating glint showed in back of her eyes for a moment, then she arched her knees higher, twisting her body so that the robe opened right up to her waist.

"Stay a little longer, huh?" Her voice was hoarse. "We could make love—or something."

I'd gotten as far as the three steps that led up to the hallway when I heard the glass splinter, so I went back. Her arm swung listlessly a couple of inches above the broken glass as it lay in a small pool of bourbon, and she was snoring heavily with her head slumped onto one shoulder.

By the time I'd gotten one arm under her knees and the other under her shoulders and managed to lift her clear of the chair, I was panting. Dead weight, all those entrancing curves added up to a surprisingly heavy package. I carried her into the house and dumped her gently onto a couch in the living room, modestly rearranging the robe before I left.

As I wedged myself into the Healey, the sun was sliding fast out of the sky, and over in the direction of the Harvey house a patch of blood-red cloud sat brooding. A lot had been done to tame the canyon in back of Bald Mountain during the last hundred years, but even so, it still looked pretty rugged.

I wondered how it had looked to Nigel Harvey when he first brought his daughter to this strange place, the other side of the world. Maybe it looked real good to him, just the place to keep a suspected witch and murderess out of trouble and well hidden from sight. I had to hand it to Delia on one point: she'd been well out of sight these last hundred years—buried at the foot of the oak tree—but she'd never been out of the Harveys' minds.

Chapter Six

The sun had slid over the horizon by the time I got to the Harvey house, and the light was just beginning to fade. I walked toward the front porch and was about halfway there when an excited voice called out "Lieutenant!" I turned around and saw Ellis Harvey coming toward me quickly, an excited look on his gaunt face.

"I'm very glad you're back, Lieutenant!" He greeted me like I was an old friend or something. "I have something to show you, something that will interest you very much, I'm sure."

His bony fingers grabbed my elbow and hustled me around the side of the house and then across the straggling lawn that ran from the back terrace for maybe a hundred yards before it was finally engulfed by the encroaching weeds and tall trees. We reached the edge of the lawn, then Ellis urged me down a small, overgrown gravel path for maybe another forty yards before his tight grip jerked me to a halt.

"There!" He pointed dramatically. "That's it, Lieutenant, the oak tree."

It looked like any other oak tree to me, except for the large area of barren ground around it.

"This where Delia's buried?" I said.

"Right at the foot of the tree," he said, nodding.

"'I lie at the foot of the oak, where no flowers bloom,'" I quoted.

"'Condemned to lie beneath the oak, wrapped in everlasting awareness,'" Ellis outquoted me, then saw the questioning look in my eyes. "Justine told me about the tape recording at lunch," he said casually. "I walked down here about an hour back, Lieutenant, and saw it!"

"What?" I said impatiently.

"Come a little closer." He dragged me another ten feet nearer the tree. "There, you see it? Right at the foot of the oak!"

For a moment I figured he'd completely flipped, then squinted and did see some small object there. "What is it?" I grunted.

"See for yourself, Lieutenant!" He pulled my arm mercilessly until we were only a few feet away and I could see the object clearly.

"What the hell is an oil lamp doing out here?" I asked him.

"That's what I said to myself, the very words," he answered enthusiastically. "Then—when I examined it more closely—I recognized it!"

"As an oil lamp?" I looked at him dubiously.

"I think I mentioned last night that whenever a storm is forecast we put oil lamps into every room because we have so many power failures, Lieutenant?"

"Right."

"It's a little chore I like to do myself—so I know each lamp individually, like old friends as it were? That lamp"—his finger stabbed dramatically toward the base of the tree—"is the same lamp I put into Delia's room last night after I'd opened it up for Henry Slocombe!"

"So?"

He looked shocked. "Lieutenant, when you forced your way into that room, did you see any lamp there?"

"No, I guess I didn't," I admitted.

"Then how did it spirit itself out of that locked room and down here to the foot of the tree? Don't you see now? The only possible explanation is that Delia herself brought it with her, as some kind of warning—or proof even—that she had exacted retribution from the one foolhardy enough to challenge her curse!"

"You're certain it's the same lamp you left with Slocombe last night?"

"I would swear on oath it's the same," he said solemnly.

I went over and picked up the lamp, then looked at him. "How about the other lamps still in the house? Have you checked them over today, Mr. Harvey?"

"I make it a habit first thing the next day after a storm to refill them all, trim wicks, and so on," he said gravely. "Who knows how soon the next storm may come?"

"You remember how much oil they'd used last night—on an average?"

"They were about a third full this morning," he said raptly.

"How about this one?" I handed him the lamp.

He unscrewed the filler cap and looked carefully for a couple of seconds, then frowned. "That's strange—this is a little more than half full. Slocombe must have had the wick turned right down."

"Or maybe he didn't have the lamp lit the whole time?"

"That's certainly feasible, Lieutenant." Ellis cheered up again now he felt that little problem had been disposed of. "Well, Lieutenant, do you still doubt the existence of the Gray Lady?"

"I'm not qualified to give a definite opinion on her existence, Mr. Harvey, or otherwise," I said soberly, "but I'm still not convinced she murdered Slocombe."

"Oh!" He looked genuinely disappointed. "You're a hard man to convince, Lieutenant."

"My mother was a hard woman to convince, Mr. Harvey," I told him. "That's why I'm an only child."

We walked back slowly, retracing our steps across the lawn, then around the side of the house to the front porch. Ellis led the way through the front doorway into the wide hall, then stopped uncertainly.

"Well," he said awkwardly, "you have your duty to do, Lieutenant, so I imagine you want to be about your business. Feel free to go anywhere in the house. You'll stay to dinner, of course?"

"Thank you," I said politely.

"There was another officer here early this morning." He frowned for a moment. "Sergeant—Polnut?"

"I believe you," I told him.

"Then he was replaced by a uniformed officer at midday, and he left a couple of hours back—your office called apparently and said he was no longer required to stay here. I had hoped, Lieutenant, that it was a sign you were beginning to recognize the truth—Slocombe met his death through some supernatural agency that we poor mortals can't even begin to understand!"

"Maybe I'll come around to your viewpoint yet," I said. "I heard something about you earlier, Mr. Harvey. They told me you're the man who refused a fortune because he prefers to keep things the way they are?"

"What?" He blinked at me anxiously for a moment, then his face cleared. "Oh, you're talking about the oil leases? They could be wrong, you know, in their estimates!"

"It's not very likely," I said.

"My grandfather wasn't a poor man when he first came here," Ellis said reflectively. "He invested his money well, and fortunately we haven't had a profligate in the family yet, to spend it all in one generation. We have no real need for more money—I think the tradition is more important."

"And the rest of your family agrees with you?" I asked easily.

He gave a wintry smile. "I wouldn't say that exactly, Lieutenant! My younger brother Ben—you've met him, of course—doesn't agree at all. But then he would go off traipsing around the world for all those years, living wildly above his means. I haven't much sympathy for him, frankly. The family tradition of this estate means far more to me."

"And as you're the eldest, I guess what you say goes, Mr. Harvey?"

"Up to a point, Lieutenant. It is also a tradition in the family that the estate be jointly owned by all the living members, you see, but the eldest son always has the biggest single share. I own forty per cent of the estate. Ben and the two girls each have twenty per cent."

"So you're the boss?"

"Unless the three of them should unite against me!" He smiled. "But I don't think that's very likely!"

"I'm sure," I said. "Do you know where I can find Martha?"

"She may be still in her room," he suggested. "George Farrow was visiting with her a while back, but I think he's gone now. George is a splendid young man—excellent background, solid financial foundation—but there are times, I confess, I wish he wasn't quite so much of a go-getter!"

"George believes a thousand barrels of oil in the hand is worth a hundred acres mostly bushes?" I queried.

"Nicely put, Lieutenant!" He beamed at me for a moment. "You know I must say that was one thing about Henry—tragic as any alliance between him and my younger daughter would have been inevitably, he at least appreciated my feelings about the land."

"Maybe because he was a poet?"

"I do hope not!" Ellis shuddered faintly. "I read one of his poems once—it was dreadful!" He wandered away toward the back of the house, still shaking his head sorrowfully.

I walked up the stairs and then along to Martha Harvey's room, and tapped politely on the door.

"Who is it?" she called out.

"Lieutenant Wheeler."

"Lieutenant—oh? Please come in!"

Inside, the room was a pleasant contrast to what I'd seen of the rest of the house. The furnishings were bright and cheerful, and the room felt as if it was used by a human being, not something that flew out the window on a broomstick every night.

Martha was sitting in a chair, her hands folded in her lap. She wore a severe black dress which, coupled with a complete lack of make-up, heightened the pallor of her face. Her eyes were red-rimmed and swollen, with a dull look about them.

"Please sit down, Lieutenant," she said, gesturing toward a chair opposite hers. "I owe you an apology—my sister told me I behaved outrageously in front of you last night. I really am sorry, although I don't remember a thing about it!"

"Forget it," I said as I eased into the chair. "You had just undergone a tremendous shock, and you were also under heavy sedation. Anyway, you didn't do anything."

A momentary gleam showed in her eyes as she looked at me with a mock-innocent expression on her face. "Prancing around in front of you, wearing nothing but a transparent nightgown—you call that nothing, Lieutenant?"

"It was a pleasure," I said sincerely.

"That was exactly what Justine guessed—" she smiled faintly—"and why she was so furious with me this morning, I bet! But thanks for the compliment, Lieutenant, anyway."

"You mind if I ask you some questions?" I said.

"Not at all." Her face set into a tight mask. "I was going to marry Hal Slocombe, Lieutenant, and I loved him! Anything I can do to help bring his murderer to justice I'll do gladly!"

The words were just fine, but the way she said them sounded just a little bit phony.

"You don't believe it was the Gray Lady who killed him, then?" I asked in a mild voice.

"Of course I don't!" she said venomously. "That story is for fools and little children!"

"Do you have any idea why someone would want to kill Henry

Slocombe?"

"To stop me marrying him could have been a good reason to an insane mind!" she snapped.

"Like whose, for instance?"

She shrugged. "If I knew I'd have told you before this, Lieutenant!"

I relaxed a little in the chair. "I was talking to an old friend of yours this afternoon," I said. "Loraine Farrow?"

"That alcoholic little whore!" She flushed violently, more from annoyance at herself for stepping out of character as the grieving lover than any embarrassment, I figured.

"I'm sorry, Lieutenant," she whispered, "I shouldn't have said that."

"Maybe you're right, I wouldn't know." I shrugged. "She told me Slocombe was going to marry your sister at one time."

"She's a congenital liar!" Martha snapped. "Oh, they might have been out together a few times, but there was nothing to it at all. Just a casual friendship, Lieutenant. Trust sweet Loraine to embroider it into a big deal!"

I figured right then was maybe the time for me to do a little embroidering on my own account and see what kind of a big deal would come out of it.

"Loraine told me she had it straight from Justine herself," I lied easily. "That right up until the time she confided in you she was going to marry Slocombe, you were perfectly happy in the thought of marrying George Farrow."

There was an unholy look in Martha's eyes. "Justine told her that?" she rasped.

"The way I understood it, she told Loraine you'd always been insanely jealous of her looks and figure—her ability to attract men—and you couldn't stand to see her with anything of her own without trying to take it from her. Even"—I gave Martha a sweetly apologetic look or quoting—"if it meant throwing yourself shamelessly at a man, and jumping into bed with him without waiting for an invitation first."

She made gobbling noises in her throat while a furnace roared inside her body, heating her face to a scarlet color and throwing sharp tongues of flame in back of her eyes. I sat and waited patiently with a look of sympathetic understanding on my face until she finally simmered down a little.

"Me!" she screeched suddenly. "Insanely jealous of that overblown lump of grease! Me!—jumping into bed with a man without waiting for an invitation first! I could tell some delightful stories about Big Sister in that regard! She should hear some of the stories Hal told me about her—their very first date and how she'd got half her clothes off already before she got inside the front door!"

"I didn't pay too much attention," I said confidentially. "It sounded kind of wild anyway. I mean, even an attractive girl like you, Martha, would have a hell of a job taking a man away from Justine, I'd figure, that is—if she didn't want to let him go."

Her eyes widened and the pupils dilated with scorched fury as she stared at me fixedly.

"You think I couldn't take any man away from that oversized slob if I wanted?" She laughed contemptuously. "She was crazy for Hal! She thought the sun shone out of his eyes and the world went around because it had his permission! That was why I couldn't resist showing her once and for all that she couldn't keep a thing she valued without my consent!" Her voice was a harsh, ugly-sounding thing. "I snapped my fingers—like that! And he came sniffing around my skirts like an overanxious puppy. After that, she could have thrown herself down at his feet, and if I snapped my fingers once, he would have walked right over her without even noticing!"

"You think maybe Justine hated both of you enough for her to kill Slocombe?" I asked quietly.

"Of course I do!" she snarled savagely. "Justine's a good hater—I've made sure she's had a lot of practice!"

"You got to the door of the locked room first, after the scream," I said. "The way Justine tells it, you were hysterical so she got George to help her carry you back here and she gave you a sedative." I paused for a moment. "That's the way Justine tells it. The only thing I'm sure about is that she gave you a slight overdose of the sedative, enough to ensure that you wouldn't be talking to anyone for the next nine or ten hours. Maybe she had good reason—what do you think?"

Her eyes narrowed slightly as she concentrated for a few seconds. "I was here—sitting in this same chair—waiting until it would be all over. I was frightened, scared for Hal, that something would happen to him. Then I heard him scream—" Her voice faltered for a moment. "It was a horrible sound. I'll never forget it for the rest of my life! I rushed outside to the locked door—I wanted to try and tear it down with my bare hands even—but Justine kept pushing me away and telling me it was no use. Hal was dead, she kept on telling me, and I was to blame!" She looked up at me, her face delicately tear-stained and her lips quivering gently.

"I don't remember anything clearly after that, Lieutenant."

"The way you told me just then, it sounded like Justine was already outside the locked door when you arrived?"

"I think—" she bit her lower lip pensively "—I think she was, but I can't be absolutely sure. But then I can't see how she could have gotten there first, Lieutenant. I rushed outside as soon as I heard Hal scream—

and her room is a lot further away from the locked door than mine."

"Maybe she was already there—before he screamed?" I suggested.

"What possible reason could she have had for being there before anything happened?"

"There's one excellent possibility," I said pedantically. "Because she was about to make it happen?"

"You mean it might have been Justine who—" Martha shook her head violently. "Oh, no! Not Justine! It mustn't be my sister who—" She dissolved into an impressive flood of tears.

I got up from the chair. "I'm sorry I upset you, Miss Harvey," I said gently. "But there are some things I have to know for sure—and asking personal questions is the only way I have of getting the answers."

She lifted her head with sudden interest and looked at me through brimming eyes. "What kind of things, Lieutenant?"

"Well, for instance—" I thought for a moment. "You come from a family of damned good liars, Martha, if you don't mind me mentioning it? But you don't have anything to be ashamed of—even out of a bunch of damned good liars like them, I figure you're the best!"

Chapter Seven

I used the phone downstairs and called the Sheriff. He didn't sound exactly elated to hear my voice, maybe because he'd just sat down to dinner when I called.

"You think you could get somebody to bring that recorder, and the tape, out to the Harvey house tonight?" I asked him.

"I guess so," Lavers snapped. "If it's that important to you."

"I'd appreciate it," I told him. "Maybe Polnik could do it?"

"Well, maybe he could," he said heavily. "But then, Wheeler, if you want that recorder real bad, why take chances on it finishing up in Nevada again?"

"Your logic is only exceeded by your waist measurement, Sheriff," I admitted gracefully, then hung up on

A minute later I found out Ellis Harvey was wrong—George Farrow hadn't gone home, he was in the living room with Uncle Ben, drinking. George kind of twitched a little when he looked up and saw me walk into the room, but to be fair, I had to admit the possibility that George's life was probably full of little twitches and this particular one had no special significance.

"Well, well!" Uncle Ben boomed jovially. "If it isn't Lieutenant Wheeler who's rejoined us. Help yourself to a drink, Lieutenant—on the buffet over there. The Scotch isn't bad, but for God's sake don't touch the brandy! I think Ellis buys it cheap in fifty-gallon drums from the local gas station."

"Thanks for the warning," I told him, and went over to the buffet.

"How is your investigation progressing, Lieutenant?" George Farrow asked nervously. "Or is that top-secret information?"

I finished making the drink, then carried it with me over to the couch and sat down unhurriedly. "It's top-secret information," I said coldly.

His light blue eyes watered with embarrassment. "Oh? I'm sorry I asked."

"Forget it," I told him.

Ben Harvey leaned forward in his chair, scattering cigar ash over the carpet with a negligent flick of his finger.

"I've got a question for you that's not top-secret, young feller," he snorted. "When can I expect to get my tape recorder back?"

I stared at him in genuine surprise: "*Your* recorder?"

"Of course it's my damned recorder!" The sharp blue eyes twinkled at me aggressively from behind their protective layers of fat. "Poor old Slocombe borrowed it from me last night before he went up to the locked room."

"Why didn't you tell me it belonged to you before?" I growled at him.

"Because you never asked," he said reasonably.

"You'll have it back any time now," I said.

Ben puffed rapidly on his cigar for a few seconds, ejecting puffs like an Indian smoke signal. "Poor feller," he ruminated. "So scientific with his tape recorder and all." He slumped back into his chair with a thud that shook the floorboards under the carpet. "Going up against the Gray Lady with that thing gave him about as much chance as you'd have up against a Mau Mau with a pocketknife in your hand."

I looked across at George. "I stopped off at your house on my way up here," I said conversationally, "and met your sister."

"Did you?" He twitched more violently this time.

"She's a charming girl," I went on. "We had a long talk together."

His eyeballs rolled in anguish at the thought. "Loraine kind of gets carried away when she's talking," he said desperately.

I resisted the temptation to say "Feet first?"

"It's been too long since we've seen Loraine over here, George!" Ben bellowed at him. "Charming gal! Why don't you bring her more often, boy? Ashamed of the family you're marrying into, or something?"

"No!" George yelped frantically, then dabbed his forehead with a pocket handkerchief. "It's just that—well, Loraine, she—she doesn't go out much," he finished with sudden inspiration.

"How can the poor girl go out if she's not damned well asked?" Ben shouted at him. "It's just not being fair to us other fellers, keeping a pretty little filly like that at home all the time! Am I right, Lieutenant?"

"I think it's possible," I admitted, "but not probable."

"Hah!" There was a noise like a pistol shot as he slapped his thigh delightedly. "You don't like me, do you, young feller?"

"I'm a police officer," I said sententiously, "neither liking nor disliking people is any part of our business."

"Just forget the copper business for a minute." He leaned forward in his chair again. "As an ordinary, average man, Lieutenant—you think I'm a loudmouthed old fool, right?"

"If you say so," I said politely.

"That's what I thought in the first place!" He sank back into his chair again. "I've got a feeling for those kind of things—an instinct you call it!—comes from all those years in primitive places among the savages."

George cleared his throat painfully. "Ben spent fifteen years, Lieutenant, just traveling the whole time from place to place, wherever and whenever he felt like it. How about that?"

"How about that," I muttered.

"He's got a trunkful of curios in his room," George went on determinedly. "You should get him to show you them sometime, Lieutenant. They're absolutely fascinating!"

"Stuffed Mau Maus?—unsigned oil leases?—that kind of curio?" I asked innocently.

Ben winked elaborately at George and gave his goatee a savage wrench at the same time. "He's pulling your leg, young feller!" he confided at the top of his voice. "A devious mind, that's what the Lieutenant has—right, Lieutenant?"

"Right now, I'm not too sure I've still got any kind of a mind," I told him truthfully. "Maybe the combination of your family and its ghost is getting to be more than I can handle."

He snorted with laughter. "I told you last night, remember? All that tough, factual training and experience of yours, Lieutenant—they don't mean a damned thing now you're up against something you never met before like the Gray Lady. I'm willing to bet right now that this case will wind up in your 'Unsolved' file, and by the time it does, you'll be personally convinced Slocombe was killed by some supernatural agency—a ghost!"

Justine came into the room right then, saving me the trouble of saying something stupid in answer to Ben Harvey. I got onto my feet politely and she looked right through me with one casual glance on her way across to the buffet.

"How about making your poor old Uncle Ben a drink while you're there?" His rumbling voice bounced around the walls for far too long after he'd finished speaking.

"Get it yourself, you hulking faker!" Justine said tartly. "What do you think this is?—the Gobi Desert?"

"That's the kind of girl I like!" He tugged his beard in ecstasy. "All ladylike and feminine with lovely big curves on the outside—and a vat of acid sheathed in armored steel plate on the inside!"

Justine came back from the buffet with a drink in her hand, surveyed the seating for a long moment, then shrugged her shoulders eloquently and sat on the far end of the couch away from me.

"You haven't spoken to Martha in the last hour or so, by any chance, Justine?" George asked hopefully.

She gave him a fixed smile. "I never speak to Martha whenever it can be avoided, George, you know that."

His eyes were glassy with embarrassment, the moment before they swam out of sight. "I—I guess she must be still up in her room, then?"

"She was when I left her maybe fifteen minutes back," I told him.

"Oh?" He blinked at me nervously. "You were talking with her, Lieutenant? How was she? Did she look like she was starting to calm down a little?"

"More like she was getting madder and madder when I left," I said easily. "I was telling her a wild story I'd heard about how she took Hal Slocombe away from her sister just for kicks—"

"Loraine!" George moaned and visibly shrank into his chair.

"—and how I didn't believe it," I went on steadily. "It was then she got mad at me, I think. Right after I told her nobody in their right mind would believe she could take anything away from Justine—not with her looks and figure unless she already wanted to let it go. Martha had some crazy idea that she's a hotter attraction than her older sister!" I smiled tolerantly.

George sat perfectly still with his eyes tight shut, obviously hoping he was invisible. I felt a gentle pressure against my thigh and turned to see Justine sitting right next to me.

"Lieutenant?" Her voice was a soft caress. "Let me freshen up your drink, h'mm?"

"Well, thanks," I told her.

Her fingers touched mine with brief intimacy as she took the glass from my hand and walked across the room.

"So my darling little sister was real mad when you left her, Lieutenant?" she asked happily from the buffet.

"She kept on telling me she only needed to snap her fingers and Slocombe came running like an overanxious puppy," I said. "But I told her you must have snapped off the leash before that could happen."

Justine glided back to the couch, placed the glass carefully in my hand, then sat down even closer beside me so I could feel the whole length of her warm, rounded thigh pressed hard against mine.

"Poor little Martha!" she gloated. "You were unkind to my little sister, Lieutenant. Shame on you! What else did you say?"

"It wasn't much use me saying anything else," I said apologetically. "I don't think she would have heard me—not while she was frothing at the mouth, and all!"

George bounced out of his chair with an anguished yelp and disappeared from the room at a fast gallop. A moment later we heard the heavy thumping noise as he took the stairs, three at a time.

"I don't know what your game is, young feller," Ben barked suddenly, "but you're playing it a little rough aren't you?"

"Don't pay him any mind, Lieutenant," Justine said coldly. "He got left out in the sun too long in one of those foreign places and it softened his head. You might think he's just a barrel of lard, looking at him from the outside, but inside he's exactly the same!"

"One of these times you'll go too damned far, my girl!" he spluttered at her.

"That's very possible," Justine snapped, "but not with you, Uncle, dear, so don't build any hopes!"

"*Justine!*" He heaved his massive bulk out of the chair and stalked out of the room with his shoulders set we back and his head held high. Obviously it was an orderly disengagement of combat, not a retreat.

"I think you hurt his feelings," I said tentatively.

"They're made of elephant hide!" she said. "I wish I could hurt his feelings—then maybe he'd stop fumbling around my knees at the dinner table!"

"Loraine has the same problem, she told me."

"Loraine has a problem whenever there's a man around," Justine said evenly. "I thought you hated me, Lieutenant Wheeler, from the way you were so rude to me last night?"

"I guess my nerves were a little on edge," I murmured. "Any time now, someone's delivering that recorder and the tape back here. Would you do me a favor and make sure you answer the door—then have them put it someplace the others won't see it?"

"Of course!" Her fingers squeezed my arm gently. "What are you planning? Something diabolical?"

"I want to play it over to Martha and get her reactions," I said.

"That's diabolical enough!" She sighed ecstatically.

"Would you like to help?"

"Oh, you wonderful, thoughtful man!" She kissed my cheek gently, a dreamy look in her dark eyes. "I'd adore to help! And if you're going to third-degree my little sister anytime, could I make a couple of little, teensy-weensy turns on the thumbscrew?"

The gigantic doorbell tolled suddenly, and Justine was already halfway to the front door before my eardrums had adjusted. She came back into the room five minutes later with a contented smile on her face. "It's in back of the hall closet," she told me in a conspiratorial whisper. "Nobody will ever look in there!"

"Great," I said warmly. "After dinner we'll sneak it upstairs, right?"

"Right!" she said.

There was a scampering noise and George suddenly reappeared, his eyes full of defiant determination and his lower lip quivering uncontrollably. He came right up to the couch and stood directly in front of me, his hands planted firmly on his hips.

"Martha didn't say any of those things you say she said, she just told me!" he said rapidly, his voice on the thin edge of hysteria.

I stared up at him blankly for a moment, then looked questioningly at Justine. "Who dat?" I asked her.

"Dat George." She sniffed disparagingly.

"What did he say?"

"Something confused, like always." She yawned loudly. "What do we need to talk about George for, when there's fascinating people like you and me to discuss?"

"Don't try and wriggle out of it, Wheeler!" George's voice almost vanished in the higher treble range. "Martha says you're a liar!"

"Well," I said, "I guess that's all right, so long as *she* says it."

"What the hell do you mean by that?" His voice zoomed down a couple of octaves with sudden, new-found confidence. "Answer me, Wheeler!"

"Yes," Justine said coolly. "Wheeler—answer him!"

"I said it's okay if Martha calls me a liar," I explained, "because she's a lady—well, a female, anyway—and there's not much I can do about it."

"I'm calling you a liar, Wheeler!" George said loudly, obviously drunk with power.

"Ah, that's different!" I told him, and got onto my feet with a series of slow, immensely deliberate movements.

I stood real close to George and looked down at him menacingly from a height advantage of around six inches.

"If you call me a liar, I can hit you, George, because you're no lady," I explained carefully. "It's okay to muss you up a little—maybe break a couple of small bones—if you call me a liar!"

"He did, he did, he did!" Justine said excitedly. "I heard him, Lieutenant, he called you a liar right to your face! Now kill him!"

"Is that right, George?" I growled.

His face suddenly dissolved like someone had pulled a plug and they couldn't find the lifeboats. "No!" he said thinly. "Not me, Lieutenant. There must be some mistake—honest! I wouldn't think of calling you a liar!"

"Well," I said reluctantly. "If you're sure?"

"Positive!" he squeaked.

"Maybe if you just bent him permanently to one side a little, Lieutenant?" Justine asked hopefully. "So he wouldn't forget?"

Chapter Eight

Ellis Harvey looked at me across the dining table, his dark, opaque eyes like two bruises placed carefully in the middle of his paper-white face.

"Lieutenant, may I ask you a question?" His desiccated voice sounded almost apologetic.

"Sure," I told him.

"Please don't misunderstand me—you are a welcome guest in this house—but why are you here?"

"How's that again?" I said blankly.

"Exactly what do you hope to achieve by being here?" He kept right at it with delicate but inflexible determination. "I admit I'm absorbed with curiosity. I don't think I've ever spoken to a law enforcement officer in my whole life before!"

"It's very simple," I said in a casual voice. "Last night a murder was committed in this house, and from the time I arrived until the time I left, I was kept busy with all the things that have to be done first. There's a kind of automatic formula which is concerned first with the victim, and then with the things that surround the victim—from the carpet on the floor where his body lay, to circumstances of time and place."

"Very interesting, very interesting indeed!" Ellis murmured almost enthusiastically. "Please continue, Lieutenant."

"I guess the easiest way to answer your question about why I'm here tonight," I said slowly, "is to say I want to get better acquainted with a murderer."

"Just what does that mean—exactly?" Ben rumbled at me accusingly. "I think you should explain yourself more clearly, Lieutenant!"

"Right now there's a four to one chance I've just had dinner with the murderer." I grinned at him. "The fifth chance is that the murderer ate alone in her room upstairs."

"You mean Martha?" George looked at me with a horror-stricken face.

"The way I see it," I said wearily, "it had to be one out of the five of you in the house at the time, who killed Slocombe. The more I know all five of you, the better my chances of finding the murderer among you."

"The murderer among you," Justine repeated slowly, then shivered suddenly. "What a delightful phrase that is, Lieutenant!"

Ellis shook his head slowly. "Thank you, Lieutenant, I hadn't even hoped for such a graphic explanation as the one you just gave us." He smiled faintly. "I must admit it's slightly unnerving to realize that when a man looks into your face as he speaks, he's not just being polite. He's also weighing up in his mind the possibilities that he's talking to a murderer."

"It's crazy!" George said, suddenly. Then his face flushed a bright crimson as everyone stared at him. "I mean—how could any of us have gotten inside that room and killed Hal Slocombe? I'm no great believer in the supernatural, but this time I'll go along with it all the way because it's the only explanation that makes any sense! Don't you see that, Lieutenant?" He looked at me almost wistfully. "If you want the most logical explanation of how Slocombe was killed—then you don't have any other choice but to accept the fact that the Gray Lady killed him!"

He slumped back in his chair with an exhausted look on his face and I wondered if he'd just made the longest speech of his whole life.

"Bravo, George!" Ellis said softly.

"Made a lot of damned good sense!" Uncle Ben boomed, tugging fiercely at his goatee. "You could do a lot worse than listen to what the young feller said, Lieutenant."

"Okay"—I shrugged—"why don't we do that? If the most logical explanation of Slocombe's murder is that the Gray Lady killed him—then it follows that the lady herself should stand up within a logical framework, right?"

"I lost you there, Lieutenant, right after the second word you said," Justine said apologetically.

"Maybe I lost myself?" I grunted. "I mean if the Gray Lady is the logical murderer, then you have to also prove logical reasons for her existence and for her actions, right?"

"I see what the Lieutenant is driving at," Ellis said. "Go ahead."

"The way I heard the story," I said evenly, "the man Delia didn't want to marry was murdered by some beast in the forest. Eyewitnesses claimed they saw a huge gray wolf near the scene at the time—and others claimed they saw Delia running from the woods into the house, the front of her dress stained with blood. Later, the villagers swore she was a witch and planned to burn her at the stake. Right?"

"You have an excellent memory," Justine said softly.

"So the strong inference is that Delia was a witch, capable of transforming herself into an animal—the wolf—then back to a human again?"

"I would think so," Ellis nodded.

"How did she become a witch? Did the gypsy lover teach her the black arts, or what?"

"That is what I believe happened," Ellis said simply.

"So Delia gained nothing by getting rid of her unwanted prospective bridegroom. Her father brought her out to California and built this house. Then, as I understand it, she died soon after of her own conscious choice?"

"Willed herself to die!" Ben shouted to the ceiling. "Seen it done in India a hundred times—funny fellers, those fakirs!" He shook his head doubtfully at the chandelier.

"On the day of her death, she suddenly decides she wants her room left empty for as long as the house remains standing, and puts a violent curse on anyone who dares use her room in the future. Why?"

"I agree, that's hard to understand, Lieutenant," Ellis said quietly. "I've given it a great deal of thought myself." He placed his elbows on the table and steepled his fingers, tapping them together gently. "I've come to this conclusion—Delia was initiated in the arts of sorcery by her gypsy lover. In her first major attempt to apply the knowledge— the murder of the unwanted suitor—she failed miserably. Instead of bringing herself and her gypsy lover together, it had the effect of separating them forever, and she also bungled the actual killing so badly that the villagers were ready to burn her at the first opportunity!"

"What's this got to do with the curse and her room?" I asked.

"Witchcraft, like most other things, has its penalties for failure," he said softly. "Isn't murder a classic example of the rule, Lieutenant? The penalty the unsuccessful murderer pays is his own death! I think it was something like that with Delia. When she left England with her father, she already knew she had to pay the price of her own failure by dying herself.

"On the last day of her life, I think she had a sudden strong desire to use her powers of witchcraft one more time, before it was too late. She wanted to be a successful witch once, before she lost the chance. Anything would do, so long as it gave her the chance to perform—so she used the room as an excuse for a successful curse!"

"So maybe she died happy?" George asked seriously.

"I think that was the most dreadful mistake she ever made," Ellis said in a somber voice. "For a curse to be successful throughout eternity, there must be someone watching to ensure it is so. When Delia put her curse on that room, I think she condemned herself to an eternity of guardianship at the same time." He glanced at me momentarily. "'Condemned to lie beneath the oak, wrapped in everlasting awareness,'" he quoted softly.

"So when that poor feller Slocombe said he'd defy her curse and spend Walpurgis Night in her room, she rose from her eternal vigil and wreaked a swift and terrible vengeance!" Ben Harvey said in a wondering voice. "It's all there, Lieutenant, as plain as the nose on your face!"

"On that tape, Slocombe said you were convinced that Martha was in some way a reincarnation of Delia herself," I said to Ellis. "The incredible likeness between her portrait and Martha for a start—their mothers had both died giving birth to them. He said that you saw a parallel situation to Delia's, with Martha, George Farrow, and Slocombe himself. George was the prospective bridegroom all over again, and Hal Slocombe, the gypsy lover. Is that right?"

"It is," Ellis said in a taut voice. "That was why I bitterly opposed Martha's marriage to Slocombe—it would have ended in stark tragedy!"

"But it really wasn't a parallel," I grated. "It's the situation in reverse. If it were a parallel, it would be George who was murdered, not Slocombe!"

"You miss the point, Lieutenant," Ellis said gently. "In these things, although minor details may differ, the parallel must be exact. Remember the gypsy was more than a lover—he was a teacher of sorcery—a witch himself!"

"So?" I snapped.

"So when, in the face of my continual opposition to the marriage, Slocombe came and challenged me to let him stay in Delia's room through the night of April thirtieth—the anniversary of her death—I was finally sure of the truth. His claim that he wished to prove the whole thing a lot of superstitious rubbish was merely a blind—a cover for his real intentions."

"Which were?" I prompted.

"To pit his strength against hers," Ellis said slowly, his voice sinking to a whisper. "He had no alternative left but to stake everything on the outcome of direct battle with Delia. And he lost, Lieutenant, and as always, had to pay the price for failure."

"I'm not sure I understand exactly what you're getting at, Mr. Harvey," I muttered.

He straightened his thin shoulders and leaned back in his chair, a small triumphant smile on his lips.

"It's perfectly simple, Lieutenant, when you remember the parallel must be exact in all major factors. Henry Slocombe himself was a *witch!"*

I looked at the others sitting around the table. Ben Harvey sat rolling a cigar between his fingers, his face stern as he slowly nodded emphatic agreement; Justine's face was a mask showing neither agreement nor disagreement; and George Farrow sat with a look of ecstatic, stunned revelation on his face as if one of the great truths of all time had been suddenly revealed to him.

"Now you understand, Lieutenant?" Ellis asked in a genial voice.

"Oh, sure," I said dully. "Henry Slocombe was a witch."

It was an hour after we'd left the dining room before we had an opportunity to sneak the recorder upstairs. The chance came just after Ellis had retired for the night and Uncle Ben was launched into a lengthy account of that time in Upper M'Gonko, assured of a captive audience in poor George.

Justine went ahead of me to the door of Martha's room, while I brought the recorder along with me behind her. She tapped imperatively on the door, and Martha's voice sounded angry as she asked who was there.

"It's me, darling," Justine said happily. "Your big sister."

"Go away!" Martha's voice was sullen. "You overweight witch!"

"Coming, ready or not!" Justine called cheerfully. She opened the door, then swept into the room.

The expression of dark fury on Martha's face turned to surprise when she saw me follow Justine into the room and put the tape recorder carefully on the table.

"What do you want?" she asked cautiously.

"I want you to listen to this tape," I told her. "Then we can talk about it afterward."

I threaded the spool, flicked the switch, and adjusted the volume control so it wouldn't be loud enough for anyone to hear downstairs. It wasn't exactly a riot to watch Martha's face while the tape played through. Even Justine lost her taste for it after the first couple of minutes. I'd never figured Martha to be madly in love with Slocombe, but at times they must have been fairly close, and listening to his voice pleading with the ghost must have been an exquisite form of sadistic torture for her.

The scream of terror at the end brought Martha onto her feet, her hands clenched to her ears, sobbing uncontrollably. Justine picked her up in her arms like a babe, then sat in a chair and nursed her until she quieted down.

"Was there any real point in making her listen to that, Lieutenant?" Justine asked in an ominous voice.

"Yes," I said tiredly. "There was a lot of point. When did you record that tape, Martha?"

She got to her feet and walked slowly across the room to the window. "Over the last two weeks," she said in a small voice. "In bits and pieces. Hal would sneak the recorder up here and we'd do a couple of lines every night. But there's some of it missing."

"Like what?"

Martha turned around to face me, a bewildered look on her tear-stained face. "There's a whole lot missing," she said firmly. "The way we did it, Delia—that was me, of course—relented finally, and told Hal she would lift the curse so we could get married and live happily ever after—well, you know the kind of thing?"

"The idea was Hal would burst out of the locked room joyfully, to tell everybody the great news at the psychological moment?" I said. "Then play back the tape for your father to hear and after that everything would be roses, roses, all the way?"

"That was the idea," she said sadly.

"Hal wrote the script?"

"He worked harder at that than at anything he'd ever done before, I think," she whispered. "Some of those lines he wrote for Delia to say were the best poetry he'd ever written, I thought. I guess that's funny when you think about it."

"There's a whole chunk missing, you said? Has anything been added, maybe?"

She thought for a moment, then her face tightened with fear. "At the end," she whispered slowly. "When Delia whispers in that horrid, rasping sound! When she says about the Gray Witch walking by night! *That's not me!*" She sobbed deep in her throat, then ran across the room to her older sister's protective arms.

"Take it easy, honey," Justine told her in a soothing voice. "Just take it easy!"

"Justine? You think while Hal was playing the tape through inside the locked room—the *real* Delia appeared, and that's her voice on the tape now?" Martha whimpered convulsively and clung tightly to her sister.

"Of course not!" Justine said, without any conviction in her voice at all. "Of course not!"

I packed up the tape recorder ready to be moved, then looked at Justine.

"Take it along to my room, Lieutenant," she said softly, "and wait for me there. I'll be along in a little while." For maybe ten seconds I tried hard to think of something encouraging to say to Martha, then gave up and carried the recorder out of her room, along the corridor to

Justine's room. I sat on the end of her bed and smoked a couple of cigarettes while I thought about the Harvey family in general, and then in particular. It wasn't the kind of mental exercise to strengthen the brain muscles—it was more likely to stretch them tighter and tighter until there was a nasty twanging sound when they snapped.

I heard a soft movement in back of me, and looked to see Justine step lightly into the room and close the door gently behind her.

"Poor kid!" she said compassionately. "She's okay now, I think. I've given her a sedative and she was asleep before I left." She walked over and sat on the bed beside me, a troubled look in her eyes.

"I've been such a bitch to her!" she said in a low voice, "It doesn't make me feel very good right now."

"I wouldn't worry too much," I said tersely. "After all, Martha's been such a bitch to you, too, right?"

Her head lifted angrily and she stared at me in frigid silence for a few moments before she spoke.

"Just what do you mean by that, exactly, Lieutenant?" Her voice was like a whiplash.

"It's pretty damned obvious," I grated. "Anything you had, Martha always wanted so bad she had to take it away from you any way she could. But once she had it for herself, she'd lose interest in whatever it was. She's always had to keep on proving to herself that she's smarter than you, prettier than you, sexier than you. The acid test was Hal Slocombe and she won that with a knockout in the first round, right?"

"It's a fascinating theory," Justine said in a brittle voice. "Just how did you formulate it, exactly, Lieutenant?"

"I just listened while other people told me what happened between you and Martha," I snapped. "There's no trick to it. All you have to do is concentrate while they're speaking to you."

"Who's speaking to you?"

"Loraine Farrow—Martha herself."

"And you believed them?"

"Sure." I shrugged irritably. "Why not? Slocombe started out as the big thing in your life and wound up wanting to marry your kid sister, didn't he? I guess you didn't have any choice about that!"

Her open palm slammed down across the side of my face like a steam hammer, the force of it toppling me over sideways onto the bed. I lay there for a couple of seconds listening to the bells, then hauled myself slowly up into a sitting position again.

"What the hell was that for?" I snarled at her.

"All those stinking lies you told George before dinner, about how you told Martha she didn't have a chance compared to an attractive woman like me!" she said tautly. "And I believed you. If you'd asked me to sleep with you at that moment, Lieutenant, I'd have walked straight up here and got into bed! For the first time since I don't remember, you gave me back my confidence while Martha was around. I could relax, enjoy myself, even laugh a little and play crazy, like that horsing with George and his calling you a liar. But it was a big fake, wasn't it?"

"Justine," I mumbled, "I never figured to—"

"Don't bother with more lies," she said stonily. "You had it figured exactly. You'd already arranged for the tape recorder to be sent out. Then you realized you'd need help to smuggle it in the house and up to Martha's room without the others knowing about it! So suddenly Justine is elected to become the big deal in the lieutenant's life, long enough for her to function effectively as an apprentice cop. But when she's outlived her usefulness, why should the big lieutenant bother about letting her keep her illusions? Tell her the truth—it's about time the overweight slob realized, anyway! Tell her straight out—give it to her right between the eyes, she's big enough to take it!"

I figured if I shrank anymore I'd simply disappear. "I'm sorry," I said humbly. "You have a murder and then you have to find the murderer, and sometimes you get too close to it. Then you forget about the feelings of other people involved. Somehow, just because they're involved in murder, you feel it gives you a right to use them in helping you find the murderer. You forget they can still be hurt just as easy as anyone else—they can still bleed real easy, like everyone else!"

"You're still lying, aren't you, Lieutenant?" There was stark contempt in her voice. "In your head, you're still figuring percentages the way you've been doing since you first got here tonight! Please go now— suddenly I'm very tired, and slightly nauseated."

I got up from the bed, picked up the recorder, and started toward the door.

"Lieutenant?"

"Yeah?" This time I didn't bother to turn my head.

"Remember when I said I'd misjudged you?—you were really a subtle son of a bitch?" she said gently. "Now I guess I was right the first time—you are just a cheap son of a bitch!"

Chapter Nine

When I looked into the living room, George had vanished and there was only Ben Harvey sitting there with a huge balloon glass in his hand and a look of contentment on his face. I figured it must be his secret drinking glass and he kept it hidden someplace until he was sure he was alone and not likely to be disturbed. He was facing away from me, and the combination of the giant balloon and the fat cigar between his fingers looked much too good to disturb. I stepped back silently into the hall, still holding the recorder.

"Still snooping, Lieutenant?" Uncle Ben's roar shattered the silence into supersonic dust.

I walked back into the living room and saw his artful grin.

"Didn't think I knew you were there, eh, young feller?" He chuckled throatily. "It's a little trick I picked up from the Zizi tribe—you don't listen so much with your ears as with your feet—and you pick up the vibrations!"

"There are times, Uncle Ben," I told him, "that I suspect the furthest you've been overseas is to Catalina Island."

"Hah!" He waggled the glowing end of his cigar at me. "I'd like to see you stand up to one of those Zizi all-night tribal dances, young feller!"

"What's the incentive?" I grunted.

"They distribute the virgins around three A.M.!" He leered at me triumphantly.

"I brought your recorder back," I told him, and dumped it on the table, then removed the tape and put it in my pocket.

"Good!" he bellowed. "I hope you haven't fouled up the works or anything. I value that machine, paid a high price for it!"

"Three Zizi ex-virgins and a couple of shrunken heads?" I suggested.

Ben threw back his head and roared like a wounded bull. I went over to the buffet, made myself a drink, then sat down and waited for him to stop laughing.

"Hah!" He pulled a handkerchief out of his pocket and wiped his eyes carefully. "Shouldn't say things like that, young feller! Can spoil a man's cigar—and his brandy."

"I was curious," I told him, "about that tape recorder of yours. Did Slocombe ever borrow it before last night?"

"He seemed to be borrowing the damned thing all the time," Ben grunted. "I don't know what the hell he was doing with it, and as he didn't tell me, I didn't like to ask—if you know what I mean?"

"Sure," I said. "Just to satisfy my own curiosity, Mr. Harvey—what kind of a man was Slocombe?"

"Why don't you ask Martha?" he growled. "She wanted to marry the feller!"

"I've already got bits and pieces," I said. "He'd never done a day's work in his life—he was a poet, and a real lousy poet, at that!—he had more arrogance than twenty normal men, and that made him irresistible to all the girls. His major hobby was collecting female scalps—" I shrugged helplessly. "How about throwing in your bit?"

Ben Harvey studied the glowing tip of his cigar for a few seconds.

"He was an educated bum," he said finally. "I'm glad for Martha's sake she can never marry him now!" He gave his goatee three sharp tugs, the buried his nose in the brandy balloon.

"I only saw him when he was a corpse, but he looked like a man, anyway, and that's more than you can say for poor old George!"

"What?" His nose reared out of the glass, and the look of indignation on his face was exactly how you would imagine Santa to look if he found one of his reindeer loaded on Christmas Eve.

"Don't you underrate George Farrow!" he thundered. "There is a hell of a lot more to that young feller than meets the eye, let me tell you! He's got a head on his shoulders and—"

"Once he's married to Martha, he'll throw her twenty per cent of the estate in favor of the oil leases?" I finished for him.

The blue eyes, all but submerged in the rolls of fat, leered at me knowingly. "Well"—he tugged at his beard innocently—"you could be right about that, Lieutenant, who knows?"

"You know, for sure," I said. "Then you'll only have Justine to worry about, once George and Martha are married. Get Justine on your side, and your brother Ellis is going to find himself a lonely—if stinking rich—old man, right?"

"Oh, Ellis isn't that old," Ben Harvey said in a mild voice. "He's only just sixty—lot of life left in him yet!"

"But he won't want to spend it counting barrels," I said.

"I guess he's old enough to make up his own mind about that," he murmured.

"I guess so." I shrugged. "Did George go on home?"

"Some time back," he boomed. "He's got a hell of a lot more sense than some young fellers I know—disturbing their elders and betters in the middle of the night!"

"George is real smart, all right," I said absently. "That's the trouble with the whole damned bunch of you in this house—you're all so much smarter than you make out."

"What?" The enormous nose reared out of the brandy again, and I saw the look of outraged indignation on his face at the fresh interruption. "You say something?" He bellowed at a painting hanging on the wall twelve feet in back of me.

"Sure—good night!" I snapped, and walked out of the living room."

A sudden crack of thunder shook the hallway, and for a split second I thought the storm was coming back, then realized it was Ben Harvey's answering good night from the living room. I walked briskly toward the front door, then stopped dead right in front of it. All the frustrations that had been building up inside me over the last twenty-four hours suddenly got themselves unionized and marched all over me, keeping in perfect step the whole time.

I reached out and opened the front door wide, then slammed it shut again, and stood looking at it for a couple of minutes, listening to the union organizers representing Amalgamated Frustrations make some short, passionate and inflammatory speeches to the back of my mind.

Then I turned around and eased gently—like thistle-down on the breeze yet!—past the open door of the living room, and catfooted up the stairs. There didn't seem to be much point in knocking politely on Justine's door so I didn't; I just opened it and walked straight into her room.

She was standing in front of a full-length wall mirror with her back toward me, vigorously brushing her hair. I figured if a knee-length nylon nightgown had made Martha shameless the previous night, according to her sister, then there just weren't any words left to describe Justine's own choice of sleeping attire.

The pants were bikini-size, made from black nylon, and they just managed to straddle her magnificent hips with one large bow of white lace perched on each hip and fluttering bravely like flags of victory. I guessed the matching bikini bra had been intimidated from the start, what with so much territory to be covered, the way nearly all of it jutted proudly straight out over a terrifying sheer drop, and all. So the poor little ole bikini bra just clung desperately to the foothills, and let the mountains take care of themselves.

Justine saw my reflection in the mirror, and spun round with a startled expression on her face. "Lieutenant! What are you doing here? I thought you'd gone, ages back."

I leaned my back against the door and lit a cigarette carefully. "I got to thinking," I told her. "There were a couple of things on my mind."

"I'm sure they couldn't be of any interest to me," she said icily. "So why don't you take them somewhere else, Lieutenant?"

"Wheeler," I corrected her. "It's Al Wheeler, and maybe I am a son of a bitch most of the time but—goddamn it!—I'm not *cheap!*"

"It's a matter of opinion, I would say," she snapped.

"Like you said, I used you against Martha when I figured it would help," I said in a carefully neutral voice. "And I used her against you when I figured that might help me get a little of the information I was looking for. This is legitimate, if not friendly."

"I am very tired, Lieutenant!" she said, with immense deliberation. "I would like you to leave now—immediately. Or will I have to do something stupid, like scream my head off?"

"You can scream your head off any time you want," I said, generously. "It won't make any difference to me, honey. I don't leave until I've said the things I want to say."

She shook her head in frustrated anger. "All right! Then please make it brief, Lieutenant."

"This play-off jazz is one thing. You, Justine Harvey, are something different again—very different. I thought you should know that."

"You're drunk?" she said suspiciously.

"I'm not drunk," I growled, "just ashamed for you!"

"You're what?"

"A girl who's got everything—a fantastic combination of brains, looks, and a figure to take my breath away—should let her kid sister give her a king-size inferiority complex?"

She just stood there staring at me with her mouth wide open, like she'd never seen me before, or I had two heads.

"You make me mad," I snarled ferociously at her. "You give me a strong urge to toss you over my knee and paddle that delightful rear end of yours until you learn some sense! Only two things stop me doing it right now—I'm scared I might paddle it out of shape and that would be a crime—and I'm also scared that once I started in on the project, my intentions suddenly wouldn't be good anymore!"

The mountains lifted suddenly, causing the foothills to tremble and the bikini bra to say goodbye to all it held dear.

"Al Wheeler—Al?" Her voice was uncertain. "Those were the things you had on your mind? The things you had to say to me?"

"Right," I said.

"Well, I enjoyed hearing them!" She turned back toward the mirror and raised the hairbrush to her head. "Thank you, Al Wheeler, and good night!"

"Huh?" I stared uncomprehendingly at her back.

"I was touched—moved, even, by your noble display," she said tartly. "I'm sure you had the highest motives, Lieutenant. Like a sudden realization that spending the night in my room would be preferable to the long drive home?"

"No," I said quietly. "That wasn't the idea at all, and you know it."

The hairbrush moved in faster strokes for a few seconds, then slowed down again. "I'd like to believe it," she said finally. "I really would, Lieutenant Wheeler. Only it's a little too much to ask of me right now."

"Why?"

"Because then I'd have to believe that you were being sincere!" She turned her head toward me suddenly, and her dark eyes held a derisive gleam. "Lieutenant Wheeler—the sincere cop!—everyone's cheerful pal! You see what would happen if I started in believing you sincerely meant just one word you said? In no time at all, I'd have to believe every word you said was sincere!"

She turned her head back toward the mirror and brushed vigorously for another ten seconds, then the hairbrush suddenly froze in mid-air. "I have a lovely thought for you," she announced in a flat voice. "Lieutenant Wheeler—the hand that children love to hold when they cross the intersection!"

A split second later she exploded with a gust of hysterical laughter. "I can't help it," she groaned weakly, "I keep on seeing all those sticky little hands reaching out toward you—trustfully, while—" she moaned helplessly and wrapped her arms around her middle "—while you try to beat them off with a nightstick!"

Her whole body shook with silent laughter as she sank slowly down onto her knees. I watched bleakly for maybe a half-minute, until she had it under control, except for the occasional wild spasm.

"I'm—sorry!" she gasped. "Maybe it isn't funny at all?"

She stumbled back onto her feet and shook her head ruefully. "Now I come to think of it, what's to laugh at?" Her face had an apologetic look on it as her eyes met mine. "A big bunch of small, sticky hands all reaching out toward the kind lieutenant—and you, beating them off with a—Aha! Ha! Ha! Ha!—I—Oho! Aha! Oh!" She sank back onto her knees in a kind of moaning delirium, her body shaking worse than ever.

While I still stood watching her with a wooden face, I heard a distinct, snapping sound. "There goes my mind!" I observed casually to anyone around who cared to listen. And it was true—it started out from depths those unionized frustrations had never even heard of, as a kind of blind fury; but by the time it blew straight out the top of my head, it was real educated.

Without hurrying, I walked across the floor to where Justine was kneeling, still moaning uncontrollably, grabbed myself a fistful of her hair, then dragged her over to the bed. I sat down carefully and made sure I was comfortable before I yanked the fistful of hair up off the floor and over my knees. There seemed to be an awful lot of hair, but after a while her face appeared, wearing a thunderstruck expression. But that passed on and was replaced by the nape of her neck in due course. I kept on feeding various portions of her anatomy across my knees until her rear end was strategically poised high in the air. Then I clamped one hand firmly onto the small of her back so she couldn't wriggle suddenly and throw off my aim, and raised my other hand high above my head. It made a gentle swishing sound as it cut through the air in a curving arc, a nice contrast to the explosive report that followed.

There was some interesting counterpoint harmony drifting up from the floor, too. It was mainly composed of high-pitched yelps of agony— frantic pleas for mercy—dire threats of retribution—all punctuated here and there by short, explosive giggles.

After a while my arm got tired so I slowed down a little, and after another little while, I slowed right down to a stop. Then I realized I was bathed in a warm, pleasant glow—that pleasant, self-righteous feeling a guy always gets after taking vigorous exercise he knows has done him good. The rear end felt like it had suddenly grown a lot heavier since I first lined it up across my knees, so I put the flat of my hand against her hip and gave a sudden push.

Justine was suddenly a furiously writhing, untidy heap on the floor in front of me. For one heart-stopping moment, I thought I'd drastically rearranged all her anatomy; then a wave of relief surged through me when I realized the bikini bra had long since quit trying and now hung coyly from her left ear.

Her hands fumbled in front of her face, parting the long dark hair that hung down over it until one baleful eye was suddenly exposed.

"I'll cut your heart out!" she said thickly. "I'll marinate your liver and feed it to the rats! I'll—"

"—sit down carefully for a long while yet." I suggested.

Her hands frantically shoveled hair back from in front of her face to where it belonged and, after a time, the second baleful eye joined the first.

"I'll have them stake you out over a barbecue pit," she hissed venomously, "and I'll roast chestnuts in your navel, you hear?"

"You want to hear something real funny?" I asked her happily. "Get a load of this! There's me, the kindly lieutenant, see?—standing at the intersection while all these kids reach out with their grubby little hands toward me—and I keep trying to beat them off with a—"

"Oh, *shut up!*" she snarled savagely.

I got onto my feet and offered her my hands, then pulled her gently onto her feet, while she pulled painful faces and made sharp ejaculations of misery the whole time.

"You know something?" I told her. "I'm not mad anymore."

"I am—you brute!" Her hands made a delicate exploration behind her back. "I think I'm going to need a skin-grafting job, you sadist!"

She swayed gently toward me, the mountains collided with my chest, and her mouth clamped against mine. Maybe ten seconds later, Justine murmured deep in her throat and completely relaxed her body against mine. I wasn't prepared for the sudden extra weight and the backs of my knees were pressed tight against the edge of the bed, so something had to give, and it was Wheeler.

I found myself sprawled across the bed, pinned like a bug in some weirdo's private collection by the solid weight of Justine sprawled on top of me, her mouth still firmly clamped to mine, while the tip of her tongue made a couple of experimental forays.

Some time after the circulation had been cut off completely at my knees and elbows, she opened one eye drowsily and surveyed the scene. "Hah!" she said significantly. "That was a sneaky way of getting a girl onto a bed!"

"Stupid, too," I gasped. "Would you mind taking a quick look at my forearms and see if gangrene's set in yet?"

Justine sighed irritably and rolled gently over me onto the bedspread. Right after I'd gotten my blood flowing around the extremities again, I made the exciting discovery that Justine was not only right beside me, but she was a girl, too! So I kissed the nearest available portion of girl, then worked my way upwards, using the kind of dedicated concentration a man needs to reach the top.

When I was just leaving the gentle hollow of her neck, Justine opened both eyes and looked at me calmly.

"Now, at last, we find the real Al Wheeler!" she said in a superior voice. "Sincere at last while he sneaks up on a defenseless girl. A sincere seducer—that's him!"

"I wasn't sneaking up on you," I said defensively. "If you wanted to know where I was, all you had to do was open your eyes to find out."

Her eyes widened in horror. "Are you suggesting I'm the kind of girl who'd watch shamelessly?"

"I could make a couple more suggestions," I said tersely, "but I guess you wouldn't like them much, either."

"Never mind the suggestions!" She closed her eyes contentedly. "You just keep right on sneaking up on me, huh?"

Chapter Ten

Around noon the following day I was sitting in the sheriff's office staring moodily at his repulsive face while he suggested a hundred good reasons why a lieutenant should report for work earlier in the morning than 11:30. The most important reason, I remembered, was that he gets fired if he doesn't.

When he simply had to take a deep breath or crumple in on himself like a can caught in a vacuum, I dove into the momentary silence with a whole spate of words, both short and long. When I'd finally exhausted every facet of the previous day's activities—excluding the interlude with Justine which was strictly after-hours therapy in any case—it was the Sheriff's turn to stare moodily at my repulsive face.

"You went out looking for motives," he said, with no enthusiasm at all, "and nobody can say you didn't come back with a barrel-load!

Listening to you about this case, Wheeler, I keep remembering a device I saw in a research lab once."

"An instant blonde?" I asked with interest.

"A small circular cage, designed like a miniature treadmill," he said flatly. "They had a live rat in it—the more it ran, the more it stayed still—it wound up chasing its own tail!"

"I'd resent that if it wasn't true," I said gloomily. "But you have to admit, Sheriff, we got the whole focal point of the case neatly set out for us by Ellis Harvey last night!"

"What was that?"

"Henry Slocombe was a witch?" I said despairingly.

"I don't want to pull rank, or anything like that, Wheeler," Lavers said heartily, "but I feel I must ask you a couple of direct questions. First: Are you going to do anything further about this investigation, or just sit there like a taxidermist's mistake? And if your answer to that question is in the affirmative, my second question is: When?"

"The thing is," I brooded, "about all of them are lying, but for different reasons. Two days back when you called me in the middle of the night, you said they could be just a bunch of nuts, and that premise still holds good right at this minute. So how do you tell who is a nut and who isn't? How do you figure out if a nut is lying just because it's a nutlike thing to do, or he's lying to try and stop you pinning a murder rap on him?"

"Wheeler!" Lavers muttered hoarsely. "Would you mind doing your mental arithmetic someplace else, before the little men in the long white coats come and take *me* away?"

"I can figure out how it was done," I said, still brooding. "Except that lamp still bugs me! At least three of them have excellent reasons for why. So *who* becomes a stupid question even to ask right now!"

I felt a sudden firm pressure under each arm, and the next moment I was being carried out of the office by a couple of beefy uniformed cops. At the last moment before we went out the door, I managed to twist my head around and get a brief glimpse of Lavers smiling grimly at me.

"Write when you get work!" he shouted encouragingly, then the door to his office slammed shut with violent force.

"How about this chair, Lieutenant?" one of the cops asked politely, while they held me hovering a couple of feet in the air above it like an eggbound helicopter.

"That'll do just fine!" I snarled.

"Yes, sir!" they said in unison, and just let go.

Five minutes later when I hobbled out to the Healey parked at the curb, I had a mutual bond of sympathy for Justine's rear end that hadn't existed before.

During the long drive out to Old Canyon Road, I had nothing else to do but think about what the hell to do next, and finally came to an obvious conclusion. The only thing left was to grab somebody's arm and start twisting until they shouted "Uncle!" The obvious choice was George Farrow.

I had stopped for a quick lunch in Pine City before I drove out, so it was around three in the afternoon when I arrived at the Farrow house. It was another beautiful day, with the sun burning fiercely out of a cloudless sky, and I had that weird feeling I'd suddenly stepped back into the exact pattern of the previous day.

After I pressed the buzzer I watched hopefully through the plate-glass panel just in case I really *had* stepped back into the earlier time pattern, but this time no stark naked redhead sauntered carelessly along the hall. I pressed the buzzer again and waited impatiently. Now I'd made up my mind to twist George's arm, I could hardly wait to grab hold of it.

Another couple of minutes dragged by, and I gave the buzzer a final blast. I'd just turned away from the front door when a hoarse voice croaked, "Who is it?"

"Lieutenant Wheeler!" I snapped briskly. "Sheriff's office."

"You bastard!" the voice said feelingly.

That left me with a choice. I could either just stand there, or not only stand but punch the side of my head at the same time. While I was still making up my mind, the problem was suddenly resolved by someone opening the front door. I turned back toward it, wondering what kind of an old crone owned a voice as hoarse as that, and saw a bent-up redhead standing there, holding a bloody beefsteak to her left eye.

"Loraine?" I said doubtfully.

"This is all your fault!" she said bitterly. "You had to go shooting off your big mouth all over the Harvey house! 'Loraine says!' You should have put it to music—it was like a signature tune the whole damned night, wasn't it?"

"Loraine, honey!" I said sympathetically. "What the hell happened?"

She turned slowly and limped down the hallway with painful slowness, her body leaning forward as if she couldn't stand up straight. I helped her down the three steps and out onto the patio, where she groaned miserably as I gently lowered her onto a chair. "Get me a drink!" she snarled as soon as she was sitting down.

I got one for myself at the same time and took them back out to the patio. She took the beefsteak away from her eye while she drank from the glass, and I saw she had the emperor of all black eyes, multihued with all the colors of the rainbow.

"What happened?" I asked again.

"I told you already!" she snarled. "I gave you a few facts about the Harveys in strict confidence yesterday afternoon, and you spent the rest of the night quoting me at the top of your voice all over the Harveys' goddamn house! George was fit to be tied when he got home—I've seen him in rages before, but this one scared me to death. He stormed around like a maniac, shouting and screaming at me the whole time, and most of it just didn't make any sense."

She lowered her glass and raised the beefsteak back to her eye. "I was sitting on the couch in the living room—right where you left me yesterday afternoon—when he came in. The first thing I knew about it was when I collected his fist in my eye—that knocked me off the couch onto the floor, and I was dazed. That suited dear George real fine! He walked up and down me a couple of times, then decided he couldn't stand the sight of me any longer, so he kicked me across the floor until I was hidden under the table. That's where I woke up this morning."

"You're kidding?" I pleaded.

"Am I?" She jerked the blouse free from the waistband of her skirt and pulled it up around her chest.

The soft white skin around her solar plexus showed a complex pattern of discolored bruise marks, all of them about the size of a dime.

"George always wear pointed shoes?" I snarled.

"I should be real mad at you, Al Wheeler," she said in a softer tone, "but you were real nice to me yesterday afternoon, so I can't be that mad at you, can I?"

"I wish I deserved it," I said, "but I didn't do anything yesterday afternoon."

"That's what I meant," she said in a low voice. "It's not often I get treated like a lady, and never when I'm loaded! You were a kind of unique experience for me, Al, and I appreciated it afterward."

"Then I lined up another kind of unique experience for you last night," I said bleakly. "I'm real sorry about that, Loraine. The only thing I can say is, that was the last time it will ever happen."

She laughed bitterly. "I wish I had your faith in George, Al!"

"I have faith in Al," I said immodestly, "who is going to have an intimate talk with George. Where is he now? Back at the Harvey house?"

"Where else?" She drank some more bourbon. "I honestly figured he'd flipped permanently, the way he went on. If Martha didn't marry him now, he said one time, he was as good as dead already. That stinking lieutenant, he said, sniffing around all night, following up all the dirt you'd given him, and it was taking him places he shouldn't know about. Does any of that make sense to you, Al?"

"In a roundabout way," I said. "Anything else he said, you can remember?"

Loraine thought hard for a few seconds, then shook her head tiredly. "I wasn't really in the best condition for remembering!"

"Did you get a doctor?"

"Doctor? I've got some pride left!" she said in a brittle voice. "You'll ask if I called the police any minute! They'd take one look at the records and figure I fell down an elevator shaft someplace when I was loaded!"

"You sure you're all right?" I prodded. "I could get an ambulance out here and have them take you over to my apartment. You could rest up awhile there, get George out of your hair for a couple of weeks, anyway?"

"Why, Lieutenant?" she croaked happily. "Just what kind of a proposition are you making me?"

"I promise I won't get in your hair, either. Seriously, how about it?"

"I think I'd like it very much," she said softly. "On one condition though!"

"Name it?"

"You take back your promise."

Fifteen minutes later I was on my way to the Harvey house, having left Loraine packing a bag while she waited for the ambulance to pick her up. I drove the Healey hard all the way, but it didn't help to work off the head of steam I'd built up after seeing Loraine.

I parked out front of the house and climbed out, then took my time about lighting a cigarette, hoping my nerve-ends would quiet down a little before I got inside the house.

Ellis Harvey opened the front door to me and smiled vaguely.

"Come in, Lieutenant! You're getting to be one of the family, almost!"

"That's real nice," I said without any enthusiasm. "You know where I can find Justine?"

He blinked slowly. "I did see her, only a few minutes back. Now, where was I?" His bony fingers beat a thoughtful tattoo against the parchmentlike skin of his face, and it made a faint, scraping noise that sent my nerve-ends running for cover. "Ah, yes!" he said happily. "She was out on the back lawn, reading a book—or was she knitting?"

I found her a couple of minutes later, sprawled on her stomach in the grass, reading a book. She wore a huge pair of dark glasses and a playsuit that fitted much too tight wherever it made contact with Justine, which wasn't very often.

"Hi." She took off her dark glasses for a moment to look at me as I sat down beside her on the grass. "How was the drive home all by yourself in the romantic dawn, and all?"

"I survived," I said.

"Well! Bully for you!" she said coolly, and went back to her book.

"Justine, honey," I said softly. "Remember last night you said the only sincere Wheeler was the 'sincere seducer'?"

"Bedroom intimacies bandied about in the open air?"

"There's one more area of sincerity I got," I said tightly. "Like I can be a sincere cop, too."

She flipped the book shut, then rolled lazily over onto her side and looked up at me. "Why all this passionate declaration in the heat of the afternoon, Al?"

"We had something kind of special going for us last night," I told her. "I don't want to lose it, Justine, honey."

Her hand squeezed mine warmly. "Not a chance!" she said confidently. "You're the man who's changed sneaking-up-on-a-girl tactics from a science into a pure art!"

"You don't understand," I grated. "Any moment now I'm about to become Al Wheeler, sincere cop, dedicated seeker of truth—the whole bit. And maybe you won't like it."

She took off the dark glasses and dropped them onto the grass. "I'll take my chances on that," she said.

"Okay," I said. "I don't know anything more today than I did yesterday—anything worthwhile, that is—but this afternoon I suddenly got smart. I could stay around here for six months and I still wouldn't be any the wiser. Because everybody's told me everything they can to help solve the murder—short of involving themselves."

"You make it sound like you've come to a dead end, Al."

"Only a barrier," I said. "I have to break it down, and maybe a few people will get bruised here and there."

"So go ahead," she said crisply. "Are you going to arrest me right off?"

"You ever play charades, honey?" I asked her. "That's how it feels inside this house—everybody's playing charades—pretending to be something they're not. You on the night of the murder for instance— with the long white robe and the silver-mesh belt and all that jazz about *It*, and *They*, and the occult references to demon gods. The first couple of hours I was here, I had you figured for a genuine nut—but then the little things started to show up that didn't match the pattern. Like the overdose of sedative you gave Martha—how disturbed you were when she walked in on us, still floating on the dope, and accused you of murdering Slocombe."

Her dark eyes had been watching me steadily with intelligent interest up to the time I mentioned Martha, then they had slid away for a moment, and when she looked back into my face, there was a tight, opaque veil across them.

"Martha maybe doesn't know you that well as a person, but she sure knows you as a rival. She'd stolen Hal Slocombe from under your nose—he was no great bargain, but that wasn't important to either of you! And when he was dead, she felt instinctively that you had either killed him yourself, or had a part in it."

"Do all dedicated cops talk as much as you do, honey?" she asked easily.

"This was what worried you, after you knew Slocombe was dead— that Martha would immediately suspect you. But if you were completely innocent it shouldn't have really worried you at all."

"So you believe I had a hand in Hal's murder, at least?" she asked in a cold, remote voice.

"But you didn't know it would be murder at the time," I said. "So that absolves you of any guilt."

"How kind of you to wash my sins away, Lieutenant!"

"Let's do this just once—and do it fast," I snarled, "and you listen real good, Justine Harvey!"

"Yes, sir!" She gave me a burlesque military salute, and I backhanded her across the mouth hard enough to send her sprawling back into the grass.

She sat up slowly and dabbed the blood from her lower lip with the back of her hand, her eyes wide open with shocked surprise.

"Are you listening?" I asked coldly. She dabbed her lip again and nodded silently.

"The family owns the estate, and the estate's sitting on a fortune in oil. Ellis is not interested in more money—only the family tradition of the house and its land remaining unchanged—and he owns forty per cent of the estate. Uncle Ben, who came stumbling home from foreign parts because he was broke and had no choice, desperately wants to sell. The money from the oil leases is his one chance of ever regaining his old life—and he owns twenty per cent. Martha goes any way at all, but if she's married to George, he'll see that she votes to sell. So there's a deadlock—Ellis against Uncle Ben and Martha, once George is her husband. That puts you right into the middle—you're the key, Justine. So they pressured you to make a deal. Whatever you wanted you could have—just name it."

She smiled wanly. "I don't know why you bothered talking with me if you know all the answers already."

"This offer of a deal came right at the time Martha had taken Slocombe away from you and they were talking marriage," I said. "So you made a deal—you'd vote to sell out—if they made sure Martha never married Slocombe."

"It sounds kind of mean when you say it out loud, doesn't it?" she said hesitantly.

"They weren't giving you a thing," I said. "They couldn't afford to have Slocombe married to Martha—he was on Ellis's side. Whatever you'd asked for, they still had to prevent that marriage!"

Justine winced. "The prize sucker of all time, that's me!"

"No, that's Hal and Martha," I said. "Once you were part of the conspiracy, they told you their plan, right?"

"In detail!" she said dryly.

"Ellis had often remarked on the resemblance between Martha and Delia—the portrait likeness, their mothers both dying giving birth to their daughters. You would all start building this up in Ellis's mind, harp on it constantly. Then, after a while, you'd convince him there was a parallel between Delia's situation with her gypsy lover and the man she was supposed to marry, and Martha's situation with George and Hal Slocombe.

"And it worked just fine. Ellis became adamant that Martha must never marry Slocombe under any circumstances."

"I guess there's nothing I can tell you you don't know already," she said. "But there's something you can tell me, Al. Who *did* kill Hal?— and how did they do it?"

"If I get real lucky I might be able to tell you in maybe a couple of hours' time, honey," I told her. "How's the rear end situation?"

"Painful!" she said. "And also embarrassing. The rest of the family keep wondering why I stand up for all meals now—but they don't have the nerve to ask!"

Chapter Eleven

I was sitting in the living room, where I'd been almost since the time I left Justine on the grass and walked back inside the house, and that must have been at least an hour back. The trouble with investigation is it's a mutual thing—you can't investigate people if they aren't around to cooperate.

Another ten minutes limped by, then I heard a light patter of footsteps down the stairs, and George Farrow almost skipped into the room. For once in his life he looked pleased with himself—he almost beamed at me.

"How are you today, Lieutenant?" His eyes swam toward me in a friendly, puppy dog fashion. "It's a great day, isn't it?"

"Real great," I agreed. "You don't happen to have seen Uncle Ben around anyplace?"

"He takes a nap almost always in the afternoons," he said.

"That's a pity," I said. "We got to talking last night after you'd gone, and I got to admit he had me going there with some of his stories!"

"He's a wonderful guy!" George said warmly.

"Promised to show me his curio room—that's what I came out here for this afternoon, to tell you the truth." I glanced at my watch. "I can't stay more than another quarter-hour at most. Well—" I shrugged "—I guess it's too bad!"

"I know where his curio room is," George said eagerly. "I know Uncle Ben doesn't give a damn if he's with you or not when you look it over. Like me to give you a quick run-through?"

"Fine!" I said. "I'd appreciate it."

We went out of the living room, grinning at each other like we were real buddy-buddy. I'd been worried earlier I was coming on a little too strong with a sudden switch like that—but George lapped it up greedily and came panting back for more. I followed him into the back of the house, through the kitchen where the cook gave us a disapproving stare, to an internal flight of stairs.

"It used to be the place they stored the coal, before they put in central heating," George said, leading the way down. "Now it's old Uncle Ben's hideaway!" He laughed shrilly for maybe the next twenty seconds, and I figured he'd flipped until I realized he thought he'd made a joke.

It was more like a cheap junk shop than a hideaway, which sounds kind of fancy and vaguely immoral. There was stuff littered all over the floor—sea chests, gaudy parasols, woodcarvings, a stuffed tiger mounted in a rampant position, but now anything but, because half his stuffing had dribbled out onto the floor through a rip in his hide.

There was a small bureau beside me, and I pulled open the top drawer a little too far. The kind of deadly native trinkets they wouldn't try and give away in a dime store came cascading out all over the place in a hideous profusion. Necklaces made from chipped sea shells, animal teeth, you disclaim it, they had it.

"Great, isn't it?" George beamed at me moistly, chewing his quivering lower lip with genuine excitement.

"I think it stinks!" I told him.

"What?" Already, his eyes were heading for the beach.

"I think it stinks," I repeated. "I'm entitled to say what I think about Uncle Ben's jewelry and junk, the same way you're entitled to say what you think about me."

"I am?" His eyebrows went for broke and tried to climb the sheer wall of his high-domed forehead.

"Sure!" I snarled. "Like you said—that stinking lieutenant sniffing around all night, following up all the dirt—"

He started to back off toward the stairs, his face the color of dirty ashes.

I sniffed audibly. "Funny thing, George, I can smell more dirt right now than I ever have before. Just like a pile of garbage!" I walked toward him, still sniffing loudly. "You know something?" I asked in a low voice. "I think it's you, George."

He held out his hand in front of his face, waving it blindly in the air. "Don't you touch me!" he whimpered. "Don't you dare touch me!"

Maybe, at bottom, a sadist waits hopefully within everyone for the chance to be let out. I had a sudden feeling of revulsion as I realized I'd just begun to enjoy George's blind terror. But I couldn't forget the whole thing, for Loraine's sake.

"George!" My voice sounded suddenly harsh. "Let's get this over fast. You ever touch Loraine again, I'll beat you into a pulp. You understand?"

"Yes, yes!" he whimpered eagerly. "I understand just fine, Lieutenant. I won't ever do it again. I don't know what got into me last night— honest! I—"

What the hell could you do with a jellyfish that suddenly developed spiked boots to trample over its sister? Let him know how a spiked boot feels, anyway, I figured helplessly.

"Can I go now, Lieutenant?" he whined hopefully. "I won't ever forget, I promise!"

"This should help your memory," I said sourly.

I slammed four stiffened fingers into his solar plexus hard, but not that damned hard. He doubled up with both hands clasped to his middle like he was about to die; and while he was still jackknifed I threw both arms back as far as they'd go, then brought them together smartly. George's head was between them, and the heel of both hands hit his ears simultaneously. It's an old wrestling gimmick that's not real nice, but not real nasty, either. It hurts like hell for maybe five minutes and there's no damage done, except a cauliflower ear at worst.

George reeled around the cellar screaming his lungs out like somebody had sunk a red-hot bayonet into his insides or something. The next time he reeled past close enough, I grabbed his tie and pulled him up real close so that our faces were maybe two inches apart.

"It's like a sample, George," I told him. "One bruise on Loraine, and you get the full treatment." I pushed him away from me toward the stairs, and he staggered up them at an amazing speed. By the time he reached the top step, he'd forgotten to scream, even.

I lit a cigarette and took a slow walk around Uncle Ben's curio room, and the more I saw of it, the more I wondered what kind of a maniac world he'd been traveling in for fifteen long years.

On my third time around, I heard the stairs creak, then a booming voice asked, "Looking for something, young feller?"

Ben Harvey eased his massive bulk down the stairs, testing each one carefully before he put his full weight on it.

"Where do you keep your Mau Mau souvenirs?" I asked him.

"Over there." He pointed toward the farthest corner. "Wait for me. That's the damned trouble with everyone today—always in too much of a hurry to enjoy themselves!"

I waited while he moved off the bottom step carefully and started across the cellar toward me.

"Charades!" I shook my head wonderingly.

"What's that?" He tugged his goatee impatiently. "Don't mutter at me, young feller, anything I hate it's a mumbler!"

"I think you got your image kind of confused, Ben," I told him mildly. "Trouble is, when you've got a good act going for you, it's hard not to ham it up a little, here and there. Then, in no time at all, you're hamming it up all the time."

The blue eyes behind their portals of fat suddenly lost their twinkle. "What the hell are you talking about?" he barked at me.

"The whole bit, Ben," I said. "The ghost that also came on just a little too strong—your locked-from-the-inside room with a corpse on the carpet. Your roaming days are over, Uncle Ben!"

"Don't know what the hell you're talking about," he rumbled. "Hah! I just remembered—what you did to George." He shook his head reprovingly. "That wasn't nice, Lieutenant!"

"What George did when he beat up on his sister, that wasn't nice, either," I said. "Taking the living throat out of a man who thinks you're his friend—that wasn't very nice, either, Uncle Ben."

He pulled harder on his beard for maybe ten seconds, then his face cleared suddenly. "I've got it!" he roared triumphantly. "You're trying to tell me something!"

"I'll tell you the truth, Uncle Ben," I said coldly. "I'm a little tired with the whole bit, and I'd like to move it fast. So why don't we stop playing 'Billy Baffles, the Master of a Thousand-and-One Disguises'?"

"I'm listening," he said evenly.

I took it from the start up to where I'd left it with Justine, and then continued: "That was okay as far as it went—you had Ellis implacably against the marriage of Martha and Henry Slocombe—but was it enough? There was always a chance they might suddenly decide to elope—and, anyway, it wasn't enough just having Martha not married to Slocombe. She had to be married to George before that twenty per cent of the estate was safely lined up against Ellis."

Uncle Ben spoke for the first time since I'd started the story. "Are you implying that I am the mastermind in back of this scheme?" he asked interestedly.

"Mr. Baffles—please?" I looked at him sorrowfully.

"Please continue!" He tugged his goatee savagely.

"So you dreamed up the idea of Slocombe challenging Ellis to let him spend Walpurgis Night in the locked room. Ellis couldn't refuse because everyone would think he didn't believe in the story of the Gray Lady himself—and he didn't want to see the whole thing laughed out of existence.

"Then you took Slocombe to one side and told him your brilliant idea, how he could get to marry Martha and at the same time not hurt Ellis's feelings. You'd make up a tape for him which, as far as everyone would know, would be actually recorded while he was in the locked room. The touching forgiveness from the Gray Lady and the removal of the curse. You had Martha busy playing Delia, and Slocombe busy playing himself.

"On the big night, I figure you made some excuse about having a little technical trouble with the tape so you couldn't give it to him before he entered the room. But that was no problem, you'd long ago taken a wax impression from Ellis's key and had a duplicate made, so you could let yourself in with no trouble.

"You'd carefully edited that tape—junking the hearts and flowers bit from Delia, and substituting your own whisper for Delia's voice as she's about to murder Slocombe."

"Aren't you being just a little slapdash here, Lieutenant?" He gave his beard an inquiring tug. "I took a wax impression of the key Ellis had, then had a duplicate made, you say smugly. Can you prove it?"

"No," I said, "and I don't need to. Anybody could have got at the original key if they made an effort."

"Very well!" He inclined his head stiffly. "Let us hear some more of your fantasy, Lieutenant!"

"At midnight there is a dreadful scream from inside the room, followed by a thud. Hysterics all over the place and George calls the police. I shoot in the door, and find Slocombe's body. We investigate—Ellis can tell us the exact time the scream was heard because he was looking at his watch—and I wonder who gave him that idea? The five of you were in separate rooms at the time. The girls got to the door first because they were already on the top floor."

"And if they rushed out of their rooms when they heard the scream— which is exactly what they did do—it would have been impossible for the murderer to have rushed from the room and down the stairs without being seen!" Ben Harvey stated confidently. "Or don't you agree, Lieutenant?"

"I entirely agree with you, Uncle Ben," I said firmly.

There was a momentary gleam of surprise in his eyes. "Then why are you accusing me of masterminding the whole thing when I'm obviously innocent?"

"Because Henry Slocombe wasn't killed at a minute of midnight," I said easily. "He was killed between eleven twenty-five and eleven thirty—a half-hour earlier."

"Then who screamed at a minute of midnight?" Uncle Ben asked in an icy voice.

"I think probably *you* did," I said. "Whoever provided the scream for the end of the tape, anyway. When you were sure the others were settled in their various rooms, you went up to the locked room and let yourself in with your duplicate key. Slocombe was expecting you with the tape, and my bet is you killed him while he was still thanking you for your kind help."

Ben Harvey's face showed only the polite attentiveness of the courteous listener who generously gives his full concentration to the speaker.

"Then you put your tape onto the recorder," I continued, "and started it running. Time was no problem—it would be another thirty minutes before the scream would happen. You had one impossible problem— how to relock the door from the outside with your duplicate, and still manage to leave the key in the inside lock. Obviously one key would push out the other. But you figured, to get into that room the police would either have to shoot in the lock or batter down the door. With the pounding a three-inch thick solid oak door would withstand—from either bullets, or a ram—nobody would think twice about the key being shaken out of the inside lock and dropping to the floor."

"Very ingenious, Lieutenant," he said stiffly. "How about the lamp that disappeared from inside the locked room and reappeared the following day at the foot of the oak tree where Delia is buried?"

"That bugged me for a while." I grinned. "I was damned sure that lamp wasn't inside the room when I broke into it. You took it, Uncle Ben, just to confuse the issue still further—and if it helped strengthen anyone's belief in Delia's supernatural powers, so much the better. But like I said—you had me going with that lamp, while I was still convinced that Slocombe wasn't killed until a minute of midnight, because under those circumstances nobody would sit placidly in the *dark!* Then later on, I realized he didn't need a lamp after eleven thirty because he was dead."

Uncle Ben gave his goatee a sharp, questioning tug. "A fascinating theory, Lieutenant, and I'm flattered you give me credit for having masterminded such an ingenious plot. But I have the feeling you'll need a little more than just a theory, Lieutenant. Won't you need a few hard facts?"

"You're right, Uncle Ben," I said. "The tape recorder is yours—and you're the expert on it. Neither Martha nor Slocombe could have spliced the finished tape, let alone edited it and re-recorded it onto a new, unbroken reel of tape. Then you've got about the strongest motive of all—need of money. Justine will testify about the deal you made with her in return for her twenty per cent voting with you to accept the oil leases."

"Your case doesn't sound very strong," he said calmly.

"I hadn't finished," I said. "You could frighten the hell out of George by threatening to handle him the same way you handled Slocombe, if he ever double-crossed you. But once you're in jail awaiting trial, guess who will be asking George nice, polite questions?"

I shook my head slowly. "It's nothing to boast about, Uncle Ben, but since about twenty minutes back, I figure all I have to do is look at George and he'll have hysterics."

He took a pigskin cigar case out of his pocket, selected a cigar with great care, then went through an elaborate ritual of lighting it.

"I do see what you mean about George," he said sadly. "He was a mistake, but what else did I have to work with? I blame it all on Martha's excruciating bad taste in men, Lieutenant!"

"Do me a favor, Uncle Ben," I asked. "Tell me—was George in on the murder plan before it happened?"

"Good God, yes!" He looked genuinely shocked. "Why do you think he was sitting in the living room the whole time? To watch the stairs and see who went up and who came down!"

"You'll sign a statement on that one?" I asked him.

"The promising pupil should go wherever his master goes, don't you agree?" He rumbled with laughter. "I'll make sure George comes along even if I have to drag him by the ear. Now, you tell me something, Lieutenant? What put you onto it in the first place?"

"You couldn't ask a cop to buy the ghost story, now could you?" I said plaintively. "It was pretty obvious there was no problem in getting hold of a duplicate key to the room, too. But it was a lot of other things. I can imagine one nut in a family swallowing this witch's curse stuff, but when a whole bunch of you is, in chorus, then I begin to smell a rat. Collectively, you hit a phony note every time you opened your mouths. After that, it was just a problem of reconstruction."

"Would you care to guess at the weapon, Lieutenant?"

"There was that terribly strong, fetid smell inside the room," I said. "Then later I heard you mention the Mau Maus and it triggered a memory—the 'Leopard men,' I think, who wear the skin and head of a leopard when they attack—but they replace the animal's original claws with razor-sharp curved steel."

"I am amazed!" he said bleakly.

"You had a whole bunch of ingenious bits and pieces," I told him, "but there was one piece of sheer genius, and for that I shall always remember Uncle Ben Harvey!"

"Oh, really?" He tugged the goatee in a sudden spasm of delight.

"Henry Slocombe was a witch!" I said solemnly.

He threw back his great head and bellowed with laughter. The sound grew and grew, until it filled the cellar, echoing and re-echoing, so that even the floor seemed to vibrate in sympathy. I laughed right along there with him, but I didn't throw my head back because I was too busy watching his right hand, which had slid deftly into the voluminous coat pocket as he started to laugh, then had poked around, sometimes with the fingers straight, and then balled into a kind of fist.

I had disliked Uncle Ben at first sight, and the fact that he deliberately made himself out to be a warm-hearted friend of Henry Slocombe so the man could more easily be manipulated to the right place to have his throat ripped out didn't do anything to make me revise my first opinion.

"All right, Wheeler!" a shrill voice, right up on the edge of hysteria, screamed suddenly. "I've got a gun on you—stay right where you are, and put your hands in the air!"

I paid no attention to George's interruption at all. I figured so long as he aimed his gun at me, I had nothing to worry about. Life and death were much more intimately concerned with what went on inside Uncle Ben's pocket.

The movement was so fast that his hand blurred as it leaped out of his pocket. At the same fraction of a second, that familiar fetid animal stench assaulted my nostrils, and the hand, as it cleared the cloth, was monstrously enlarged to twice the normal size, with the cruel steel talons winking reflected light as they streaked through the air toward my throat.

At the first movement of Ben's hand, I'd made a convulsive backward leap and the back of my knees slammed painfully into the lid of a tin sea chest; the rest of my body kept on going in a backward arc until I finally crashed flat on my back on the far side of the sea chest.

Somewhere I had a confused impression of steel talons plunging through a downward arc that had missed my throat by no more than six inches, and there had been a couple of shots fired while I was hurtling backward over the sea chest. I gouged the thirty-eight from the belt holster, and scuttled on all fours to the more secure cover of a massive teak chest that stood maybe six feet in back of the sea chest. I made it without hearing another shot fired, and crouched low, while the faces of the wood carved mandarins watched without curiosity.

I heard the light patter of feet come down maybe the last six or eight stairs, then scamper across the floor, and the hysterical whimpering sound grew rapidly louder. It seemed like a good time to find out what was going on. George anywhere, I figured, would be a lousy shot— George running would just simply be George running.

So I lifted my head above the lid of the teak chest and looked.

Uncle Ben was slumped against the wall, his right hand still enmeshed in the barbaric leopard's claw, while his left hand was pressed tight against his side, a steady trickle of bright red blood seeping through his fingers.

George came running toward him, a gun held awkwardly in his hand and the tears drowning his eyes, even. All the time that frenzied, inarticulate whimpering sounded deep in his throat.

"Uncle Ben!" He came to a slithering halt in front of the massive hulk that looked like it had shrunk a little already.

"It was an accident!" George whimpered. "I aimed at that stinking lieutenant and somehow—"

"That stinking lieutenant's throat would be missing if you hadn't yelled at him from the top of the stairs!" Ben said in a bitter voice.

"I told him to stay right where he was and put his hands up!" George's whimpering hit a new high of frustrated fury. "He just *ignored* me!" he wailed in furious humiliation.

"You fool!" Ben shook his head despairingly as he looked at him. "Oh, you poor, bloody fool, George!"

"Come on, Uncle Ben!" George's hands pawed at Ben's coat ineffectually as he tried to drag him toward the stairs. "We have to get out of here! Quick!"

"You know something, you useless bastard!" Ben said savagely. "The lieutenant's about twenty feet in back of you, watching, with a thirty-eight in his hand. And he'll hit whatever he aims at!"

George suddenly froze into a rigid, unmoving statue, and the whimpering sound vanished at the same moment. I watched him for around thirty seconds just in case for the first time in his life, he'd dreamed up a new angle that could be dangerous.

Then I moved out slowly from behind the teak chest and started toward them. "Okay, George," I said evenly. "Drop the gun!"

The statue still presented a rigid back toward me.

"I'll count to five, George," I said evenly. "If you haven't dropped it by then, I'll shoot. One—two—three—"

"It's no use, Lieutenant," Ben said curtly. "He's in some kind of a trance. He looks like he's dead already."

"George could fake anything," I said coldly. "I'll give him one more count—"

"There could be an easier way to find out," Ben grunted.

He raised his right hand slowly and the steel talons glittered brightly again as the glove came close to George's face. Then he let the nearest claw slide down George's cheek, and I saw the bright red ribbon spring into sudden life behind it.

"He doesn't even flinch!" Ben said disgustedly. "I had a chance—not much of one—but at least it was a chance. If I'd caught your throat I could have been on the way south by now, with still a small chance of making it into Mexico!"

His face puckered in loathing and disgust as he stared at George's frozen features. "But he has to try and help me! Screams out at the top of his voice right at the crucial moment—then aims his damned gun at you and puts two bullets into my side!" His voice shook with impotent fury. "Now he figures it's all too much for him so he goes into this goddamn trance. You know something, Lieutenant? I'll bet he winds up in a state sanitarium and is out again inside two years—while right now my lifeblood drains away through the holes he put into me!" His voice suddenly rose into a towering roar. "Well, this is one time George Farrow won't walk away from it!"

The steel gleamed in a short, deadly arc that was over almost before it had begun: but now the brightness had vanished, replaced by a glistening dull wetness. I put a bullet through the roof of Uncle Ben's mouth while he was still screaming abuse at George Farrow, and he slumped forward onto the floor, his shoulder bumping George's as he fell.

For a couple of seconds, George's rigid body swayed backward and forward like a tin soldier, then finally toppled backward and crashed onto the floor. The two of them lay, side by side, head to head, feet to feet, looking like two good buddies who'd died fighting together—and I hoped Uncle Ben was someplace he could see it because it would drive him berserk.

We stood on the porch watching the procession of headlights a half mile back on the road, all heading our way.

"Martha's taking Father to some friends in San Francisco," Justine said. "I think the change will do him good. When he gets back I'm sure he'll want to sell out to the oil leases—the house will hold too many bitter memories for him now."

"It could be what he needs," I said. "If you live too close to a tradition it can get to be like an ingrown toenail."

"You have the most romantic thoughts, Al!" She giggled comfortably.

"Where are you going?" I asked her absently.

"Pine City. Stay with a friend. You," she said coolly.

My face lit up like a sun-kissed California orange for maybe two whole seconds, then somebody cut the switch. "I am about to go out of my mind! You can't stay with me—I already have another girl established in my apartment since this afternoon."

"Oh, no, you don't!" she said smugly.

"I don't?" I said hopefully.

"They took Loraine straight to the hospital this afternoon. She has three broken ribs."

"She's going to miss George," I said pensively.

"Like three broken ribs," Justine agreed. "We can drive back in your cute little sports car, can't we, Al?"

"Sure, if you'll fit," I said seriously. "You may need to hold your breath all the way so you don't buckle the windshield. I guess we'll manage."

"Tell me about your apartment, Al?" she said eagerly.

The first pair of headlights were just turning into the driveway. "It has floors, walls, ceilings—the usual things like that—and a hi-fi machine with five speakers in the walls."

"I like that," she said, nodding her head for emphasis. "You can put a whole stack of records on, late every night."

"What for?"

"I want to live dangerously, Al!" She rubbed her cheek against my shoulder softly. "With all that music I just won't be able to hear you sneaking up on me!"

THE END

The Dumdum Murder

Carter Brown

"Many a man has dated his ruin from some murder
or other that perhaps he thought little of at the time."
—Thomas De Quincey

Chapter One

We stood on the front porch and peered dubiously past the wide-open door into the dimly lit front hall that looked like it stretched into eternity. From the moment I'd cut the Austin-Healey's motor, the silence had been growing steadily louder and any moment now it was about to start screaming at me.

"Lieutenant," Sergeant Polnik's gravel-like voice rasped in my ear, "you figure there just ain't nobody home?"

"Nobody living, you mean?" I asked bleakly.

"That call to the Sheriff's office reporting a homicide, maybe it was just a gag, huh?" he asked, with no real hope at all in his voice.

I thumbed the doorbell again and listened to its maniacal peal re-echoed around the front hall for the fifth time. The door had been wide open when we arrived, I remembered, and it did nothing to reassure me.

"Why don't we go inside and find out?" I said in a too-brisk voice.

"Sure, Lieutenant, why don't we?" Polnik muttered, without moving an inch from the spot where he'd obviously been frozen.

I lit a cigarette carefully and considered the situation, figuring it probably wasn't some evil apparition that ran ice-cold fingers up and down my spine, but merely an unusual combination of circumstances.

There had been the anonymous but cultured feminine voice that had called the Sheriff's office and said, after giving the address, "We have a rather repulsive, comparatively freshly murdered corpse here. Kindly remove it at your earliest convenience," then hung up.

Then there was the house itself—looking like a reject from the movie lot where they made a great motion picture called *Sunset Boulevard*—with its sweet overpowering smell of decay that instantly reminded you it was only a couple of minutes after midnight. "The witching hour when graveyards yawn," and all that kind of hair-raising jazz. All in all, I figured the short hairs at the nape of my neck had every right to bristle, the way they were bristling already.

"I'll wait for you, Lieutenant," Polnik said happily. "Like I'll make sure nobody else gets inside the house while you're in there, huh?"

"The hell with that!" I snarled at him. "You just make damned sure I've got plenty of room to get out again."

"Yes, sir, Lieutenant Wheeler." He bared his teeth at me in the horrible grimace that was as close as he could come to a smile.

"You get into any trouble inside the house, Lieutenant," he assured me, "and all you got to do is shout."

"So you can get a head start to the car?" I growled. "*We* are going inside the house, Sergeant, and that's an order."

"Whatever you say, Lieutenant," he mumbled dismally.

So we walked into the house, my right hand firmly clamped on Polnik's elbow, propelling him along like a reluctant dinosaur.

The dimly lit hall didn't improve any on closer acquaintance; it apparently ran from the front to the back of the house in a straight line, with innumerable doorways opening off on either side. A gigantic chandelier hung precariously from the cracked plaster above our heads. Around fifty per cent of the bulbs had burned out already, and the rest were a hideous blue color casting the dim light ideally suited for a medieval torture chamber.

The Sergeant pointed toward the second doorway on our left. "Looks like somebody's in there, Lieutenant," he observed shrewdly. "Why else would they leave the light on, huh?"

"Why don't you go look?" I suggested.

"Aw, Lieutenant!" The primeval planes of his face corrugated into an unnerving resemblance of bas-relief map of some Louisiana swamp. "Why don't the both of us go look, huh?"

There was a curtain of beaded tassels across the doorway that jingled softly when I pushed my way through, still keeping a tight hold on Polnik's elbow. We found ourselves in the living room, and were simultaneously transported back thirty years in time. The furnishings were in magnificently bad taste, everything overstuffed and covered with a violent floral chintz. The room was dominated by a jumbo-sized bar at the far end of the room, all tarnished chrome with a massive, amber-tinted mirror in the back of it.

"I love my wife but oh you kid!" I said in stunned disbelief.

"Right out of Prohibition, huh, Lieutenant?" Polnik said, then glared at me suspiciously. "You never said nothing about being married before, Lieutenant?"

"I don't like talking about it," I told him in a bittersweet voice. "We honeymooned in Nome, Alaska, and she died suddenly on the fourth day."

"That's real tough, Lieutenant," Polnik sympathized. "Some kind of disease, huh?"

"Heat exhaustion," I murmured.

His eyes popped. "In Alaska?"

"I told her, I kept on telling her all the time, but she just wouldn't listen." I shook my head sadly. "Mink pajamas are strictly for the girl that sleeps alone, I told her, but no! She wouldn't listen."

The Sergeant backed away from me with that bug-eyed look riveted to his face until his heel hooked in a loose strand of the carpet—hand-woven by some myopic misanthrope—and he disappeared abruptly in back of a king-sized couch with a startled yelp. I waited patiently and maybe five seconds later his head reappeared above the back of the couch, and somehow that bug-eyed look had gotten even worse.

"Lieutenant," he croaked, "I got it!"

"Heat exhaustion?" I queried.

"It's right here on the floor," he gulped. "The cadaver, I mean."

I moved around fast in back of the couch as Polnik climbed back onto his feet, and saw he wasn't kidding. The corpse was sprawled face down on the carpet, and was very obviously feminine. Long, velvet-black hair lay over her shoulders like a shroud, and a skintight scarlet leotard emphasized the narrow waist and the proud high curve of her rump. Her elegant legs were splayed out grotesquely from her trunk at right angles on either side, so she made a perfect letter T.

"Cheez!" Polnik said emotionally. "What a waste of a dame. Must have been some kind of a nut to bust both her legs like that, huh, Lieutenant?"

"Are they busted?" I asked doubtfully.

He bent down and grabbed hold of the nearest ankle, then recoiled. "*Yikes!*" His voice was strictly falsetto. "It moved, Lieutenant, right under my hand!"

The ankle kept right on moving, and the rest of the leg with it, describing a graceful arc through ninety degrees until it was stretched out in straight line with the trunk. A moment later it was joined by the other leg, then the corpse rolled over onto its back and two glittering, sloe-colored eyes looked at us coldly.

"It's getting so a girl can't even do her exercises around here without being interrupted by a couple of sex-starved rubbernecks," the deceased observed with husky-voiced contempt.

"Hey!" Polnik's voice dropped three octaves back to its normal basso profundo. "She ain't dead, Lieutenant?"

The brunette non-corpse sat up slowly, and the taut-stretched scarlet leotard proved beyond any doubt that the proud high curve of her bosom was equal to the one she was sitting on, already.

"Who the hell are you?" she asked, with no real interest in her voice.

"I'm Lieutenant Wheeler from the Sheriff's office," I told her, "and this is Sergeant Polnik. Who are you?"

"Celeste Campbell!" she said in a ringing voice, then closed her eyes expectantly.

I stared blankly at the Sergeant and he stared blankly—what else?—right back at me. After around ten long seconds had slumped past, Celeste Campbell opened her sloe eyes again and glared bloody murder at me.

"You never heard of Celeste Campbell before?" She shrugged expressively. "*Civilians!*"

"Ah!" I said brightly. "Showbiz?"

She bent forward for a moment, then took hold of her right ankle in one hand, lifted it easily over her head, and planted the sole of her foot on the nape of her neck—and left it there.

"I'm just about the greatest contortionist in the business," she said nonchalantly.

"Female contortionist?" Polnik ventured.

She blinked slowly at him, then gave me a wondering look. "Are you sure you're not a ventriloquist?"

"You're kidding," Polnik rasped happily. "If the Lieutenant was one of them, that would make me a—" The smile faded slowly from his face.

"Somebody reported a homicide," I said in a weak voice, "and for God's sake put that leg back where it belongs before it snaps clean off."

Obligingly, she lifted the ankle back over her head and allowed her legs to resume a normal position. "Pop's waiting in the garage for you, Lieutenant." She yawned gently. "Him and the body."

"If her old man's anything like she is," Polnik growled, "he's most likely tied up the cadaver into a reef knot while he's been waiting for us—maybe sitting on its teeth?"

"Pop Livvy is not my father," she said in an icy tone. "He owns the joint, that's all."

"It was a woman who called in," I said.

"Girl," she corrected me. "Pop asked me to make the call because telephones make him nervous."

"But corpses he don't mind?" Polnik croaked.

Celeste Campbell got onto her feet, then bent backward from the waist in an effortless movement. "The garage is on the far side of the house," she said, her face looking upward at me from between her knees.

"I wish you wouldn't do that," I told her. "It makes me feel seasick."

"A girl has to stay in shape," she snapped.

"There, you don't have a problem," I admitted, then looked at Polnik. "I guess we'd better go take a look at the garage."

"Sure, Lieutenant." He made a visible effort and disengaged his focus from the stretched scarlet leotard.

"Can you drink a glass of water and make him talk at the same time?" the inverted face asked interestedly from between the rounded knees.

I grabbed Polnik's elbow again and hustled him out of the room before he had time to start his mental wheels churning on that one. We went out the front door back to where we'd started, then along the deep-rutted driveway until we reached the garage. The doors were wide open, and from the way they sagged drunkenly on their hinges, had been for the last twenty years. Inside, it was big enough to garage a couple of stagecoaches and still have plenty of room for a bus fleet.

The light came from another chandelier yet. It hung nervously from the rafters, with just one of the ten bulbs still functioning. At the back of the garage a car stood with its square rear end pointed toward us and it looked interesting, but then my attention was concentrated on the guy walking toward us at a leisurely pace.

"Gentlemen," he said in a soft, pleasant voice, "I am Pop Livvy. You've come about the murder, of course?"

If he wanted to read his lines like Noel Coward in the drawing room, that was okay by me. I nodded once and looked him over.

Pop Livvy, I guessed, would be around sixty, but both his face and body still retained an amazingly youthful vitality. A tall, slender man with a full crop of curly gray hair, his faded blue eyes gleamed with an alert compassion for the frailties of all mankind.

He wore a sweatshirt and a pair of disreputable denim pants, both faded to match the color of his eyes, and they somehow combined to give an impression of sartorial elegance. I told him who we were, and that we'd already talked to Celeste Campbell, who had told us to come to the garage.

"A darling girl, Celeste," he said sincerely, "although she's wasting her time with this contortionist act she's always working on. As an exotic dancer she could make herself a fortune in no time at all, don't you agree, Lieutenant?"

It was an intriguing thought and, for a moment there, I almost went along with it. "Mr. Livvy—"

"Please!" He gestured with one hand. "Call me Pop. Everyone does."

"Pop," I corrected, gritting my teeth, "I'd love to sit around with you and work out real exotic dance routines for Celeste, but we did come about the murder, remember?"

"I'm sorry, Lieutenant," he apologized. "I imagine you would like to see the body?"

"If it don't talk back to us like the last one did," Polnik grunted.

"Then, if you'll follow me, gentleman?"

Pop Livvy turned and walked toward the back of the garage with Polnik, and me following him cautiously. I stopped suddenly when we drew level with the square end of the parked car and knew I'd been right the first time—it was interesting, okay. It was an incredibly ancient coupé de ville designed so the chauffeur sat out in the rain, with even an elegant lantern jutting from the pillar between the front and back doors.

"What make of automobile is this?" I asked, fascinated.

"I wouldn't know, Lieutenant," Pop said. "It came with the house when I bought it in 1932. The previous owner swore that nobody else would ever use it, so he had the motor and all the working parts removed. The easiest thing seemed to be to just let it stand here."

"Maybe the cadaver came along with the auto," Polnik suggested gloomily. "And tonight, for the first time in thirty years, he takes a look inside, huh?"

"Oh, the body isn't inside the car," Pop said. "It's here—on the hood."

I suddenly lost my interest in antique automobiles and took a half-dozen strides that brought me level with Pop Livvy and gave me a clear view of the car's hood. It also gave me a crystal-clear view of the body stretched out flat on its back along the top of the hood. In back of me I heard Polnik's sudden sharp intake of breath and knew exactly how he felt.

The body belonged to a fat, bald headed guy somewhere around his late fifties with a face that made Polnik's Cro-Magnon profile look cherubic by comparison. Only it wasn't the face that gave me a queasy feeling in my stomach, it was the gaping hole in his throat and the blood—which must have poured through that hole in a torrent— saturating his chest and arms.

"Messy, isn't it?" Pop Livvy said in a gentle voice.

Chapter Two

Doc Murphy finally finished his examination and walked toward the open door of the garage where I was stood waiting. The sharp planes of his sardonic face looked a little more so than usual, and I would have sworn there was just a tinge of gray under his heavy tan.

"Messy, isn't it?" he said.

"You voice the majority opinion around here," I told him. "You have something else, like real scientific, to add to that, Doctor?"

"I can tell you what killed him, Lieutenant," he said in a complacent voice.

I closed my eyes for a moment: "King Kong finally came down off the top of the Empire State Building?"

"A bullet."

"You're kidding?"

"A soft-nosed dumdum bullet," Murphy said. "I can't prove it until I do the autopsy, but I'm prepared to bet on it right now."

"Close range?"

"Not real close because there aren't any powder burns or anything, but a maximum range of twenty feet, Al."

"How do you figure that?" I growled.

"Because that's the distance from the body to the back wall of the garage," he said. "That corpse must have been sitting on the hood of the car when it was shot—the impact knocked the guy backwards. Nobody could have moved it afterwards without leaving a trail of blood a yard wide!" Murphy sniffed loudly. "I can smell trouble for you, my dubious detective. This one has got all the signs of a real screwball case."

"Don't they all?" I muttered.

"Why would a guy be sitting on the hood of the car in the first place?" he asked gleefully. "And when you get right down to it, that car doesn't look like it's been outside the garage in thirty years, either."

"It hasn't," I told him. "The first owner had the motor removed, just to be sure."

"Oh, brother!" Murphy gurgled. "Want to bet you don't find the corpse has a maiden aunt who learned to fight dirty helping the Arabs and Lawrence of Arabia in the desert, with dumdum bullets, and all?"

"Doc," I said sincerely, "get the hell out of here, will you?"

He went, still chuckling evilly to himself, and nearly collided with Polnik who was on his way in. Murphy just managed to avoid being flattened by the Sergeant's bulk, and snarled, "Cretin!" as he executed a frantic, sideways leap.

"I don't know, Doc," Polnik said politely, "maybe he is, and maybe he ain't. You know this guy—Cret—Lieutenant?"

"No," I said truthfully, as Murphy disappeared into the outer darkness leaving only the overtones of his anguished howl behind him. "What's happening inside the house?"

"Pop Livvy got the rest of them that's living in the joint all together in the living room," he said in a hushed voice. "You want to get a good grip on yourself, Lieutenant, before you go take a look."

"How's that?" I queried.

He shook his head slowly. "It's Nut Week, I can tell you. The whole bunch look like they just stepped right out of one of my comic books." He grinned sheepishly. "Not that I read comics, Lieutenant, you understand?"

"Sure," I said, "you just look at the pictures."

"Yeah!" He gazed at me with open-mouthed admiration. "How did you know?"

"Why don't we go back into the house and talk to the rest of the nuts?" I said. "It looks like it's going to be a long night already."

Pop Livvy was waiting for us at the front door, and escorted us into the living room. One quick glance at the people sitting around waiting there was enough to tell that Polnik wasn't kidding, it was Nut Week all right.

"This is Lieutenant Wheeler, folks," Pop said to them. "I guess the best thing I can do is introduce you to everybody, one at a time, Lieutenant?"

"That would be nice," I said dismally.

"You've already met Celeste Campbell, of course."

I looked at the brunette in the scarlet leotard who was now contorting in an armchair. Her knees were on the seat, facing the back of the chair, while the rest of her was bent backward so the top of her head rested on the floor. The inverted face smiled in casual recognition, and I figured a girl had one advantage in her position—at least she didn't need a bra.

"And this is Antonia," Pop continued.

"The Great!" a vibrant bass voice added.

The voice's owner got onto her feet, and great she was, I would freely admit the fact anyplace. An Amazonian blonde who towered over my six feet by at least five inches. Her thick, tawny hair hung down her back as far as her waist. She wore a magnificent leopard-skin leotard, which I guessed she'd peeled off a passing leopard one day in the jungle when she was out chasing Tarzan. At a rough guess, her vital statistics were 44-26-45. All by herself she was enough woman for three strong men, and maybe an eager adolescent as well.

"This is Sebastian," Pop murmured. "The Man of Mystery."

Sebastian was a mere shrimp of a man around my own size. He wore white tie and tails, complete with a black cloak that had a scarlet lining. Maybe the jet-black hair was dyed just a little, but it went very well with the thin mustache and pointed beard. He looked the perfect model for an older-type Satan—one who was just a little tired of claiming all those souls day after day, but was still capable of an infinite variety of hell-raising if the occasion arose. He bowed and smiled, showing flashing white teeth, then turned toward Polnik and held out his right hand. The Sergeant automatically held out his own right hand and received a bunch of wilted roses instead of fingers.

"An illusionist, sir!" Sebastian bowed again in my direction then resumed his seat.

"And, finally, this is Bruno Breck," Pop said, finishing the introductions.

Breck was a wizened little guy around the same age as Pop Livvy, and his face had all the charm of a frilled lizard. Only his eyes were alive, mud-colored and malicious, always moving in search of a new victim. When he opened his mouth to speak, I waited to see a forked tongue dart out.

"Monologues and funny patter," he said in a high-pitched, spiteful voice. "A funny thing happened to me on my way to the theater tonight—and I think it'll need surgery." He paused for a moment but nobody laughed. "A comic, sir, in spite of their reaction. When is a cop not a cop?" He waited expectantly for a few seconds until he realized I wasn't going to be his straight man.

"When he's copped out!" he sniggered. "I knew you wouldn't like that, I never met a cop with a sense of humor in all my life!"

"How would you know if you did meet one?" I asked interestedly.

Pop cleared his throat gently. "Well, Lieutenant, now you've met all my house guests, I expect you'll want to ask some questions?"

"You know what time it was when you found the body?" I asked him.

"About eleven, I think." He looked down at Celeste's inverted face. "I came right in and asked you to call the police, dear. Do you remember what time it was then?"

"Five after," she said. "I wouldn't have done it for just anyone, Pop, you know? Not right in the middle of my evening workout."

"I know," he said gratefully, "and I appreciate it."

"What made you go into the garage at that time of night?" I persisted.

"It sounds silly." Pop's face reddened a little. "But it's gotten to be a habit with me over the years, maybe because I never learned to drive?" He looked at my blank face for a moment. "It's just that I like to sit in that automobile—in the driver's seat—and pretend it's a very special day and I'm driving Gwen someplace real exciting and all the crowds are cheering...." His voice trailed away into an embarrassed silence.

"Gwen?" I queried.

"My wife. You never heard of Livvy and Lysander, the biggest song-and-dance team in vaudeville? No—" he shook his head "—I guess you're too young, Lieutenant. It was right after my wife's death that I bought this house."

"You didn't hear any shots?" I asked.

"Oh, yes, plenty of shots," he nodded. "But I naturally didn't pay any attention to them."

"You naturally didn't pay—" I repeated. The glassy look in Polnik's eyes was only a reflection of my own, I guessed. "Why not?" I pleaded with Pop.

"We're all so used to hearing shots, Lieutenant." He smiled tolerantly. "You see, Sebastian is a sharp shooter as well as an illusionist, and he's always practicing his sharpshooting in the basement. He has it specially set up down there."

I closed my eyes again and tried not to recognize the obvious truth, that the hard lump pressing against my skull was my brain congealing into one solid mass.

"You didn't recognize the man who was murdered?" I persisted.

"No, sir," Pop said in a firm voice. "I've never seen him before."

"How about the rest of you?" I looked at the others without hope. "Anyone hear anything unusual, or see anything, maybe?"

The silence lasted maybe five seconds, then Breck's shrill voice cackled, "I saw something most unusual, Lieutenant! One time when I was on safari in darkest Africa. Of course, I'd always known that elephants have fleas, but this was the first flea—"

"When vaudeville died, I wonder they didn't hold you personally responsible," I snarled at him. "Where were you, anyway, from ten tonight onwards?"

"In my room," he snapped. "By myself."

"How about you?" I asked the illusionist.

Sebastian looked at me dreamily. "I, sir? Why, as always, I was down in the basement—sharpshooting."

"You didn't have a practice shot in the garage, too?"

"You jest, sir!" He took a silk handkerchief from his top pocket and shook it out in front of him a couple of times. "Why, sir, if I wished to get rid of anyone I would just make them—" he shook the handkerchief a third time and it disappeared— "vanish!"

"I was out," Antonia the Great said, her vibrant bass anticipating the question. "Walking in the trees."

"Huh?" Polnik rumbled. "Don't she mean, 'walking under—'"

"Don't ask!" I said frantically.

"I walk *in* the trees," Antonia insisted, addressing her remarks exclusively to the Sergeant. "Up and down the branches, swinging from one to the other. It is good exercise." She stared down at him silently for a few seconds, then a peculiar gleam showed in her eyes. "One night you must come with me, my little dumpling," she whispered, and it sounded like a jet coming in to land. "Then we can walk in the trees together!"

"Huh?" Alarm signals blazed in Polnik's eyes as he backed off away from her.

Antonia caught up with him in one giant stride. "Don't be shy, little dumpling," she said with a pantherish smile. "You are like me, I know— primitive—all muscle!" She gave him a playful punch on the chest and he keeled over onto the carpet.

"Let's save the fun and games until later, shall we?" I snarled at her. "I hate to bother all of you with a trivial thing like a murder, but that's what I'm paid for."

Celeste Campbell kind of crawled up her own legs until she was in an upright position, kneeling on the chair, then turned around and sat in it.

"I was in here all evening, Lieutenant," she said.

"Doing your workout," I grated.

"Right!" She smiled wickedly at me. "One night we should do it together, Lieutenant. You're like me, I know—all rubber!"

Right then I knew I had to make a choice, either stay there and lose my mind, or get the hell out fast. One glance at Polnik was enough to confirm my choice. Antonia had picked him up tenderly and now held him firmly in her arms, cradled to her massive bosom, while his feet kicked helplessly a foot above the floor.

"Please put my sergeant down," I said in a quavering voice. "He's the only one I've got!"

"There, my little dumpling," Antonia crooned with fierce tenderness, ignoring my plea entirely. "You just hold on tight and I'll hug you a little until the pain's all gone."

"No!" Polnik yelped. "Don't do—" Then all the air came out of his lungs, and I turned away before I heard his ribs start to crack.

"I'll be back later," I said to anyone who cared to listen. "I think."

Then I walked out of the room quickly before they could argue and didn't stop until I reached the front porch again. The cool night air dried my forehead, and the moonlit sky was reassuringly normal. I lit a cigarette and began to feel better, then heard a slight footstep in back of me which made me jump six inches straight into the air.

"I'm sorry if I startled you, Lieutenant," Pop Livvy said softly. "But I just remembered something that might be important."

"Like what?" I asked, all on edge.

"It's about the house," he said. "The former owner wants to buy it back, but I refuse to sell."

"You mean the guy who took the motor out of the car so nobody else but him could ever drive it? I figured he must have died, or something."

"He didn't die, he went away," Pop said. "Most of the last thirty years he's spent on a small island north of here, but now he's back and he just won't take no for an answer."

"Oh, really?" I said, keeping it polite.

"I would say he has a fixation about it, Lieutenant." Pop's voice sounded genuinely troubled. "Maybe it's possible there's a connection between him and the man who was killed in the garage tonight?"

"Don't you flip now, Pop!" I pleaded with him. "I had you figured as the only sane one of the whole bunch."

"I guess I'm not saying this very well, Lieutenant." He smiled apologetically. "The former owner's name is Jones."

"Kind of unique name," I grunted.

"And that island where he's spent the best part of the last thirty years is called Alcatraz."

I suddenly revised my opinion about his sanity. "Go on."

"Well, he was once a man of violence and—" Pop stopped talking and turned toward the open front door. From inside the house a sound like a herd of stampeding elephants was rapidly approaching us, getting louder all the time.

A couple of seconds later, a wild-eyed Polnik came charging out onto the porch. "Run for your life, Lieutenant!" he screamed at me and grabbed my arm on his way so that I didn't have any choice—the next moment I was galloping along right beside him. He stopped when we reached the car and almost threw me into the driver's seat, then vaulted over the hood and hurled himself in from the other side.

"Get going, Lieutenant!" he gasped desperately. "It's that man-eating dame—she's after me!"

I saw a flash of bronzed legs and leopard skin in the doorway of the house and didn't need any further encouragement. The Healey's rear wheels spun furiously for a couple of seconds, then gained traction and we were off, like jet-propelled, down the driveway. As we flashed past the front porch I heard Pop's faint yell, "Parson Jones, Lieutenant!" Then we were at the front gates and turning onto the road.

By the time we reached the highway, the car was doing a steady eighty-five, so I eased my foot off the gas pedal and watched the needle swing slowly back.

"You figure it's safe to slow down already, Lieutenant?" Polnik asked in a shaking voice.

"You're safe," I told him. "I don't see Antonia chasing us in the rearview mirror!"

"Yeah?" He sounded totally unconvinced. "How do you know she ain't ahead of us already, Lieutenant—running in the trees?"

Chapter Three

Sheriff Lavers glared at me across the top of his desk with such malignant intensity that I figured his eyeballs were about to fuse any moment. I had to admit, in the cold light of day, it sounded real wild even to me. Polnik calling in an hour back to say he was staying home because his ribs were all banged up, didn't really help much, either. Like most genuine reasons, it sounded like a lousy excuse.

"Your fertility was never in doubt, Wheeler," Lavers said, in an ominous voice, "but I never figured on it straying so far it would reach your imagination."

"I can't help what happened last night, sir," I said.

"Let's go over it again, briefly," he snapped. "There are five people living in the house, right?" He didn't wait for my assent. "The owner is the surviving half of a song-and-dance act; the others consist of a female contortionist, a giant strong woman wearing a leopard skin, a sharpshooting illusionist, and a dried-up comic, right?"

"I—"

"The corpse was found stretched out on the hood of an antique automobile that hasn't been out of the garage in thirty years because the former owner removed the motor before he left, right?"

"I—"

"You left in a hurry because the strong woman had taken a fancy to Sergeant Polnik and insisted on carrying him around in her arms like an infant child, right?"

"Well—" I gave him a glassy smile. "I admit it does sound a little unusual, sir, but—"

"Unusual?" The veins stood out on his forehead like steel cable. "What do you take me for, Wheeler? Some kind of a gullible nut? I want to know what you and that bruised sergeant really did last night? Maybe there was some kind of heroin cocktail party going on in the house, and you got invited?"

I figured it might somehow be to my advantage to change the subject. "There's something else, Sheriff," I said eagerly. "You ever hear of a guy named Jones?"

He made a kind of choking sound and I figured he was about to have a coronary right in front of my eyes. His face went a beet-red color while the pupils of his eyes dilated wildly; deep in his chest he made feeble, gurgling sounds as his right fist pounded the desk top with spasmodic violence.

"No, Lieutenant," he managed to gasp finally. "I never heard of a guy called Jones! I once met a Smith in San Francisco, and a couple of Browns in L.A., even, but Jones—never!" The last word came out in his usual full-throated roar.

Before I could get a word in, there was a knock on the door and his secretary, Annabelle Jackson came into the office. The pride of the South wore a brand-new sheath dress—a velvety-black which contrasted nicely with her honey-blonde hair. It also fit real tight, and I figured the thing I liked most about Annabelle's prominent curves was how they stood out for themselves, obviously in no need of invisible support.

"The autopsy report just came through from Doctor Murphy, Sheriff," she said briskly, and put the folder onto his desk. "I thought you'd want to see it right away."

"Thank you, Miss Jackson," Lavers grunted. "Let me ask you a question. Did you ever hear of a guy named Jones?"

Her eyes widened fractionally. "It's some kind of a joke, sir?"

"I guess you're right," he said. "Did you know the Lieutenant has a fertile imagination, Miss Jackson?"

Annabelle gave me a cold, analytical look, then nodded. "It figures!" she said.

Her heels tapped sharply across the floor, and then she disappeared back into the outer office. I watched the Sheriff's slow, deliberate intake of breath, and timed my interruption for the last moment before he was about to blast me again.

"Parson Jones?" I said dully.

"Wheeler! I won't tolerate your ridiculous, idiotic, insubordinate—" He blinked at me slowly. "Did you say, *Parson* Jones?"

"Did I?" I mumbled.

"Where did you hear that name?"

"He's the guy that Pop Livvy bought the house from, and now he's trying to buy it back again," I said. "It's a little confused in my own mind. Pop said something about Jones spending the last thirty years mostly on Alcatraz and—"

"Shut up!" he snapped. "I'm thinking."

I shut up—who was a humble lieutenant to interrupt the county sheriff's enjoyment of a unique experience in his life? After a couple of minutes' brooding silence, he suddenly yelled for Annabelle and she came running. There was a momentary look of disappointment in her eyes when she saw I was still in one piece.

"Did we get those morgue shots yet?" Lavers asked.

"Yes, sir." Annabelle shuddered deliciously. "They're horrible—all that blood!"

"It's the face I'm interested in," he said. "I want you to take one of the photos up to Captain Parker in Homicide right away. Tell him I've got a hunch that corpse was one of Parson Jones's associates from way back, and ask him to have it checked through records right away. Ask him to call me if it checks out—or if it doesn't, either way."

"Yes, sir." Annabelle hesitated for a moment. "You did say Jones?"

"Of course I did," he snapped. "Parson Jones. Anyone would think it's an unusual name or something!"

He frowned at her retreating back until she disappeared into the outer office again, then glared at me suspiciously. "You haven't been fooling around with my secretary again, Wheeler?"

"No, sir!" I said in a wistful voice. "These days I don't seem to get the opportunity."

"Well, there must be something the matter with her," he grunted. "The way she reacted when I said 'Jones,' you'd think I was making some kind of a joke."

"Not you, Sheriff," I said warmly.

For a moment he hesitated, then decided to let it pass and study the autopsy report instead. I lit a cigarette and wondered vaguely why I ever became a cop when there were so many fascinating alternatives, like the Sanitation Department.

"Probable time of death, two to three hours before time of examination," he read out loud. "What time would that make it?"

"Between ten and eleven last night," I said.

"A thirty-eight-caliber soft-nosed slug?" He shook his head slowly. "Why the hell would anyone use one of those?"

"All the possible reasons are depressing," I said, and gave him the obvious answer. "Like you hate your victim so bad, just killing him isn't enough. It means we're looking for a psychotic, or a sadist or both?"

"Maybe." The Sheriff shrugged indifferently. His phone rang and he grabbed it quickly. "Lavers." He listened attentively for what seemed a hell of a long time, then cleared his throat worriedly.

"Mrs. Polnik," he said, "you have my complete assurance that any injuries received by your husband last night were strictly in the line of duty." He slammed the phone down hastily and glowered at me. "What right have I got to order her husband into the arms of a strange woman? she wanted to know."

"Yes, sir." I carefully avoided meeting his eye.

"I hoped it might be Parker, but I guess Miss Jackson's only just about arriving in his office now."

"Sheriff," I said coldly, "how long are you going to hold out on me?"

"What?"

"Parson Jones!" I snarled. "Who the hell is he?"

"Before your time, Wheeler," he said. "I was only a kid myself. Jones was the bootleg baron of the West Coast during Prohibition, and he came up to the top real fast, no more than twenty-six or -seven, when he took control of the whole operation. For sure, the three men who stood in his way were murdered either by Jones himself, or by his direct orders. Then, maybe a year before Repeal, he got smart and decided to retire. He built a house here in Pine City in an architectural style I guess you could call 'Bootleg Baronial', moved in with his wife and their brand-new kid, and was all set to become an upright citizen. Then they nailed Capone in Chicago for tax evasion, and the writing was on the wall. Six months later they locked him away—forever, I figured—and his wife and kid somehow disappeared."

"And Pop Livvy bought his house," I said.

Lavers lit a cigar and looked at me with an eager glint in his eyes. "When they'd finished with his books, found all his dummy bank accounts and the rest of it, there was still something like a half million unaccounted for. They figured it was in cash and Jones must have it stashed away someplace, but he wasn't about to tell them where, obviously. The Feds searched the house, almost took it apart brick by brick, but they never found anything."

His phone rang again and this time it was Captain Parker calling. Lavers listened attentively, giving an occasional grunt and making notes on his desk pad while Parker kept on talking.

"Thanks a lot, Captain," he said finally. "I surely appreciate it.... Sure, Wheeler's handling the case.... No, I guess he shouldn't have much of a problem seeing that we've done most of the work for him already!" Then he hung up and beamed at me in conscious superiority.

"Take your time, Sheriff," I snapped. "I realize genius can't be hurried."

"It all adds up beautifully," he gloated. "Jones served a full thirty years' term and was released six weeks back. So what does he do? Right away, he returns to Pine City and tries to buy back his old house. And that corpse of yours was an old buddy of Jones's—name of Eddie Moran—a two-bit hood who spent more of his life in jail than out."

He settled back comfortably in his chair and blew a cloud of acrid black smoke in my direction. "It all adds up, Wheeler. Jones wants his old house back for only one possible reason. That money is still there, stashed away in the house or the grounds someplace. But the present owner won't sell, so if Jones can't get what he wants legally, he'll try getting it illegally. Right away he looks up his old buddy, Eddie Moran, and sends him to break into the house."

He puffed a couple more thunderheads my way. "To make it real easy for you, Wheeler, I can even tell you where you can find Jones right now. He's staying at the Starlight Hotel with his son! So you'd better get over there right away and start cleaning up the case."

"Why did they call him 'Parson' Jones?" I asked.

"He was prematurely bald," Lavers explained. "The top of his head was like a billiard ball, except for a real bushy growth of black hair at the back of his head, and for a couple of inches above his ears. Don't ask me why, but they said it made him look like a parson."

I got up onto my feet, ready and eager to leap the whole three blocks into the wild blue yonder which would take me to the hotel, only I had to do something about that smug, complacent look on Laver's face, and the cigar smoke, too.

"Well, thanks, Sheriff," I said in my most sincere voice. "A little minor help along the way is like real encouraging."

"What do you mean—minor help?" he bellowed.

"Putting a tab on the victim and the tie-in with Parson Jones," I said.

"You call that minor? It about wraps up the whole case for you!" he yelled indignantly.

"Jones wants to grab his loot out of the house Pop Livvy now owns," I said with enormous patience. "He can't buy back the house so he sends a goon in to get the loot, right?"

"As I told you, already," Lavers growled.

"So who knocked off the goon—Eddie Moran?" I asked.

"Why it's—it's—" Lavers removed the cigar from between his teeth so he could gape at me, open-mouthed. "That's right. It couldn't be Parson Jones!"

"It was a real good try for an amateur, Sheriff," I told him in a soothing voice. "Trouble is, it takes a hell of a lot of hard work and expertise to make a cop. But if you keep trying I'm sure you'll make it one of these years." I was out of his office with the door shut tight in back of me before his first bellow of anguished fury was launched.

Annabelle Jackson was sitting at her desk, and by bending my knees a little I could see that the tight sheath she wore rode up a whole four inches above her knees. Conscience told me it was kind of sneaky, but logic reasoned you don't get to see knees like Annabelle's every day and the sight was well worth a little exercise.

She looked up suddenly from her typewriter and caught me bending. "Al Wheeler," she said with tart disgust, "anyone would think you'd never seen a girl's legs before!"

"Before what?"

"You are impossible," she said flatly.

"I'm growing maudlin and morose," I admitted. "Because that beautiful thing that flowered between us has withered and died."

"You mean the potted plant?" she asked happily. "It died—but we can always get another cactus if you're that broken up about it."

"There was a time we used to date—and not with a damned cactus plant between us, either," I grated. "What happened to that sweet little magnolia blossom I used to know?"

"Al, honey"—the drawl in her voice was strictly burlesqued—"I do declare one night with you is enough to give a poor little Southern girl the vapors the whole ye-ar round! A girl can get real fussed and fatigued with that l'il ole hi-fi machine of yours blasting l'il ole romantic music in her ear, while you're chasing her around and around your l'il ole couch! My!" Her eyes shone with sweet Virginian innocence. "Once a girl loses her breath in your l'il ole apartment, Al, honey, there's just no telling what she's about to lose next!"

"So next time we'll go to a movie," I mumbled.

"I do declare!" She giggled hysterically. "My mama always told me never to sit in the dark with a man who's got five hands. But if you're real anxious, Al, honey, maybe one Sunday morning we could go walking—down Main Street?"

Suddenly I knew what was wrong with Annabelle—I was seeing her right side up. "Tell me something," I asked casually. "Do you contort, Annabelle, honey?"

She thought about it for a couple of seconds with a look of dark suspicion in her eyes. "If you mean what I think you mean," she said finally, "how dare you even suggest such a thing!"

"I met a girl last night who contorts," I continued. "It's done her a world of good—if you could see her you'd know what I mean. I bet you'd want to try it right away."

"Just what would—contorting—do for me?" she asked icily.

"Tone up your figure, Annabelle, honey." I smiled sweetly. "Tighten up all those sagging muscles and—"

I made it to the door before she had time to hurl the steel rule at me, but on the way to the car I had to admit to myself that she'd won on a technical knockout long before I threw the last foul punch.

Chapter Four

From the supercilious look on the desk clerk's face you would have figured he owned the Starlight Hotel instead of just working there.

"We're all booked up," he announced before I had time to open my mouth, even. "Why don't you try the Continental across the street?"

"Because the guy I want to see is staying here," I suggested in a mild voice.

"Why didn't you say so in the first place?" he snapped. "I—wait a minute!"

He moved swiftly away to greet a slightly overweight white-blonde with a brunette streak just above her right ear. Around midnight the previous night, her make-up would have looked exotic; at eleven-thirty the following morning it looked like she was about to take the warpath after some more paleface scalps—and maybe she was.

"Good morning, Miss Adele," the desk clerk said in a honied voice. "How can I serve you this morning?"

"Oh, Cedric!" The blonde gave a girlish giggle, and that was something she should have stopped around fifteen years back. "I just adore the way you always fuss over me! I just wondered, is there any mail this morning?"

"Two, I think," he said passionately. "I'll get them for you right away!"

While his back was turned toward the desk as he dug out her mail, I took the opportunity to move up right next to the blonde and slam my shield down onto the desk in front of her.

"Lieutenant Wheeler," I growled. "Sheriff's office. We got a complaint about you, Cedric!"

He spun toward me, his eyes leaping out of his head. "There must be some mistake!"

I shook my head slowly. "You're the one, all right. A former guest of the hotel filed the complaint—a Miss Petunia Appleyard—that's what she calls herself anyway, even if she has been divorced three times already."

"I never even heard of her!" he stuttered frantically. "This is all some dreadful mistake—"

"It's a dirty business, Cedric, preying on lonely, middle-aged women who keep deluding themselves that a new hair rinse and pancake make-up will make them look glamorous to a kid your age. Miss Appleyard gave us the whole score—how you started off by flattering her, making big eyes at her the whole time—personalized attention. The whole thing wouldn't have worried her so much, she said, only a kid who arrives in her room to keep a discreet, late-night rendezvous with a camera in one hand while the other goes through her purse when he figures she's not looking—"

"She must be out of her mind!" he gabbled. "She's got the wrong hotel, the wrong desk clerk, the—"

"I would like my mail!" The naked savagery in the white-blonde's voice sent a chill up and down my spine.

"Oh—er—sure, Miss Adele!" The clerk put the two letters down on the desk and she snatched them away a moment later.

"*Thank you!*" She went through her purse with deliberate slowness while Cedric's horror-stricken gaze alternated between my face and hers. Finally she snapped the purse shut and held her clenched fist about a foot above the desk.

"I would also like to thank you for your—personalized attention?—while I've been a guest in the hotel," she said in a saccharine voice. "I always believe that good service should be rewarded. This, Cedric, is for you!"

She opened her fingers and a bright, shiny penny jounced onto the desk right under the clerk's nose. Then the white-blonde turned and stalked across the lobby, her swaying hips offering a mute but unmistakable Bronx cheer.

I slipped my shield back into my pocket and smiled cheerfully at the dazed Cedric. "Where would I find Mr. Jones, please?" I asked courteously.

"Huh?"

"Mr. Jones—from San Francisco? His son is also with him, I understand."

"The penthouse suite," he said automatically.

"Thank you." I smiled again in gratitude.

I was maybe ten feet away from the desk when he recovered his voice. "*Lieutenant?*"

"What is it?" I looked back over my shoulder.

"That—that complaint Miss Appleyard made?" He couldn't keep the whimpering tone out of his voice anymore. "She must have made a mistake!"

I nodded soberly. "I think you're absolutely right, she did make a mistake, and I feel badly about it. Just forget the whole thing ever happened and go on giving everyone your personalized attention, even before you find out they're carrying a shield."

The first outraged glimmer of understanding was beginning to show in his eyes as I turned back toward the elevators. Riding the powered casket up to the penthouse, I guessed that white-blonde would have been bad for Cedric, anyway; he didn't look like he had the necessary stamina.

A Starlight penthouse suite has its own entrance hall right over the elevator, because they figure anybody paying a hundred dollars a day is entitled to some privacy. I figured Parson Jones should appreciate it after spending most of the last thirty years on the Rock. While I waited for someone to open the door after I'd thumbed the buzzer, I idly wondered what was the one thing he'd want most of all after being behind bars all that time. Then the door opened and I didn't have to wonder anymore.

A redhead with a slightly vacant look in her eyes stood there looking at me like I didn't exist. An inadequate blue silk bandana was knotted casually in the shadowed hollow between her deep, swelling breasts; hip-high tangerine velvet pants clung desperately to her well-turned legs, all the way down to her ankles.

"You want something?" She missed a couple of beats in her rhythmic gum-chewing to ask the question.

"Mr. Jones?" I said numbly.

For a wild moment there, I thought her bare navel winked at me, but a closer look showed it was a diamond set snugly in one of the cutest settings I ever saw.

"Do I look like *Mister* Jones?" she said blankly.

"No, ma'am," I assured her. "Mr. Jones is the one with a pearl button in his navel, right?"

She squinted at me suspiciously. "Are you some kind of a kook?"

"Could be," I agreed. "How about telling Parson I'm here?"

"I guess you might as well come in." She yawned heavily. "I can use the rest while you're visiting." I followed her into the chic living room with its plate-glass view of downtown Pine City, and watched her slump wearily into an armchair. Then she turned her head slowly and yelled, "Hey, Parson! You're wanted!"

"Not now, baby," a male voice bellowed right back from the bathroom. "I'm shaving!"

The redhead's jaws moved rhythmically for another five seconds, then she opened her mouth again. "I don't mean that—there's a guy out here to see you."

"Who is it?" he yelled back.

"Yeah—" she nodded slowly. "Who are you?"

"A friend of Eddie Moran's, asking after his health," I told her.

She repeated the words at the top of her lungs, and a moment later the bathroom door crashed open and Mr. Jones came almost running into the room. His hair was still exactly the way Lavers had described it—only now it was bushy-white instead of black—and somehow it managed to give his lined, sagging face a look of benign serenity. It was no trick at all to see why they'd called him "Parson."

"What was that about Eddie?" His voice, pitched at a normal level, was rich, fruity, and strictly ecclesiastical.

"I'm a pal of Eddie's," I told him. "I wondered if he's still in good health, Parson?"

He stared at me intently for a moment, then the corners of his mouth turned down in a sour grimace. "A cop," he sneered. "A stinking cop—it gets so you can smell 'em, even."

There was no choice but to tell him who I was, and he wasn't impressed; it had enough impact on the redhead to make her pause for a moment while she transferred the wad of gum from one cheek to the other.

Jones sat heavily on the couch. He took a cigar from the pocket of his silk robe and began to peel the cellophane carefully.

"You got no right to come bothering me, Wheeler," he said, and I had to concentrate on the words, because the tone of his voice sounded like he was announcing the Sunday school picnic next week.

"I'm not out on parole, I'm clean. Thirty goddamned years in stir— I'm not about to socialize with any dirty cop!"

"This is strictly from courtesy, Parson," I said easily. "I figured you might be interested to know what happened to your old buddy, Eddie Moran, last night?"

He concentrated on lighting his cigar for a couple of seconds. "Eddie?" He gave a short laugh. "Sure, I'm real worried about a guy I don't see since 1932!"

"I guess I made a mistake," I told him. "Sorry I wasted your time, Parson."

He almost let me reach the door before his voice intoned, "So what happened to Eddie?"

"It was quite a coincidence," I said as I turned around to face him. "He got himself murdered last night—in the garage of your old house."

"Come back here and sit down," he ordered.

"Hey, Parson," the redhead said, pouting at him. "I need a drink."

"So go get yourself one," he snarled. "Take the bottle in the bedroom with you—that way you got no place to fall."

"I don't wanna—"

"Beat it! I got a little business going with this cop here right now. Get lost!"

"But I don't—"

For a man of his age, Parson Jones moved with surprising speed. He came off the couch in one quick movement and grabbed the redhead's ear between a thumb and index finger, then dragged her out of the armchair and across the room toward the bedroom door, ignoring her frantic squeals on the way. They both disappeared inside the bedroom and a few moments later I heard two savage slapping sounds; the squealing stopped abruptly.

Then he came out of the bedroom, slammed the door shut in back of him, and walked back toward the couch.

"That dumb broad!" He rolled his cigar between his fingers. "But a good cigar is a smoke, huh?"

"Eddie was a real mess," I said softly. "Somebody took a load of trouble over your old buddy, Parson."

"Sure—they killed him, you said?"

"With a soft-nosed slug through the throat." I waited a couple of beats. "I never knew just one guy could bleed so much."

"Lindstrom, the lousy sonofabitch!" The red-hot hate bubbled through the benign mask of his face and warped the fruity veneer of his voice into a primitive-sounding snarl. For a split second, the booze baron who'd worked his way to the top of the heap by methodically erasing his competition was a stark reality.

"What did you say?" I prodded him.

"Nothing important—it's a lousy way to get bumped off, is all." Both mask and veneer were back, tightly sealed down.

"I don't have to get cute about this, Parson." I shrugged easily. "I can give it to you straight."

He stared at me momentarily, then his shoulders heaved convulsively. I listened politely to his guffaws for a while, then figured I'd heard enough.

"Did I say something funny, Parson?"

"I was just thinking—" he chuckled. "In the old days a small-town cop like you would be on my payroll, or dead, or worked over until he quit anyway! Times have changed, huh, Lieutenant?"

"In some ways, not in others," I said like I'd had a real profound thought. "You've still got the same problem you made for yourself thirty years back."

"How's that?"

"The missing half million the Treasury agents never could trace and the Feds never found. You stashed it away someplace where nobody would ever find it except yourself. Once you walked away from wherever it's hidden, Parson, you gave yourself the same problem you got right now. How to get it back."

"It was a pipe dream some hot newspaper guy dreamed up," he said comfortably. "There never was any half million stashed away anyplace."

"You did thirty long years the hard way," I said. "Then the first thing you do when you're out is come straight back to Pine City and try to buy back your old house. Only the present owner won't sell at any price. So then you got no choice but to break into the place. Doing it yourself would be too great a risk, and a dead giveaway if you were seen. You're way out of touch with the talent currently available for this kind of job, so the best, and only, deal you can make is with a buddy from the good old days like Eddie Moran."

"You're out of your mind, Lieutenant." He shook his head contemptuously. "Like I said—it's only a pipe dream, like the pot of gold at the end of the rainbow. It just ain't true."

"You want to come down to the morgue with me right now, and I'll show you the most sickening pipe dream you ever saw," I snapped.

"So maybe poor old Eddie had his own pipe dream?" he suggested. "And he went and got himself killed chasing rainbows!"

"Who'd bother to kill a guy chasing rainbows—with a soft-nosed bullet?"

There was the faint scratching sound of a key turning in the door, and I looked around in time to see a tall, thin guy walk into the penthouse. He carried his hat in one hand and his attaché case in the other as he entered the living room. His sallow, bespectacled face showed a keen, nervous intelligence; and I wished I made enough to be able to buy a suit like the one he was wearing, once in a while. When he saw the two of us watching him, he halted abruptly, and a small tic in his forehead started pulsating with an irregular beat.

"This is my son, Sigmund," Parson said. "This here's a cop—Lieutenant Whotsis?"

"Wheeler," I said.

"How do you do, Lieutenant?" Sigmund Jones came over and shook hands with me in a kind of solemn ritual. "From the Sheriff's office, I presume?"

"Sigmund's a mouthpiece!" Parson said in a derisive voice.

"Lawyer, if you don't mind, Father," the son answered stiffly. "Corporation work mostly. I don't touch criminal law."

"Your offices here in Pine City, Sigmund?" I asked idly.

"Only a small branch—my main office is in Los Angeles," he explained. The keen eyes in back of their protective glass walls searched my face carefully. "I hope this is just a social visit, Lieutenant?" He meant it to sound like a joke and it came out like a prayer.

"Not exactly." I gave him a brief run-down on Eddie Moran's murder, the theory about the half million his old man had supposedly stashed away, and how it looked to us. I took a lot of time and trouble to spell it out exactly the same way I'd spelled it out to his father. By the time I'd finished, that nervous tic in his forehead was working up a storm.

"I told him it's all a pipe dream—there never was a dime stashed away, even." Parson chuckled. "But you know what cops are, son, they got to make up stories to give themselves something to do besides chiseling a few lousy bucks a week out of the penny-ante rackets!"

"No," Sigmund's voice suddenly exploded with a nervous intensity. "I don't know what cops are—not in the sense you mean, anyhow. What I do know is that an ex-associate of yours has been brutally murdered! I told you that very first day that the idea of coming back to a small town like this, with the hope of buying back your old house and picking up the threads of your old life again, was utterly absurd. But you wouldn't listen to me. Now, surely after what's happened, you'll get a little common sense and come back to Los Angeles with me as I wanted you to in the first place?"

"Eddie getting himself bumped off is a coincidence, that's all," Parson said tightly. "It don't change a thing—and stop running off at the mouth about how goddamned smart you are, in front of a cop. We got any arguments, we keep 'em to ourselves, like we're family. Understand?"

"Oh, God!" Sigmund said despairingly. "How will I ever get you to realize this is 1962, not 1932! Everything's changed—totally different! Police methods have changed, improved, gotten scientific. Most of the dumb cops you keep talking about are men with a college education today! Even the men in the same—business—you were in, have changed. The successful ones are sleek, prosperous businessmen who run a corporation, not a racket! They think of a submachine gun as something that belongs in a museum."

He swung around toward his father, his sallow face flushed with emotion. "Why won't you even try to see what I keep telling you? What happened when they let you out six weeks back? Did they keep your brains still locked away on Alcatraz?"

Parson grunted like he was in pain, then jumped up from the couch, swinging his right arm in an upward arc as he came so that the back of his hand made an explosive sound as it smashed into Sigmund's face with brutal force.

Then for a timeless moment they just stood immobile, staring at each other. Finally, Sigmund took out a white handkerchief and dabbed slowly at the blood trickling from his bruised lips.

"I didn't mean—" Parson's head started to shake uncontrollably. "I—just lost my temper, that's all—son."

"In a way I'm glad you did," Sigmund said in a dispassionate, remote voice. "It freed me from any further self-imposed obligations toward you."

"Huh?" His father looked at him in blank bewilderment.

"It means that I don't have to feel responsible for you anymore," the son said coldly. "I can return to my normal life in Los Angeles without suffering any pangs of guilt." His jaw hardened for a moment. "Do you wish to hit me again before I go?"

"Sigmund, son!" Parson croaked. "Look, it was just one of those things, it don't mean nothing. So I got mad at you, is all. We forget it, have a drink—"

"Goodbye, Father." Sigmund turned away from him and walked toward the door. "Good day, Lieutenant."

"Good day, Mr. Jones," I said respectfully.

For maybe thirty seconds after the door closed behind his son, Parson just stood there and looked at it with a blank face. Then, as if he'd waited for a time fuse to burn down, he exploded. He looked around wildly for a moment until his eyes focused on the open cellaret, then he lurched across the floor toward it.

"You lousy sonofabitch!" he screamed, and hurled an unopened bottle of Scotch toward the closed door. "You garbage!" As the first bottle fragmented under the impact as it hit the door, a second was already on the way.

He kept up an unceasing tirade of obscenities until there was nothing left to throw—the cellaret was empty—then he stumbled back across the room and collapsed onto the couch.

"Did they keep my brains locked up on the Rock when they let me loose, he says," Parson mumbled "The filth! In the old days I had an empire—you hear me good, cop!—an empire! And when they dreamed up that tax-evasion rap and hung it on Capone, I knew it was the finish for me, too."

There was a momentary pause while he clumsily wiped his mouth with the back of his hand. "The booze, the bookies, the protection, the babes—I knew I couldn't hold onto any of 'em, but I had a couple of legit deals going for me. What time I had left I worked day and night to be goddamned sure they'd keep going when I wasn't around anymore. That way, I figured I could sleep nights on the Rock knowing my wife and my kid were okay."

He toweled the sweat from his face with the palms of his hands, then wiped them down the front of silk robe.

"I made real sure the both of 'em disappeared out of sight before the trial started, so none of the dirt could rub off on them. I figured at worst I'd get a three-to-ten, and they kissed me off with thirty— straight! The first couple of years on the Rock my wife would come out and see me once a month—I wouldn't let her bring the kid. Then her visits got less and less, until one day I figured she just wasn't coming anymore. I was so goddamned right, but I didn't hear until maybe three months later that she'd dumped the kid with an aunt of hers and skipped town with some lousy piano player from a crummy beer parlor.

"So all I got left then was the kid, you understand? The aunt used to write me regular, once a month, and tell me how he was making out all the way through school, then college. For maybe twenty years, that kid was my whole life!"

His mouth worked formlessly for a short time, until the words came again with a jarring abruptness.

"You saw what happened just now, cop?" he said in a lifeless voice. "I give my whole life to the kid and what happens? Once—for the first time when he's thirty-two years old already—I give him the back of my hand for getting out of line. And he walks out on me. Me—his old man!"

He came up onto his feet again, and this time his whole body was shaking, along with his head. "You say it, cop," he shouted in my face. "My son is a dirty fink!"

"Maybe he's a man, Parson," I said slowly. "If you understand the meaning of the word?"

I rode the elevator back down to the Starlight's lobby, and was almost to the front entrance when I saw a familiar, bespectacled face hovering over an egghead magazine. So I changed direction and walked over to where Sigmund Jones was sitting comfortably in a corner alcove.

"Hello, Lieutenant." He smiled briefly. "I have an hour to kill before my plane leaves for L.A.—and I hate waiting around airline terminals. How was he, when you left?"

"Are you hoping for a miracle, Mr. Jones?" I queried.

"Not anymore, Lieutenant," he said quietly. "The whole relationship— if it ever existed—is shot now."

"You mind if I ask you a question?"

"It depends on just how personal you get." He smiled again.

"When I described exactly how Eddie Moran was murdered, in graphic detail, Parson blew his stack for a couple of seconds. He mentioned a name, Lindstrom. Does it mean anything to you?"

"It does in Los Angeles," he said slowly. "There, Lindstrom is one of the newer boys in Father's old line of business—a classic example of what I was trying to explain up in the penthouse a little while back. That's all I know of the man."

"Well, thanks anyway," I told him. "I wouldn't even ask you outright if you know for sure that Parson has got a half million in cash stashed away someplace in that house, or its grounds. But we could suppose for a little while?"

"Go right ahead—suppose!" he said.

"In that case he sent Eddie Moran to pick it up for him," I suggested, "and somebody committed cold-blooded murder to stop Eddie getting away with it. That presumes the murderer is also after the money but doesn't know where it's hidden, and for some reason we don't know about, had to kill Moran before he'd found the loot."

"I guess so," Sigmund said in a dubious voice.

"Just stay with it one more time around," I said "Sooner or later, the murderer is going to run out of patience, get tired of watching and waiting for Parson to try and get the money himself. So then he'll go looking for Parson and the murderer will either kill him trying to get the information, or kill him right after he's gotten it. If you see what I mean?"

"Oh, surely, Lieutenant!" he grated. "Either way my father winds up on a slab in the morgue alongside his old buddy, Eddie Moran!"

"Right," I nodded. "So right now I'm wondering if you'd care to add anything further to your statement on Lindstrom?"

He blinked owlishly at me from behind the thick lens of his glasses for a few moments, then shook his head in a wondering gesture.

"The tricks memory can play on a man, you wouldn't believe it! Now, like a flash, it all comes back to me."

"I'm happy for you, Sigmund," I said gently. "Now give!"

"I just remembered Lindstrom left L.A. three weeks back, and he's been right here in Pine City ever since," he murmured. "He even had a private meeting with my father about four nights back."

"You wouldn't know where I could find him, I guess?" I said in a wistful voice.

"I'm sure the desk clerk here can give you his room number." Sigmund grinned suddenly. "I do distinctly remember it's on the tenth floor."

"Mr. Jones," I told him with respect in my voice, "you are one of the best finks I have ever had the pleasure to meet."

"Thank you," he said doubtfully. "What is a fink?"

"If you ever get around to speaking to your father again," I said, back-pedaling fast, "Why don't you ask him? I think he considers himself to be an expert on the subject."

Chapter Five

It was a beautiful, lazy afternoon when I left my apartment and dumped an overnight bag on the Healey's other seat, then pointed its nose in the direction of the house currently owned by Pop Livvy. I took it real easy because I wanted to enjoy the afternoon and think at the same time, if that was possible.

Lindstrom, I decided right after lunch, could wait. He had no way of knowing I'd been tipped off about him, and to visit with him was the one sure way to destroy any tactical advantage I had at the moment. So I'd driven back to the apartment instead, called Pop Livvy, and asked would it be okay with him if I slept out at his house for a couple nights just in case of any more trouble. He said that would be just dandy, so I packed my bag.

The only minor remaining problem was that I hadn't bothered to let the County Sheriff know what I was doing yet—mainly because he'd presume I had some logical reasoning behind it and he'd want me to explain it, which would be downright embarrassing. So for the rest of the drive I concentrated on figuring some reasonable motivation for what I was doing. Thirty minutes later I finally quit. If things got that tough I could always plead insanity, and take my chances with some pointy-eared analyst who sincerely believed he could interpret my whole sex life from my reactions to a few itsy-bitsy ink blots.

It was the first time I'd seen the house in daylight, and Lavers' description of the architecture as "Bootleg Baronial" started to make a lot of sense. I shepherded the Healey over the corrugated ruts at the open front gates, and studied the house again with a fascination that steadily increased as I came closer and closer to it.

Outside as well as in, the house was a fantasy, an absolute in vulgarity, a total triumph of bad taste, a monstrosity—it really defied description, because anything you called it would be at least partially true. It looked like the probable result of a Hollywood magnate commissioning Orson Welles to design and build a Moorish castle, regardless of expense, for a mammoth production of *Othello*; then after it was finished, the magnate decided to film an updated, surrealistic version of *Saint Joan* instead, and gave Salvador Dali a completely free hand in redesigning.

I left my car out front and toted my bag up onto the front porch. The front door was wide open the same way it was the previous night, and I wondered if they ever bothered closing it. Once inside the vast hallway, I tiptoed nervously, ready to drop the bag and run like crazy at the first faint sound of a jungle mating call.

I stuck my head cautiously through the beaded curtain and peeked into the living room—just in time to see a flash of scarlet disappear over the back of a couch, followed almost immediately by panic-stricken cry of anguish. Like a real brave lieutenant, I leaped into the room, dragging the thirty-eight from my belt holster as I went. It seemed like good strategy to approach the couch in a wide, swinging arc, just in case the murderer was all ready and waiting with another snub-nosed bullet especially made for me.

When I finally gained a vantage point that gave me a clear, unobstructed view of the back of the couch it was strictly anti-climax. No killer, no nothing, only a jumbo-sized scarlet ball—the kind of jazz they toss around on Muscle Beach once they're sure someone is watching. I holstered my gun in disgust and turned back toward the curtained door when that damned ball whimpered at me.

"Help!" it whimpered pitifully. "I'm stuck!"

So what the hell, I thought bitterly? If I've flipped my trolley already, what's to hurt by taking a close-up look? On closer inspection, the ball had a remarkable resemblance to Celeste Campbell, except for the inescapable fact that no human body could withstand that kind of treatment. I got real close, maybe six inches or less, and had to admit the nearest curve of the ball was an almost replica of Celeste's proud arched rump. I patted it fondly, and the ball gave a kind of spasmodic twitch causing it to roll a little closer still.

That was the clincher—it was strictly a ball. Girls have legs attached to one end of their rumps, and backs attached to the other. Whoever met a dame with a mouth and two staring eyes situated four inches above her rump, at most? There was a simple, logical explanation—I was having a nightmare in the daytime while I was wide awake. The kind of thing that can happen to anybody, and was nothing to worry about. Then, almost on cue, the mouth opened wide while the eyes riveted me with a baleful stare.

"This is no time for a bottom-patting routine," a murderous voice hissed at me. "Can't you see I'm stuck, you—you lecherous lieutenant!"

"I hear it but I'm not about to listen," I said determinedly. "Go away, you figment of my torrid imagination!"

"It's Celeste Campbell, you cross-eyed cretin!" The voice nearly choked on its own fury, "I was practicing a new exercise on top of the couch and overbalanced. For Heaven's sake get me unscrambled! I can feel my bones bending, even!"

"Sure thing, Celeste," I told her happily. "Where do I start?"

"Any place, you idiot!"

"Okay, here we go," I said, and plunged into the fray.

"*Aaah!*" She gave a sudden, piercing scream. "*Not* there, you revolting—"

"I'm sorry, Celeste," I said. "But from where I am, it all looks the same."

"Well, try some other place!" she snapped.

On the second plunge I managed to get a firm grip on a forearm, and gave it a determined tug. It was like one of those intricate metal puzzles where one tiny piece is the whole key to the solution. As I tugged, Celeste gave another of those unnerving screams, then suddenly unraveled back into a normal-sized girl.

"How about that?" I said, feeling childishly pleased at my success.

She sat up slowly, rubbing her arms with tender solicitude for all those bent bones slowly straightening back into shape, and glared at me. "Why couldn't you do that the first time?" she stormed. "That was a real mean trick you pulled on a defenseless girl, you dirty-minded detective!"

"Okay, if that's the thanks I get for saving your life!" I got up onto my feet, with an injured look on my face and stalked toward the beaded curtain.

"Hey!"

"What?" I snarled, without bothering to look back at her.

"What's your first name?"

"Al."

"Okay, Al," she said, her voice a shade warmer "You can call me Celeste. I don't see why not—I have practically no secrets left."

"Hey!" I stopped dead, momentarily transfixed by the obvious truth of what she had just said. Then I spun around and started back toward her at a loping gallop.

"Take that gleam out of your eye, Al!" she said tartly. "Right now I'm in enough trouble with these aching bones, already!"

"Maybe I can find some liniment around the house?" I suggested, my voice both hopeful and enthusiastic at the same time.

"You think I'm a horse or something?" She shook her head firmly. "Just go someplace else for a while, Al, please? I'll issue regular bulletins on the aching bones situation, I promise."

"All right," I reluctantly agreed. "But promise you won't do any more contorting for a while, huh?"

"Don't worry!" She massaged her thighs gently. "I'm about to become an exotic dancer anytime now!"

I pushed my way through the beaded curtain back into the front hall, just as Pop Livvy walked into the house.

"Welcome, Lieutenant." His faded blue eyes smiled warmly at me. "I saw your little sports car parked outside and came right back. Let me show you to your room." He picked up my bag and started off down the hallway at a rapid pace. I had to almost run to catch up with him.

My room was the fifth door down from the living room, and I counted it twice to make sure, figuring a sure way to suffer a fate far more painful than death would be to walk into the female Tarzan's room by mistake.

Pop dumped my bag on the comfortable-looking bed, then smiled at me again. "I guess why you're here is your own business, Lieutenant," he said easily. "But while you are here, I'll give you the house rules. Any time you hear someone beating the hell out of an iron pot with the aid of an iron spoon, you start running toward the dining room because it means somebody's prepared a meal. We mostly eat regular meals, so don't get worried! The bar's reasonably well-stocked, so make yourself a drink whenever you feel so inclined."

"Sounds great," I told him. "Thanks a lot, Pop."

"Oh, yes." He shook his head slowly. "I almost forgot the most important house rule—it's really the only one we stick with all the time. Everybody can do exactly as they please in the house, whenever they please. There's just one thing that nobody's allowed to do— complain about another guest."

"I'm real glad to hear that," I told him. "Now I can relax and be my usual obnoxious self."

From somewhere right in back of me came a sudden blood-curdling cry of the jungle that froze the marrow in my bones. With a supreme effort of will I managed to turn my head, just in time to see the room shrink to midget proportions as a raging giantess towered over me.

"Hi, Antonia!" I said in a falsetto squeak. "Been running in the trees again, huh?"

She wore a different outfit from the one I'd seen before, I quickly realized. A tiger-skin bikini bra and pants—I guessed she'd peeled it off a passing tiger one day in the jungle while she was out, still chasing Tarzan. On the very slim chick, I always figure a bikini looks real cute. With Antonia the Great's vital statistics, the result was terrifying. I'd never seen so many square yards of healthy female flesh at the one time before.

"Where is he?" Her eyes flashed dangerously as she bent her head to look into my face. "What have you done with him—my little dumpling?"

I could feel my eardrums start to buckle with the impact of that vibrant bass voice at close range. "You mean Polnik?" I gurgled.

"Who else?" she asked passionately. "My own beloved ape man!"

She punctuated that with a deep, lusting sigh, then had to replenish her air supply, so threw back her head and inhaled deeply. Right then, I knew exactly how it felt to be trapped by an avalanche. I watched helplessly as the twin, snowy-white mountains advanced toward me at remorseless speed. Right in back of me was the wall, so I had no place else to go—trapped and alone—without even a St. Bernard to do the bartending yet!

At the impact I thought I detected a definite yielding sensation from the opposing forces, and foolishly thought the worst was already over. Then Antonia gulped another fifteen cubic feet of air into her lungs, and the mountainous peaks surged forward again with overwhelming force. The avalanche hit me high in the chest and—in a moment of incredulous disbelief—I felt my feet leave the floor. The next moment my back slammed hard against the wall and there I was—pinned helplessly like a bug in some screwball's private collection. My brain reeled under the sudden horrific thought that maybe this was exactly what had happened. It was possible—probable, even—that Antonia did have her very own private collection, only she pinned men into her scrapbook, not bugs.

"Antonia, dear," I heard Pop's voice a thousand miles away. "I think you're crowding the Lieutenant, just a little?"

"But he has not told me what he has done with my little dumpling?" she argued heatedly.

"I think that's mostly because he can't breathe at the moment," Pop explained. "Back off a little, dear, and I'm sure he'll tell you."

The next moment I was plunged into free fall. My heels thudded painfully back onto the floor, and my pectoral muscles offered a heartfelt vote of thanks to the warden for the last-second reprieve.

"The Sergeant is home sick," I said huskily. "Bruised ribs, but it's his old lady's bruised ego, mostly, I guess. He should be back on the job tomorrow, Antonia-uh-the Great."

"Poor little fellow," she crooned. "Tomorrow I shall carry him in my arms over the mountain to the farm in the valley on the other side. He can sit in the shade and rest—and watch while I wrestle the bull."

"Polnik will flip at the whole idea," I gurgled. "And when you're carrying him down the mountainside, let him swing though the trees for a while, would you? He'll *love* it!"

"It will be a whole day of love for my little dumpling," she said in an ardent voice. "Tell him to be early!" Then she stepped out into the hallway, and the room suddenly expanded back to its normal size.

I staggered over to the bed and sat down heavily on it. I fumbled a cigarette from the pack and was about to strike a match, when someone fired six heavy-caliber shots into the soles of my feet. Cape Canaveral never had it so good—no preparation, no countdown, not even a launching pad. I just went straight up into the air. On the return, the free fall was just fine, only I hit the edge of the bed, instead of the center, and wound up on the floor with what felt like a completely remolded spine.

Pop Livvy coughed apologetically. "It's just Sebastian sharpshooting in the basement," he murmured. "You'll get used to it in no time, Lieutenant."

I hauled myself painfully off the floor, then carefully lowered my new-model backbone onto the bed. "Pop," I said bleakly. "You mind if I ask you a straight question?"

"Go right ahead," he said. "Asking straight questions is your business, isn't it?"

"What kind of a place is this you're running here?" The plaintive note in my voice sounded kind of over-done, even to my own ears.

He chuckled softly. "I guess when you first walk into it, you must figure it's some special kind of nut house! Well, if you got the time to listen, Lieutenant, I got the time to tell you the story."

"You go ahead," I told him, and managed to light a cigarette without being clobbered by another major calamity.

Pop Livvy perched comfortably on the end of the bed, looked at me for a few seconds, then clean through me. I saw the warm, nostalgic glow make his eyes glisten as he started to speak.

"It all seems to have started such a long time ago, now," he almost whispered. "When my world was young and if anyone had called me 'Pop' in those days, I'd have figured it was because I never looked anywhere near my rightful age. I was a hoofer in those days, working the straw-hat circuit, loaded with ambition and maybe a little talent to match it.

"I won't bore you with the detail, Lieutenant. One day I met the new singer who'd just joined the company, and she was the most beautiful girl in the whole world. I fell in love with her that first moment I saw her, and it never changed. Gwen Lysander—with large dark eyes, and her soft black hair floating like a cloud around her head. I guess it was a kind of mutual feeling—in no time at all we were engaged and that was wonderful. But after a while we got nervous about our future, our marriage. Vaudeville was the only life we knew, and we didn't want to change it. Then Gwen had a brilliant idea. I was a dancer, she was a singer—so she'd teach me to sing, and I could teach her to dance."

Pop smiled softly. "The crazy thing was, it worked. Six months later we were a professional song-and-dance team. Livvy and Lysander. And I shouldn't say it, but we were good, the best. Another year and we played the Palace and made a big hit. After that we couldn't look back.

We'd been married almost two years when we had this wonderful offer to go to London, England. It was another dream come true and we grabbed it—there was even talk of a Command Performance where we might top the bill!

"A couple of weeks before we were due to sail, Gwen had word her mother was dangerously ill, and naturally she wanted to go to her right away. Gwen's hometown was in the Midwest, a long way out of New York, and there was still a lot to be done before we could leave for London. So we decided she should go to her mother while I stayed in Manhattan and cleaned things up there."

The warm nostalgic glow suddenly vanished from his eyes, like someone had snapped a switch. "There was a train wreck and Gwen was killed in it. The ironic part was, I found out later, her mother had died six hours before the wreck.

"Without Gwen, nothing mattered anymore to me. They wanted me to get a new partner, but I could never have danced with anyone else— or harmonized, either. Money was no problem, I had plenty, so I just kind of drifted for a while. South to Miami, then New Orleans, through Texas, and finally I wound up on the West Coast. I liked it a little better than most other places, because it didn't have any painful memories. So I stuck around, not doing anything much."

"This must have been around the time they were closing the net on Parson Jones?" I said, more for something to say than anything else.

"I guess it was," Pop said, nodding. "One day some friends of mine took me out in their brand-spanking new automobile, and we came right by this house. They stopped and pointed it out to me as the crazy castle a bootlegger built, and now he was on trial for tax evasion and the house was on the market for a ridiculously low price, but how could anyone find a use for something as absurd as that?

"The more scornful they got, the more annoyed I got, for some reason I didn't fully understand. There had to be a good use for any house, I kept telling myself, more so for one this size. Then suddenly I knew exactly how it could be used. I bought it the next day, moved in three weeks later. Bought everything along with it, the furnishings—the lot. I was going to make it a home—a real home—for vaudevillians. For the use of all our friends, the people who'd been so kind to us through the years. They could use it exactly as they pleased, come and go as they liked. It was somewhere to go if they'd been sick and needed a rest—if they had a new act they wanted to rehearse—if their luck had run out lately and they couldn't find the rent."

Pop stopped talking for a few seconds, then looked up at me shyly. "In my own mind, I dedicated it to the memory of Gwen Lysander. I knew she would have thought it was a wonderful idea, and it was the best thing for me, too. Never lonely, still a part of the business even though I'll never make another public appearance.

"Times change, of course, and the people change with it. Vaudeville died, but show business went right on. I'd always get a percentage of misfits and screwballs, but they never worried me and I never worried them. Right now I've got the four of them, as you know, Lieutenant. Celeste is going to be a big talent when she gets over this ridiculous contortionist routine—"

"I have a feeling that may be quicker than you think, Pop," I said smugly.

"—The other three will always be with me," he went on. "I'm glad of it because if it wasn't for them I'd be a lonely old man. And if it wasn't for the house, how would they survive? Can you imagine Antonia working in a supermarket? Or Sebastian running a shooting gallery? Bruno making anyone laugh with those dreadful jokes of his?"

"It was a wonderful idea, Pop," I said sincerely. "How long is it now since you first started here?"

"Thirty years." He smiled to himself. "Half a lifetime for me, and more than a lifetime for Gwen."

"Thirty years," I repeated. "Pop—what have you been using for money all this time?"

"What?"

"How have you managed to survive all this time?"

"It hasn't been a problem." He shrugged. "I told you I had plenty of money after Gwen died."

"But that was 1932!"

"Well,"—a trace of irritation sounded in his voice—"I made some lucky investments—and a lot of our guests paid their own way, you know? Even now, I only have one non-paying guest out of the four. So, you see, Lieutenant, with a little luck you don't need that much money to keep going!"

"That's what the County tells me every year," I grunted. "Thanks a lot for telling me the story, Pop. It's one of the nicest I've heard in a long time."

"You'd better go get yourself a drink, Lieutenant," he said. "You must be dry, just listening to me talk all that time—and I only made it all up as I went along, for your benefit, anyway!"

"My parents saw you once at the Palace, on the only trip they ever did manage back East," I told him. "They figured Livvy and Lysander were the greatest!"

"You're lying, Lieutenant," he said with a smile. "But I appreciate your motives."

"You go around usurping a cop's prerogatives, Pop Livvy, and you'll be in big trouble," I threatened him. "It's not an exciting job most of the time, and the pay is lousy, but it does give you certain privileges—and those privileges are jealously guarded by every cop in the whole country. So don't ever tell me I'm lying again, you hear?"

"Sure, Lieutenant, I hear!" He got up from the bed and walked across the room, grinning to himself. I let him get almost out the door before I pulled the clincher.

"The week they saw you," I said in a real casual voice, "you introduced a new song that had been especially written for Livvy and Lysander. What was the name of it again—'Never Laugh At Love'?—They gave you a standing ovation when it was over, my mother told me."

He blinked a couple of times, then tried to apologize for not believing me in the first place; underneath he was real pleased, and he went down the hallway whistling the tune under his breath. The big nostalgic thing we'd had going in my room lasted another three whole seconds, then was painlessly dispatched by the nut under my feet resuming his sharpshooting practice with what sounded like fifteen rounds of rapid fire.

Chapter Six

At first glance, the basement looked like the main workroom of Murder, Incorporated. The ceiling, and the four walls, looked as if they had been constructed from bullet holes, barely held together by thin wisps of plaster. Tin cans were strewn everywhere, on tables, benches, underfoot; a gun rack on the far wall bristled with a startling variety of small arms, including a couple I had never even seen before.

Sebastian himself had been transformed from the Man-of-Mystery, elegant in his white tie and tails and flamboyant scarlet-lined cloak, into a Man-of-Action, even more romantic in his white silk shirt and polished cotton pants. If the great illusionist was the suave playboy sophisticate, he'd look pretty damned stupid stalking big game in his boiled shirt and scarlet-lined cloak. Whereas the great sharpshooter looked just right for the jungle, and also as if he might be one of the cherished few who could knot a shoelace around the collar of his white shirt, and have the maître d's bow him out of their most exclusive establishment throughout the capital cities of the world.

During the first five minutes I'd been in the basement, I was so busy measuring up the Jekyll and Hyde of Sebastian's character, that I hadn't heard a word he'd said. Now that I had it I figured out that Hyde (the sharpshooter) had it all over the opposite side of his nature, I could relax.

"—So all my life I seek perfection, Lieutenant," Sebastian said, like he'd just finished a passionate declaration of faith. "And now—after I have given you reasons—I hope you understand my feelings?"

"Perfectly!" I pursed my lips and nodded my head slowly in measured approval.

"That is why I can never perform in public," he went on. "To cheat my public, who trusts me, by anything less than perfection would be nothing less than barefaced fraud! You agree, Lieutenant?"

"Oh, sure," I said hastily. "As a matter of interest, when was the last time you did perform in public, Sebastian?"

"In 1947," he said. "It was a bad mistake."

"What happened?"

"A stupid accident." His white teeth flashed in a satanic snarl. "At the beginning of each performance I would invite three men onto the stage, give them each a cigar, then later stand them in line ready for the climax of my whole act!"

He stroked his pointed beard fondly. "I would stand with my back toward them, fire over my shoulder with only a pocket mirror to help my aim, and shoot the burning cigars from their mouths—One! Two! Three!—like that! Always to hysterical cries from the ladies in the audience, and then, a few seconds later, the tumultuous applause at the successful conclusion."

He snarled again, and the white teeth flashed with an even greater ferocity as he tugged cruelly on his beard.

"This one night," he said in a low, intense voice, "there was a big, fat man with buck teeth in the audience. You do not get too many like that and the audience loves to see them onstage—so many deluded idiots still believe that because a man is fat he must automatically be good-natured and jolly. Give him buck teeth, and they're convinced the greatest joy in his life is to be exhibited publicly so everyone may have the privilege of laughing hysterically at the face and figure he has to live with for the rest of his life!"

"You're absolutely right," I said quickly. "But, what happened?"

He brooded over the memory for a while before he could bring himself to speak again. "So this fat man was one of the three who came onstage to be my assistants. I handed them each a cigar and lit it for them, then of course became immersed in my act. When the time came to line them up for my grand finale, I never had time to look at them closely. It was my one tragic mistake. I learned later that it was the first cigar the fat man had ever smoked in his whole life, and he held it between those hateful, protruding teeth the whole time, puffing incessantly without rest."

Sebastian shuddered faintly. "It still haunts me, the memory of it!

You must understand, with my back turned toward them and using only a pocket mirror, my view was terribly restricted. I had made it a habit to line up the gun sight with the glowing end of each cigar, safe in the sure knowledge that the long cigars I was always careful to hand out would still be four inches in length as an absolute minimum. This, of course, gave me a safety margin. It seemed no different that night—One! Two!—Three!

"I turned, ready to acknowledge the usual tumultuous applause and instead was greeted by a screaming mob who swore I'd deliberately murdered the fat imbecile, and were not only willing but eager to lynch me on the spot."

He declined my offer of a cigarette with a miserable shake of his head, so I lit one for myself.

"If it's not an indelicate question," I said carefully, "had you killed the fat man?"

Sebastian snorted in outraged fury. "The fool had smoked the cigar down to a butt, precisely five-eighths of an inch long—I had the chance to measure it sometime later that night. The buck teeth protruded outward, obviously. This gave me an extra safety margin of a quarter-inch, at most. The bullet hit him squarely in the teeth, and apparently people in the twelfth row, even, were sprayed by fine fragmented particles. That was what caused the riot—after that, they were naturally convinced I'd killed the man!"

"So, other than losing his teeth, the guy wasn't hurt at all?" I queried.

The wry twist to Sebastian's mouth, acknowledged the grim jests of fate. "He claimed damages from me later. I can still recall the document he presented me with, word for word." He closed his eyes tight shut, then began to recite slowly: "'In full settlement for damages inflicted on me by Sebastian, The Deadly Marksman, during night of April 17, 1947. One full set of teeth: four dollars and fifty cents. Said teeth bought off Swickey's General Store on March 20, 1947, receipt attached.'"

"And you've never performed in public since that night?" I queried.

"Never!" he snarled. "And never will, until I achieve the absolute perfection I seek."

"How's the absolute perfection coming along right now?"

His face brightened immediately. "Would you care to see a demonstration, Lieutenant?"

"Fine," I told him.

Sebastian bounced onto his feet and went about setting up the tin cans in a burst of furious energy that made me tired just watching him. By the time he was through, the basement looked like the canned goods section of a supermarket. I had a nasty feeling I was going to be sitting there all night, waiting for him to shoot the last can back onto the floor again.

He walked leisurely across to the gun rack, selected a long-barreled thirty-two, checked it carefully, then walked back to where I was sitting and bowed gracefully. "Lieutenant!"

"I consider it an honor to be given a personal demonstration by the greatest marksman in the world!" I told him, not to be outdone in the courtesy bit. Then I settled back to watch, grimly determined not to move a muscle of my face even if he didn't hit a single can he aimed at.

Then for the next thirty minutes I sat all by myself and watched a virtuoso display of gunmanship that I guessed could be matched by only two other men in the whole country. Sebastian did about everything that could be done with trick shooting, except have the slug return back into the barrel it had just been fired from, maybe. He fired from every conceivable position—over his shoulder, through his legs, flat on his back with the target directly behind his head—and finally over his shoulder again but without using a mirror this time, and blindfolded.

I spent maybe five minutes congratulating him and he lapped up each and every word like he'd been starving for the last fifteen years, and, in a way, I guessed he had.

"You are a magnificent audience, Lieutenant," he said finally. "It has been a delight to perform for you."

"You put on a magnificent show, Sebastian," I told him, "and I'm grateful." Then, because I knew we could start the whole routine all over again if I didn't watch it, I asked the first question that came into my mind.

"What's the hardest trick shot in the world?"

"Ah!" There was a brief, satanic flash of teeth, then he fondled his beard again and smiled knowingly at me. "What is your opinion, Lieutenant?"

I thought about it for a while. "Catching a bullet in your teeth, I guess."

"So?" His grin widened.

"Or is that always faked—sleight-of-hand—that kind of jazz?" I asked.

"It is very often faked, Lieutenant," he said seriously. "But it can be done, though there are not many who can do it." He paused for the effect. "When it is genuinely performed, it is the second hardest trick shot in the world!"

"So what's the hardest, then?" I obligingly fed him the line.

Right then he went straight into his Jekyll-Hyde routine, and emerged as the Man Of Mystery again.

"I'm afraid that must remain my secret for the time being, Lieutenant," he said in a suave voice. "Remember what I told you about my search for absolute perfection—therein lies your answer!" After that he simply clammed up on the subject.

We went from the basement to the monstrosity of a bar in the living room and settled in for a couple of pre-dinner drinks.

"When you—uh—retired in '47," I said, "was that when you came here?"

"Yes," he said. "The first time."

"And you've been here ever since?"

"From time to time." He looked bored with the conversation. "It is bad for a man not to get away from his work at least occasionally, Lieutenant. I find the constant striving for perfection becomes exhausting if you stay at it too long over a period of time."

"Pop Livvy's setup here fascinates me," I murmured. "How about Bruno Breck? Is he here permanently?"

"Like me, only from time to time, but we always come back to Pop. He's like a brother—better, maybe."

"Antonia comes and goes, too?"

Sebastian shook his head softly. "Antonia is always here. So much better for her—the world outside can be bitterly cruel to one like her. She has only her great strength, you understand, Lieutenant? And that is not enough to survive in the harsh realities of a predatory world."

"I guess you're right," I agreed. "That only leaves Celeste."

"She has only been here three months," he said shortly. "It is her first visit, I don't think she will stay much longer—youth is too impatient!"

"You're right," I told him for around the fiftieth time in the last hour or so. "Where do you like to go when you relax and leave this house for a while?"

He shrugged with the weary nuance of the international playboy who finds the whole world boring because he moves around it with the same people who bore him to death back home.

"I like Rio," he grudgingly admitted. "Paris can be fun if you don't stay there too long at a time. Tahiti was fun until they commercialized it—another ten years and it will be a second Honolulu!" He gave a well-bred shudder at the thought.

A sudden sharp cackle of malicious laughter made us turn around. Bruno Breck was standing just behind us, his muddy eyes darting sharp, expectant glances at both of us in turn. Somehow he looked even more like a lizard tonight, and I would have sworn that was impossible the first time I saw him.

"Getting some inside tips from the international traveler, Lieutenant?" Bruno sniggered. "You've come to the right man, that's for sure. Sebastian's been about every place you can go, haven't you, Sebastian?"

Something had happened to the playboy sophisticate; I realized he'd suddenly vanished. Neither the Man of Mystery nor the sharpshooter had replaced him either. This was a brand-new character sitting beside me, wearing the same old mustache and beard, but I just didn't know who the hell he was. His fingers trembled slightly as he raised his glass to his lips—maybe that was a clue?

"I hate to spoil anybody's fun, Lieutenant"—Bruno's shrill venom sank straight between my shoulder blades "—but I've been listening to him talk for some little time now, and I think there's a limit—don't you agree?"

"Does it make any difference?" I grunted sourly.

"Why of course it does, Lieutenant! You are our guest here tonight and I feel a personal responsibility toward you—we all do! That's why I think Sebastian went just a little too far, why I just had to force myself into your conversation."

"He is right," the stranger beside me said in a hoarse, nervous voice. "I let myself get carried away!"

"Maybe you'll all get lucky and the same thing'll happen to Bruno one of these nights," I grated.

"Hey, Lieutenant!" The high-pitched, synthetic laugh grated on my ears. "You're being naughty, but I don't mind. Have you ever been to Paris, Sebastian?"

"No!" The guy next to me whispered.

"Tahiti—Honolulu—any of those places?"

"No!"

"When you take a vacation from all of us here in Pop Livvy's house, where do you go?"

"San Diego, mostly. Los Angeles a couple of times." The hoarse whisper beside me had a frightening undercurrent of tension hovering around the breaking point.

"Well, that's a whole lot better, Sebastian!" Bruno cackled. "From the way you were shooting off your mouth there, the Lieutenant could mistake us for a bunch of millionaires!"

"Excuse me." I put my glass down onto the bar top. "I have to take care of a couple of things." I turned deliberately toward the mute figure huddled over the glass in front of it.

"Thanks again, Sebastian," I said, "for that magnificent display of trick shooting I was privileged to watch down in the basement!"

"What!" He turned his head quickly toward me, and for a fleeting moment there was something close to terror showing in his eyes. Then he laughed weakly: "Oh—that? Shooting up a few old tin cans is nothing special, Lieutenant."

"Now you're being too modest, Sebastian!" Bruno chirped. "The

Lieutenant was obviously impressed, and he's a man who knows something about guns."

"I tell you it was nothing!" Sebastian drained his glass then pushed past me brusquely, and almost ran from the living room.

Bruno giggled delightedly. "Lieutenant, you think it could have been something I said?"

"I still have those couple of things to look after," I said in a frigid voice. I was about to walk past him, then suddenly changed my mind. "As a matter of interest, Bruno, where do you spend your vacations away from Pop Livvy's house?"

"I haven't had any vacation from this house in more time than I can remember, Lieutenant," he said easily.

"I guess, since you were so generous with your advice to Sebastian," I suggested gently, "you wouldn't object to a word of advice from me?"

"Lieutenant—" he giggled, "—I'd be delighted!"

"An expert liar is always striving for the appearance of truth and honesty," I told him, with a real sincere smile on my face. "So all the time he's lying, he carefully uses the hesitations, the averted glance, the occasional mumble, the awkward silences, that all honest people unfailingly use when they're telling the absolute truth. You're just a little too smooth—there's a fraction too much high gloss—and that's why you aren't an expert liar yet."

I patted his bony shoulder consolingly. "But I'm sure you'll improve real fast with practice, Bruno, and that's one thing you're getting plenty of so far tonight—right?"

For a split second I had the rare experience of looking into a man's eyes and seeing a true reflection of what went on inside his mind. The cold ferocity of his hate hit me with almost a physical force; then, the next split second, it had vanished and his eyes were their usual muddy color.

"You're being very naughty tonight, Lieutenant!" Bruno gave a shrill cackle of delight. "I bet whenever you arrest some nobody for a minor misdemeanor, you always walk them down an alley first before you take them back to the Sheriff's office, right?"

All hell broke loose before I had time to answer, and it took around twenty seconds before I identified the frantic noise as the sound of an iron spoon being beaten against an iron pot. I only discovered it was Antonia beating the dinner gong when I arrived in the dining room. I should have guessed, of course; to a girl who could lift me bodily off my feet by just taking a deep breath, caving in my eardrums would be mere child's play.

Chapter Seven

I sat in solitary splendor at the jumbo-sized bar in the living room and sipped my drink sparingly while I tried hard to avoid seeing my own reflection in the amber-tinted glass on the far side. My watch said it was a couple of minutes after eleven, and the whole house was deathly silent. Now, I found myself almost hoping Sebastian would let off fifteen rounds of rapid firing under my feet—even a mating call straight out Darkest Africa would have been acceptable.

A cigarette meant brief activity, I reflected as I lit a fresh one, but it did nothing to break the monotony. After dinner, the whole household seemed to just disintegrate. Celeste had left the table and gone straight to her room; Antonia had gotten busy with the dishes in the kitchen; Bruno had pleaded a headache, and Sebastian hadn't even showed up for the meal.

The faint jingling sound as someone brushed through the beaded curtain made me sneak a look at the amber-tinted glass. Pop Livvy's faintly distorted reflection slowly grew bigger as he walked across the room toward me.

"Thought I'd join you for a nightcap," he said pleasantly.

"Fine," I told him.

"We don't seem to have entertained you too well tonight." He busied himself making a drink. "It's unusual in this house—most nights there's always someone doing something into the early hours of the morning."

"Maybe they're tired," I suggested. "It was a rough night last night."

"I'd almost forgotten that," Pop admitted. "You wouldn't think it possible, would you? That a man could forget finding a corpse only twenty-four hours back!"

"It all belongs inside the mind, I guess?" I wondered, vaguely. "Some kind of a safety mechanism. If a memory looks too disturbing emotionally, then the mechanism automatically seals it off, no matter how recent it might be?"

"It sounds real impressive," Pop said in an admiring tone. "So that explains how I'd forgotten about it so quickly—the memory was still too emotionally disturbing?"

"I guess," I said. "And you only found the body. Imagine the potential dynamite in a murderer's memory of the act!"

"I can only say I'm glad I'm not the murderer," he said, then cleared his throat resolutely. "Lieutenant, you mind if I ask you a straight question?"

"Go ahead."

"Why are you here, truthfully? It's a pleasure to have you as my guest, of course. But why, officially, are you here?"

"It's a good question, Pop," I said. "The answer is maybe a little confusing. I'm not here officially in the sense the County Sheriff gave me an order to come. But I'm in charge of the murder investigation, so even though it was my own idea it's still more or less official."

"I see what you meant about it all being a little confusing, Lieutenant." He grinned. "Then can I ask why you decided you should spend a few nights here?"

"Eddie Moran was murdered in your garage, Pop." I shrugged. "So the first logical place to look for the murderer is inside this house. I didn't have a chance to even take a quick glance at them last night."

"But now you have the opportunity to get real close to them?" he murmured. "That sounds like good sense to me, Lieutenant."

"Sebastian's been with you, most of the time anyway, since 1947," I said. "How about Bruno?"

"Maybe a year earlier—on and off—much the same as Sebastian."

"Do you know if Bruno's ever actually worked as a comic—professionally, I mean?" I shook my head dubiously. "His jokes worry me. Nobody could be that bad without trying."

"An emcee, professionally, I'm sure about," Pop said, then thought hard for a few moments. "I can't honestly say I'm sure he's ever been employed professionally as a comic."

"How about Antonia? Where did she come from?"

"She's the daughter of a very old friend of mine who died suddenly about three years back." Pop shook his head regretfully. "It won't surprise you to know he was a circus strongman. His wife had died a few years earlier, so Antonia was completely alone. Working with her father in the circus, she'd been protected—circus folk always take care of their own. But with her father gone, she wasn't good enough to hold down a job as a performer—so I brought her back here with me. She's a wonderful cook, she does no real harm, and she has her dream of returning to the circus as a star performer one of these days. I suspect it's not vitally important to her to make it become reality—just so long as she can hold onto the dream."

"I understand," I said. "How about Celeste?"

"She's only been with us two or three months." Pop took time out to taste his drink. "Like I told you this afternoon, once she gets away from this crazy contortionist idea and starts thinking about exotic dancing, nothing will hold her back."

The beaded curtain jingled again and I automatically glanced up into the tinted mirror—and was hooked! A dark-haired, absentminded

Chinese girl was gliding across the room toward us. Chinese, because she wore a beautiful hip-length Mandarin coat of green silk with delicate embroidery woven across the front panels; and absentminded, because she'd apparently forgotten to put on the bottom half of the outfit.

I swung away from the bar so I could appreciate the real-life shapeliness of those tapered legs in preference to their amber-tinted reflection in the mirror. As she came close I had to revise a couple of first impressions. The Mandarin coat was the top half of a pajama outfit, and she hadn't forgotten the bottom half after all. She was wearing a Hong Kong version of a baby doll outfit—which meant she wore a pair of matching briefs under the mandarin coat. But the overall effect was still dynamic.

"I decided I needed a drink." Celeste yawned, and sank onto the bar stool beside me. "As a special privilege, Al, you can make me something nice."

"Like what?"

"Gin and tonic, maybe?"

"Coming right up." I slid off the stool and walked around to the business side of the bar to make her drink.

Pop Livvy winked slowly at me out of an expressionless face, finished his drink, and stood up. "I'm tired," he said vaguely. "See you in the morning. Good night."

"Good night, Pop." Celeste watched him out of the corner of her sloe eyes until he vanished into the hallway. "Pop's a nice guy," she observed. "Tactful, too!"

"Sure is," I agreed, and put the drink down on the bar top in front of her.

"Aren't you coming back around this side?" There was a wicked glint in her eyes. "Or maybe you figure it'll make you too nervous being that close to me when I've got practically nothing on at all?"

"What's to get excited about over a dame with aching bones?" I said calmly.

She lifted her arms over her head and massaged the back of her neck gently with both hands. It was a very feminine, very graceful movement, but it was only indirectly the cause of my sudden, traumatic reaction. The lift of her arms had automatically lifted her bosom at the same time, and the arrogant thrust of those proud curves against the thin green silk was enough to send me almost out of my mind.

"If my bones ache," Celeste gloated, "I'll bet they don't ache half so bad as your eyes right now! Can they come any further without falling out of the sockets, Al?"

"Celeste," I said morosely, "you're nothing but a tease, and it wouldn't worry me except you've got such magnificent equipment for teasing."

She brought her arms down from above her head and I wasn't real sure if I should be glad or sorry.

"I just had a wonderful idea," I told her. "Now's a perfect chance to start in on some of your new exotic dancing routines! For a start, you can just keep taking off your clothes, a different way each time; and in a couple of hours I'll let you know which way, exactly, is the most effective."

"When I have to face up to such open-hearted generosity, I feel ashamed," she murmured. "Have you ever figured out how many alternative methods a girl can choose from when she takes off her clothes—apart from the usual method, I mean?"

It was a fascinating problem in its own right, and I thought real hard about it for a few seconds before I gave up.

Celeste glanced over her shoulder at the silent vastness of the rest of the living room. She shivered slightly. "Al?" she said with little-girl plaintiveness. "Why don't you whiz up a fresh batch of drinks and let's take them someplace else. Two people in this room just isn't enough people!"

"I go along with everything you say," I told her sincerely. "But how the hell do I whiz up a batch of gin and tonics?"

"It doesn't really matter what it is you whiz up," she said indifferently. "I'll drink it."

"There speaks my brave little neo-alcoholic," I growled. "Right now, are you drinking to quench your thirst or for the alcoholic content?"

"The alcohol of course," she said impatiently. "Doesn't everyone?"

I found an empty shaker and made us a sizable bunch of Manhattans—enough to take the chill off a quick-frozen corpse in the Arctic Circle, I figured, if we got through the whole batch. When I started out with the shaker and glasses, Celeste was already almost to the beaded curtain. By the time I caught up with her, I had a great respect for Hong Kong designers. They sure knew what to do about a girl's rump okay—cover it tightly with a thin, green silk and let nature take care of the rest.

Celeste walked down the front hall ahead of me without any hesitation at all, so I figured she knew where she was going and what I should do was concentrate on not getting lost on the way. She opened the third door from the living room, and I fervently hoped it was her own room as I followed her inside—I knew it wasn't mine, for sure. Then I saw the scarlet leotard draped across the back of a chair, and relaxed.

Once I'd set up a temporary bar on top of her bureau and made sure the door was shut securely, I began to feel the party mood kindle a warm glow in my insides.

"Celeste," I told her frankly, "you are a ravishingly beautiful creature who I am crazy about right now. And please, bones—don't ache?"

"You think just because a girl takes off most of her clothes, walks in and interrupts your solitary drinking by giving strict orders for you to pick up an ample supply of alcohol, then takes you straight back to her room—you can try and make something out of it?" she said coldly. "Is that the idea, Wheeler?"

"What else, Campbell?" I asked.

"That's fine," she said easily. "I wouldn't want this pajama outfit to fool you into bringing out your mah-jongg set!"

After the first drink, we figured it was kind of silly to be sitting facing each other on separate chairs the whole time, so we moved over to the bed, where we could sit together.

After the second drink, we figured it was kind of stupid to have to go back to the bureau each time our glasses were empty, so I brought the shaker across to where we sat. By the time we'd finished the third drink we agreed unanimously that even a shaded table lamp can give a blinding intensity of light under certain circumstances, and the only sensible thing to do was switch it off.

When the fourth drink had gone, Celeste did say something about a fifth, but I pointed out to her with clear, concise logic that to achieve it would involve my turning through an arc of 180 degrees, leaning down through an arc of 90 degrees, to find the shaker which was on the floor someplace. And even more than that, it would involve the two of us in a complete rearrangement of various personal items such as arms, legs, and so on. Under the remorseless pressure of my coldly brilliant analysis, Celeste said the hell with the fifth drink! and how come I managed to look normal when I was dressed—like where did I hide those third and fourth hands all the time?

I'm kind of hazy about the exact time, but it was early morning—a little after sunup, maybe. A violent shaking brought me awake with painful speed, and the first thing I saw was Celeste's enormous eyes looking down at me with a reproachful gaze.

"Hey!" she said in an outraged voice. "My bones ache!"

I got back to my own room around six-thirty; showered, shaved, and dressed, and was all ready to sneak out of the house about seven, when Nemesis swooped down onto me in the front hall, scooped me up in its arms and carried me into the kitchen.

"You silly lieutenant," Antonia said with an almost fond tone in her voice. "Trying to sneak out without having any breakfast first!"

Being literally seized and carried off by a six-and-a-half-foot-tall Amazon at seven in the morning when you didn't even suspect it could happen, is a kind of unnerving experience. It wasn't helped by the fact that Antonia obviously hadn't bothered to get dressed yet, and was still wearing her nightgown. A very respectable nightgown that covered her from neck to feet in a no-peeking, nylon-cum-silk material. The trouble was it looked exactly like the kind of tent they use for signing peace treaties in, when they can't fit everyone in the local palace.

I guess the whole early-morning experience had made me slightly psychotic—but the more Antonia hovered over me offering more food than I normally eat in a week, the more tempting that tent looked, as a safe refuge. From a nightgown it became a tent; and from a tent, it became a prospective haven to quieten the Freudian havoc produced by the experience of being carried helplessly in the arms of a gigantic female who might conceivably put you back into diapers at any moment she thought fit.

By the time I'd refused another half-dozen eggs and settled for a fourth cup of coffee, I'd screwed up my courage to the point where the next time Antonia turned her back on me, I was going to make one dive under that tent-flap and hide inside the tent, where she'd never think of looking for me.

"Lieutenant?" She patted my cheek playfully, and impacted a wisdom tooth at the same time, I was sure. "You had enough to eat?"

"Enough isn't the word for it," I said feebly. "I've had my lunch, dinner, and tomorrow's breakfast, already."

"That's good," she said, and giggled suddenly. For a moment I thought it was a dam-burst, and was about to take for the hills.

"You won't forget, will you, Lieutenant?" She looked down at her toes and they wriggled coyly in mutual recognition that they all belonged to the same monster.

"Forget what?" I croaked.

"You know!" A nudge from her elbow slammed me into the unyielding corner of the table with painful results. "You promised," she said, and blushed.

Any moment now my hair would turn white, I knew it instinctively. But some inner fortitude made me face up to my moment of truth.

"Promised what?" I whimpered.

"You'll see he gets here nice and early today?" She giggled again. "So I can carry him over the mountain to watch me wrestle the bulls?"

"You mean—Polnik?" I yelled in hysterical relief.

"My little dumpling!" she said, and sighed heavily.

My psychosis disappeared like that! Along with it went the frantic desire to hide myself away under the protective covering of the nightgown tent. Afterwards, I figured it was just as well because I would have been trampled to death in the first couple of minutes.

"Good-bye, Lieutenant." Antonia's whisper followed me like a hurricane down the front hall. "Tell my little ape man his baby-love is waiting for him!"

Driving back toward Pine City, I wondered just what it was exactly Polnik had done to deserve this sudden outburst of affection from Antonia the Great? Whatever it was, it must have been something real lousy, I figured.

Chapter Eight

I stopped by at the Homicide Bureau first before I went on to the Sheriff's office. An old buddy of mine was working in records, and that saved me the trouble of having to endure Captain Parker's heavy-handed humor to get what I wanted. Officially the lost cooperation between the City bureau and Sheriff's office was expected—and always achieved. In reality, they looked on us as the local hicks, and as we had no legal right to demand their full cooperation, this was something always to be endured with a brave smile on your face.

My old buddy's name was Don Bastin, and he said it would be a breeze to run the checks I wanted. So I gave the names and physical descriptions of everyone currently living in Pop Livvy's house, including Pop himself. Don promised to call me whenever he had anything and I continued on my way rejoicing—more or less.

It was still only a quarter of nine when I walked into the Sheriff's office, and it was definitely a unique experience for me to be there in the morning before the Sheriff himself, and the kind of experience I figured I should try again sometime—like in a couple of years maybe.

The look on Annabelle Jackson's face when she arrived around twenty minutes later and saw me already there—real nonchalant, like I'd been delivered with the furniture—almost made the whole bit worthwhile.

"Al?" She goggled at me. "You're sick!"

"I know this office couldn't get along without me, honey," I said comfortably. "But I can't be here all the time and it's important my inferiors—like yourself and Lavers—have some sense of responsibility. So, once in a while, I figure I should check up and find out." I glanced at my watch. "You're four minutes late, Miss Jackson. Please don't let it happen again!"

Her face flushed angrily. "I've a good mind—"

"Pure, I'll go along with," I interrupted. "A good mind implies intelligence, logic, and so on." I gave her what you could call a frank smile. "Let's face it Annabelle, even in their wildest dreams nobody would say you had a good mind—"

I hadn't realized that the early morning trauma with Antonia the Great had still left me with some psychoneurotic symptoms, until I experienced a wild panic at the sight of Annabelle Jackson bearing down on me with a threatening look in her eyes. The phone's sudden, insistent ring a few seconds later was the one thing that saved me. My gibbering mind had completely reverted and I was back with that nightgown-tent complex, and had already decided to dive for cover and keep hidden until the whole world had gone away. I thanked Providence for that incoming call, when I realized Annabelle was wearing a real tight gabardine skirt. There just wouldn't have been enough room for the two of us underneath it—and how could you explain later that you'd recently been frightened by a female Amazon whose idea of fun was wrestling live bulls?

"County Sheriff's office, Lieutenant Wheeler speaking, Miss Annabelle Jackson is available if necessary—for conversation, that is. Sheriff Lavers is out at the moment, expected in at any time. Can I help you?" I babbled in the phone.

There was a pregnant silence—the kind of long pause while Daddy loads his shotgun—then a slightly stunned voice quavered, "I was calling the Sheriff's office."

"You did amazingly well," I said heartily. "You got it first time."

"Oh?" The speaker sounded like she'd lost interest for one reason or another. "This is the Starlight Hotel. Please connect me with Lieutenant Wheeler."

"This is he," I said.

"You're kidding!"

"You want to take a look at my shield, I'll bring it right over and cram it down your throat," I told her in a frigid voice.

"Mr. Jones is calling, Lieutenant, please hold the line." From the tone of her voice, someone was slowly strangling the switchboard girl to death. It seemed a kind of unorthodox way to run a hotel, but maybe they catered to their guests' every whim, I figured. "Lieutenant?" The rich, fruity tones unmistakably belonged to Parson Jones.

"What can I do for you, Parson?" I asked, with politeness but no enthusiasm.

"I been thinking," he said slowly. "Ever since you told me what happened to Eddie Moran. Maybe you're right, cop. I'm thirty years out of date, and I guess Prohibition will have to make a comeback first, before I get a chance!"

"Philosophy at ten after nine in the morning, Parson?" I said dubiously. "What happened? That redhead walk out on you or something?"

He gave a distinctly nonecclesiastical chuckle. "No, she's still here!

Listen, Wheeler, maybe we should have another talk. Who knows, it could do us both some good, huh?"

"Fine," I agreed. "When?"

"How about ten-thirty?"

"Okay."

"Do me a small favor, cop?" he asked. "I don't want to come over to your office because it'll stink up my nostrils with the smell of the Law, and I had thirty years of that already. How about coming over to the hotel? No offense, you understand?"

"Sure, Parson," I told him. "If I were you, I figure I'd feel the same way. I'll be there at ten-thirty."

I hung up, looked up, and saw the stony countenance of Annabelle Jackson watching me with a baleful stare.

"And how was your weekend, Annabelle, honey?" I gave her a bright, encouraging smile.

"Today is Wednesday, in case you've forgotten," she stated in an icy, clipped tone of voice. "And we were discussing my mind, remember? You were kind enough to point out that a 'good' mind is one that has intelligence and logic. Nobody in their wildest dreams, you said, would think of describing my mind as good—then the phone interrupted you." She took a step closer toward me and kind of flexed her biceps, "I'd just like you to finish off that remark, Lieutenant, if you don't mind?"

"Why should I mind?"

"You may well find out." She smiled thinly.

"All I was about to say was, nobody in their wildest dreams would think of describing your mind as good, Annabelle, honey," I said at a very fast rate of words per minute. "Good, if you'll pardon the expression, is simply not a good enough word to use about your mind, honey. Excellent, brilliant, superb—*these* are the adjectives one looks for to describe the mind of Annabelle Jackson!"

I folded my arms across my chest and gave her a brilliant smile, so sincere it made my gums ache. Only I think it was all wasted—the Southern belle didn't notice it, even. She just stood there with a baffled expression on her face, and it said a lot for Annabelle that she still looked attractive with her mouth hanging wide open.

Then she gave her head a sudden shake. "Well"—her voice sounded the same way her face looked—"you sure crawled out from under that one, Al Wheeler!"

"I have to talk to the Sheriff," I said nervously. "So I guess I'll wait in his office until he gets here, if you don't mind?"

I executed a sideways crablike walk, toward Lavers' office which enabled me to pass his secretary without getting real close.

"Hey!" A wicked gleam suddenly flared in back of her big, blue eyes. "Lieutenant—you've changed!"

"I'm one of those change-daily guys," I muttered. "It's not unusual."

"That's not what I meant and you know it!" Her eyes narrowed as she studied my face with intuitive feminine cunning, "You've changed, all right! Something must have happened since yesterday—you've had an experience?"

"Annabelle!" I protested. "You don't really think I've just been standing around all these years waiting to have an experience and finally made it yesterday?"

"You know what I mean!"

Her eyes narrowed even more so, then the gleam in her eyes changed from wicked to downright diabolical. She walked toward me slowly, smoothing the tight skirt down over her oscillating hips as she came, making a soft, purring noise deep in her throat. That did it! She only needed to make just one purr to trigger off my trauma again—purring women to cats to tigresses to jungle to Antonia. I backed off frantically as Annabelle advanced, until finally my back collided with the closed door to the Sheriff's office.

"Why don't we have a date tonight, Al honey?" She took a leisurely deep breath, and smoothed the silk blouse down over her sculptured bosom. "Have dinner up at your apartment, play your hi-fi machine?" Her meaningful smile was so loaded, I wondered bitterly why it didn't fall from her lips and thud onto the floor. "I've given up any athletic activity, Al, honey, so I promise you don't have to chase me around your l'il ole couch anymore. What do you say, h'mmm?"

"No!" I used a pocket handkerchief to dab my wet forehead.

"I knew it!" she said gleefully. "You've flipped, Al Wheeler! Oh, brother! That I should live to see the day that you—the uncrowned king of the Pine City boudoirs!—would be scared of women!"

"You're out of your mind!" I snarled, dabbing frantically at my forehead.

"I guess it had to happen." She gurgled in delight. "Someday there had to be an evening of the score!"

"Me—scared of w-w-women? Ridiculous!" I wished my teeth wouldn't chatter that way every time I used *that* word.

"So you're not scared, eh?" she said in a malicious voice. "Okay—kiss me!"

I had one small thing to be grateful for: If Annabelle insisted on turning herself into my personal demon, at least she wasn't a very smart one. She stood there expectantly with her eyes closed, long enough for me to slip into the Sheriff's office and lock the door.

Maybe fifteen minutes later I heard his heavy tread pounding through the outer office, so I quickly unlocked the door, then resumed my seat. Lavers came in, closed the door behind him carefully, then took a casual glance around his office before he went across to his desk and sat down. It was like I didn't exist. I gave him a couple of minutes to study the papers on his desk, then cleared my throat loudly. After the third time I cleverly realized it wasn't about to work, and my only hope was a frontal assault.

"Good morning, sir!" I'd figured to raise the level of my voice a little above normal, so he'd have no chance of pretending he didn't hear me. Only somewhere along the line I made a miscalculation, and my voice erupted into the room in one great volcanic blast of sound that would have driven a riveter in search of earplugs.

But it turned out to be a good fault, like they say about overdeveloped girls. Lavers jerked backwards in sudden alarm and shock, and cracked his skull against the back of his chair hard enough for it to make a pleasing dull sound.

"I got into the office early this morning, Sheriff," I said casually, just in case he hadn't noticed. "Thought I should check a couple of points with you."

There's no ham like a big ham. The County Sheriff proved it with the most elaborate double take I'd seen in around twenty years—since, in fact, they stopped using that particular bit of business.

"Well!" Lavers reacted violently as he looked at me directly for the first time. "If it isn't Lieutenant Wheeler, just stopped by to visit with us! What an unexpected pleasure! Staying in town long, Lieutenant? Or just passing through—as usual?"

"You're a riot, Sheriff, you really are!" I said icily. "I just can't wait for next week. What is it?—*Tobacco Road?*"

He searched the top drawer of his desk for a cigar—and the appropriate words to go with it, I guessed. He apparently found both. "The night before last we had a homicide, you may recall?" He bit off the end of his cigar with such violence, I figured he could have fantasied it into the end of my nose.

"Yesterday morning," he continued on a rising note of fury, "you left this office to start your investigation by questioning Parson Jones. Correct, Lieutenant?"

"And I didn't come back," I said impatiently. "Why don't we take a raincheck on the rest of this routine, Sheriff? You bawl me out, build your blood pressure another five points, and finally we get around to talking some sense about the case. I was kept busy yesterday—real busy!—and there's a hell of a lot coming out of this investigation that I never even suspected could be there, and I don't like any of it. You want to hear it now?—or bawl me out first?"

He had a slightly popeyed look on his face when I'd finished. After he'd blinked a few times and then studied his cigar carefully in case it concealed any secret messages from Agent X—he finally got his face back to normal.

"I guess I'll hear it now, Wheeler," he said. "What you said about my blood pressure just now. You really think so?—five points, huh?"

"At least!"

"Then maybe I should insist we always keep our relationship on a friendly basis!" A spasm of revulsion at the thought contorted his face. "So talk," he grunted.

I told him about the meeting with Parson Jones in his penthouse suite and the fight between Parson and his son. About Lindstrom, the hood from L.A.—who was hip, according to Sigmund Jones—and that he'd had a secret run-down on the people living out at Pop Livvy's house, and I tried like hell to make them sound just like people—a little eccentric maybe—but people. It still didn't do any good. By the time I'd finished, Lavers' eyes were two bewildered stones dropped dead-center into twin saucers brimming with disbelief.

For a while after I'd finished, the Sheriff just sat there with the flat of his hand pressed hard against his forehead. He made a concentrated effort and found some words. "I don't think I want to talk about the— people—living in that house just yet, Wheeler if you don't object? It's still kind of early, and I hate to lose my mind before the morning coffee break. What about this Lindstrom?"

"I never went near him," I said. "I figured we might as well keep a small advantage in knowing about him already, while he still thinks he's out of it."

"What about Parson Jones?—the money? You think it's true, and there's a half a million dollars stashed away in that house someplace?"

"Maybe, Sheriff," I said. "To be honest, I got a thousand theories that fit, and any one of them could be right. There's something else bothering me right now. I hate to say wheels within wheels, but that's what it is. There's a tremendous involvement here between all the suspects. I find one relationship between two of them, for example, and I get the feeling that's the one I'm meant to find, to cover their real relationship on a completely different level. Somehow they're all involved in a giant complex of material and emotional involvement—if that makes any sense—and the complex is about to explode."

For a cop to run off at the mouth like that was to leave himself wide open, and I knew it. But Lavers didn't bother taking the opportunity to chop bits off my hide.

"What happens if this—complex—of yours does explode, Wheeler?" he asked quietly.

"I have a feeling the end result will make Eddie Moran's morgue pictures look like part of a program designed for uplift in kiddies' culture," I said.

"What can we do about it?" he grunted.

"That's a hell of a good question." I grinned bleakly. "How's Sergeant Polnik today?"

"His wife called again around five last night," Lavers said. "According to her he'd be back at work this morning—and would I please refrain from ever giving him *that* kind of assignment again."

"I was about to suggest that's exactly what you do give him, Sheriff," I said.

"I don't run this office for Mrs. Polnik's convenience," he snapped. "What do you mean, exactly?"

"Send him straight out to the house and tell him to stay there until I get there this afternoon."

"Is that where your complex is about to explode, Wheeler?" he asked.

"If that's where Parson's money is stashed."

"You figure just Polnik is enough?" he said, dubiously. "I can put a twenty-four-hour detail on stakeout there—four men all the time—without too much trouble."

"I know, Sheriff." I lit a cigarette, using it for a time lag the way he used a cigar. "But then we load the odds too much our way and frighten them off. So they wait—and we wait. Somebody has to get tired first and for sure it'll be us. You can't keep a twenty-four-hour stakeout going indefinitely."

Lavers puffed his cigar furiously for a few seconds. "The way you tell it," he growled finally, "you make it sound like a game of Russian roulette!"

"And Polnik gets first pull at the trigger?" My watch said five after ten. "I almost forgot to tell you, Sheriff. Parson Jones called this morning. He's been thinking about how Eddie Moran died, he said. I'm going over to the hotel to talk with him at ten-thirty."

"Maybe Parson is having the first shot, and not Polnik?" He grinned.

"I just hope he understands the rules of the game," I said anxiously. "That he puts the gun barrel to his own head, *not* mine!"

Chapter Nine

I stepped out of the elevator into the private entrance to the penthouse suite at precisely 10:29, and hoped Parson Jones would properly appreciate my punctuality.

At 10:32 after having about worn out both the buzzer and the top of my thumb, I came out to the reluctant conclusion he wasn't about to appreciate anything because he wasn't there. I mentally called him a number of suitable names I would never dream of using to describe a real parson, then took the elevator back down to the lobby again.

The superior look on the desk clerk's face vanished abruptly when he saw me heading toward the desk. By the time I reached it, he was waiting for me anxiously, eager to give of his full, undivided personalized attention.

"G-Good morning, Lieutenant!" His smile quivered around the edges but he was obviously doing his best. "How can I help you?"

"You see Mr. Jones—from the penthouse suite—go out anywhere this morning?" I asked.

He thought for a moment, then shook his head. "Sorry, Lieutenant."

"He's got a—redheaded friend—"

Cedric grinned understandingly. "Sure, Lieutenant. Miss Poppy Lane?"

"Have you seen her this morning?"

"No—and Miss Lane I would remember, Lieutenant!"

"I don't get it," I said, brooding over the sudden warning nudge in back of my mind. "He called me and made an appointment for ten-thirty. I've just about worn out the buzzer up there."

"Why don't I check around the hotel, Lieutenant?" Cedric suggested eagerly. "I maybe can get a line on something."

"Fine," I told him.

I spent the time he was busy with the phone by improving the shining hour—playing a rocking improvisation on strict tempo to accompany my own version of "Melancholy Baby," whistled in three flats. The improvisation was really something—a hotel desk top is a good, reliable percussion instrument and there were moments, when I had a drum roll going, where I was using three fingers of each hand at the same time.

Cedric hung up and galloped back to me, like it was his first morning with the Pony Express and nobody told him you got a horse, too.

"Room service took up breakfast for two at nine-thirty, Lieutenant," he said. "I spoke to the waiter and he said they were both still in bed then. I checked the switchboard—there was your call made about nine ten, another outgoing call at nine forty-eight—"

"Who to?"

"Mr. Jones asked for a direct line, and dialed the number himself. Then an incoming call at nine fifty-eight which he also answered—it was a man's voice is all the operator remembers, Lieutenant."

"Thanks, Cedric," I told him. "You did a nice job—got the makings of a good cop, even. Do one more little thing for me—let me have a passkey for the penthouse."

"But, Lieutenant, I'm not supposed—the assistant manager is the only—" Suddenly he shrugged his shoulders and grinned at me. "Okay. I guess one favor deserves another."

He turned and lifted a passkey from the board, then dropped it onto the desk in front of him.

"Thanks." I picked it up, then looked at him, curiously. "When did I ever do you a favor?"

"Yesterday, remember? You fixed my wagon with Miss Adele—the silver blonde?"

"That was a favor?"

"Lieutenant, you don't know the half of it!" His grin widened. "The hotel detective caught her red-handed last night—in one of the other guests' rooms—lifting a couple of hundred out the wallet the guy had absentmindedly left on top of the dresser!" Cedric closed his eyes and shuddered. "They would have figured me as her accomplice, or something!"

"It's nice to know I go around doing people favors all the time without even realizing it," I said. "You can have the passkey back in about ten minutes."

"Lieutenant? If the assistant manager wants to know—"

"Tell him I twisted your arm until you had a choice between handing over the key, or getting your arm busted," I suggested. "Tell him I said if he likes to come up to the penthouse, I'll be happy to twist his arm, too."

The second time out of the elevator into the private entrance was an anticlimax. I had a momentary vision of walking into an empty penthouse to find a rude note from Parson Jones telling me he'd left Pine City, and exactly what he thought I was in an indeterminate number of four-letter words.

The hunch grew stronger after I opened the door and stepped into the living room of the suite. It couldn't have been more empty. "Anybody home?" I said loudly. Nothing happened, so I called out again, louder this time, hearing the faint embarrassment in my own voice that everybody gets when they figure they're talking out loud to themselves. Then there was a sound—so faint I wasn't even sure whether I'd imagined it or not.

"Who's there?" I yelled, and listened so hard, my eardrums hurt. I was sure the second time there was a faint, rustling sound that seemed to come from the bathroom. I played it safe, straight out of the book, with a gun in my hand. Nothing happened when I kicked the bathroom door open and waited, flattened against the wall for maybe ten seconds; and I got precisely the same result when I leaped through the open doorway into the bathroom itself.

I put the thirty-eight back into the belt-holster and felt thankful for one thing, anyway—at least I hadn't had an audience to watch me playing cops-and-robbers with myself the last five minutes. Then the rustling started again, someplace real close to me, and there was another sound with it vaguely like a bumble bee that needed to get its buzz working properly again.

The only place I couldn't see into was the shower stall, and that was where all the noise was coming from. Miss Poppy Lane made an untidy bundle on the tiled floor, with knotted towels tied around her wrists, knees, and ankles. The intermittent buzzing sound came from trying to bite her way through the toweling gag wadded into her mouth. Her usually vacant eyes were filled with a jam of urgent messages as she stared up at me. I figured she must have been about to take a shower, or just finished, when whoever it was grabbed her. Apart from the toweling used to bind her, she was nude, and goose-pimples were showing up in the oddest places.

I picked her up from the tiled floor, carried her out into the living room and dumped her in an armchair. For the first minute after I removed the gag from her mouth, I seriously considered replacing it in self-defense. The redhead talked more nonsense faster than anyone else I'd ever heard in my whole life. And where had she been, to learn all those words?

By the time I'd untied her wrists, knees, and ankles, I could feel my brain coming loose under the constant fire of her vindictive babble, delivered like machine gun fire.

I hauled myself up onto my feet and glared at her "Shut up!"

Her mouth dropped open, but no sounds emerged and I let the blissful silence lap around me for a few seconds.

"Miss Lane," I said, with tremendous restraint. "I want you to be very clear about this. The sound of your voice doesn't enchant me. The nonsense you've poured out like a flood ever since I removed that gag doesn't interest me. All I want is to ask some questions and listen to your answers, preferably brief. Is that absolutely clear?"

"Listen, cop!" she said sullenly. "Don't try and push me around, or I'll—"

I held the gag securely back in position until she gave up struggling and glared at me with a murderous expression in her eyes.

"I can tie you up again, honey, toss you back into the shower stall, then tell the management you don't want to be disturbed," I said evilly. "Chances are you could just stay there a couple of days. This is your last chance to do like I told you before."

When I took the gag away, she just sat with her lips shut right.

"You want to put some clothes on before I start asking questions?" I asked her.

She looked down at herself, then shrugged. "Why bother? You've seen it all already—there isn't any more. And I can tell you're not my type." She shrugged disdainfully. "A lotta guys would give their right arms to see me this way!"

I let it ride—what the hell—there are guys who figure riding a canoe through the rapids is a fun project.

"Parson called me and made a date for ten-thirty," I said. "Tell me what happened after that—in sequence, huh?"

"I don't know about the calls," she said, shrugging again. "He always used the phone out here where I couldn't hear what he said. He was kinda funny that way. The flunky brought the breakfast, and right after he'd eaten, Parson got up. Next thing I knew he was back in his bedroom, all dressed and everything. He told me you were coming and I'd better get the hell out of it for the rest of the morning. 'Go shopping, or something,' he said, 'and you got thirty minutes to be dressed and out.'

"I came in here to have a shower." Her eyes flashed with indignation. "Right after I stepped into the stall, I heard somebody come busting into the bathroom, and I figured it couldn't be Parson because—well, you know—he's a little bit old for all that impetuous stuff. When I put my head around the stall to take a look, there was this big guy with a scarf around his face coming right at me. I opened my mouth to scream and he hit me!"

She looked down anxiously at her solar plexus, then gave me a beaming smile. "How about that!" she said joyfully. "It didn't even bruise."

"Then?" I grunted.

"He knocked the wind right out of me," she continued angrily. "Then, while I was bent double, he grabbed a couple of towels and tore them into strips, and put the gag on. By that time, I was too hurt and too plain scared to argue, or do anything. I just didn't know exactly what he had in mind!"

"So he tied you up and put you back into the shower stall?" I prodded, wanting to keep her strictly in line with what did happen, rather than what made her show up to best advantage.

"Yeah," she said. "Right after he'd dumped me back into the stall— Cheez! those tiles get cold!—I heard somebody else come into the bathroom, but they didn't come close enough so I could see who it was. They were talking, though. Their voices sounded real scary—all muffled through those scarves, I guess? The one who'd just come in said how was everything—and the one who'd just tied me up said everything was fine, he'd just finished taking care of me and he wished they had more time because he'd like to take care of me properly."

She looked away from me with becoming modesty on the last line. "Then he asked about Parson, and the other one said Parson was no problem because he was out cold. They started arguing then about how they'd get him out of the hotel if they had to carry him—things like that—and they were still arguing when they went out of the bathroom." She shrugged. "That's it, Lieutenant!"

"You figure you'd recognize the man who tied you up if you saw him again?"

She thought for a moment, then shook her head firmly. "He was just a big guy with a scarf around his face. Most of the time I was so scared I didn't even look at him!"

"When they were arguing just before they left, did they mention anything about how they figured on getting Parson out of the hotel?"

"Not that I remember."

"Okay. Thanks, Poppy." I said wearily. "You've been a big help. Maybe you'd better go get dressed now, the place could be swarming with people real soon."

The redhead disappeared into the bedroom, and I picked up the phone to call Lavers. He listened silently until I'd finished the story, then grunted a couple of times.

"If he's been kidnapped it's a Federal offense," he said in a mild voice. "That automatically brings in the FBI. Did you think about that?"

"Not until you mentioned it," I admitted.

"Well?" he asked in a laconic voice.

"I'm not completely convinced it is a genuine kidnap," I said truthfully. "Parson Jones could have figured this was a cute way of getting out from under our noses—leave the girl all tied up to make it look authentic, and just disappear."

"What about the girl?" he asked. "You try breaking down her story yet?"

"If she is lying, it's going to take a lot of time to break it down," I told him. "She's got a nice, simple story that's real hard to knock a dent in, even. I don't have the time to try, Sheriff. It might be better if you have her brought in for questioning."

"All right." His voice got brisk. "I'll send a car over right away, and arrange for a stakeout in the penthouse. Polnik's on his way to the house incidentally. And for the time being we don't talk to the FBI because it could be a frame."

"Right." I said. "That seems to cover it."

"Is there anything else?"

"Not that I can think of," I said truthfully. "I'll keep in touch."

"That, I'll believe when it happens," he said, and hung up.

The uniformed men arrived a couple of minutes before Poppy Lane swept out of the bedroom, fully dressed in another of those bandanna and hip-high pants combinations. I eased myself out of the penthouse before she started to react with a torrent of words again, about being taken in for questioning. I had a fascinating elevator ride to the lobby, wondering how Lavers would react when he first saw that diamond-studded navel.

Cedric nearly burst a blood vessel from curiosity when I came back and dropped the passkey onto the desk. I figured he deserved to get some kind of a story, so gave him an expurgated version.

He had the kind of quick mind that immediately comes to grips with the essentials of a situation. "How about that, Lieutenant?" He breathed heavily. "The redhead was stark naked, huh?"

"What's Mr. Lindstrom's room number?" I asked him.

"He's not in the hotel anymore," Cedric said, casually. "Checked out yesterday."

"Any forwarding address?"

"I'll check."

"See if you can find out what time he left, huh?" I suggested.

It took him around thirty seconds to come back with the information. "No forwarding address, Lieutenant. He checked out around three yesterday afternoon."

"Thanks." I thought about that for a moment. "You have an airline schedule anyplace?"

"You name it, we got it, Lieutenant!" He deposited one on the desk in front of me with the triumphant flourish of a minor diplomat who's found the secret treaty was only lost, not stolen.

I spent the next fifteen minutes with the kind of routine work that's real exciting, if you don't wind up in a padded cell. But it paid off. None of the airlines had carried a passenger named Sigmund Jones to L.A. the previous afternoon, and none of them had even had a booking in that name.

After I'd told Cedric goodbye and thanked him again for his help, I went out of the hotel and got into the Healey. I just sat there for a while, hoping sooner or later something would happen, like I might even start in with some objective thinking. Nothing much happened. It was interesting Lindstrom had checked out suddenly yesterday afternoon, within an hour of Sigmund Jones tipping me off about him. It was also interesting Sigmund himself hadn't taken that plane ride to L.A. All in all, I figured I had a whole bunch of interesting facts, but I was in the same situation a guy would be when he knows the vital statistics of the blonde who lives right across the hallway from him, and they're surely interesting—but just knowing them gets him no place at all.

I sat for another ten minutes vaguely hoping something—anything—would happen, and finally it did. A traffic cop came along and tried to give me a parking ticket.

Chapter Ten

Around three in the afternoon I went back to the office after having spent the last couple of hours dawdling over a lunch I couldn't afford in a downtown restaurant. Annabelle Jackson looked up at me with a knowing, malicious gleam in her eyes as I went past her desk, and by the time I reached Lavers' office I was almost running.

The County Sheriff was obviously not a happy man. If there had been twelve buttons on his desk, each one releasing a nuclear weapon to destroy one of the capital cities of the world, I figured right then he'd have pressed the whole twelve, twice, to make sure he didn't accidentally allow anyone to survive.

"Where the hell have you been all day?" he snarled almost before I'd gotten into his office. "Isn't there anyone else around here who's supposed to do any work besides me?"

I sat down cautiously and lit a cigarette. "You have any luck with Poppy Lane?" I asked.

He shuddered. "I don't understand how Parson Jones could put up with that for more than a couple of hours at most. I never heard a woman talk the way she does! She doesn't take time out to get her breath, even! And the language! You were real cute, Wheeler, saying you didn't have the time to break down her story and why didn't I bring her back to the office for questioning!"

"Did you have any luck?" I said, and knew too late it was a stupid question.

"I don't remember distinctly," he said in a shaking voice. "After the first fifteen minutes, everything kind of vanishes into a nightmarish haze inside my mind. I do have an impression that Miss Lane broke down three or four stories of mine, and around a dozen others belonging to the uniformed men who were present!"

"Where is she now?"

"I sent her back to the hotel," he snarled. "If she'd demanded money to go I would have gladly given it to her, but fortunately she didn't. If she belonged to me I wouldn't waste my time and money putting a diamond in her navel, I'd buy her a diamond choker—and use it!"

"Yes, sir," I said.

"Did you find Parson Jones yet?" he rasped.

"Not yet," I admitted, then hurriedly told him about Lindstrom checking out the day before from the hotel, and that Sigmund Jones hadn't taken a plane back to L.A. that afternoon.

"You think this is significant?"

"I've been thinking about Sigmund," I said slowly. "He's a corporation lawyer in L.A. is all I know about him, and that's taking his word for it. When he was arguing with his father, he told Parson he was out of date—an antique—that people in the same business today were, in fact, corporations. The way he talked about what a smart hood Lindstrom was, you could have thought he even admired the guy. Lindstrom's a corporation, Sigmund told me. Now I'm wondering if Sigmund's his corporation lawyer."

"And if he is?" Lavers snapped.

"Maybe he's working with Lindstrom to get their hands on that half million his old man maybe has stashed away?" I said. "Maybe that's why Sigmund's been so close to his old man, from the day he was released right up until the brawl they had yesterday morning. Playing the dutiful son didn't get Sigmund anyplace, so maybe he's changed his tactics and now he's started playing it rough?"

"It could have been Sigmund and Lindstrom who kidnapped him this morning," Lavers said, doubtfully. "But that dreadful Lane girl would have recognized Sigmund right away."

"Only one of them dealt with her directly," I reminded him. "The other one never came close enough for her to get a glimpse of him, even."

"So what he couldn't get out of his father by being nice to him," Lavers said grimly, "he figures now to beat out of him."

"It opens up a whole new field for Father's Day, doesn't it?" I suggested.

"It still doesn't give us any real help," he grunted. "If you're right, we haven't got any idea where they're holding him. Not a clue—not one lousy little lead! Maybe we should call the FBI?"

"Sheriff," I gritted my teeth soundlessly. "What's the reason for kidnaping anybody at all?"

"To hold them for ransom—extortion, what else?" he snorted.

"What ransom do they want from Parson Jones?"

"The information about where he stashed that money—what else!"

"Right." I nodded. "And we do know if it's anyplace, it's in the house Pop Livvy now owns—the one Parson tried to buy back from him in the first place. You see what I'm getting at, Sheriff?" I almost pleaded with him. "We don't know where they are right now, but it almost doesn't matter, because we know damned well where they have to go to collect the loot!"

"I hope you're right, for both our sakes, Wheeler," he said, scowling at me. "I—" His phone rang and he answered, then gestured to me to take it.

"Don Bastin, Al," a pleasant voice said in my ear. "I've been trying all day with those names you gave me, but no luck at all so far. They all look to be clean—for sure they are in Pine City and L.A. You want me to keep trying?"

"I guess not, Don," I said. "Thanks, anyway."

"You know me, Al," he chuckled. "Anything for a friend, so long as it doesn't cost money!"

Lavers watched me return to my seat. "You're going out to the house tonight?"

"When I leave here," I agreed.

"It could happen tonight," he said. "I'd better get a couple of cars into the area, real close, and we can shut it up nice and tight."

"So tight they'll take one look and drive right back to wherever they came from," I snarled.

He drummed a pencil on his desk top for a while. "I'll make you a deal," he said finally.

"Like what?"

"Keep Polnik there with you tonight, and I'll forget the rest of it."

"Okay, we have a deal, Sheriff," I told him. "I guess I'd better get started."

"Don't let that childish hero-complex get the better of you, if anything breaks, will you, Wheeler?" Lavers pleaded, gruffly. "The Administration just can't afford another premature pension, or burial expenses, even!"

I had his door wide open ready to run before I said it, "Sheriff?"

"Something I can do to help?" he asked almost eagerly.

"A small thing, but it's real important," I said. "Would you call Mrs. Polnik and explain why her husband won't be home tonight?" Then I ran.

It was around five when I got back among the Bootleg Baronial architecture, and into the tight little world that freewheeled around Pop Livvy as its natural gravitation point. As usual there was nobody outside of the house, so I went straight into the living room, looking for a drink.

The room was empty except for one beautiful brunette who sat at the bar, her long hair curling around her shoulders like a negligent cloud.

"I made you a drink," Celeste said, without turning her head as I walked toward her. "I've been keeping it warm for you—or cool— whichever you prefer."

I sat on a barstool beside her and looked at her appraisingly.

Something was different about her but I couldn't figure out what, then I suddenly realized it was the first time I'd seen her fully dressed. She wore a fresh-looking white silk blouse and a wide skirt patterned with a real jazzy overprint. A wide cinch belt of white leather made her waist absurdly small, and the overall effect was also absurdly attractive, I had to admit to myself.

"You approve?" Her sloe eyes had been watching my face like a hawk.

"I think it's very becoming," I told her. "It's also an occasion. I never saw you in a whole outfit of clothes at one time before."

She moved a glass in front of me on the bar top. "It's a Manhattan, I think," she told me, with unnerving vagueness.

"Is it really some kind of celebration?" I asked her.

"For me, Al, it is." She smiled provocatively. "For you, honey, it may be strictly old-hat."

"So tell me."

"When you were a kid, Al," she said in a dreamy voice, "did you ever play 'Mothers and Fathers'?"

"You'll have to have me under oath before you'll get an answer to that one!" I told her.

"Well, I'm playing a game something like that, all by myself," she went on in the same dreamy voice. "You see, this is the very first time in my whole life that the man I went to bed with one night has come back to me the very next night." She closed her eyes for a moment and hugged herself delightedly. "It's almost like we were married, Al. So that's the game, you see? I've been sitting here the last hour pretending I'm your loving wife, just waiting, all breathless and anticipating, for her adorable husband to come home!"

"Oh!" I said bleakly.

She opened her eyes again and squinted at me cynically. "You can relax, old lecher! I wouldn't marry you—or anybody—for a long time yet!"

"Is that a fact?" I said gratefully, and stopped holding my breath.

"Oh, I'll get married someday, I guess," Celeste said airily. "But not for years and years and years yet—maybe when I get to be real old—like twenty-eight, maybe?"

"You figure it's right to keep the best years of your life to yourself, and go hobbling down the aisle on your stick, with maybe a blue rinse through your gray hair?" I asked her. "You should make up your mind to marry while you're still real young—like twenty-seven, maybe?"

I tasted the drink she'd made me and put down the glass hastily. It wasn't a Manhattan, that was for sure. From the taste, I didn't much care to think about what it could be—it opened up much too big an area of possibilities.

"What kind of a day did you have?" I asked her. She shrugged. "Just a day. I tried out a couple of exotic dance routines, so I guess that makes me an exotic dancer now, right?"

"What were you yesterday?" I asked her, anxiously.

"A contortionist, naturally!"

"That's okay, then!" I felt an overwhelming sense of relief. "I would've hated to miss out on the chance of making love to a contortionist by one lousy little day!"

"Oh—" she shook her head reprovingly, "—you're charming, Al Wheeler! Full of lovable qualities, like booze, cigarette smoke—how come you managed to seduce a sweet, innocent girl like me?"

"I just got lucky, I guess," I said. "Didn't anything exciting at all happen today?"

"Your dummy came and visited with us!" she suddenly remembered. "You're a genius, Al! How do you manage to throw your voice all the way back here from Pine City?"

"You mean Sergeant Polnik," I said. "Is he around now?"

Celeste shook her head. "Haven't seen him since around eleven this morning."

I started to get worried. "You got any idea where he went?"

"Oh, sure," she said, nodding. "Up the mountainside cradled in the arms of his beloved."

"Antonia?" I gurgled. "You mean she really did carry him up the hill?"

"And over the top and far away," she said. "They looked like something out of one of those old, old musical comedies. Well, they would have if Antonia hadn't been wearing her bull-wrestling outfit—and your sergeant had been smiling, even!"

"Bull-wrestling outfit?" I said in a shaky voice.

"I guess it's really a one-piece swimsuit," Celeste admitted. "Antonia calls it her bull-wrestling outfit because it's a bright scarlet color, I guess."

"Antonia in a one-piece swimsuit," I muttered, glassily.

"All latex," Celeste said. "It's a couple of sizes too small for her, but it stretches, of course."

"And Polnik should have been smiling?" I whimpered.

"Well, he could have tried to just look happy, or something, and not hurt poor Antonia's feelings," she said indignantly. "It looks plain stupid, anyway, a grown man like him screaming for help at the top of his voice. Somebody might have thought he meant it."

"I would!" I said fervently. "And they didn't get back yet?"

"Not that I know of." She looked at me with a hint of frost in her eyes. "You're jumpy tonight, old lecher. This little loving wife routine of mine put your nerves on edge, maybe?"

"I'm worried about Polnik," I said.

"You being that worried about him," she said sweetly, "could make me start worrying about you. Except now I don't have to—not while my bones are still aching!"

The beaded curtain jingled and in thumped Polnik, looking large as life and twice as repulsive, with that big, fat grin on his face.

"Hi, Lieutenant!" He boomed as he pounded across the room toward us. "How's everything?"

"I heard you were last seen screaming for help?" I snarled. "What did you get—the Marines?"

"Yeah!" He grinned sheepishly. "I guess maybe I got kind of excited this morning when Antonia grabbed me and started up that hill. I figured maybe she figured to just keep on going, and what the hell would happen to my old lady, and all? But it was okay, everything turned out fine, Lieutenant. We walked in the trees for a while—"

"I winced. "*Through* the trees, Sergeant!"

"Are you kidding, Lieutenant? *Antonia?*"

"Well," I said reluctantly. "Maybe you're right."

"I guess she kind of unnerved me at first," Polnik confessed shyly. "I mean, a girl and all, being strong the way she is. But underneath she's only a kid, Lieutenant. I mean, like a real small kid." He shuffled his feet awkwardly. "That first time I figured she was a man-eater or something, but all she wants is somebody to make a fuss over—like playing with dolls."

"Now that's the Lieutenant's lifelong interest!" Celeste giggled. "Seriously, you're right, Sergeant. Antonia has the mind of a nine-year-old child, locked in the body of a giantess. Sometimes she forgets her own strength in a childlike enthusiasm, but there's nothing bad about her."

"Now you got here, Lieutenant," Polnik said. "I guess I can beat it back to town, huh?"

"The Sheriff—" I started.

"Got a big night tonight!" he said happily. "It's my old lady's birthday and I got a wonderful surprise party set for tonight, and she don't know a thing about it!" He beamed at me. "Everybody's coming from the whole block!"

"Sounds great," I said.

"So, if it's okay with you, Lieutenant?"

"Sure," I grinned. "Wish your old lady a happy birthday from me, huh?"

I watched his broad back all the way across the room, until he brushed through the beaded curtain into the hall. Then I picked up my drink again.

"Maybe I *am* worried about you?" Celeste said in a brooding voice. "You looked real sorry to see the Sergeant go!"

"I think maybe I am," I said sincerely. "Or I'm about to be."

Chapter Eleven

I had a new viewpoint about Antonia and I watched her carefully through dinner that night and saw what Celeste had said about her earlier was completely true. Basically she was a nine-year-old kid, imprisoned in a body five times too big for her. And once I understood that, I suddenly lost that psychoneurotic twitch that had started me gibbering if any female even looked like she could be aggressive.

Nothing seemed to have changed from the previous night. Pop Livvy was his usual pleasant self; Bruno Breck his usual unpleasant self; and although Sebastian did come to the dinner table this time, he didn't say more than two words throughout the whole meal.

Because I'd kept my promise and sent Polnik out to see her, Antonia fussed around me through the whole meal, serving me gargantuan portions of everything. I wondered what would have happened to her after her father died if Pop Livvy hadn't brought her to this house and looked after her. I had a strong feeling he was still owed for that— Antonia would never be able to repay him, so that made it up to somebody else to square the account.

"Lieutenant?" Bruno's shrill, unpleasant voice jerked me out of the reverie. "We're all dying to know! How's the investigation coming? You haven't caught the killer yet?"

"Not yet," I agreed. "But there was an interesting development today. Parson Jones was kidnaped."

"Who by?" Sebastian asked urgently.

"Two unidentified men—but we've got a good idea who they were."

I told them about Sigmund and Lindstrom—how it looked like Sigmund had tired of playing the dutiful son to get what he wanted and now was about to beat the information out of his father if necessary.

"If it's really true that Jones did hide a fortune someplace all that time back, Lieutenant," Pop said quietly, "and the other two force him to tell them the hiding place, what do you think will happen then?"

"Pop—" I grinned at him. "You're kidding me? If somebody told you where a fortune was hidden, what would you do?"

"Go and get it, of course," he said. "Forgive me, it was a stupid question!"

Celeste and myself were the only ones who went back into the living room when dinner was over. This time I made the Manhattans, and she even admitted they just could be a fraction better tasting than the ones she made. I would have enjoyed the couple of hours we spent at the bar if I hadn't had six other things on my mind. Finally, a little after ten, I told her I had to go talk with Pop for a while.

"That's okay." A troubled look showed in her tawny eyes. "You haven't listened to a word I've said all night. If I'd taken off my clothes and stood on top of the bar, I'd bet you wouldn't have noticed, even!"

"Don't bet too hard on that one." I grinned at her.

"Is it trouble, Al?" she asked in a soft voice. "Can I do anything to help, maybe?"

"I think it could be trouble," I said carefully. "And the best way you can help is by staying out of it. If anything does happen, you stay in your room, okay?"

"Won't you be there to make sure I do?"

"Not tonight, honey," I said sadly. "Don't ask me if I'm out of my mind because I'm not sure myself."

"I'll bear with it," she said, grinning. "But if nothing's happened by morning, Al Wheeler, I'll—"

"Where would I find Pop? You got any idea?" I interrupted her. "I have to talk with him before he goes to bed."

"What a romantic bum you are!" Celeste wrinkled her nose in disgust. "Have a look around the garage, he walks quite a bit most nights, then sits out there for a while before he goes to bed. I hate you, Al Wheeler, but take awful good care of yourself, huh?"

A couple of minutes later I found Pop, like she'd said, leaning against one of the sagging garage doors. "It's a beautiful night, Lieutenant," he said softly.

"No," I said. "It's a lousy night, Pop, and it's about to get worse."

"I don't think I understand?"

"Sigmund Jones and Lindstrom," I said. "They know by now. Parson's not in shape to hold out on them for more than ten minutes at best. So they'll come to pick up the loot, and my bet is they'll do it tonight."

"I still don't understand you, Lieutenant." In the dim light of the one surviving bulb, his face looked absolutely calm and unworried.

"Pop," I almost pleaded with him, "I am trying to do you a favor. It's almost sure it'll be too late by morning, so listen hard, huh?"

"I'm a good listener!"

"A man breaks the law, that's one thing," I said quickly. "Then he associates with others who do a lot worse things in lawbreaking than he ever did—and they get caught—the Law doesn't differentiate between them. But if the same guy was maybe disgusted by the crimes his associates committed and turned State's evidence against them—"

"I wouldn't think much of him as a man," Pop said in a clear, hard voice. "Informing on his friends!"

"It could depend on his other responsibilities," I said evenly. "Maybe he has a wife and kids—or maybe he's assumed that responsibility—like you and Antonia, for example?"

"Not even for Antonia," he said flatly.

I lit a cigarette, then shrugged hopelessly. "Well, I tried."

"You did, Lieutenant." He smiled warmly at me. "And I appreciate it very much. I also don't know what you're talking about." He walked past me slowly in the direction of the front porch. "Good night, Lieutenant."

For maybe five minutes after Pop Livvy had disappeared back inside the house, I stood in the garage getting more and more tired of waiting for something to happen with each passing minute. At the end of the fifth minute I had a brilliant, if not original, idea. I could make some trouble of my own, as opposed to standing around waiting for somebody else to make it.

The lights were on in the basement, so I pushed the door open and walked in. Sebastian was sitting by the gun rack, carefully oiling a venerable-looking Colt .44. His head jerked up quickly when he heard the door squeak, the pointed beard quivering nervously. He relaxed when he saw it was me, but not that much, I noted.

"I think I guessed it, Sebastian," I said enthusiastically.

"Guessed what?" He looked at me curiously.

"You told me that catching a bullet between your teeth is the second greatest gun trick in the world, remember?"

"Sure," he said. "It's true."

"But you wouldn't tell me what was the greatest gun trick in the world." I grinned triumphantly. "So I've figured it out for myself."

"So?"

"So the greatest gun trick in the world would be firing a bullet that a volunteer from your audience couldn't *help* but catch in his teeth," I said slowly. "A man who could make the right gun and the right bullets, and trust his expert aim to always lodge the slug between the volunteer's teeth—this man would be a genius!"

"The greatest in his field the world has ever known!" Sebastian said hoarsely.

"I have the first step clear in my mind," I told him. "But no more."

"*You* have the first step in your mind?" His white teeth flashed in sardonic amusement. "I should be fascinated to hear your secret, Lieutenant."

"You take any normal heavy-caliber slug," I said. "Then you file away the outer casing until you get down to the lead itself. The first essential is a soft-nosed bullet."

Sebastian put the Colt .44 back into the rack with great care, then looked at me coldly. "It sounds inspired, Lieutenant. Where did you get the idea?"

"From a body stretched out along the hood of an automobile, strangely enough," I said. "I could show you some of the morgue pictures if you want, but you can't see anything for the blood!"

Sebastian stood motionless watching me, then his eyes flicked toward the gun rack momentarily, then refocused on my face.

"What you need for the experiment is a man who's expendable, don't you agree?" I said softly. "The ideal situation would be if you had to kill somebody for your own protection in any case—there was no question about it—then he'd be available to try out the idea. If it didn't work, it would save you the trouble of killing him later." I grinned at him. "The hard part is to find somebody you genuinely have no choice about killing in the first place!"

I stepped back easily until I bumped the door, then fumbled behind me for the knob. When I had it open, I still backed out so I never took my eyes off him for a moment.

"The annoying thing is," I told him for an exit line, "there just aren't enough Eddie Morans to go around!" Then I closed the door gently.

Pop was at the bar when I came back into the living room with a tall glass in front of him. Celeste had gone, I was glad to see, and I hoped she'd take the rest of my advice and stay in her room, whatever happened.

Even when I climbed up onto the bar stool beside him, Pop gave no sign that he was aware of my existence, even.

"It had to be in the car someplace," I said conversationally. "Did you find it by accident, or did you go looking?"

"Are you talking to me, Lieutenant?"

"Parson told me he owned a couple of legitimate businesses that he kept going after they hit him with the tax rap," I said. "Maybe one was an auto repair shop? I bet that fancy car was never in the garage while the Feds were pulling the place apart. When they'd given up looking, Parson had it driven into the garage and the motor removed to make damned sure it was never driven out again. He never dreamed they'd give him anything like thirty years—he was betting on doing seven, at most. Did you get a reduction on the price of the house if you agreed never to disturb the auto that the former owner wished to leave in the garage for his own sentimental reasons, or some such?"

"A thousand," Pop whispered.

"How did you find the money?"

"I had a dog and he tore the upholstery on the back seat one day," he said, still staring straight ahead of him. "I opened one of the rear doors and about twenty thousand dollars lay at my feet!"

"You used the money to keep the house going," I said. "What did you need Bruno and Sebastian for?"

"I wasn't big enough to cope with so much money," he whispered. "It frightened me, I felt lonely. They both looked like they could deal with any situation that could possibly crop up. With two partners I only carried a third of the responsibility!"

"You have any idea how much there was?"

A ghost of a smile showed on his face for a moment. "I can see you don't know my partners, Lieutenant. We've counted it a thousand times! At the beginning there must have been about four hundred and fifty thousand. When the other two joined me, there was three hundred and sixty thousand."

"How much is left?"

"A little under one hundred thousand."

"Sigmund Jones and Lindstrom are going to be disappointed when they get here," I said softly. "I'm real glad you changed your mind, Pop, and decided to take me up on that offer."

"It was what you said about Antonia that decided me, Lieutenant," he said in an expressionless voice. "You were right, I can't desert her, however unpleasant the alternatives."

He turned his head and looked at me for the first time since I'd sat down beside him, and there was a cold glitter in the faded blue eyes that I'd never seen there before.

"Your offer would involve at least a few years in jail, Lieutenant," he said harshly. "So it's out of the question, I have to accept one of the more unpleasant alternatives!"

"What does that mean, exactly?" I asked.

"Tell him, Bruno," he snapped.

Bruno's head lifted suddenly above the bar top as he got up from where he'd been crouching on the other side of the bar. His muddy eyes glittered as he watched my face, and the thirty-eight in his right hand was rock-steady.

"Lieutenant," he cackled gleefully, "you're a scream, you are really! Did you think you were going to scare us all to death, or something, with those wild stories about Lindstrom and Parson Jones's kid being on the warpath?"

The beads jingled and I saw Sebastian come into the room. I watched him approach the bar through the amber-tinted mirror. He stopped beside Pop Livvy and looked at both his partners with a fixed, semi-hysterical stare.

"He walked into the basement," Sebastian muttered. "Stood there grinning at me while he talked. He knows everything! My wonderful gun trick—the soft-nosed bullet!—Moran, everything!"

"Of course he does, you cretin!" Bruno said shrilly. "Who was it had to show off their shooting skill to him with a personal demonstration? Who was it had to tell him about Europe and all the other expensive foreign cities he visited all the time?"

"I don't like it!" Sebastian muttered. "Moran was different—a cheap hood! But a lieutenant of police?"

"Why is the Lieutenant here?" Bruno sneered at him. "To protect us, what else? Who will grieve the most if he is killed trying to protect us—we three, of course!"

Pop Livvy picked up his king-sized drink and drank steadily until the glass was empty, then replaced it on the bar.

"The Lieutenant tried to do me a favor," he said thickly. "I give it back. Make it quick and clean, Bruno—and no testing your bullets this time, Sebastian. I will wait in my room."

He walked stiffly away and the silence lasted until he'd reached the hall.

"'Make it quick and clean, Bruno'!" Bruno mimicked savagely. "'No testing your bullets this time, Sebastian'!" He giggled shrilly. "Stupid old fool! We'll handle it our way, Lieutenant, you can bet on that! It won't be either quick or clean, and you can bet on that, too!" He stiffened suddenly, staring over my shoulder.

I saw in the mirror that Pop had returned and was standing in the doorway, holding the beaded curtain with one hand.

"I changed my mind," Pop said stiffly. "Bring the Lieutenant out to the garage—now!—and we'll get it finished with." Then he went back to the hall.

"Who does he think he is?" Bruno said venomously. "Maybe we should—"

"Do as he says," Sebastian said in a nervous voice. "Let's get it over first. Argue afterwards, if you want!"

After Bruno had lifted my gun and put it on the bar top, we went out of the living room and down the hall to the front porch. Bruno's gun barrel pressed hard into my spine. Sebastian followed a couple of paces behind us.

Pop was waiting in the garage, standing at one side of the antique automobile. "Bring the Lieutenant down here," he said in a flat voice as soon as we reached the open doorway.

It happened so fast it was over before I realized anything was wrong. Bruno gave a shrill squeal of fear, then I heard his gun thump onto the floor, and that was it.

"Back over against that wall!" a hard voice said. "Make it fast, huh?"

I turned around and saw that the tall, hard-faced guy who'd just spoken had a thirty-eight in his hand. This would be Lindstrom, I figured, and beside him was Sigmund Jones, a look of mild interest at the proceedings showing in his bespectacled eyes.

Both Bruno and Sebastian had their backs hard up against the garage wall, and they both looked like they could die of fright before anything worse could hit them.

A rear door of the antique car swung open suddenly, and a third man climbed out. He grabbed Pop's arm and hustled him toward us quickly.

"Get over to the wall with the others," Lindstrom said curtly to Pop when they reached us, and watched him carefully until he was standing beside Bruno.

"I figured you'd stick your nose in once too often, cop!" a rich, fruity voice said.

The man who'd just gotten out of the car was Parson Jones, so now I knew the kidnaping was strictly a phony, if that was any consolation.

"How much, Father?" Sigmund asked in a taut voice.

"The rats had been at it," Parson said savagely. "We're lucky if there's a hundred grand left, even!"

"Then it's one of them who killed Eddie Moran, for sure," Lindstrom said.

"They steal three hundred and fifty grand of my dough!" Parson almost choked at the enormity of it. "Then they rub out an old buddy of mine I send around to just take a look!"

"You can cry later, Parson," Lindstrom snapped. "We've got a hundred grand—and a problem."

"The Lieutenant," Sigmund said softly.

"Where's the problem?" Parson snarled. "He's a good cop, he figured it out and tried to take them on his own. He got them, too—a real good cop! But the last one got him at the same time. You got four cadavers who don't talk to anybody. We got a hundred grand between us—and no problem!"

"That's good thinking, Father!" Sigmund said in an admiring voice.

"Like the good old days," Parson said with a chuckle.

"That reminds me," Lindstrom said casually. "I brought something along special for you, Parson, from the good old days. Go get it, will you, Sigmund?"

Sigmund was gone maybe a minute, then his tall, lean figure came hurrying back through the doorway carrying a bulky package. Parson took it from him and eagerly tore off the wrappings, then bellowed in delight.

"From the good old days, huh?" he yelled.

"Eddie Moran was your buddy," Lindstrom observed with no inflection in his voice. "I figured you might want to do it yourself."

"You were dead right," Parson said thickly, and patted the stock of the Thompson submachine gun with something close to affection.

"You're not serious?" I gaped at him. "You can't mow down three men with—"

"Shut up, cop!" Parson snarled. "You're going to get it, too, only them three have got a priority! One of them killed Eddie!"

Bruno suddenly pulled away from the wall and ran toward us. "Hold it!" Parson yelled, and swung the Tommy gun to cover him.

"Don't shoot, don't shoot!" Bruno screamed. "Listen, Mr. Jones! You don't need to kill me—you only want the one who killed your friend, right?"

"Maybe!" Parson said. "Which one was it?"

Bruno's arm stabbed out in a straight line pointing toward Sebastian. "That's him, Mr. Jones! He's the one who killed your friend!"

The Tommy gun suddenly came to life in a deafening roar of sound, like a bunch of steam hammers gone berserk. A line of holes magically appeared in the garage wall, and ran in a straight line toward Sebastian. A split second later his whole body jerked violently, then pitched forward onto the concrete floor. The dotted line continued implacably along the wall to where Pop Livvy stood, unmoving, his face composed. Then, in turn, he gave a sudden, violent jerk before he crumbled to the floor.

"You got him, Mr. Jones!" Bruno screamed ecstatically. "You got him all right! He was the one who—" The scream changed abruptly from ecstasy to stark terror as the Tommy gun opened up again.

The noise died as abruptly as it had started, and Parson Jones turned away from his contemplation of Bruno's body threshing wildly on the floor, back to where we were standing.

"That takes care of those three," he said, with thick satisfaction in his voice. "Now there's only the cop and—"

"There's you first, Parson!" Lindstrom snapped, and triggered his thirty-eight at the same time.

It wasn't much, but for sure it was the only break I was about to get. While Lindstrom's full concentration was directed toward killing Parson, I made a standing jump that cleared the distance between me and Lindstrom. I slammed into him hard, and we both crashed to the floor.

As we rolled over and over, I heard the terrifying stammer of the Tommy gun burst briefly into life, and a thin scream over it.

Lindstrom had lost the gun when he hit the ground, which made us even. We kept on slowly rolling, first one on top and then the other— punching, gouging, kicking—then something plucked my shoulder, and the next moment I was skittering across the floor in the opposite direction from where Lindstrom was.

I finally slammed into something heavy that brought me to a full stop, which I later realized was Sigmund Jones's body. The last burst his dying father had fired with the Tommy gun had stitched a neat row of holes straight across his son's chest.

I managed to stagger up onto my knees and take a look to find out what the hell had separated me from Lindstrom so effortlessly, then thrown me ten yards across the floor like a bowling ball.

She was standing with her back toward me, and her thick, tawny hair spread like a fan from the crown of her head down to her waist. Wearing that neck-to-feet white nightgown, she looked about ten feet tall in the dim light of the garage, like some pagan goddess of revenge.

She cried continuously, the way a child cries—a pathetic, desolate sound that in itself cries out for comfort.

"Bad!" Antonia wailed in a kind of mounting hysteria. "You killed Pop! You killed my friend!"

As I lurched onto my feet, I saw her bend down and grab hold of Lindstrom's right ankle. Then she straightened up again suddenly and, using him like a flail, she methodically beat out Lindstrom's brains against the garage wall.

It was a week before Lavers would even speak to me. He figured the whole thing was my fault—"Like a battlefield!" he said when he first saw the garage, and he was right—but the Tommy gun had been Lindstrom's idea.

If I was so smart and knew so much about the setup out at the house, why the hell hadn't I made some arrests before the shooting started? He'd yelled this at me, and brushed aside the fact that suspecting the truth is one thing, and proving it a much more difficult proposition.

Celeste had been safe in her room, hiding under the bed, when I'd finally gotten back inside the house, and she'd helped me calm Antonia down before Lavers and the rest of them arrived.

Afterwards they put Antonia in a sanitarium. Celeste figured she was genuinely happy there the couple of times she'd gone out to see her. One of the psychiatrists who examined her on admission said it was a kind of inevitable tragedy that had to happen sooner or later; when a child's mind gives way to primitive emotion, the parents normally control it; when Antonia's childish mind did the same thing, she had the use of an immensely powerful body as a force of destruction.

The one ray of sunshine in my life right then was Celeste; she couldn't stay on at the house by herself and had no wish to, either, so she'd moved into my apartment on a temporary basis. It made for a little crowding here and there, but I liked crowding Celeste just fine.

And best of all was the wonderful status symbol she created for me when she moved into the apartment. Right away it made me stand out from the herd—a man of distinction, even. I hate to boast—but how many guys do you know who are living with a female contortionist and an exotic dancer at the same time?

THE END

Alan Geoffrey Yates Bibliography (1923-1985)

**As Carter Brown/
Peter Carter Brown**

Series:

Al Wheeler (no U.S. edition unless
otherwise stated through to
Chorine Makes a Killing)

The Wench is Wicked (1955)
Blonde Verdict (1956; revised for the
U.S. as The Brazen, 1960)
Delilah Was Deadly (1956)
No Harp for My Angel (1956)
Booty for a Babe (1956)
Eve, It's Extortion (1957; revised as
Walk Softly Witch!, 1959, and
further revised for the U.S. as The
Victim, 1959)
No Law Against Angels (1957;
revised for the U.S. as The Body,
1958; 1st U.S. Wheeler)
Doll for the Big House (1957; revised
for the U.S. as The Bombshell,
1960)
Chorine Makes a Killing (1957)
The Unorthodox Corpse (1957;
revised for the U.S., 1961)
Death on the Downbeat (1958;
revised for the U.S. as The Corpse,
1958)
The Blonde (1958; reprinted in the
U.S., 1958)
The Lover (1958)
The Mistress (1959)
The Passionate (1959)
The Wanton (1959)
The Dame (1959)
The Desired (1959)
The Temptress (1960)
Lament for a Lousy Lover (1960)
[includes Mavis Seidlitz]
The Stripper (1961)
The Tigress (1961; reprinted in the
UK as Wildcat, 1962)
The Exotic (1961)

Angel! (1962)
The Hellcat (1962)
The Lady Is Transparent (1962)
The Dumdum Murder (1962)
Girl in a Shroud (1963)
The Sinners (1963; reprinted in U.S.
as The Girl Who Was Possessed,
1963)
The Lady Is Not Available (1963;
reprinted in U.S. as The Lady Is
Available, 1963)
The Dance of Death (1964)
The Vixen (1964; reprinted in the
U.S. as The Velvet Vixen, 1964)
A Corpse for Christmas (1965)
The Hammer of Thor (1965)
Target for Their Dark Desire (1966)
The Plush-Lined Coffin (1967)
Until Temptation Do Us Part (1967)
The Deep Cold Green (1968)
The Up-Tight Blonde (1969)
Burden of Guilt (1970)
The Creative Murders (1971)
W.H.O.R.E. (1971)
The Clown (1972)
The Aseptic Murders (1972)
The Born Loser (1973)
Night Wheeler (1974)
Wheeler Fortune (1974)
Wheeler, Dealer! (1975)
The Dream Merchant (1976)
Busted Wheeler (1979)
The Spanking Girls (1979)
Model for Murder (1980)
The Wicked Widow (1981)
Stab in the Dark (1984; Australia
only)

Larry Baker

Charlie Sent Me (1965; revised from
Swan Song for a Siren, 1955)
No Blonde Is an Island (1965)
So What Killed the Vampire? (1966)
Had I But Groaned (1968; reprinted
in the UK as The Witches, 1969)

True Son of the Beast (1970)
The Iron Maiden (1975)

Barney Blain (no U.S. editions)

Madam, You're Mayhem (1957)
Ice Cold in Ermine (1958)

Danny Boyd

Tempt a Tigress (1958; no U.S.)
So Deadly, Sinner! (1959; reprinted
    in the U.S. as Walk Softly, Witch,
    1959, 1st U.S. Boyd; different
    version of the Wheeler title)
Suddenly by Violence (1959)
Terror Comes Creeping (1959)
The Wayward Wahine (1960;
    published in Australia as The
    Wayward, 1962)
The Dream Is Deadly (1960)
Graves, I Dig (1960; revised from
    Cutie Wins a Corpse (1957)
The Myopic Mermaid (1961, revised
    from A Siren Sounds Off, 1958)
The Ever-Loving Blues (1961;
    revised from Death of a Doll, 1956)
The Seductress (1961; published in
    the U.S. as The Sad-Eyed
    Seductress, 1961)
The Savage Salome (1961; revised
    from Murder is My Mistress, 1954)
The Ice-Cold Nude (1962)
Lover Don't Come Back (1962)
Nymph to the Slaughter (1963)
Passionate Pagan (1963)
Silken Nightmare (1963)
Catch Me a Phoenix! (1965)
The Sometime Wife (1965)
The Black Lace Hangover (1966)
House of Sorcery (1967)
The Mini-Murders (1968)
Murder Is the Message (1969)
Only the Very Rich (1969)
The Coffin Bird (1970)
The Sex Clinic (1971)
Angry Amazons (1972) [includes
    Randy Roberts]
Manhattan Cowboy (1973)
So Move the Body (1973)

The Early Boyd (1975)
The Savage Sisters (1976)
The Pipes Are Calling (1976)
The Rip Off (1979)
The Strawberry-Blonde Jungle
    (1979)
Death to a Downbeat (1980)
Kiss Michelle Goodbye (1981)
The Real Boyd (1984; Australia only)

Paul Donavan

Donavan (1974)
Donavan's Day (1975)
Chinese Donavan (1976)
Donavan's Delight (1979)

Max Dumas (no U.S. editions)

Goddess Gone Bad (1958)
Luck Was No Lady (1958)
Deadly Miss (1958)

Mike Farrel

The Million Dollar Babe (1961;
    revised from Cutie Cashed His
    Chips, 1955)
The Scarlet Flush (1963; revised
    from Ten Grand Tallulah and
    Temptation, 1957)

Rick Holman

Zelda (1961; 1st U.S. Holman)
Murder in the Harem Club, 1962;
    reprinted in the U.S. as Murder in
    the Key Club, 1962)
The Murderer Among Us (1962)
Blonde on the Rocks (1963)
The Jade-Eyed Jinx (1963; reprinted
    in the U.S. as The Jade-Eyed
    Jungle, 1964)
The Ballad of Loving Jenny (1963;
    reprinted in the U.S. as The White
    Bikini, 1963)
The Wind-Up Doll (1963)
The Never-Was Girl (1964)
Murder Is a Package Deal (1964)
Who Killed Doctor Sex? (1964)

Nude—with a View (1965)
The Girl from Outer Space (1965)
Blonde on a Broomstick (1966)
Play Now… Kill Later (1966)
No Tears from the Widow (1966)
The Deadly Kitten (1967)
Long Time No Leola (1967)
Die Anytime, After Tuesday! (1969)
The Flagellator (1969)
The Streaked-Blond Slave (1969)
A Good Year for Dwarfs? (1970)
The Hang-up Kid (1970)
Where Did Charity Go? (1970)
The Coven (1971)
The Invisible Flamini (1971)
The Pornbroker (1972)
The Master (1973)
Phreak-Out! (1973)
Negative in Blue (1974)
The Star-Crossed Lover (1974)
Ride the Roller Coaster (1975)
Remember Maybelle? (1976)
See It Again, Sam (1979)
The Phantom Lady (1980)
The Swingers (1980)

Andy Kane

The Hong Kong Caper (1962; revised
    from Blonde, Bad and Beautiful,
    1957)
The Guilt-edged Cage (1963; revised
    from That's Piracy, My Pet, 1957;
    published in Australia as Bird in a
    Guilt-Edged Cage)

Ivor MacCallum (no U.S. editions)

Sweetheart You Slay Me (1952)
Blackmail Beauty (1953)

Randy Roberts

Murder in the Family Way (1971)
The Seven Sirens (1972)
Murder on High (1973)
Sex Trap (1975)

Mavis Seidlitz

Honey, Here's Your Hearse (1955; no
    U.S.)
The Killer is Kissable (1955; no U.S.)
A Bullet For My Baby (1955; no U.S.)
Good Morning, Mavis! (1957; no
    U.S.)
Murder Wears a Mantilla (1957;
    revised for U.S. as same title, 1962)
The Loving and the Dead (1959; 1st
    U.S. Seidlitz)
None But the Lethal Heart (1959;
    reprinted as The Fabulous, 1961)
Tomorrow Is Murder (1960)
Lament for a Lousy Lover (1960)
    [includes Al Wheeler]
The Bump and Grind Murders
    (1964)
Seidlitz and the Super Spy (1967;
    published in the UK as The Super-
    Spy, 1968)
Murder Is So Nostalgic (1972)
And the Undead Sing (1974)

Unrelated Novels/Novelettes (all
    non-U.S. unless otherwise noted)

Death Date for Dolores (1951)
Designed to Deceive (1951)
Duchess Double X (1951)
Forever Forbidden (1951)
The Lady Is Murder (1951; reprinted
    as Lady is a Killer with Murder by
    Miss Take, 1958)
Three Men, One Love (1951)
Uncertain Heart (1951)
Your Alibi Is Showing (1951)
Alias a Lady (1952)
Blackmail for a Brunette (1952)
Blondes Prefer Bullets (1952)
Hands Off the Lady (1952)
Kiss Life Goodbye (1952)
Larceny Was Lovely (1952)
Meet Miss Mayhem (1952)
Murder Sweet Murder (1952)
She Wore No Shroud (1952)
Sssh! She's a Killer (1952)
Chill on Chili/Butterfly Nett (1953)

Cyanide Sweetheart (1953)
Dead Dolls Don't Cry (1953)
Dimples Died De-Luxe (1953)
Judgement of a Jane (1953)
Kidnapper Wears Curves (1953)
The Lady Wore Nylon (1953)
The Lady's Alive (1953)
Lethal in Love (1953; reprinted as
    The Minx is Murder, 1956)
Madame You're Morgue-Bound
    (1953)
Meet a Body (1953)
The Mermaid Murmurs Murder
    (1953)
Model for Murder (1953; different
    from 1980 Al Wheeler title)
Moonshine Momma (1953)
Murder is a Broad (1953)
Penthouse Pass-Out (1953; reprinted
    as Hot Seat for a Honey, 1956)
Rope for a Redhead (1953; revised as
    Model of No Virtue, 1956)
Slightly Dead (1953)
Stripper You're Stuck (1953)
Widow is Willing (1953)
The Black Widow Weeps (1954)
Felon Angel (1954)
Floozie Out of Focus (1954; reprinted
    with A Bullet for My Baby, 1958)
The Frame is Beautiful (1954)
Fraulein is Feline (1954; reprinted
    with Moonshine Momma &
    Slaughter in Satin, 1955)
Good-Knife Sweetheart (1954)
Honky Tonk Homicide (1954;
    reprinted with Chill on Chili &
    Butterfly Nett, 1955)
Homicide Harem (1954; reprinted
    with Good-Knife Sweetheart &
    Poison Ivy, 1955; with Felon Angel,
    1965)
The Lady is Chased (1954; reprinted
    as Trouble is a Dame, 1957)
A Morgue Amour (1954)
Murder—Paris Fashion (1954)
Murder! She Says (1954)
Nemesis Wore Nylons (1954)
Pagan Perilous (1954)
Perfumed Poison (1954)
Poison Ivy (1954)

Shady Lady (1954)
Sinsation Sadie (1954)
Slaughter in Satin (1954)
Strip Without Tease (1954; reprinted
    as Stripper, You've Sinned, 1959)
Trouble is a Dame (1954)
Wreath for Rebecca (1954)
Venus Unarmed (1954)
Yogi Shrouds Yolande (1954;
    reprinted with Poison Ivy, 1965)
Curtains for a Chorine (1955)
Curves for a Coroner (1955)
Cutie Cashed His Chips (1955;
    revised for U.S. as The Million
    Dollar Babe, 1961, as Farrel series)
Homicide Hoyden (1955)
Kiss and Kill (1955; reprinted with
    Cyanide Sweetie, 1958)
Kiss Me Deadly (1955; reprinted as
    Lipstick Larceny, 1958)
Lead Astray (1955)
Lipstick Larceny (1955)
Maid for Murder (1955)
Miss Called Murder (1955)
Shamus, Your Slip Is Showing (1955;
    reprinted with A Morgue Amour,
    1957)
Shroud for My Sugar (1955)
Sob-Sister Cries Murder (1955)
The Two Timing Blonde (1955;
    reprinted with Honey, Here's Your
    Hearse, 1957)
Baby, You're Guilt-Edged (1956;
    reprinted with Pagan Perilous,
    1959)
Bid the Babe Bye-Bye (1956)
Blonde, Beautiful, and – Blam!
    (1956)
The Bribe Was Beautiful (1956)
Caress Before Killing (1956)
Darling You're Doomed (1956)
Donna Died Laughing (1956)
The Eve of His Dying (1956)
Hi-Jack for Jill (1956)
The Hoodlum Was a Honey (1956)
The Lady Has No Convictions (1956;
    reprinted with Slightly Dead,
    1959)
Meet Murder, My Angel (1956)
Murder By Miss-Demeanour (1956)

My Darling Is Deadpan (1956)
No Halo For Hedy (1956)
Strictly for Felony (1956)
Sweetheart, This is Homicide (1956)
Bella Donna Was Poison (1957)
Cutie Wins a Corpse (1957; revised
    for U.S. as Graves, I Dig!, 1960, as
    Boyd series)
Last Note for a Lovely (1957)
Lethal in Love (1957; different than
    1953 title)
Sinner, You Slay Me (1957)
Ten Grand Tallulah and Temptation
    (1957; revised as The Scarlet
    Flush, 1963, Farrel series)
That's Piracy, My Pet (1957; revised
    as Bird in a Guilt-Edged Cage,
    1963, as Kane series)
Wreath for a Redhead (1957)
The Charmer Chased (1958)
Cutie Takes the Count (1958)
Deadly Miss (1958)
Hi-Fi Fadeout (1958)
High Fashion in Homicide (1958)
No Body She Knows (1958; with
    Slaughter in Satin, 1960)
No Future Fair Lady (1958)
Sinfully Yours (1958)
A Siren Signs Off (1958; with
    Moonshine Momma; revised for
    U.S. as The Myopic Mermaid,
    1961, as Boyd series)
So Lovely She Lies (1958)
Widow Bewitched (1958)
The Blonde Avalanche (1984)

As Tod Conway (western stories)

As Caroline Farr (house name
    shared with Richard Wilkes-
    Hunter and Lee Pattinson)

The Intruder (1962)
House of Tombs (1966)
Mansion of Evil (1966)
Villa of Shadows (1966)
Web of Horror (1966; reprinted in
    the U.S. as A Castle in Spain,
    1978)
Granite Folly (1967)

The Secret of the Chateau (1967)
Witch's Hammer (1967)
So Near and Yet... (1968)
House of Destiny (1969)
The Castle on the Lake (1970)
The Secret of Castle Ferrara (1970)
Terror on Duncan Island (1971)
The Towers of Fear (1972)
A Castle in Canada (1972)
House of Dark Illusions (1973)
House of Secrets (1973)
Dark Mansion (1974)
Mansion Malevolent (1974)
The House on the Cliffs (1974)
Dark Citadel (1975)
Mansion of Peril (1975)
Castle of Terror (1975)
The Scream in the Storm (1975)
Chateau of Wolves (1976)
Mansion of Menace (1976)
Brecon Castle (1976)
The House of Landsdown (1977)
House of Treachery (1977)
Ravensnest (1977)
The House at Lansdowne (1977)
Sinister House (1978)
House of Valhalla (1978)
Heiress Of Fear (1978)
Room Of Secrets (1979)
Island of Evil (1979)
A Castle on the Rhine (1979)
The Castle on the Loch (1979)
The Secret at Ravenswood (1980)

As Raymond Glenning (stories)

Ghosts Don't Kill (1951)
Seven for Murder (1951)

As Sinclair Mackellar

Prompt for Murder (1981)

As Dennis Sinclair

Temple Dogs Guard My Fate (1968)
Third Force (1976)
The Friends of Lucifer (1977)
Blood Brothers (1977)

As Paul Valdez
(stories & novelettes)

Hypnotic Death (1949)
The Fatal Focus (1950)
Outcasts of Planet J (1950)
Jetbees from Planet J (1951)
Escape to Paradise (1951)
Fugitives from the Flame World
　(1951)
Kidnapped in Chaos (1951)
Killer by Night (1951)
Suicide Satellite (1951)
The Time Thief (1951)
Flight Into Horror (1951)
Murder Gives Notice (1951)
The Corpse Sat Up (1951)
The Maniac Murders (1951)
Satan's Sabbath (1951)
You Can't Keep Murder Out (1951)
Kill Him Gently (1951)
Feline Frame-Up (1951)
Celluloid Suicide? (1951)
The Murder I Don't Remember
　(1952)
Kidnapped in Space (1952)
There's No Future in Murder (1952)
The Crook Who Wasn't There (1952)
Maniac Murders (1952)
The Mad Meteor (1952)
Operation Satellite (1952)

As A. G. Yates

The Cold Dark Hours (1958)

As Alan Yates

Novel:

Coriolanus, the Chariot (1978)

Stories & Novelettes:

Client for Murder (*Leisure Detective
　#7*, 195?)
The Corpse on the Carpet (*Leisure
　Detective #8*, 195?)
Farewell, My Lady of Shalott!
　(*Action Detective Magazine #6*,
　1952)
Hush-a-Buy Homicide (*Leisure
　Detective #9*, 195?)
Margie (*Action Detective Magazine
　#5*, 1952)
Merger with Death (*Leisure
　Detective #12*, 195?)
Murder in the Family (*Leisure
　Detective #11*, 195?)
Murder Needs Education (*Action
　Detective Magazine #2*, 1952)
Murder! She Says (*Detective
　Monthly #2*, 195?)
My Love Lies Murdered (*Action
　Detective Magazine #7*, 1952)
Nemesis for a Nude! (*Leisure
　Detective #10*, 195?)

Genie from Jupiter (*Thrills
　Incorporated #14*, 1951)
Goddess of Space (*Thrills
　Incorporated #20*, 1952)
No Pixies on Pluto (*Thrills
　Incorporated #22*, 1952)
Planet of the Lost (*Thrills
　Incorporated #17*, 1951)
A Space Ship Is Missing (*Thrills
　Incorporated #16*, 1951)
Spacemen Spoofed (*Thrills
　Incorporated #23*, 1952)

Autobiography

Ready when you are, C.B.!: The
　autobiography of Alan Yates alias
　Carter Brown (1983)